A Mother's Guide to Cheating

Also by Kate Long

The Bad Mother's Handbook

Swallowing Grandma

Queen Mum

The Daughter Game

Kate Long
A Mother's Guide to Cheating

**SIMON &
SCHUSTER**

London · New York · Sydney · Toronto

A CBS COMPANY

First published in Great Britain by Simon & Schuster UK Ltd, 2010
A CBS COMPANY

Copyright © Kate Long, 2010

3 5 7 9 10 8 6 4 2

Simon & Schuster UK Ltd
1st Floor
222 Gray's Inn Road
London WC1X 8HB

www.simonandschuster.co.uk

Simon & Schuster Australia
Sydney

A CIP catalogue record for this book
is available from the British Library

Hardback ISBN 978-1-84737-750-0
Trade Paperback ISBN 978-1-84737-751-7

Typeset by M Rules
Printed in the UK by CPI Mackays, Chatham ME5 8TD

For Alexandra WILLOW Lister
9 May 2005 – 15 June 2008

Thanks to the following for their help with research: John and Margaret Green, Kat Dibbits, Susan Donley, Joyce Carter, Judith Magill, Judy Strachan, Joan Turner, Anna Eveley, Joanne Ash, Tracey and Den Hartshorn, Ruth and David Riley, Amanda Dubicki, Reg Moorland, www.grandparentsapart.co.uk and Ben Long.

Also, thanks as ever to the WW girls for their excellent feedback, to Suzanne Baboneau, and to Peter Straus.

A Mother's Guide to Cheating

CHAPTER 1

Photograph 46, Album One

Location: the back garden at Pincroft, Bolton

Taken by: Dad

Subject: The rear of the house, flat and rendered, looks over a straight-sided lawn bordered by bare black earth. Can a garden look packed-away? This one does. The beds remain unfilled, and will stay that way till spring. Round the front, though, it's a whole different story: Carol's mother Frieda has planted blocks of purple and white pansies, there is an Alpine rockery and even a little sundial. But the front of the 1930s semi boasts a gable with a tile pattern, and a bay window, and a proper porch, and is on view to passers-by. This is 1963. Appearances matter.

At the top edge of the picture is Carol White, aged eight. She is raking up fallen beech leaves, as a punishment. She has on her black wellies, brown crimplene trews, a yellow jumper, and a face like thunder.

Asked, the day before, to go round and pick snails off the hedge, Carol instead attempted a rescue. She should have drowned the snails in her bucket, but when it came to turning on the outside tap, she couldn't bring herself to do it. They were, when she examined them, unexpectedly beautiful, the radiating flecks on their shells reminding her of the patterns in her own irises. Then there were the little jelly feelers, so friendly and sad. Nothing else to do but line an Oxo tin with leaves, and tumble the snails on top, with the lid open a crack for air.

For such slow creatures, snails (it turns out) can cover a lot of ground in six hours. The square of bedroom carpet has had to be scrubbed, the wallpaper wiped down and the candlewick bedspread put on a hot wash. There it hangs at the opposite edge of the picture, a soggy curtain in tufted salmon.

'What did you think you were doing?' cries Frieda, her voice shrill with martyrdom. 'As if I haven't enough on, trying to keep this place decent.'

No good trying to explain. In her mother's book, cleanliness will always trump invertebrate welfare. If it wasn't for Dad, Carol thinks, she'd pack her satchel and go live in the forest like the Babes in the Wood.

2007

Sometimes I think I had a premonition. That the moment I picked up the phone, I had this sense something was wrong. But more likely, it being a Wednesday evening, I'd have been rushing round trying to get washed up and cleared away before going to the gym, and not thinking about anything other than where I'd put my water bottle and whether it was too late to walk – in which case I needed to shift the wheelie-bin and get the car out of the garage.

I do remember I couldn't tell who was speaking at first, because Jaz was in such a state. Then I managed to make out 'Mum', and that's when I started to get frightened. I said, 'Jaz, love, what's the matter?' She just cried harder. I said, 'Jaz, are you all right?' which was a daft question because of course she wasn't all right, she was absolutely beside herself, incoherent. And she's normally so cool, so laid-back; that or in a temper about something. Not tears, though, she's never been one for tears.

So I said, 'What's happened? Whatever's the matter?'

She said, 'He told me, Mum, he told me straight out.' Which I couldn't make sense of. All I knew was that something was dreadfully wrong.

It's amazing how you can go from calm to terrified in a few seconds, like revving up a car. I made myself ask, 'Is it Matty?' Because that was the very worst scenario I could imagine; the call every grandparent dreads. I remember looking down at my hand where it was holding the edge of the chair and the knuckles were white, and at the back of my mind I was making all these mad bargains with heaven and fate – anything.

'It's not Matty,' I heard her say.

My legs nearly gave out with relief. Thank You, God, thank You, God, I was saying in my head. At least if Matty was all right, if my Matty was safe and sound, I could cope with whatever was coming.

'Tell me, love,' I said. 'Whatever is it? Surely we can sort it out?'

'No, Mum,' she said. 'It's all shattered, all of it.'

They say families follow certain patterns. Like, if you're knocked about as a kid, you might end up marrying someone who knocks you about, and if your mother's a cold fish, you're going to find it hard to bond with your own children. I'd have said that was phooey: thinking of my own mum Frieda, and how she was with me, and how I've been with Jaz, there's no comparison. But then, you don't know what children take in when they're young. You can run yourself ragged for them, and they'll still seize on the one thing you did wrong. Which in my case was to marry a cheat.

Which, it turned out, was what Jaz had done.

Normally it takes me fifteen minutes to get to the other side of Nantwich: I did it in eight. I don't know what I was expecting when I pulled up outside the house. Smashed windows, a pile of Ian's belongings on the front steps, maybe. Instead, everything looked normal: planters full of dead lobelia, plastic cart of Matty's in the middle of the drive, gate off its hinges. One day, I thought, Ian might actually get round to fixing the place up. Or not.

Jaz had left the door on the latch for me, so I went straight in. There's always a lot of clutter in Jaz and Ian's hall and it's narrow to begin with, so I had to go carefully, stepping over shoes and squeezing round the pushbikes and pausing to pick up clothes I'd dislodged from the radiator. Piles of stuff on the stairs, as usual; it would drive me round the bend if I lived here. I don't ever criticise, though. That would be asking for trouble.

As soon as I called her name she appeared in the kitchen doorway.

'Oh, love,' I said.

She's always been a beautiful girl. I've tried never to make a big deal of it, but other people would comment, especially when she was little. 'Child model,' Mrs Wynne next door used to say. 'You should send her photo off.' Even when she started with her piercings and her long clothes, my daughter still turned heads.

Now, though, standing in front of me in this gloomy hall, she just looked a mess. Her eyes were red and swollen, marked with tracks of mascara, and her long, thick hair was all over the place. The baggy black jumper made her seem much younger than her twenty-seven years.

I moved forward to give her a hug, but she started to talk in a way that kept me back.

'Complete fucking *bastard*,' she said. 'I can't believe what he's done. Just goes, "Yeah, I've slept with someone". Like it was nothing. Like it was *fucking nothing*.'

Even though there was no questioning her distress, I had some trouble taking in the image. Ian – casually announcing his infidelity? Surely not. One of us must have it wrong.

'Are you saying – he's admitted he's having an affair?'

'Of course he's *fucking* admitted it! That's what I've been *telling you*!' She struck the doorframe with the flat of her hand, and I saw tears drop off her chin.

So that was it. There didn't seem to be any doubt. Ian, the boy everyone liked: shyly spoken, posh, gawky. Decent, we'd thought. Straightforward. Good for Jaz. That big wedding four years ago, all for nothing. Marquee, open-topped car, special bamboo holders for the flowers. Dress that she wanted altering right at the last minute. I still had the pillars off the cake sitting on my kitchen shelf.

'Oh, love,' I said again.

'I hate him, Mum. I *hate him*. If he was here now, I swear I'd fucking kill him. I would, I swear. I'm not joking. I'd *fucking* kill him.'

'Where's Matty?' I asked cautiously.

Jaz looked at me as though I was mad. 'He's up-fucking-*stairs*. In his cot. Where did you think he was? On the *fucking moon?*'

I didn't dare ask if he was OK in case she took it the wrong way, but suddenly I was desperate to see. 'I thought I heard him calling,' I fibbed, and scooted back down the hall.

By the time I got to the top of the stairs, my blood was pounding. Matty's door was a few inches ajar and the night light showing. With extreme care I pushed the door open further, wincing at the shush-scrape of the carpet, and stuck my head round.

The sight of him asleep always makes me catch my breath. He was lying on his back with his fists balled, the way he used to when he was a tiny baby, and his lips were slightly parted. Dawg was underneath him, grey cloth tail poking out. 'You're going to have to get him one of those toddler beds soon,' I'd said to Jaz only the week before. 'And you reckon he'll stay there, do you?' had been her reply. 'You think he'll lie down, stick his thumb in his mouth, and that'll be it till the morning?' She said she wanted to wait till he could climb out of the cot unaided before letting him loose with a bed. So I went along with it. He's her child, after all.

I stood there in the calm dim glow of his moon-shaped lamp and watched his little chest move up and down, up and down, till I felt ready to go back downstairs. To be honest, I could have stayed there all night.

She was sitting at the kitchen table, head in hands, her coloured scarves draping down over plates and mugs and papers and books. When she heard me, she sat upright and I thought, At least she's stopped crying.

'Where's Ian?' I asked, drawing back a chair.

'Fuck knows.'

I waited for her to go on.

'It was a text.' Jaz looked as though she was about to spit. 'We were in here, talking about his day, everything normal. A bog-standard tea-time. Next thing his phone bleeps, but he doesn't open it, he takes it off into the lounge, really shifty. And you know that way he has of pushing his glasses up when he's nervous about something? It was such a weird reaction he might as well have waved a fucking flag, though I don't think he realised. Too much on his mind. When he went up to run Matty's bath, I got out the phone and checked.'

The lights on the baby monitor flickered briefly, settled.

'What did it say? Can you tell me?'

She shrugged as if she was past caring. 'It said: *What did you dream last night?*'

I was seeing it with her, imagining the letters on the screen.

'Well, perhaps it wasn't necessarily—'

'Then some kisses.'

'Oh.'

'Then a name.'

Without warning she got up, grabbed a mug off the table and slammed it onto the quarry tiles at her feet. It shattered like a bomb.

'Her fucking *name*. Now I'll always know it!'

'Good God, Jaz. You'll wake Matty.'

Her eyes, when she looked at me, were wild and stary, and for a moment I didn't know what to do. What *do* you do when everything you thought was safe is just falling apart?

Then I thought, Sod it, someone's got to get a grip.

I began to stack the dirty plates on the table, because I can't think straight when everywhere's untidy. While my daughter stood in the middle of the room grasping her own hair, I ferried crockery to the sink, ran the hot tap, and set to gathering pieces of broken cup. 'You can't leave it like this,' I said. 'If Matty walks in here with no slippers tomorrow morning—'

She bent and took a single sliver of white china between her finger and thumb.

'Come on, love,' I said. 'Let's clear away and then I'll make us a hot drink and we can go sit in the lounge. It'll be better there.'

I guided her to the bin, then handed her a damp cloth so she could wipe up all the very tiny fragments. As I washed and stacked, I kept an eye on her.

'Don't touch my papers,' she said at one point, when I reached across the table for a dirty spoon.

As if. Even when she lived under my roof I never dared interfere with her stuff.

Once I'd finished the dishes it was tempting to go through the whole kitchen, collect up all the books and toys and carry them next door, put away the pans and bowls that had been left out, stick the pot plants in for a good soak and wipe the soil off the windowsill. Some of her leaflets and postcards had fallen off the cork board; there was a pile of assorted boots on the doormat. I longed to put these small things right.

Instead I brewed two teas, picked up the baby monitor, and led Jaz through to the sofa. We sat for a while watching the television play mutely, pictures of a bossy-looking woman preparing vegetables in a low-beamed kitchen.

'Don't,' she said, when she saw me eyeing the hearth, and the tumbler containing six wax crayons in an inch of orange squash.

'It might tip over.'

'And you think I care?'

The woman on TV yanked a chicken open and paused, smugly. I wondered where Ian was and what he was doing right at this moment.

Jaz said: 'When I asked him about the text he looked – frozen. Like he had no idea what to say. I mean, he obviously wasn't expecting the question. So I asked him again and he came right out with it. I suppose he didn't have time to think up a story. No time to prepare a defence.' She laughed bitterly. 'He could have said it was a mistake. People get phone numbers wrong, don't they? Why didn't he go for straight denial? I might have bought it.'

'You wouldn't.'

'No, you're right, I wouldn't. *Fuck* him. Why didn't he *delete* it?'

I said, 'Did he tell you much else?'

'Only that he'd seen her twice. He met her in the pub near where he works. The first time they did anything, they only kissed. Apparently. The next time, he went back to hers. It was a lunchtime. So much more con*venient*.' She flopped back against the Indian throw. 'What I don't get, Mum, what I don't get is – you know, actually I don't get fucking *any* of it. It's so, it's out of the blue, I wasn't expecting it, I didn't think there was anything wrong. There's nothing wrong with me, is there?'

That made me want to cry. Really I needed to hold her, but she was still too spiky; she'd have pushed me away and I couldn't have stood that on top of everything else. I said, 'Jaz, there's nothing wrong with you. Ian must be having some kind of, I don't know, crisis.'

'I'll give him a fucking crisis,' she said.

By now the woman chef was sharing her chicken with some laughing friends at a pristine table. 'See my glorious world,' she was saying. I'd have turned the bloody TV off if I'd stood a chance of finding the remote.

'Did he say he was sorry?'

'Yeah. And that he'll never see her again, it meant nothing, one-off, blah blah. Like they do.'

'It's not always talk,' I said. 'Sometimes they mean it.'

Jaz gave me a withering look.

'I'm sure he'll come back.'

'He'd better not.'

'I don't mean straight away, obviously. When things have calmed down. Then you can talk, and try to get to the root of—'

She sat up and leaned towards me. 'You're not getting it, Mum. Ian's gone because I've thrown him out.'

'Well, yes, I see. And I know that just at this moment you'll be feeling—'

'Mum, read my lips,' she said. 'This marriage is over. Over. Ian's made his position clear. *I'm* not good enough – *this* isn't good enough for him.' She swung her arm round to take in the room with all its evidence of family life: the stack of toddler vests balanced on the chair arm, the tumbled Duplo, Ian's computer magazines mixed with her foreign language dictionaries, and cardboard wallets dumped all along the top of the sideboard and the coffee-table and the windowseat.

'Oh, I'm sure it is enough, love, it's—'

'The one thing I won't do,' she cut in, 'let's be totally clear on this, is live with a man who doesn't put his marriage first. A man who lies and cheats. A man who thinks he can get away with treating me like a fool because I'll always turn a blind eye, I'll always forgive him. Make like I'm a *fucking* door-mat. 'Cause that's not me and I won't have it; I've never taken shit from anyone and I'm not about to start now.' The baby monitor crackled and she nodded at it angrily. 'Plus, I'm not bringing Matty up in that kind of a household. No way. I'm not putting either of us through that pantomime. Damaging him. He doesn't need a childhood like *that*.'

And I thought, So here we go. I might have known it would come down to this. Somehow it turns out to be my fault, again.

CHAPTER 2

Photograph 294, Album Three

Location: Acton Scott Historic Working Farm, Shropshire

Taken by: Carol

Subject: Twelve-year-old Jaz stands within a semi-circle of interested geese and ducks, her back against the wall of a pigsty. She is wearing a frilly cap and an apron, and carrying a bucket of grain. If it weren't for the jeans and the trainers showing at the bottom, she could be a dairymaid from the 1800s – which is the general idea. She has already had a go at making butter pats, and been taught the correct way to hold a chick. She's watched a demonstration of spinning and carding, and how you'd saddle a carthorse. The sun is out and it should be a top day, except that Phil is AWOL again after a fight and Carol is as blue as a wife can be.

Not that she's letting on to Jaz. 'Dad's having to work extra hours,' she's told her, and so they make free in the gift shop and eat triple-scoop ice creams and hire a rowing boat and order a Victorian cream tea. Every ounce of Carol's strength goes into keeping that smile.

Meanwhile, Jaz plans what to do when they get home. She will run her own bath, put her nightie on, then attempt *to make her mother a hot drink. Perhaps she can add a snack and bring a tray through, the way her mum does when anyone's ill. It is all Jaz can think to do in the face of her mother's despair, and even now she's guessing it's not enough.*

The obvious course of action was to take Matty for a few days. 'Give you time to get yourself together,' I told Jaz, the morning after both our lives had caved in. 'He was due to come to me on Saturday, anyway. It's no trouble.'

'Would you?'

'Of course. You need some space.'

She nodded.

'And you need to speak to Ian,' I added unwisely.

'I'm never speaking to him again,' she snapped. 'So you can forget that idea.'

Don't be daft, I nearly said. There's all kinds of stuff you need to sort out. Even if you both decide the marriage is finished, there'll be maintenance and access and divvying up your assets, and you can't do all of it through a solicitor – well, you can, but it costs an arm and a leg. And, in any case, I don't believe the marriage is over: I think you'll get through this, maybe with some counselling, and come back together for the sake of little Matty. I think Ian's had a stupid bloody selfish slip, that's all it is, and after you've both done a lot of soul-searching, and he's apologised and you've had a good old shout, probably lots of shouting, you'll move on. It might take months, but you will get there.

I didn't say any of that, obviously. Sometimes I think my head'll explode, all the unspoken words in there.

I keep Matty's room ready, because not only is he with me most weekends for a stopover, give his mum and dad chance to have a lie-in, but you never know when there might be a crisis.

'Is that new?' Jaz asked, putting the changing bag down on the chest of drawers and pointing to a wall light in the shape of a gecko.

'It is. I meant to store it away for a Christmas present, but then I thought, well, it seems a shame not to have it out, let him have the enjoyment of it now.'

'You're hopeless.'

'I know.'

I straightened the cot cover and plugged the monitor in. Between our feet, Matty sat and rolled a wooden truck back and forth like someone planing floorboards.

'Car,' he said.

'And tonight,' I said, sinking to my haunches, 'you're going to stay with Nanna. Won't that be nice? We can read *Dear Zoo* and *On the Road*. And you can have a boiled egg.'

The truck crashed against the leg of the cot and Matty cackled.

'You're talking to yourself,' said Jaz.

'He has a special egg cup,' I said, hauling myself up again. 'Mrs Wynne brought it me back off holiday. It's shaped like a Highland cow.'

Jaz drew her hand over her face.

'Look,' I said, 'you need to go back home now and get some sleep. I bet you were up all night, yeah?' I'd sat up till 3 a.m. myself, watching the night sky from Jaz's old room, wondering who the hell my daughter had married. But there was nothing to be gained from sharing that. 'Stick the answerphone on and put your head down for a few hours. You're fit for nothing at the moment.'

'Yeah,' she said. 'I should be working. There's a translation I need to finish for Uniflect.'

'Can't it wait? Look, I'll make us a cup of tea.'

'I'm still drinking this one, Mum.'

'Can I get you something to eat?'

'I'm not hungry.'

'Syrupy porridge? I've got some in. Or I could do cheese on toast; Matty likes that.'

'Brrrm brrrm,' said Matty.

'I'm not hungry.'

'How about if I do some, and then you see how you feel?'

Jaz looked as if she was about to speak, then she turned away and began to tug at a lock of hair.

The problem, I felt like saying, is that I don't know what to do. I'm grown up, I'm the mum, I'm supposed to know. But I don't.

I bent down and picked up Matty's beaker. 'Cheese on toast it is, then. And an egg in the cow cup?'

'Egg,' said Matty.

Jaz turned back to me, her face pinched and white. 'Actually,' she said, 'there is something I'd like. Do you mind if I crash out upstairs for a while? I can't face driving back right now. I just want my old bed for a few hours.'

I tell you, I could have wept.

After we'd eaten – after Jaz had sat and stared at her food, and Matty had spread his over a wide area – I took her up and closed the curtains.

'Sit there while I make up the bed,' I told her, and she plonked herself in front of the dressing-table. I got fresh sheets from the airing cupboard and grabbed the pillows off my own bed because they're the decent ones.

'You've taken my posters down,' she said, as she watched me shake out the duvet cover.

'Well, yes. It's my guest room, now.'

I could see her eyes swivelling round, clocking all the changes. 'And you've repainted the ceiling. And the lamp-shade's new. And that's not my duvet.'

I said: 'Love, I couldn't leave it untouched for ever. If I have people to stay, they don't want to be looking at pictures of half-naked men waving guitars about or leaning on gravestones.' I tried a laugh. 'Could give them nightmares.'

'Well, I hope you haven't thrown them away.'

'Of course I haven't. They're on top of the wardrobe in Matty's room.'

'And what about my lampshade?'

I paused, pillowcase in hand. 'What about it?'

'Did you keep that?'

'No, it went to the tip. I didn't for one minute think you'd want it.'

'I customised it,' she said. 'I painted it myself.'

'Black, with crosses and roses. It didn't really go with any-thing any more. And it was very battered. You wouldn't have wanted it up in your house, would you?'

'Dunno. But you could have offered it to me before you chucked it out.'

I shook the pillow down and dropped it onto the bed.

'Did you keep my old curtains?'

'They're in the loft,' I said quickly. I didn't dare tell her I'd cut them up to make a garden kneeler.

'Good.' She continued to watch me in a glazed, spacey way. 'I suppose I should be helping with that.'

'You stay where you are. Just this duvet to sort out and we're done. Then you can put your head down. Matty and I might go for a walk so you can have total peace.'

'Yeah.'

'Do you want to borrow one of my nighties?'

For a moment she actually smiled. 'I'll give that one a miss,

15

Mum. I've got a T-shirt on under this jumper; I can sleep in that.'

I left her to get undressed, and when I came back she was under the covers. I drew the curtains closer to block out the little triangle of light at the top, and went to sit on the bed next to her. 'Can I get you anything? Cup of Horlicks? Do you want the radio out of my room?'

She shook her head and closed her eyes. 'Oh – you have still got Kitten?'

'Of course. I'd never throw Kitten out. He's in Matty's cot.'

'Can I have him?'

'Now?'

'Yeah.'

I stepped across the landing and retrieved the cat-doll from under a pile of bright, newer teddies. 'You're in demand again,' I told it. 'I hope you're more use than me.'

'Thanks,' she murmured, when I placed it in her hand. She never opened her eyes, and I think she was asleep two minutes after. You sod, Ian Reid, I thought as I closed the door on her quietly. You utter, utter sod.

Matty didn't want to go for a walk; he'd been watching a cookery programme on CBeebies, and it was baking or nothing.

'Shall we make rolls for tea, then?' I asked, because I knew I had a packet of bread mix in the cupboard, and all you do is add water and knead. Matty made a drilling noise which I took to mean yes, so I got down the big mixing bowl that was my mother's, and carried a chair in from the lounge for him to stand on.

'You'll need to let Nanna measure out the water,' I told him. I didn't want him near the tap. Laverne-next-door's cousin's little girl was very badly scalded with a hot tap last year. That story's haunted me ever since I heard it. Her mother was only in the next room, ironing.

I opened the packet, and a little bit of flour puffed up into the air. 'Oh,' said Matty, impressed. I patted the sides for fun and another tiny cloud rose up. Matty squealed. I slid the packet slightly over towards him, smiling, and without hesitation he stuck out his palm and walloped the side. Bread mix exploded out of the top and the packet fell over, spilling a long white plume across the kitchen surface.

'Oops,' I said.

'Oops,' echoed Matty.

'My fault,' I said. 'Nanna's fault. Silly Nanna. What was I thinking.'

I began to scrape the mix back up but, as I did so, Matty leaned in over my arm and sneezed spectacularly. The air in front of us became at once thick and misty. Flour hung in suspension, like smoke, like the pall after a bomb's gone off. 'Uh-oh,' he said.

'Uh-oh indeed. My goodness. What a mess.'

'All-gone.' He waved his arms.

'Not really, Matty. Not even slightly, in fact.'

While I wetted a piece of kitchen towel, he began to blow at the flour like a maniac, spreading it as far as his lungs could reach. I thought, I'm going to be cleaning this room till midnight.

'Gotcha,' I said, swooping in and lifting him off the chair, out of range of the bread mix. 'Now, mister, let's see if we can clean you up. Oh, good grief. It's all in your hair, down your T-shirt. You've even got it on your eyelashes. If your mummy sees you like this . . . Close your eyes. Close your eyes, Matty. No, don't wipe it on your trousers. I've got a cloth. Close your eyes while Nanna sorts you out.' As he twisted away from me I could see that my front was covered in streaks of flour too, and that a pale film had settled over everything even as far as the sink, which meant it must be on all the plates in the plate rack and the cups above and the storage jars, and the lot would need taking down and washing.

And at the same time I was thinking, His nails need a proper scrub with a brush if I'm going to let him help knead the dough, and is there enough mix left, should I weigh it out and scale down the amount of water, and when is he due a nappy change, and I was just asking him again to stop blowing at me when the phone rang.

It took me about twenty rings to brush the worst of the mess off myself, shepherd Matty into the living room and shut the kitchen door behind us, pull the toy box out again from under the coffee-table, and locate the phone. If it was Ian, I was going to tell him what I bloody well thought of him. No, I couldn't do that because Matty was at my elbow. I was going to be icily polite, then, and tell him Jaz would ring back when she was less upset, then hang up. No, I'd be better just hanging up, full stop. Unless that was too rude. Except he'd gone beyond rude with what he'd done, even if he was the father of my grandchild.

Then, as I reached for the handset, I had this flash that it might, in fact, be Phil, and I wondered what the hell to say to him, because Jaz had said to me twice now, *Don't tell Dad yet*. But if he asked after Jaz (and he always did), or if he heard Matty in the background, I wasn't going to lie. I wasn't going down that route. There'd been enough lies in our family.

So when I pressed the accept button, I was already worked up, and not fully on the ball. Which is why I made such a hash of it; why I managed to make everything a whole lot worse.

CHAPTER 3

Photograph 271, Album Two

Location: the hallway, Sunnybank, Shropshire

Taken by: Carol

Subject: Jaz, ten, in a blue sequinned party frock. She stands stiff and furious, the Deco glass of the front door fanning behind her in an accidental headdress. It's clothing that's the issue: Jaz would prefer to wear a black strapless top with jeans, and has stated this preference energetically for the last hour. But Phil says the outfit's too old for her and, just for once, Carol's backing him up. 'Nobody else'll be in a dress,' complains Jaz. 'Dresses are lame.' 'Then wear your jeans with a nice blouse,' says Carol. If looks could kill, Carol would be eviscerated on the spot.

But this is not actually the argument. This is an add-on, an extra layer on top of something else. What Jaz is really sulking about – has been for weeks – is that she's been banned from the travellers' camp that's appeared on the wasteground behind the local GP surgery. 'Why would you want to keep going there anyway?' asks Phil. 'Because they're interesting,' says Jaz. And, when she catches him making faces behind her back, adds, 'More interesting than either of you, anyway.'

Phil laughs his head off, but it's a line that cuts Carol to the quick.

'Hello? Am I speaking to Carol Morgan?'

The tone was formal, and I thought it might be a cold-caller. At the same time, Matty was holding up a pot of Play-Doh for me to unscrew, pushing it into my chest.

'Who is this?' I said crossly.

'David.'

I still wasn't with it.

'David Reid,' he said. 'Ian's father.'

There were, I saw now, white footprints across my blue carpet and a shower of white over the arm of the sofa. When I turned to look in the mirror, there was flour in my hair and also caught in the top folds of my blouse. A tilt of the head dislodged another flurry.

'We should talk,' went on David, his tone ultra-cool. I stopped seeing the marks on the furniture and pictured him instead at the wedding in his morning suit, and his snooty girl-friend buzzing around in the background as though it was her son getting married. *I've moved the flowers so they're in the centre of the table, Carol.*

'Talk?' I said.

'Nanna,' said Matty, thumping the pot against my breast-bone. '*Nanna.*'

'Is Jasmine with you?' he said. 'Is she around? Because Ian's been trying to call her, and she won't answer. Is that Matty?'

'Jaz is with me, yes. But she's having a lie-down, I'm not disturbing her.'

'If you could. Ian needs to speak to her urgently.'

'He'll have to wait. She's not ready.'

'You should know, he's staying with me at the moment. He's very upset.'

I snatched at the Play-Doh pot and flung it at the hearth. The top pinged off, and Matty scrambled after it.

'Upset?' I said. 'Upset? I should damn well think he is. Jaz is pretty "upset", too. She's devastated. What Ian's done to her is –' I almost said 'unforgivable', but stopped myself in time – 'despicable. At the very least she needs some time to come to terms with it.'

'There's nothing to be gained from silence,' David was saying. 'The sooner they get together and talk it through, the better.'

'She needs *time*,' I repeated.

'I disagree. The longer she shuts him out, the harder it's going to be.'

'For who, exactly?'

There was a pause, then David spoke again. 'For everyone. Look, I've always had you down as a very reasonable person, Carol, so if the two of us could—'

'Oh, *reasonable*, is it? Depends what your definition of reasonable is, doesn't it? I suppose you want me to go upstairs, wake her and tell her it's all OK, Ian's sorry, and she should be a good girl and take him straight back. Four years they've been married, four years, and if he can't keep his hands to himself in that time then they've no chance. She might as well ditch him now. Everything on a golden plate, he's had, you've seen to that –'

'I resent the implication there.'

'– and it's still not good enough. I don't know who he thinks he is, what right he has to – That lovely girl up there – God, what's wrong with people that they can't *hold on to what they have and be grateful?*'

I realised I must have been shouting, because Matty had stopped playing and was looking at me. I put my hand against my mouth, ashamed, and at that moment the living-room door opened and Jaz walked in.

'What's going on?' she said. 'I could hear you on the stairs.'
I shushed her, but it was too late.

'Can I hear Jasmine?' came David's voice, thin and power-less out of the receiver. 'Jasmine? Jasmine?' I held the phone to my chest, muffling him.

Her face fell. 'Oh God, what have you been saying, Mum?'

'I don't know,' I said. 'It just came out.'

'Well, it shouldn't have. This is my crisis.' And she took the phone away from me and switched it off.

There've been several notable occasions when I've opened my mouth and come out with the opposite of what I wanted to say. Sometimes, if I can't sleep at night, I play those times back and then I have to get up and stick the radio on and have a milky drink or maybe do a few stretches. Must be nice to be one of those people who aren't bothered.

After Jaz had taken Matty upstairs to change him I felt the urge to haul out her wedding album, compound the misery of the moment. The album (hand-tooled, gilt-finished) lived in the space under the bureau, in a special white box. Last time it had an airing was the night Jaz came round to tell me she was pregnant.

I wiped the dust away with my sleeve and lifted the lid.

Inside, it smelled of the past. Leather, cream card, tissue paper edged in gold: all those layers protecting, and not one of them any use in the end. Here at the front was Phil – open-faced, amiable cheat. It's eight years since I finally threw him out – an age ago – yet if I look at his picture for too long, time's compressed to nothing. He was standing under the archway at the entrance to the church, Jaz clutching his arm. Later she'd told me she was so nervous she thought she might be sick, right there in the porch, but Phil had distracted her with a story about how he'd sneaked into the hotel earlier and drawn a penis on the inside of David's place-card. She'd been so busy being annoyed, she'd forgotten to be scared. So Phil had been some use. And at least he had turned up, without Penny in tow, and had given Jaz away properly. He even behaved himself at the reception, if you didn't count trying to kiss me at the end of the evening.

On the next page was the immaculate David with his lovely consort, Jacky, like a couple out of *Cheshire Life*. 'I tell you, I'd have sold my bloody flat to pay for this wedding if I'd known he'd be so up himself,' Phil said to me afterwards. 'Lording it over everyone.' I'd thought that was a bit unfair at the time; put simply, David had money, and we didn't.

I suppose you want me to go upstairs, wake her and tell her it's all OK, Ian's sorry, and she should be a good girl and take him straight back, I heard myself say again. Lord above, why had I come out with that, when ultimately I wanted them reconciled?

I turned the page quickly.

Now it was Dad's lost and vacant eyes staring back at me. We'd picked confetti off his front, lifting his arms out of the way to get at the little horseshoes. 'I think he enjoyed himself,' I remember saying to Jaz as we got him ready to wheel back. 'I'm sure he knew what was going on.' You tell yourself all sorts.

The next page was a close-up of the happy couple: Ian now, to my eye, slightly shifty behind his metal-framed glasses, as though he'd pulled off something that he didn't deserve, and Jaz tragically radiant beside him. Her long hair was drawn back at the temples, mediaeval-style, and she had a circlet of artificial daisies on her brow. 'We do some very nice tiaras,' the woman in the bridal shop had said. But Jaz wouldn't budge. 'I want it to look as though I've picked them fresh from the fields.' The shop woman wrinkling up her nose when she thought I wasn't looking. God knows what face she'd have made if she'd known we were having black ribbons too.

A memory came suddenly of a teenage Jaz getting ready to go out one night, popping her head round the living-room door and asking whether she could borrow my jacket, and me saying, 'Which one?' Jaz tilting further so her body was hidden by the jamb, mumbling, 'Oh, just that velvet one.' So I knew she already had it on. 'But you've got a velvet jacket of your own,' I'd said. 'Not like yours. Mine's a blazer-type. Yours is all silky and drapey.' She'd come in then and showed me, lifting up the tails, waggling the bell sleeves. I seem to recall her with crimped hair, or that may have been another time. 'That's because it was very expensive, Jaz. It's meant for special occasions.' Of course she won, beauty over age, and the jacket became hers. *You want to borrow it back from her*, I imagined Phil saying, and then David's voice sliced in again: *I resent the implication there.*

I let my gaze fall one last time, then closed the album against the brightness of her smile.

Thing about Matty is, he's at that terrifically portable stage. True, I can't take him to the gym, or when I do my swimming, or on any of the Beavers excursions (or to work, of course, which is another bone of contention with Jaz). But aside from that, as long as the place we're going to can supply him with a container plus some small objects to put in and take out, he's fine. Failing that, there's entertainment to be had from anything that can be rolled, anything that can be hidden under, any object that can be used to strike another object, and all pipework and cabling.

So when I go to see Dad, Matty makes himself at home wherever we're based. If we're in the central lounge, he'll explore the toy box they keep there for visiting grandchildren, and submit to being ruffled and cooed over by any number of elderly strangers. If he's in Dad's room, he'll make a bee-line for the yucca in the corner with its fascinating white gravel. As long as you check he's not putting any of it in his mouth, you can pretty much leave him be. Give him a mug to fill and he's occupied for half an hour.

These days, Sunday mornings are a good time to visit, because I always have Matty with me then; he's stayed over Saturday nights since he was weaned. I have him till tea-time, till *Songs of Praise* he's all mine. And visiting my dad is now part of the routine. What used to be a potentially upsetting part of the weekend is transformed, because I tell you, it's a heck of a lot easier to go along with Matty than it is to go on my own. He's a fresh, new thing in the land of the old. He's something to focus the conversation on, something to distract from the horribleness that is watching your father leave you by degrees.

This week we arrived to find Dad propped up in bed, having his tea out of a lidded cup. 'Well, I'm glad you're here,' went the hearty nursing assistant, 'because we're doing very nicely indeed today.'

'Yes?' I wondered whether Dad had done something remarkable.

'His chest's completely clear, what do you think about that? None of the nasty coughing that kept him awake before. He's had three really good nights, and today he's full of the joys of spring, aren't you?'

Dad, glassy-eyed and weary underneath her strong arms.

'Great,' I said.

Once she'd finished and left, the first job was to go round the room moving pills, pads, hearing-aid batteries, unsuitable sweets, coins, pen tops. I plonked Matty with his changing bag by the yucca and gave Dad a kiss, and then I sat down to assess the state of play.

She was right, I thought, when I got a proper look at him. He was a better colour, and he was sitting up straighter than last week. The blue shadows under his eyes had almost gone.

'I've brought Matty,' I announced brightly, as I always did. Matty paused at his name, then carried on shovelling stones with his fingers.

'He's staying with me for a few days,' I went on.

Dad blinked.

'So we're both enjoying that.'

'Bee,' said Matty, pointing at a fly on the wall above him.

'Not a bee,' I said. 'Just a fly. Dirty fly. Bleah.'

Dad cleared his throat, like someone about to speak.

I waited, but nothing came.

'Anyway, it's great to have him, but it is making life a bit tricky, because I'm having to take him to nursery the mornings I'm in the shop, and it's the wrong direction so that adds an extra half an hour to the journey. Cutting across from Nunheath isn't an option because I have to come back for Josh next door; I can't suddenly tell him to start taking the school bus. Although I suppose he could, but it's messing his mum about, and she's enough on. You remember Josh's mum? Laverne?'

We used to joke about Laverne, how thin she was. 'Not as far through as a tram ticket,' Dad used to say. 'She daresn't step over a grid in case she falls through.'

Matty laughed suddenly. 'All-gone,' he said.

'What has, sweetheart? Oh.'

He'd found a cup of cold tea I'd managed to miss on first inspection, had tipped it onto the floor in the space between his legs and was measuring the effect of liquid on nylon fibre. I took the cup off him and placed it out of reach. Then I dabbed up the pool with a handful of tissues. Not for nothing do they have mottled-pattern carpets here.

'Hey, I've got your Scooby car with me,' I told him. 'And let's see if Nanna doesn't have a packet of raisins for a good boy.' I extracted both items from my bag, then came and knelt beside him so I could lay the raisins out in a row across the little table. He likes it when I do that, and I needed him to be occupied, to let me think for a minute. There's a fine line between being a distraction and a nuisance.

Above me, Dad sighed. I got up and went back to the chair.

'I was thinking on the way here,' I said, leaning forward in the hope I might catch his interest, 'do you remember when Jaz was little, and you let her help make a bird scarer for your veg?'

For a second I thought he was nodding in acknowledgement, but it was just a wobble of the head.

'Do you remember,' I went on, 'all the milk bottle tops and foil pie cases and strips of tinsel she tied on? And there was a budgie bell and a couple of old forks, strung on about a mile of twine. How many pegs did you use in the end? I know it was more bird scarer than garden when she'd finished. I've a photo of it somewhere. And we were watching out the kitchen window, it had only been up an hour, and this jackdaw came down and started taking the tinsel off. Pulling away at it, like it was a worm. Do you remember, Dad? I thought she'd hurt herself with laughing so much. You said, "I reckon you've made a bird disco, Jaz". She thought that was fantastic.'

I paused, because you can do that with Dad. Silences are OK. Over in the corner Matty was busy squashing raisins under car wheels, but overlaid with that was an image of his mother, aged about nine, clapping her hands to her face with delight.

'It's different being a grandparent, isn't it?' I said. 'I know there were times, when she was growing up, Jaz would talk to you when she wouldn't to me. Not that I minded. What I say is, thank God there was someone she *would* talk to.'

Outside the room a trolley rattled; someone shouted a greeting. Matty's car fell off the table, scattering raisins.

'I went to a talk on nineteen thirties' suburban architecture last week,' I said, because as well as long silences, non-sequiturs are also fine when you're talking to Dad. Whatever pops into your head, really. 'Gwen from the gym invited me. It was good, you'd have loved it. All houses like Sunnybank, and Pincroft. The speaker was saying how few Thirties buildings still have their proper metal windowframes, and I felt like sticking my hand up and shouting, "Mine has!".'

Dad's eyes were empty, but I never let that put me off. Because it's like they say about comas: you can have someone lying there apparently unconscious, and then when they wake up they can tell you word for word what they've heard people saying around them. And Matty, months before he could speak, could point to all sorts. You'd go, 'Where's the light?' And his arm would ping straight up. 'Where's the car?' And he'd swivel to the window. So just because Dad's so quiet doesn't mean he's not still with us at some deep level. And the strange thing is, I can tell this dad things I would never have been able to before.

I reached out for his hand.

'Do you ever wonder,' I said, 'what would have happened if you'd taken different decisions in your life? I do. If I'd stuck with Phil, say, and made more of an effort to blot out what was going on, how Jaz would have turned out. Or should I have kicked him into touch right at the start, when I first found out? Would that have been better? I wish now I'd confided in you, but coping with someone else's upset on top of your own . . . And Mum would have gone, "I told you so". Sometimes I used to imagine you coming round to our house and punching him in the face. I want to punch Ian. I want to sock him in the jaw.'

The shadows on the wall were focusing and unfocusing as the sunlight altered; Matty's fly crawled across the headboard.

'Jaz must think it's all men ever do. Sorry, sorry, Dad. Not you, obviously.'

Someone far off was playing Glenn Miller.

'Or David. Oh, did I tell you he'd rung? I made a hash of that, too. Typically. They'll put it on my headstone: *Tried Hard, Made Everything Worse.*'

And just as I was thinking I shouldn't have mentioned graves, the sun came out, making a tiny brilliant spotlight from my watch appear on the wall just by Dad's shoulder. Matty lifted his head, transfixed. 'That?' he said. For fun I jiggled my wrist so the spot danced about, and within seconds he'd left his pot of gravel and was up by the bedhead, tugging at the nearest pillow in an attempt to reach it.

'Careful,' I said, torn between delight and concern.

Matty slapped his palm against the wall. Slowly Dad turned his head, like a man trying to locate a sound in thick fog.

I made the beam slide down to the end of the bed, out of Dad's way, and Matty followed it, patting the bedcover. There I let the light play on his fingers and he stood still for a moment, puzzling. At the same time, Dad shifted so his right arm came out from under the covers, and now you could see both sets of flesh within touching distance: the chubby unblemished, and the freckled slack.

The scene held me. Were Dad's eyes watching Matty, or were they fixed on some point beyond him? If I had my camera, if I took a photo now, would the picture turn out happy or sad?

CHAPTER 4

Photograph: newspaper clipping between the pages of a Christmas 1967 Woman's Realm *inside Carol's bureau, Sunnybank.*

Location: the square outside the Red Lion, Tannerside

Taken by: the Bolton Evening News

Subject: The Big Switch-On *reads the caption.* Tannerside's Tree of Light is illuminated by councillors Bob White and Tommy Pharaoh.

At the base of this twenty-foot Douglas fir, the two men shake hands. There's been a good turn-out despite the drizzle — too many people for them all to fit into the shot. Carol, Councillor White's daughter, just squeezes in, though she's not actually that keen to appear in the local rag wearing this stupid tam o' shanter her mother forced over her ears before she was allowed out. 'You want to try looking smart, for once,' said Frieda.

For all the icy wind and headgear humiliation, Carol's enjoyed the walk up, just her and her dad together.

'How you doing?' he asks.

'Happy as a sandbag,' Carol says.

A standard and much-loved exchange.

When they draw near the cemetery and a car slooshes through a puddle, soaking them both, Bob goes, 'There's nowt like good manners, and that was nowt like it.' It's a turn of phrase which never fails to make Carol laugh.

He has dozens of these sayings. They are who he is. Every time she drops something, he chirps, 'Did it bite you?' If she complains that something's not fair, she gets, 'Neither are th' hairs on a black pig's bum.' Then there are his nicknames: people from Horwich are 'sleepers'; from Standish, 'pow-yeds'; from Bolton, 'trotters'; from Wigan 'purrers'. Purrers sounds nice, thinks Carol, the first time she hears it. She pictures Tenniel's drawing of the Cheshire Cat, perched on the gates of Mesnes Park. But 'purring', Bob enlightens her, means kicking someone with clogs on. It's all good fun.

The only saying she can think of that her mother uses is, 'Go rub it better with a brick.'

Ian caught up with us eventually. He was waiting for me one morning when I got to The Olive.

'Carol,' he said, pushing at the bridge of his glasses. 'I need to see you.'

'Not here, not now,' I said, fumbling with the keys in my eagerness to escape inside. What if Moira popped in to check a customer order or a delivery, walked through the door and found a family drama unfolding in the middle of her shop? Tears and accusations amid the wooden mushrooms.

'Carol,' he said.

'It's Jaz you should be talking to,' I told him. The key slid home and turned. 'Go round there. She's in.'

'No, she isn't.'

I was genuinely surprised. 'She was in an hour ago because I stopped off to pick up some more of Matty's clothes. She must have nipped out for something. I'd try again.'

And with that I slipped inside and locked the door against him.

He loitered for five minutes and then walked off. Good, I thought. I got on with my jobs: turning on the lights, the till, checking the post and answerphone, unpacking a load of cat-motif mugs for examination and then flattening the cardboard box ready to go in the bin out the back.

After that I flipped the sign round and opened the door. Ian was standing on the pavement opposite.

'You can't come in,' I called, stupidly.

'You can't stop me, I'm a customer,' he said, and walked straight over, crossed the threshold, installed himself by a display of slate clocks. No one else was around. We don't usually get anyone till ten at the earliest, so why Moira always wants the place open at nine-thirty sharp is beyond me.

Ian glanced at the shelf nearest, then picked up a marble egg and weighed it in his hand the way everyone does who touches them. 'I'm not hanging round there indefinitely, Carol. She's in but not answering the door, and she's got the deadbolts on. She won't pick up the phone either.'

'She will. I was chatting to her last night.'

'We've got caller display. She won't pick up when she knows it's me.'

'Ring from a friend's, use a different mobile.'

'I tried that. She hung up.'

'Can you blame her?' I said.

I watched his expression flicker for a moment. Ian isn't the kind of man who's built for deceit; he's nowhere near cool enough.

'No, of course I don't blame her. But we can't carry on like this. I have to explain.'

'To her, though, not to me.'

He put the egg down – I was relieved about that – and approached the counter.

'You need to hear, Carol. You need to help. You understand Jaz better than anyone.'

It was an astute compliment on his part. 'Well,' I said.

'I know what I've done, I know just how badly I've messed up. I love Jaz, and Matty; they're the only things I care about. Not that woman, she was nothing. What happened was a slip. It absolutely didn't mean anything. It'll never happen again.'

'Why did you do it, Ian?'

He shook his head. 'I don't know.' And he did look bewildered, as though he truly couldn't fathom it.

'You need to take responsibility,' I said.

'That's what I'm trying—'

'She's very, very upset.'

'Yes. She must be.'

'Devastated.'

'Tell me what I can do, Carol.'

I let myself imagine, for a moment, what might have happened if someone had taken Phil aside all those years ago and told him. Whether Phil could have been straightened out. I turned my head away from Ian, and across the floor of the shop, ground-in specks of glitter winked and sparkled at me; we'd had some frosted twigs in over Christmas and they'd shed like billy-o, we'd been hoovering every day. Christmas, when Matty wasn't even walking.

I had a chance to make things good.

'She is dreadfully hurt,' I said.

Ian hung his head. 'I feel terrible. Please, tell me what to do.'

'OK, then,' I said, sitting myself on the edge of the counter because by now my legs were trembling. 'Firstly, don't corner her. Don't stake out the house or ring every half-hour. She doesn't react well to being pursued. Send her a letter – I'll give it to her if you're worried she'll just stick it in the shredder, though I don't think she will. Give me a letter and I'll make sure she gets it. In it you say what you've told me: that you love her and Matty; that she's not done anything wrong, it's entirely your fault; that it was a stupid, joyless one-off and it will *never ever happen again*.' He was nodding emphatically. 'That last bit's really important. You must never let her down again, Ian. She won't give you a second chance.'

She might not even give you a first, I thought, but I kept that to myself.

'Will it work? Will she have me back?'

'I don't know.' In my head I saw Matty, pyjama-ed, rolling his toy car up and down the newel post in their hall. 'But you have to give it a try.'

After he'd gone I turned on the shop's CD-player and listened to some Celtic harp. I felt drained, as though I'd been doing some hard physical labour. The urge to ring Jaz was enormous, but I made myself stay off the phone because I knew I'd only blurt out something I wasn't supposed to. Though I did call the nursery and check on Matty. 'Is anything wrong?' the girl asked me when she came back from the toddler room. 'Nothing,' I said. Then, because I didn't want to sound weird, I said, 'He looked a bit flushed when I dropped him off this morning.' 'Well, he's fine now,' she said. 'He's playing Funky Footsteps.'

We had four paying customers all morning – you can see why Moira frets – so I had plenty of time to go over events. Mainly I thought about Ian: how much did we ever really know about him? The first time Jaz mentioned him was the Christmas after she started at the Rocket café. 'I met him on a protest, Mum,' she said, and when I told Phil he went, 'Of course she did.'

We thought we knew what was coming. The Sullen Boys, Phil used to call them, the thin, shifty youths who refused to meet your eye and slipped away upstairs the moment you paused to draw breath. The bedroom door would shut and you'd be crashing around in the kitchen, trying not to think about what was going on above. Couldn't believe it when Ian turned up in a shirt and tie, normal hair, voice like a BBC newsreader. His table manners were lovely. 'Were you protesting, too?' I asked him over the washing up. 'No, I was trying to get into my office,' he said. We were so busy admiring what he wasn't, we never thought to probe what he was.

And he seemed so kind. One time he came and dug out my pond while I was at work, for a surprise. I came back to find a moulded liner, like a giant tortoise shell, propped against the back fence. I love that pond. When I spied my first load of frogspawn a few months later, he was the person I rushed to tell.

Phil reckoned Jaz was the happiest she'd ever been, and we were happy for her. How much had we all invested in this charming, earnest, motherless young man, taking him into the family, knotting him into our hopes and dreams. The day Matty was born, I'd thought my world was complete, that everything was stable at last. Goes to show how wrong you can be.

Jaz had Matty that night, so it was a chance for me to catch up on jobs before I drove up to Chester library for a lecture on Clarice Cliff. The clematis wanted tying back before it snapped, and I'd some raffle ticket stubs to fill out and give back to Laverne, an outrageous estimated gas bill to chase up, plus my hair desperately needed a wash and blow-dry. I knew I'd have to scoot if I was going to make it out of the house for half-six.

The phone went while I was leaning over the bath side with my head under the shower.

I threw a towel round my sopping hair and ran to pick up.

'Carol?' It was David Reid.

'Yes; what?' I said abruptly, because once again he'd caught me on the hop.

There was a slight hesitation.

'Ian and I were talking at breakfast this morning. I gather you're acting as mediator.'

'Ahm, I suppose, yes.'

'He's very relieved. Jasmine's still not taking his calls.'

'No.'

'So what's been the reaction? Do you think we might be making progress?'

The towel was sliding to one side and cold water was trickling down the back of my neck. I said, 'I've not spoken to Jaz yet, but I'm seeing her for tea tomorrow and we'll talk then. To be honest, just at this—'

'Good,' he said, sounding like a headmaster. 'That's good. I'm so glad you decided to help.'

I felt a hot flare rise up inside my chest.

'*Well, someone's got to try and make something out of this mess,*' I said. Then I hung up and stood with my hand over my eyes for a moment. It wasn't David's fault; he hadn't deserved that. But then, what a bloody imperious thing for him to say. I was right, I was wrong. I was very hot, suddenly. When I looked across the room I could see myself in the mirror: *Middle-aged Woman in a Turban, Flushed*. You'd think I'd have learned by now to be wise and serene. I put my palms to the sides of my face and lifted the slack skin tauter.

The next second, the phone rang again.

I snatched at the receiver. '*Yes?*'

'God's sake,' said the voice of my ex-husband. 'No need to

be like that. I only wanted to ask what's going on with our
Jaz.'

Too late now for Clarice Cliff, but I reckoned I could still make
it to the gym if I put a spurt on. I needed to work out my
temper on something. And to be with other women, have a
giggle, listen to some music and get out from inside my own
head.

Why didn't you tell me, Carol?
Because Jaz said she wanted a chance to think.
So how come she's just told me now?
I don't know, Phil. I don't know why Jaz would do that.

Upstairs, then, for my T-shirt and leggings. My trainers were
supposed to be in the bottom of the wardrobe, but weren't.
Were they by the back door? What was this? My top slipped off
the hanger and crumpled to beggary—

Is she right?
What do you mean?
Has he been playing away?
Of course he has. He's confessed.
Fucking hell.
That about sums it up, yes.

A different top, then, with longer sleeves. That would be
too warm, but no choice. At least the leggings were in an OK
state.

What are we going to do?
I don't see what we can do. I'm looking after Matty.
You do that anyway.
*Not this much. Everything else is on hold, I can't get on with my
ordinary stuff. I'm not complaining, Phil, I love him being here. I
just want it to go back to normal, for us all.*

Answerphone on, trainers located and laced—
Have you talked to her?

Obviously I've talked to her, I've done nothing else for over a week. But she's confused at the moment. I think it has to come down to Jaz, whether she wants him back or not. Then we have to support her either way.

What do you reckon she should do?

Whatever she thinks is best for her and Matty.

Bottle of water, bottle of water, keys keys keys—

Ian's a shit.

Well, yes.

Keys. Coat—

And that's when the phone rang again, and it was Jaz on the machine, and this time I knew I wasn't going anywhere.

CHAPTER 5

Photograph 311, Album Three

Location: Chester Rows

Taken by: Carol

Subject: Jaz and Solange Moreau, school French exchange student, stand arm in arm, grinning. Solange is neat and minxy in her mini-skirt and boots: obviously French mothers are more liberal regarding their daughters' attire. Jaz is much more suitably kitted out in jeans, sweater and long, lime-green scarf. Next to them is Jaz's friend, Natalie, standing apart, looking suspicious. Behind them all is Phil. He's pulling the same stupid expression as the one in his school photograph of 1968.

Carol has enjoyed having Solange to stay: she is drawn by the girl's fractured English, and the fact that she's away from home at such a young age. And the attraction seems to be mutual. Not an hour ago, Solange produced from nowhere a lovely set of soaps bearing an impossibly expensive label, and handed them over. 'For my vacation mother,' she explains prettily. 'Well, aren't they beautiful?' says Carol, impressed. 'But you shouldn't have. However did you afford them?'

When Jaz translates, Solange laughs and laughs, as though it's the funniest line she's ever heard. Carol can't see the joke, and nor, judging by their expressions, can Jaz or Nat. Strange creatures, teenage girls. There's been a terrible atmosphere in the house for nearly two days now. She presumes they've had some kind of a fall-out. Whatever it is, it can't be Carol's fault, because she's bent over backwards to make the visit a success.

Not to worry. Solange returns to France tomorrow, and then everything will be back to normal.

Jaz said she'd gone to pick Matty up from nursery as usual, and he had not been there.

'It's all right,' she went on, before I could begin hyperventilating. 'I mean, he's with me now.'

She paused, and I could hear him chuntering in the background. 'Oh, God, love,' I said.

And she told me this: that while she stood shaking in the hallway, among all the little coats and bags, the nursery manager came with a message about Matty's daddy collecting him twenty minutes ago. No, he hadn't mentioned where they were headed. But Mr Reid had forgotten Matty's jumper, so maybe Mrs Reid could take it. Jaz hadn't waited to argue, she'd simply grabbed the jumper and dashed out onto the pavement, scanning up and down in case she could see Ian's car. For a few minutes she ran the length of the road and back again without knowing what she was doing. Then she gathered herself to ring Ian's number on her mobile. It took two goes before he answered, at which point he calmly told her to cross the street. So she did, and through the window of a grotty little café she saw them: Matty in a high chair eating a bowl of chips, Ian with a newspaper open in front of him. 'He *waved* at me, Mum, like it was no big deal.' When she went in, he invited her to stay and have a coffee with them. But she was too agitated to sit down. 'I didn't know where the hell you were!' she told him. 'You could have taken him anywhere.'

And Ian said simply, 'He's my son, Jaz. I can take him anywhere I want.'

My stomach flipped over when I heard that. Not just because I was annoyed with Ian for not waiting, for ignoring what I'd told him – *Don't confront her, don't corner her*, I'd said – but because of the implications. And I knew, before Jaz finished the story, exactly how she would have reacted. My throat got tighter and tighter as she told me what she'd said to him, there in the café while the other patrons sat and watched, while Matty played with his chips. All the words she'd been holding back, brooding over for the last few days, flooding out. Matty hearing it, breathing it in like poisonous smoke.

'What did Ian do?' I said at last.

'I didn't give him a chance to do anything. I picked up Matty and left.'

I saw in my mind's eye a howling toddler dragged from his chair and bundled into the car, Ian dashing outside, watching them drive off while Matty sobbed and kicked in his booster seat. It was unbearable.

'I was going to tell you, he came to the shop today.'

'That was bloody sneaky of him.'

'I don't think he knew what else to do. He was desperate to see you.'

'You sound like you feel sorry for him,' said Jaz, dangerously.

'I don't—'

There was a clattering noise in the background. 'Fucking hell,' Jaz said under her breath. 'Matty? Matty! Leave it. Come here. *Come here.*'

I said, 'Bring him round to mine, give yourself a bit of peace. Have a nice bath. Or I'll pop over now and pick him up. I can be with you in ten minutes. Yeah?'

Silence. I was picking up my keys again, ready.

'No,' she said. 'He's staying with me. From now on, I'm not letting him out of my sight.'

'Make the most of it while she's small,' people used to say to me when Jaz was young. 'The time goes by in a flash.' It's one of those mantras parents pass between themselves. I remember saying it to Laverne when her Josh was at primary school. I've come out with it in supermarket queues, to young mums waiting in the nursery foyer, to Mrs Wynne-on-the-other-side's granddaughter, to friends and acquaintances and strangers. I said it to Jaz and Ian six months in when they were beside themselves with lack of sleep. 'None of it lasts long,' I told them, 'none of these stages you're convinced will go on for ever. In the blink of an eye they're gone.' You get to my age, you suddenly feel the urge to warn everyone, to explain that you were there once, and you were left gaping at how quickly your children passed through. Even now I'll sometimes be clearing out a cupboard, or moving a piece of furniture, and I'll discover an object belonging to girl-Jaz. This can be an unexpected treasure, or an irritant, like the time a Kinder dragon got into the hoover and broke the roller mechanism. But other days such finds are a blade through the heart, and I could lie down and weep that this tiny sock no longer has an owner; that the milk teeth which made the marks on this discarded plastic spoon now live in my china cabinet inside a pot with a fairy on the lid. That moment when you go to take your child's hand, as you've done for years, and she shakes you off because she's too old: that's a killer.

Thank goodness for grandchildren, our second chances.

It was easier in the mornings without Matty, I had to admit. It wasn't just the dressing, the feeding, the clearing up – procedures which often had to be repeated, from scratch. It was the run to nursery that really stretched me. To get him there, settle him, unpack his stuff, come back, pick up Josh from next door, drop him outside the high school and be at the shop on time, I had to be out of the house by 7.45 at the latest. Any accidents, any tantrums or fevers or suspicious rashes, and we were all scuppered.

So although I missed him, it was certainly less complicated to have only myself to get ready. I got half an hour's lie-in, ate my breakfast at one sitting, listened to the news and managed a proper job with my make-up and curling tongs. Josh would be relieved too, I thought, to avoid all that last-minute rush. Or be forced to listen to Matty-anecdotes the whole journey.

He was sitting on the wall when I got outside.

'You should have rung the bell,' I said.

'Needed some fresh air.' He got to his feet and shouldered his sports bag.

Needed to get away from his mother, I guessed. Laverne was fine as a neighbour, but I shouldn't have liked to share a house with her. Small, stringy, artistic, over-attentive, she buzzed round her son's lumbering frame like a mosquito. Where was Josh's dad? I used to wonder. Not that I ever dared ask her. There was a brittleness there I didn't want to test.

'Mum OK to pick you up tonight?'

'Uh-huh.'

Laverne didn't want him going on the bus in case of what she called 'rough elements'. And since I drove past the school gates every morning, at exactly the right time, it was no bother to take him. He was a nice lad. Meanwhile Laverne would don a leotard and sweatpants and head in the opposite direction to teach dance at the Opel-Warner Studios. So I saw a fair bit of Josh, holed up as we were in my Micra every weekday morning, and I guessed he talked to me far more than he talked to his mum.

When he was twelve or thirteen he went through a phase of coming round a lot. He'd say he wanted to watch a particular

43

programme but his mother had the TV on another station. Or he'd appear as I was cooking tea and cadge half a meal. At first I thought she wasn't feeding him properly – Laverne has a great horror of fat and fat people – but it wasn't always food he was after. Often he'd just sit in the living room with a drink of squash. 'You want to watch out,' Phil said when I told him. 'He's obviously got a crush on you.' 'Oh, obviously,' I remember saying. 'Because it's so normal for a twelve-year-old to fancy someone of forty-nine.'

It wasn't anything like that. The lad just wanted some peace. Which was fine by me, but I could tell Laverne wasn't suited, so in the end I knocked the visits on the head. He was all right about it; he knows his mother.

'What are you up to today, then?' I asked, as the car pulled out of the Close.

He pulled at his shirt where it had bunched under the seat belt. 'OK morning, triple-bad afternoon.'

'Not the Hungarian chemist?'

'Yup.'

'Is he really from Hungary?'

'Dunno. Round there. Transylvania, could be.'

'How are his teeth?'

'I try not to look.'

'Does he avoid mirrors?'

'I would if I had a face as ugly as his.'

'You really don't like him, do you?'

'Nope.'

We waited at the roundabout while a lorry carrying sheep crossed onto the Shrewsbury road.

'When I was at school,' I said, 'the teachers used to hit us over the knuckles with a ruler.'

'Oh, he'd use a ruler if he could get away with it.' Josh mimed a slashing action. 'He's bad enough as it is.'

We moved onto the bypass.

'Right, there was this one time, yeah, when he was showing us how we had to be careful with phosphorous. He had these tongs and gloves and he was making a big deal about how it burns your skin if you just touch it, like it's really corrosive. He got this kid he really hates to come up and pass him stuff, yeah, and then he asks him to hold his hand out and sticks this lump of phosphorous right in the middle of his palm.'

'Oh good God.'

'Except it wasn't phosphorous, it was something else, something that it didn't matter if you touched it, dunno what, but this boy didn't know. He just freaked: he was leaping about and screaming, shaking his hand, running to the sink, and the Hungarian was peeing himself laughing. He made all the other kids join in too.'

'That's appalling.'

'He said it was to make sure we remembered never to touch chemicals with our bare hands.'

'Well, I think that's disgraceful behaviour from a teacher. That boy's parents should complain.'

'It's not that easy, though. He'd just be even more of a git, I reckon.'

'Someone should say something.'

The traffic was getting heavier as we came into the middle of town. Knots of children in school blazers could be seen at intervals, crowding the footpath, calling to each other.

'We had to go in once and complain about a teacher,' I said. 'When Jaz was in Year Nine.'

'Yeah?'

'He tried to wriggle out of it, put the blame on her. But I knew.'

I clicked my indicator on and pulled into the side of the road, between two other parked cars. All Josh had to do from here was walk 400 yards and he'd be at the school gate.

'Never mind, hey.' He undid his seat belt and turned to reach for his bag. 'Come the revolution, they'll all be up against the wall.'

'Have a nice day,' I said to him as he climbed out.

'I won't.'

Which is how we always part. I watched him slouch away, then I stuck my indicator on, checked my mirror, and pulled out into the stream of traffic.

'I was thinking about Jasmine and Mr Woodhall,' I said to Dad. The room was so quiet that I could hear the ticking of the star-burst clock above the door. Dad sat in a high-backed armchair, looking like a man who might be listening. Perhaps he'd noticed Matty wasn't there, perhaps he hadn't. 'Do you remember,' I said to him, 'that teacher who made her cry?'

I pictured a corridor on a darkening afternoon, harvest displays, a cleaner pulling a vac out from a cupboard, some of the classrooms unlit. *I have to ask*, Mr Woodhall had said, *is there anything going on at home we should know about? She seems like a very angry little girl at the moment.* And I went, *Well, of course she's angry! You made her share something you'd told her would be private.* He shook his head and pressed his lips together, slid Jaz's book across for me to read.

Dad gave a little cough, and at the same moment one of the care assistants appeared at the door to ask if I owned a V reg Astra. 'No,' I said. She went away.

I said to him, 'I feel as though I'm walking a tightrope. Ian's got every right to see his son, but it's saying that to Jaz. She's still beside herself, she can't think straight. I'm worried she'll set up a situation—'

Dad's fingers flexed briefly under mine.

'And you see, if I didn't work, I could have Matty for her all the time; she'd like that. She's always telling me about other people's parents who provide round-the-clock free childcare.'

I pictured the shop, and Moira. I loved driving into town every day, chatting to customers, Friday lunches at Healey's, going through the reps' catalogues. Then Mr Woodhall's face loomed across my memory again, triumphant: *'I take it you didn't really stab your husband to death and then take Jasmine to Disneyland afterwards?'*

I stood up quickly, still holding Dad's hand. He looked in my direction for a moment, as if to ask what I was doing.

'Breaking a dream,' I told him.

But the film played on. Mr Woodhall pushing the book across to me, the house point chart on the wall behind him a column of red stars, a jar of teasel heads on his desk.

'How could you have made her read something like this out in front of everyone?'

'Oh, I can't make Jasmine do anything, Mrs Morgan. You should know that. No, she volunteered to share this.'

I looked down at my father's scalp, the marked and uneven skin, the sparse grey hairs. If he would only talk to me, I'd not find myself falling into these thoughts. Don't pick up my gloom, I told him silently.

'Hey,' I said, sitting myself closer to him, 'remember how good our Jaz was that time I broke my arm? Wasn't she a love? Did all the shopping for me, came in from school every night and got straight on with tea. It brought out the best in her, being in charge like that. For that month she was smashing. It makes me wonder—'

'What?' another person would have said. *'What does it make you wonder?'*

And I'd have gone, *'Oh, nothing.'*

The clock ticked; Dad sighed. Jaz's childhood ran away before my eyes.

CHAPTER 6

Photograph 329, Album Three

Location: a fairground, Pwllheli

Taken by: Carol

Subject: a teenage Jaz swooping down in the seat of a ferris wheel, with Nat next to her, both mid-scream. Nat is leaning into Jaz and looks to be properly frightened; Carol guessed she didn't want to go on this ride but didn't dare back out. Jaz, on the other hand, knows no fear.

At the edge of the picture is the claw end of the giant inflatable hammer that Phil's been forced to carry all afternoon. Carol thinks she might wrench it from his grasp and club him with it, any minute now. Except that would be a comic gesture, and it is not a comic situation.

The whole holiday, they have been sniping at each other. The caravan they rented has acted like a microscope, hugely magnifying all that's wrong with their marriage. There somehow isn't the space to argue, and anyway, they can't in front of Nat.

Today has been the worst. Every time the wheel carries the two girls upwards, Carol and Phil start to row. By the time Jaz is at the zenith, they are all but spitting at each other. As she's lowered into view again, it's smiles all round.

As if their daughter's blind and stupid.

One day, Jaz thinks, she's going to meet someone to whom she can confide all this, someone she can totally trust. Someone who will never let her down.

I was going to dress up to see David: my blue skirt from Autograph and a cream blouse, heels. But then I thought, I can't be bothered with all that. I'm not being intimidated. Let him see me as I am.

Typically, the place he'd chosen turned out to be a hotel restaurant, not a pub. The waitress put us in a sort of conservatory, blond wood and sage fittings.

'I knew you'd wear a suit,' I said.

David looked surprised. 'I've come straight from work.'

'So have I.'

He made no comment. We can't all be property moguls, I felt like saying. Someone has to meet society's need for pot pourri and napkin rings.

'It's a tad pretentious here, but they do a decent lunch menu,' he said. 'Do you want to look at the wine list?'

'I'm not sure it's a good idea to add alcohol into the mix.'

'Why? You're not planning to shout at me again, are you?'

The moment teetered while I decided whether to take umbrage. That's why we've come to this place, then, I thought. Protective camouflage. I said: 'I didn't shout. Anyway, it depends.'

'On what?'

'On you.'

'I'll order mineral water.'

When it came, I let him pour. I asked the waitress for pasta, but I knew I was too worked up to eat.

'So,' he said, 'to business. What are we going to do, Carol? What practical steps can we take to help get Jaz and Ian back together? You are still agreed that's the way forward?'

'I think so. I don't know. Yes. In the long term.'

'OK.'

'No one can wave a magic wand here. He had an affair.'

'Not really an affair.'

'Yes, David. He slept with another woman. If you're not going to call a spade a spade, then we'll get nowhere. This is a complete waste of time.'

He looked down at his serviette. 'I'm sorry. That wasn't my intention.'

'You do believe it was a one-off?'

'God, yes. My son's not capable of any kind of sustained duplicity.' He made it sound almost like a failing.

'Do we know anything more about this girl?'

David shook his head. 'She's not important. Honestly. This – slip – was about a moment rather than an individual. We won't hear from her again.'

'Ian told you that?'

'He did, yes.'

'Forgive me,' I snapped, 'but it's a standard line. Adulterers tend not to go, "Oh, yeah, this is only the start, you ain't seen nothing yet".'

'All I can do is ask you to go with me on this.'

In the intervals between talking I could make out background music. 'Three Times a Lady'. *Love* stretched over five ludicrous syllables.

'I suppose,' said David, 'what I'm trying to avoid is any kind of hysterical reaction – no, listen a moment. It's important to keep a perspective.'

'Hard to have much sense of perspective when your husband's screwing around,' I said. 'I don't believe you have any idea how it's affected Jaz. She's absolutely crushed. Unless Ian understands what he's done—'

'Oh, he understands.'

'Does he? You don't seem to.'

The waitress came back and we both sat mutely while she moved cutlery around. Smile smile, we went, like a couple who'd come on a date or something.

When she'd gone, David said, 'All I'm trying to do is take the long view. After the immediate emotional reaction's died down there'll come a point where they see the bigger picture. When Ian's not consumed with guilt and fear, and Jaz isn't beside herself with anger.'

'And hurt.'

'And hurt. Then they'll start to see the shape of their marriage as a whole, and Matty's needs, and be able to weigh up the true impact of . . .' He faltered over the word.

'See? You can't even call it what it is,' I said. 'Who are you to start dictating the action?'

'For God's sake, Carol, haven't you been listening to a word I've said? I'm dictating nothing! That's why I'm here. So we can talk it through together, and agree. I want you on board with this. Without you, any reconciliation plan of mine simply will not work!'

The smart old lady at the next table looked across, and I felt ashamed.

It's your manner, I wanted to tell him. You sound like you're running an executive meeting.

'I appreciate you're feeling very let down,' he went on. 'Don't make the mistake of assuming I'm not. I know full well Ian's been a bloody fool.'

'Have you told him that?'

'Of course I have. He's under no illusions. I just don't think there's much to be gained from continuing to shout the odds. However natural recrimination might be, ultimately it's unproductive.'

'You're like a damn robot,' I blurted.

He blinked.

'Sorry,' I said.

Before he could reply, the waitress arrived and set our dinner down in front of us. I bent, shame-faced, over my cloggy pasta and wished I was back in Moira's shop. At all the tables around us, people ate and drank and had a nice time.

'If we can be practical for a moment.' David laid his fork down and looked at me. 'I'd say the most pressing issue's actually Matty.'

'Oh, it is.'

'He's really the prime consideration and, in a sense, our most useful bargaining tool. But we have to tread with extreme care.'

'Yes, I meant to say about that—'

'After the business at the nursery, Ian's very concerned about access.'

'Well, he shouldn't have wound Jaz up that way. It was asking for trouble. He was supposed to be waiting for me to have a word first.'

'He misses his son,' said David. Behind him, the window began to spot with rain.

'Yes, I can understand that. But he shouldn't have taken Matty with no word about where he was going. You hear about these men snatching their kids and emigrating with them. Or worse. Jaz was frightened. People react strongly when they're frightened.'

David shook his head. 'The way it happened was a mistake. He only went across the road. He was watching for her; when he saw her car he was going to step out and flag her down, but I think Matty needed his nappy changing at the crucial moment and he missed her arriving. I gather she was later than usual.'

'Don't make it sound like it was her fault.'

'I'm not. I'm explaining what happened.'

The waitress appeared, wanting to know if everything was all right. I could tell you a tale, I thought.

When she'd gone, I said, 'It was bad luck, then.'

'Yes. I think he had it in mind it was going to be a kind of reconciliation. Meeting on neutral territory, and with Matty there. She refuses to see him, you know; all Ian wants to do is apologise, but she won't let him. I don't see how they can move on.'

'You've already made that point,' I said.

It was getting Jaz to the state where she could talk rationally, make fair and sensible bargains. David hadn't a clue.

Afterwards we were ushered into a lounge area for coffee. We sat at opposite ends of a huge striped sofa, and I could tell from the way the waitress eyed me that she thought we were a couple: Love in the Middle Years. 'You're way off the mark there, pet,' I nearly said to her. Which started me thinking about Phil and trying to picture him in a place like this, how he'd stand out. Not because of his clothes or manners; he wasn't a yob. But he never picked up on atmosphere. He'd have been winking at the staff, asking for a diet water, sticking his forks into potatoes and pretending they were dancing feet.

'Did you know Matty's latest obsession?' I said, before my mind could get hijacked by unwanted images. 'His thing about doorbells?'

'Go on,' said David.

'Well, when you go to someone's house, he has to be lifted up to ring the bell. He gets very upset if you do it first.'

'What if there's no bell?'

'You have to pretend. He presses a moulding or something, and you have to go "ding dong" for him.'

'Thanks for the warning. I'll bear it in mind.'

'You get some funny looks.'

'I should imagine so.'

The coffee came in dolls' cups, together with a bowl of giant sugar crystals like shards of quartz.

'Do you take Matty out much?' I asked, picturing for a moment that suit in the muddy park, or under onslaught from an ice lolly.

'We've been out together, en famille. We generally go for a walk when I pop round to check the house.' He paused, frowning. 'You see, Carol, that's another issue: it's my house, I own it, and yet it's my son who's been kicked out. She's actually taken it upon herself to change the locks. I could be damned awkward about that, if I wanted to be.'

I took refuge in a sympathetic expression.

'Ian's very important to me,' he went on.

'Obviously.'

'I mean, having lost his mother—'

'Yes, I can see that.'

'For years it was just the two of us. A house of men. He's a good lad.'

'I think he does love Jaz.'

'Oh, he does, he does. If you can make her see that, Carol.'

'I'll do my level best.'

'Because this isn't a game. She really doesn't want to get into point-scoring. That's not meant in any way as a threat, I'm just stating facts. If Jaz starts being obstructive, she'll find Ian more than capable of matching her.'

I had to look away to stop myself saying, 'Why in God's name did he start all this, then?' What kind of men was I dealing with, in this father and son? How far could I trust either of them? Then again, what other choice was there? Across the room from us, on a matching sofa, was a smart elderly couple; he was fiddling with the clasp of her bracelet, and she was smiling over something he'd said. On our left two young businessmen studied a laptop. The tall windows sported swagged drapes; a chandelier hung from the centre of the ceiling. I really should have dressed up a bit more for this place. Had he meant me to feel outfaced?

'Anyway, to sum up,' said David's voice from a long, long way away, 'can I take it that you and I are, essentially, singing from the same hymnsheet? That you're willing to work with me in bringing about an eventual reconciliation? Would that be a fair assessment, Carol?'

'Yes,' I said faintly.

'Good.' He leaned forward and re-filled my coffee cup, even though I hadn't asked him to. 'Excellent. Because in that case, leave it with me. I think I might have an idea.'

CHAPTER 7

Photograph: unnumbered, loose in the back of Jaz and Ian's wedding album, Sunnybank.

Location: outside the church porch

Taken by: Carol

Subject: the bridal crowd, post-official photographs, but before everyone's gone in for the eats. Jaz is in the foreground, looking at Ian. Behind her is David, his eyes on Jaz, and in the opposite corner, Phil watches David. A fascinating range of expressions is covered in this string of vision.

Twenty minutes ago, Phil drew Jaz aside and told her a bald lie: that he overheard her new father-in-law say her dress looks cheap. Since the wedding dress is the only item funded exclusively by the bride's family, the slur is a double whammy. Where a different girl would have flounced off to tell her mother, or tackled David on the spot, Jaz absorbs the information into herself silently. That's always been her way. She internalises everything. The words spiral down through her consciousness like black ink dropped into a glass of clear water.

Why did you do it? Phil is already asking himself. He has no idea what prompted the invention, except that David's a smug bastard, and things have been so shitty lately with Penny sulking about him coming to the wedding, as if he wouldn't see his own daughter married, and bloody awful it was, too, leaving her this morning in floods of tears. Christ knows what she'll have done by the time he gets back. If he goes back. Funny, but living with someone turns out to be not at all the same as having an affair with them, and their flat's too cramped and none of his things are to hand. He misses his shed. And here's David swanking about with that smart bitch at his side.

He didn't mean to hurt Jaz. He never means to hurt anyone. Carol understands that. If he can find Carol, talk to her, it'll be OK. What he really needs at this moment is a pair of arms round him.

We always called it 'the shed', but it was almost the size of a garage, sturdy and brick-built and with a concrete floor. Phil used to reckon it had been a coal-hole-plus-lav, knocked through, but houses like Sunnybank came with internal bathrooms, so I think it was always a general outhouse.

Phil's kingdom, this had been, the place he retreated to when the atmosphere got too tense, or he felt outnumbered. When he reigned here, it was terrifically ordered: tools in one section, decorating materials in another, car stuff here, garden implements there. He installed metal shelves and kitchen base units, bought plastic boxes on wheels and racks that you screwed to the wall. The ceiling was high enough for him to board over half of it and use it to store miscellaneous junk, and woe betide anyone who ignored his system. Even his screwdrivers were lined up in order of size. 'I'll shift it all, I'll shift it,' he used to say. 'I'll come round and take my stuff away, just give us chance.' Eight years he'd been feeding me that line.

Since he'd gone, the place had become a dumping ground. Any item I was too unconfident to sling got shoved in the far corner with the rolls of wallpaper and paint trays. Then having to clear Pincroft generated a load more bags and boxes I couldn't part with, and that I didn't have the time or courage to sort properly. For months I'd been setting myself targets – a box a week, say – and then, at the last minute, I'd find myself putting the job off, casting about for something easier to do. Because the idea of getting rid of anything without Dad's permission seemed like the grossest act of betrayal. Breaking up your parents' home: it's a job that comes to us all, one of those rites of passage, and it's just horrid.

But today I was going to roll up my sleeves and make a start. Here was one area of my life over which I had some control.

I dragged in a patio chair to work on, unfurled three bin bags (Keep, Throw, Charity Shop), and set to on the first box. On the top were bundles of bone-handled cutlery wrapped in my mother's fancy tablecloths. I thought how many hours she'd worked at those cloths, how she'd taught me all the stitches one after another, stem-stitch and satin- and chain-stitch and French knots, separating lengths of embroidery thread and laying them across the arm of the sofa. Her Singer box of trimmings, braid and ribbon was in the second layer down, along with a Tupperware container of sewing-machine accessories, and her embroidery hoops I was always so afraid of cracking. Two nickel-plated candlesticks in the shape of leaping deer were next – they'd sat on the box-room mantel for as many years as I could remember – and then a plastic bag of recipe books, most of them fat with clippings from magazines and packet-sides. I let a page fall open at random: *Date Delights* said the article heading, above a marginal advert for Nostroline nasal spray. Might I, one day, be moved to cook a Date Delight? Or Cornflour Foam, Cheese-and-Rice Shape? It seemed unlikely. But to consign all her work to the wheelie-bin was unthinkable.

Further down the box there was a green dragon tea service, incomplete but lovely to see again, and also a Lustreware fruit bowl with a great crack through the centre. I held the bowl in my hands for a while, turning it this way and that to gauge how visible the damage really was. Too visible, I decided, but even then I couldn't bring myself to put it in the throwaway pile. That bowl had been on our sideboard throughout my childhood. I could see my mother dusting it now.

And then, towards the bottom of the box, was real treasure: two yellow Kodak envelopes. That meant two virgin batches of photographs, unviewed and uncatalogued. My heart gave a little jolt of anticipation. Another night where I'd be able to get the albums out and go through them, refining our family story.

The prints, when I opened the flap, were an out-of-fashion size, mean and small by today's standards. They weren't especially old ones, but then I wouldn't have expected them to be. Pictures of my girlhood were few and far between.

This first set seemed to be of a family barbecue in the garden here, with another, more random selection towards the back of the pile. Eagerly I pushed the shed door further open to let more light in, and settled myself against the work bench.

Phil's picture was at the front, a Phil with thicker hair and a sharper jaw-line, but the same easy, charming smile. 'Git,' I told him, and the word hung satisfyingly in the air for a moment. But even just speaking that one syllable started a little hot fizz in the middle of my chest. Thinking of your ex is like scratching eczema, a woman on *Oprah* once said. Let yourself get started, and you'll end up a terrible mess.

I slid the picture away to uncover instead a bright-eyed Dad with a very young Jaz perched on his knee. What age was she there? I could only dimly remember the hair-in-plaits phase; she was usually too impatient for anything other than a light brushing. Knowing Jaz, she'd have had those ribbons off minutes after the picture was taken.

The next photograph fixed the date more clearly, because it was of Mum, which had to mean pre-1986. And then it clicked: my thirtieth birthday. Which made Jaz five, Mum about to be diagnosed. Another year on and she'd be dead. I held the photo up to peer more closely. What I was looking for, I suppose, was whether there was anything in her face to show that she knew. Her eyes were slits against the sun, her mouth turned down at the corners. There was still no getting past that expression.

I put her picture to the back and carried on. More pictures of the party, the lawn in its pre-pond days, the kitchen before we had it extended, Dad actually lifting Jaz right up and swinging her round. And here was my very best friend Eileen – good God, Eileen! – raising a glass and obviously in the middle of saying something. 'Oh, I miss you,' I said, 'like you wouldn't believe. What I could tell you if you were still here.' *I know*, she went. *It's a bugger.*

I sat for a minute, holding the pack and thinking how fast twenty years can go. Some days I feel all ages and no age, as though I'm hovering over time, somehow. I can be back at school in a blink, with everyone I knew and all the same jokes and worries and obsessions. Astonishing how you can be the girl at the leavers' assembly – winking at your pals while the Headmistress drones on about the world awaiting you – and also the grandmother sitting on your own in a cramped shed sorting through the dregs of your dad's life. *Failure is a natural part of existence* (I could actually hear old Miss Wilson saying it, see the rope of beads swinging from her bosom), *but it's how we deal with failure that matters.* It's the only line of hers that's stuck; that and the one about strangers judging you by your fingernails. I always hear her voice when I'm rooting for an emery board. Eileen used to do a very good impression of Miss Wilson.

The packet began to slide off my knee, and that brought me back to myself. *Get your skates on*, said Eileen.

The last photo of the batch was me with Phil, our arms round each other. I had my hair in a bob with a side-swept fringe, and I was wearing extraordinary blue eye-shadow. Phil was puckering his lips as if for a kiss.

A slight surface unevenness caught the light and made me turn the print over: *Pretty Woman*, my dad had written, in his loopy hand. I never labelled my photographs, so seeing Dad's caption was a shock, like suddenly hearing his voice in the shed with me. Hastily I went back and flicked through to check for other hidden messages, but there was nothing more, which left me feeling both disappointed and relieved. What might he have written on the back of Phil's? I didn't want to imagine.

The next batch proved to be a strange selection: Jaz, older, about ten, on a grey horse (when had Jaz ever been on a horse?); two shots of a frog out of focus; a sunset; Jaz's best friend Natalie astride a gate, balancing on a milestone, hanging by her hands from a tree, pulling a nasty face; Jaz throwing herself about in a field; a black dog tied to the post of a rotary clothes-line; a yellow toadstool. 'Funny girl,' I said to the one of her dancing. 'What were you up to there?' As I went through the set again, I wondered whether Jaz had ever felt the way I did about growing up, or whether she saw her childhood as a distinct period which was now closed, a life compartmentalised into School, University, Before Matty and after. Pre-Infidelity, Post-Infidelity.

It struck me that I could call Jaz this evening and tell her about finding them. 'Shall I bring them round?' I could say. Or, 'Do you fancy popping over?' Important, this, because since the nursery incident she'd been too busy to see me. I knew the drill: left her alone, stayed occupied, kept off the phone, even though I missed Matty like hell. You have to give Jaz space, and then you have to supply her with an opening. It's the way she's always been.

I slid the photos back, put the envelope to one side, and carried on sorting.

The banging started as I was unrolling a teacloth of spoons. It wasn't clear at first what the noise was or even where it was happening. Only when I stepped out of the shed did I understand it was coming from the front of my own house. Thumping, violent thumping, as though someone was trying to break in. What the hell was going on? I ran up the path, rounded the corner, then stood and stared.

A big fat woman was kicking the bottom panel of my door.

No, not a fat woman: a pregnant one. Dorothy Wynne's grand-daughter, Alice.

Kicking because her arms were full of a limp child.

'It's Libby!' she shouted when she saw me. 'Something's wrong.'

I ran to open up, and she stumbled over the threshold and laid the infant girl down in the middle of the hall carpet.

'What's happened?'

'I don't know what to do,' she said in a rush. 'I went to wake her up from her nap two minutes ago and she wouldn't come round; she was all, like she is now, floppy, wouldn't open her eyes, and she's so hot. Look at her, she's burning up, she's red.'

The little girl's lips were parted and her eyelids closed but fluttery. Her cheeks were scarlet patches, as though someone had slapped her.

'Get her top off,' I said. I was thinking, We need to look for a rash.

Alice unzipped the little fleece and dragged it, with T-shirt and vest, up over Libby's face while I fed her arms through the sleeves. The child was completely unresisting. Her head lolled back like a baby's. 'How long's she been like this?'

'She was like it when I went to wake her. I went up and she was . . . her eyelids were all fluttery.'

'What about before?'

'Fine, OK, just normal.'

'Strip her completely,' I said. 'Underwear and all.'

There was a clattering on the step. When I looked up it was Mrs Wynne, leaning against the jamb with her stick. She was trembling and panting, and normally I'd have leaped up to usher her onto a seat. But not right now. Instead I bolted upstairs for Matty's ear thermometer. *Be working*, I told it, *be working*. The relief when I heard it beep and the digital panel lit up.

When I got back down, Alice had started to weep with fright. I could see at once, though, that the little girl's limbs and torso were white and unmarked. 'Shut the front door and take your grandma through to the lounge,' I said, because I could see Alice was in no state to hold a thermometer steady.

I helped her to her feet, and in the brief space the two women were out of the hall, I managed to take a reading. Libby's temperature was high, but not dramatically. I felt her tummy, and it was soft.

'What do you think?' said Alice from behind me.

'I think I've been here before. How old's Libby?'

'Five.'

'Jaz was younger, but I'm pretty sure it's the same. Listen, was Libby maybe a bit cooked? She'd plenty of layers on. Was her room very warm? I know your grandma likes the heating high.'

Alice gave a nervous giggle. 'Sweltering.'

'Then I suspect,' I said cautiously, 'it's what they call a febrile convulsion. If young children get too hot they can have these mini-fits; Jaz had a couple of similar dos when she was tiny. It looks scary, but it soon passes off.'

'Does that mean she's going to be OK?'

'You stay with her and talk to her while I get some warm water.'

I brought back two clean towels, plus a plastic bucket of Matty's which had been the first container to hand, and set to work wiping Libby down. 'You too,' I said to Alice. 'It'll cool her gently.'

Within moments, Libby had started to whimper, and then cry, a normal, blessed noise. Her mother's face crumpled with relief. 'Oh, sweetheart, sweetheart, shush shush, Mummy's here. I'm here, you're all right.' She scooped the naked child up and started to rock her.

'Obviously she still needs checking over, for your peace of mind as much as anything.'

'Yes, yes,' said Alice.

'Shall I call the surgery for you? I can run you down there, too, although actually a walk in the fresh air might perk her up. Do you want to pop her vest back on now? I'll go call the doctor's, and have a word with your grandma—'

'I'll do anything,' Alice broke in, 'if she's OK. Anything, do you know what I mean? If she's all right, if she's just all right.'

'Yes,' I said.

I left her rocking and went to phone the GP.

It was dropping dark by the time I got back from the surgery. It hadn't seemed right to send Alice on her own, and Mrs Wynne wasn't up to the job. 'Thank you, oh, thank you,' Alice kept saying, the way you do when you've been frightened out of your wits and then someone gives you the all-clear.

I stepped into the hall but I didn't switch the light on. I went and sat on the stairs and contemplated the stained-glass panels in the door. The colours at this time of day were muted and dusky, the dimples and surface imperfections highlighted silver by a porch lamp on the house opposite. Jaz used to trace the lines of lead with her fingertips while I was doing her coat up, handing over her schoolbag, nagging her to be careful crossing the road. A hundred thousand years ago.

'You were so calm,' Alice had said afterwards. And she'd put her hand to her pregnant belly and sighed, as though the weight of the world was across her young frame. 'You just knew what to do, and there I was flapping about in a panic. I suppose it gets easier, does it?'

In the gloom of the hallway I leaned my arm against the stair-gate and remembered the other times Jaz was ill: a dash up to hospital when she caught a chest infection at four weeks; chicken pox that revealed itself on the first day of a holiday; nights up with croup; a gash from a knife we'd told her not to touch; the Bad Time. I thought of a moment during delivery when the midwife announced the baby was in distress and they'd have to induce. And years later, that awful morning I went into her bedroom to wake her and she wasn't there.

Which was when the phone rang, out of the gloom. I got down off the step and picked up the receiver. It was Jaz.

'I tried calling earlier.'

'Ah.'

'But you were out,' she said, her tone accusing.

'That's right.'

'It was your afternoon off. I thought you'd be home.'

Headlamps passed. I thought of Alice, crouched here in this hall, rocking. 'There was a mini-crisis next door and I got involved.'

'Trust you, Mum.'

'Can I help it if people see me as calm and competent?'

She laughed, but not unkindly. 'Talking of crises,' she said.

'Do you want me to look after Matty?' I asked, my heart doing a giant leap.

'Yeah, if you could. I've lost a bloody filling and I need to get it sorted quick, but there aren't any spaces at nursery. They're so inflexible at that place, which is ridiculous when you think how much it costs.'

'Tell me when.'

'Tomorrow afternoon. Can you sort something with Moira?'

'I can swap a Saturday, probably. I'll give her a ring now but I shouldn't think there'll be a problem.'

'Thank God. This tooth's driving me nuts. I can't stop poking at it, even though it hurts like fuck. And coming on top of everything else—'

'I know.'

'Sometimes it's the little things that finish you off.'

'Don't worry,' I said. 'It'll be fine.' I closed my eyes and became part of the darkness. 'I'm always here if you need me.'

CHAPTER 8

Photograph: unnumbered, loose inside an old Bunny-Bons toffee tin, the shed, Sunnybank.

Location: the swimming pool, Stackholme Grammar, Bolton, 1968

Taken by: Mr Soper (Physics)

Subject: The swimsuited girls of 2A stand in a double row against a wall of mustard-coloured tiles. They have been told, time without number, how lucky they are to have their own pool on the premises; the poor children of St Joseph's have to be bussed all the way across town to the municipal baths. But the municipal baths are clean and modern, whereas Stackholme pool was built in 1912, looks like the annexe of a museum and feels, to those girls shivering in their navy costumes, like a walk-in refrigerator. Painted iron pillars ending in scrolled acanthus leaves hold up the ceiling, polished wooden benches line the sides. In the foyer, pictures of teams long dead hang on fraying string, behind speckled glass.

Rumour has it that their swimming teacher is really a man. Certainly Mrs Monks' arms are thick and beefy, and she has no obvious waist, but whether she shaves her chin every

morning has never been established. Male or female, she's a
bastard. Another rumour says she can't actually swim herself,
but this turns out to be wrong.

One month before this photo is taken, Carol and her best
friend Eileen's class is getting ready to practise crouching dives.
There are twenty-five girls lined up along the length of the
pool, and Carol is the last on the right, near the shallow-end
steps. Mrs Monks' whistle shrills, echoes, and the row of navy
swimsuits topples in like a Busby Berkeley routine.

It is Eileen, emerging further up the pool, who spots something is wrong.

'You should never have made her dive past the five-foot
mark!' she says, as a dripping Mrs Monks lays Carol out on
the side. The girls watch fascinated as bloody saliva spools
from Carol's mouth and settles into the grooves between the
tiles.

'She's fine,' snaps Mrs Monks. 'Go and get me some tissues.'

And Carol is fine, of course she is, good heavens. She's
bitten her tongue so badly she won't be able to talk for a
week, and one of her bottom front teeth is loose, but that's
nothing, really. She needs to pull herself together. Wasn't she
watching where she was going? There's no apology, no letter
home to Bob and Frieda White to warn them of the possible
after-effects of a blow to the chin. The only concession Mrs
Monks makes is to allow Eileen to wait behind while they tidy
Carol up.

'Cow,' says Eileen as they trudge across the rec together.
'If I hadn't been watching, you could have died.'

'Ugh,' says Carol.

'We should go see the Headmistress about it.'

'Gugh,' says Carol.

'Don't worry, though,' says Eileen. 'I'll always look out for *you, you can be sure of that. If you ever go under again, I'll know.'*

All Carol can do is hold the paper towel to her lip.

It being a sunny day, I had Matty out in the garden with a washing-up bowl full of water and a selection of containers. Laverne's back door was open and she was playing some classical music – piano, very clean and sharp – which kind of went with the afternoon. Meanwhile Matty filled a margarine tub, poured it first into a roseless watering can, and from there into a colander. I stalked around him with my camera, crouching and rising by turns to catch the moment the silver stream fell, and playing with the shutter speed so that sometimes it was the water in focus and sometimes his face. His concentration was impressive; a Nobel physicist couldn't have been studying harder.

'Wish I was doing that,' said Josh's voice from behind me.

I took the viewfinder away from my eye and turned. He was leaning against the fence, looking like a boy with nothing to do.

'Be my guest,' I said. 'Matty won't mind.'

Josh's mouth twisted into something like a smile. 'I don't mean literally, like, on my knees with my hands in the water, yeah?'

'What do you mean, then?'

'I mean, I wish I was that age again. Sometimes. Like, when you've got no cares and everything's done for you, life's a doss.'

He stroked his smooth chin. Yes, I thought, I bet it's tough being a teenage boy these days.

'Not much freedom, though, Josh; that's the pay-off. He has to go wherever we go, eat what we put in front of him, stay in his cot till we lift him out.'

'Yeah, but. Freedom's overrated.'

'You only say that because you've got it.' Yet even as I spoke I pictured Laverne and the way she hung on him all the time, and how he didn't actually have much freedom at all, which meant that once again I was talking rubbish. *Mum doesn't say right out I can't do stuff*, Josh once told me. *She just makes me feel so guilty, I go off the idea.*

We watched Matty tip liquid from a height like a fancy Spanish wine waiter, then open his hand and drop the watering can in the bowl. Waves slopped over the plastic sides, and the paving stones around the base were stained in a jagged fan shape.

'What they do at school,' said Josh, 'is they try and splash your trousers while you're in the bogs, you know, at the front, then they can go round saying you've peed yourself.'

'Charming.'

'Have you got any washing-up liquid?'

'Why?'

''Cause you can put some in the bowl and give Matty a straw, yeah, and let him blow a load of bubbles. It's good, that. They go everywhere, you get like a mountain.'

'Nice idea, but he's too young.'

'It's not difficult. You only have to blow.'

'There's a good chance he'd suck, and then we'd all be in a mess.'

The image amused Josh, and he snorted with laughter. Before he could object, I'd brought up my camera and snapped him.

'Oy!' he said, shielding his face too late.

'Sorry. I couldn't resist.' I pressed review and brought up the picture on the screen for him. 'It's a nice one. I'll delete it if you want, though.'

He craned his neck. 'God. Do I look like that?'

'Like what?'

'Shrek.'

'You do *not* look like Shrek.'

'Colour me in with a green felt tip.'

I took the camera back. 'I'm not rising to the bait.'

At which point Laverne swept out. 'What bait would that be?' she said. She's got this way of holding her head up – a dancer's posture, I suppose. You could mistake it for snootiness. I know it's just tense muscles.

'Josh doesn't like having his picture taken.' I passed the camera across again. 'But I think he takes a good portrait.'

Laverne clutched the camera and stared at the screen for several seconds. After a moment she took a deep, intense breath. 'Oh, Carol, yes.' Behind her, Josh made a strangling gesture on his own neck.

'Shall I do you a copy?'

'Please, no,' said Josh.

'That would be lovely.'

'Uh-oh,' said Matty suddenly. 'Nanna, uh-oh.'

While we were admiring my composition, he'd taken the car sponge and held it above his head so that half a pint of water had streamed down his arm and soaked into his navy T-shirt. His torso gleamed like a sealion; he was sodden.

'Oops,' said Josh, and there was glee in his tone. I think he might have been expecting me to shout.

'Uh-oh indeed,' I said, looping my camera strap over a fencepost and going to inspect the damage. 'Good heavens. Where's all this water come from? Whatever are we going to do?'

Matty did his shrug sign, palms spread.

'His mum's going to be a bit fed up,' I heard Laverne say.

'Children should get messy sometimes,' I said over my shoulder.

'But he's drenched!'

'I've got spare clothes.'

'You think of everything.' Laverne sounded unconvinced by the argument.

'Of course. That's a grandma's job.'

I knelt down on the film of spilled water and began to peel away Matty's shirt, exposing his pale, rounded tummy. It didn't seem any time since Jaz had brought him home from hospital with the clip still on his umbilical stump; now his belly button was a smooth neat hole. Months passed like minutes.

'I remember when Josh was that age,' said Laverne.

I tugged at the waistband of Matty's trousers. 'How's that nappy going on, while we're at it?'

In the background, Josh made a disgusted noise, and a second or two later I heard their back door click shut.

I felt Laverne's eyes. 'Matty means the world to you, doesn't he?'

'Yes,' I said. 'He does.'

The garden seemed full of Laverne's presence, and for a moment I had the strongest impression it was Jaz whose eyes burned into me, observing, appraising.

I don't know why you clean the house more thoroughly for people you hardly ever see. Maybe it's because there's more chance of fooling them into thinking you lead a life of poise and order, whereas your regular visitors are too familiar with the truth. Whatever, I was burning round the house like a madwoman, shifting pockets of dust that had lain inoffensively for months. And as I went along, I thought of David's high-arched Victorian hallway with its parquet floor, wondered who it was got down on their hands and knees with a tub of polish every week to bring a shine to that. Then the picture became Mum and the way she used to clean at Pincroft: unnecessarily, in ways you'd laugh at nowadays. Every morning, all cushions

taken outside and beaten, every door handle polished reli-
giously, the front step edge chalked white with a donkey stone.
When she dusted pictures, she'd to take them off the walls and
do the backs as well. Beds were stripped to air daily, and each
week she'd haul the mattress off its iron frame for brushing and
turning. Up at six in winter darkness to clear out the grate,
dragging sodden freezing sheets out of the top-loader and feeding them through the electric mangle; you could see why she
was always tired. Then again, it's only what her own mother
had to do.

I lifted the ornaments off the mantelpiece one by one:
Matty's baby photo, Jaz's clay pot, Mum's Sylvac vase, Mum's
Beswick budgie, the cigarette-and-match dispenser Dad had
made himself out of oak in the days when he smoked. Always
good with his hands, my dad. Then I ran the cloth over the
buff tiles that Jaz hated so much (she'd cheered that time I
dropped the poker and chipped the corner off the hearth, as if
for one minute that would've meant getting new). Finally I put
everything back again, remembering how there used to be a set
of teardrop-shaped wooden mice at the window end that Phil
had brought back from a so-called sales trip. They'd gone in
the fire when I found out where he'd really been. All my life
spread out on this bloody mantelpiece.

The duster I threw in the washing machine, then I went
upstairs to make myself presentable. There was still an hour to
go, so no point getting jittery. Except I was beyond jittery,
already.

When I glanced out of the bedroom window I could see Josh
and Matty on Laverne's neat back lawn. Matty was chipping
at the grass with a teaspoon, and Josh was standing at the far
end, running a remote-controlled jeep backwards and forwards.
I leaned against the curtain for a minute and watched them,
trying to slow my breathing and not think too much about the

fact that Ian and David and Jaz were on their way here. 'They can sit down and talk things through; we can act as referees,' David had said. But 'referee' implied impartiality. I put my fingertips to my forehead and closed my eyes.

The doorbell rang.

'An hour, there's another hour to go,' I muttered as I ran down the stairs. A tall shape moved behind the coloured glass.

'I thought,' said David as he stepped inside, 'that if I got here early, we could go through our strategy together. Compare notes.'

'Oh, right,' I said. 'You'll have to give me a minute.' Then I fled back upstairs, leaving him standing there in the hallway. I'm not normally so rude; it must have been the shock.

In front of the dressing-table I rubbed foundation in at top speed, drew on my lipstick in a panicky sweep and dragged a comb through my hair. 'Referee,' I said experimentally into the mirror. 'Refereeing.' It sounded an odd word when you said it aloud.

When I came back down he'd taken himself into the lounge and was on his mobile. 'If you want,' he was saying, without enthusiasm. 'Not really. OK, then, whenever.'

He snapped the phone shut as I walked in.

'Clinching another property deal?' I'd spoken before I could stop myself. 'Sorry, ignore me.'

But he shook his head mildly. 'Just a friend. A complicated friend.' While I dithered over whether to ask, he turned and pointed to my gallery of Jaz photos above the bureau. 'That one's interesting,' he said, indicating the one of her peering through leaves, her hair hanging down, sunlight needling the green canopy behind her head. 'Was she an expert tree-climber, by any chance?'

'She was. Like a fearless monkey. I used to die a thousand deaths watching her.'

'You've got a good eye for composition.'

'I used to go to classes, up at the high school.'

He faced me again. 'Could I possibly have a drink, Carol?'

'Oh, of course. Yes. I should have asked. Tea? Coffee?'

David raised his eyebrows at me.

'I might have some red wine in the larder.'

'That would do it,' he said.

'I'll get a glass.'

'Aren't you having any?'

My first instinct was to say no, and then I realised I did want some wine, very much.

We sat in opposite armchairs with the buff-tiled fireplace between us and the bottle on the cold hearth. I noticed the way he leaned back, relaxed: a man at ease with himself. Meanwhile I could have run up the walls. 'You're wearing a suit again,' I said.

'Possibly more appropriate than an apron.'

'Bloody hell.' I dropped my gaze to my lap and saw gingham. 'You could have said.'

'I just have.'

I put my glass down and untied the apron strings.

'So,' he said. 'How are things with you?'

'Well, Jaz is still all over the place, but Matty's on good form. He's discovered the birdfeeder and he likes nothing better than to put bread out and watch the jackdaws squabble.'

'What about yourself, Carol? How are you doing?'

'Me? Gosh. You know! Staggering along.' I gave a nervous laugh, and reached for the first thing I could think of. 'In desperate need of a lawnmower, actually.'

'Oh?'

'Phil's taken mine – to fix, he claims – and shows no sign of bringing it back. But that's standard. I don't know why I expected anything else.'

'You seem to get on with him pretty well, though.'

What mad gremlin had made me bring my ex into the conversation? 'It depends what you mean by pretty well. You know how things were at the wedding. We're civil. We don't throw things at each other.'

'Better than me and Jacky, then,' he said. 'I lost a few plates to her before she left.'

Jacky gone? That was a turn-up for the books.

'I didn't realise.'

'About six months ago, now.'

'I always had you two down as suited.'

'Apparently not.' David raised his glass and stared through the wine, like a mystic. 'She said she wasn't happy, and then she went.'

'I'm sorry.'

'There's no need to be. I'm—'

'Seeing someone else?' I don't know what made me cut in like that. Nerves, probably.

'Well, I suppose.'

'Oh, great.'

'I don't know if it's that,' he said, oddly.

I imagined him at some dinner-party, surrounded by other suits and Jacky-lookalikes. Luckily his phone beeped as I was wracking my brains for an appropriate reply. He took the mobile out again, checked the screen, sighed, and switched it off.

'Anyway,' he went on, shifting forward in his seat. 'To the matter in hand.'

'Yes.'

'Starting from the point,' he said, 'that basically we want Ian and Jaz back together.'

'With the proviso he apologises, and that he never ever strays again.'

'Strays,' David repeated.

'What?'

'It's rather an old-fashioned word.'

I didn't like to say it was what Phil always used.

'But yes, obviously,' he went on, 'Ian's got to give. So has Jaz. Important, I think, for her not to end up using it as a stick to beat him with later on. Forgiving someone entails moving on.'

'Except it'll take time to get over.'

'Understood.' He put his fingertips together.

'The person who's most important here,' I said, 'is Matty. He's at the centre of all this, he's the one caught up in the middle. Matty changes everything. If it weren't for Matty—'

If it weren't for Matty I'd say to Jaz, 'Kick the bugger into touch. You don't want to waste your life on a cheat. Find someone who deserves you, or it'll eat up your self-esteem to nothing. Life's hard enough without being taken for a fool by the person who's supposed to be your number-one support.'

David nodded once, but I didn't know if it was in sympathy, or to check me. 'It seems to me, then, that if we can keep the discussion from getting too heated, and we can keep stressing the positives of staying together, then we should be able to make a little headway.' He paused. 'I know what you're thinking: easier said than done.'

'They're not going to walk out of here hand-in-hand, are they?'

'I never said they were. But maybe we can point them in the right general direction, or at least plant the possibility in their minds. You look doubtful, Carol. Don't be. We have to try. Someone has to get them off the starting blocks.'

'But what if we do more harm than good? Maybe we shouldn't be interfering. They're adults, after all.'

'Adults who've backed themselves into a corner and don't know how to get out. Adults who need our help.'

'Will it help, though? You don't know Jaz like I do; if you try to pressure her, she might go the other way out of sheer cussedness.'

'I think you're underestimating her.'

Underestimating my daughter? Mild as it was, the accusation sent me into a flurry of panic. What kind of a mother made such disparaging claims? Whose side was I supposed to be on? Appalling. And yet, Jaz *did* sometimes behave that way, and David needed to be aware of that. Was I wrong to warn him? For all he'd set this meeting up, had he really grasped the situation? Why should his approach be any better than mine?

From the garden came the sounds of Matty's squeals, Laverne's bright tones, faint saxophone music. Jaz would be taking Matty back home after this, whatever the result. His bag was packed and on the stairs.

'See, I believe Jasmine has more about her than that,' David went on. 'I've always had a lot of time for her. I like people who have something a bit unusual about them, not-your-average. She's clever, and she thinks for herself. It was a great shame she didn't get her degree in the end. She told me she was predicted a First.'

'That's right.'

'I'm not surprised. How long was she ill?'

I took a deep breath, because this was always a tricky question to answer. To measure the exact length of Jaz's depression, I'd have to be clear on when it began, and I've never got to the bottom of that. Sometimes I think it started before she went to university, in that lead-up to A-levels when I worried myself sick in case she was taking drugs, and Phil claimed it was hormones, or my fault, depending how well the divorce negotiations were going. At what point does moping about and general moodiness become a clinical condition? And, do you know, no one's ever been able to answer that for me.

I said, 'She came home from Leeds – she'd just started in her second year – because she said she wanted to change courses and they wouldn't let her, she was too far along. I can see her now: her face was grey and she had this awful rash round her chin. All she did for that first week was lie in bed. I didn't know what to do. It was the worst time, actually, because my dad had just been diagnosed with dementia and, to be honest, I was more focused on that. I thought Jaz was just a bit down.' *I thought Jaz was being self-dramatising and lazy, and heaping pressure on me for the hell of it.*

David was watching me closely, as though he could see the big cloud of guilt gathering over my head.

'But she was officially diagnosed?'

I nodded. 'Not for a while, though.' I'd stood in her bedroom doorway and yelled at her to get up and shape herself. Me, her mother. 'If she'd got help sooner . . .'

'She was recovered by the time she met Ian.'

'Oh, yes. She was working, in the Rocket café. Now a tanning salon.'

'I dimly remember it.'

'It only lasted two years. Too far off the High Street, and vegetarian wholefood's a niche market round here anyway. But she did like the place, she got on well with her colleagues. Then again, she enjoys being a freelance translator; she can pick her own hours, take on as much as she feels she can cope with. It leaves her more time to do other things.'

'She has a lot of friends?'

Again I hesitated. Jaz's friends. I wasn't about to go into that business during her teens when she claimed she was being bullied, and Phil and I marched round to the school only to be told that Jaz herself was one of the perpetrators. 'Six of one,' the Headmistress had said, 'and half a dozen of the other. A – well, a boy – some silly gossip, I'm not entirely clear what kicked it off, but I'm not taking any action against individuals. In my experience, these things usually work themselves through without too much adult intervention.' After that, Jaz didn't go out so much, and you'd not to mention certain names in her hearing. Nights I lay awake, worrying. 'I thought you wanted her to stay in more,' Phil had said. Which shows his grasp of the situation.

'Her best friend's Natalie,' I said to David. 'Nat. The one who was chief bridesmaid.'

'Ah yes.'

The sort of girl who's pleasant to your face and flicks Vs behind your back, I could have added. Who'd laugh if you fell over and hurt yourself. Who – and I'll never ever forgive her for it – played dumb the time my daughter ran away. Standing there in her school uniform, shrugging at me, looking at the floor.

I said, 'She's quite different from Jaz, but they got together at primary school and they've been pals ever since. So I suppose you could say she's a loyal girl. She works as a receptionist at a garage on the industrial estate.'

'It bothers me sometimes,' David broke in, in a way that made me realise he hadn't been with me for the last few seconds, 'that Ian's rather isolated. He didn't keep in touch with his schoolfriends when he went to Bristol, and then he didn't keep up with the Bristol lot either. He socialises with people from the office. I've told him, it's not ideal.'

Blimey, speak your mind, I thought. I'd never dare say that kind of thing to Jaz.

'Well,' I said, 'I do think you need a best mate. It's part of who you are.'

Then I heard Eileen's voice going, *Remember Bentham's Outfitters?* and I was back there with her, standing by the changing rooms in our school uniforms, and making faces at the ladies as they peered out. Our rule was, all the ones who looked a sight, we gave the thumbs up, big smiles, encouraging nods. To all the ones who looked nice, we'd fake dismay or horror. Eileen had gone so far as to imitate being strangled. One giant woman in purple satin we wolf-whistled. It took an elderly lady in a neckbrace to stop us. 'Who do you think you are?' she hissed. 'You should know, that lady you're laughing at has a degree in Biochemistry.' 'Yes,' said Eileen, 'but she also has a moustache.' Then we'd legged it. Your friends aren't just important for now. They validate your past.

'But it's harder for young people today,' I said. 'Making proper friends. Somehow they don't want to lose face, they take themselves so much more seriously. Get to my age and it doesn't matter as much. You don't care. I'll talk to anyone, me.'

'That's because you've got natural warmth.'

The compliment, coming out of nowhere, caught me on the hop, and I felt myself blush. But before I could flounder, David stood up.

'On your marks,' he said. 'That's Jasmine's car. They're here.'

CHAPTER 9

Photograph 290, Album Two

Location: Jaz's bedroom

Taken by: Jaz

Subject: hamster Mojo's monument, restored after some nocturnal disruption by cats or foxes. Carol has donated a clump of snowdrops, together with a sneaky clove of garlic pushed into the soil, which she hopes will deter grave robbers.

The day Mojo dies, Jaz, ten, announces, 'I'll never smile again.' And for a week afterwards, Carol fears it might be true. Never has a rodent been so mourned. At the weekend, in desperation, Phil marches to the pet shop in town and buys a new hamster, a baby Russian Dwarf the size of a kumquat and almost obscenely cute. Even the woman behind the counter clucks and coos as she pops him in his little carrier. Jaz will be delirious. What child wouldn't be?

When Phil and Carol call her down to see, they are united in confident anticipation. The tiny creature is sitting in his dish, quivering.

Jaz stalks over, takes one look, turns and flees back upstairs. When her mother goes to investigate, all Jaz will say is, 'It's not Mojo.' 'Mojo wouldn't mind,' says Carol. But Jaz isn't for budging. There's only room for one hamster in her heart. Mojo was the one, and no other will do.

To say the pet shop is not keen on returns is an understatement, but when Phil threatens to set the animal loose in the precinct, and Carol explains they aren't after their money back, the owner relents.

'Any normal kid would give their eye teeth for one of them little furry buggers,' says Phil as they trudge back home. 'Not our Jaz, though, oh no. Nothing so straightforward. You wouldn't credit it, would you?'

I would, actually, thinks Carol, but sensibly decides to keep her mouth shut.

'Come in, come in,' David went, sweeping the door open. I felt a little flash of irritation as he nodded them past, into the hall: whose house was this?

'We're in the lounge,' I added.

Jaz was looking better than I'd seen her for a while. She'd tied her hair back and put a skirt and jacket on, almost like someone attending a job interview. Ian, on the other hand, looked ill. 'Carol,' he muttered as I took his coat from his thin shoulders. I touched his arm briefly, furtively, then moved away before he could show any kind of reaction.

'Can I get anybody anything?' I said.

'We're fine,' said Ian.

'Drink? Tea, coffee, glass of Merlot?'

'No, we're fine.'

'Something to eat?' I couldn't seem to stop myself.

'Mum,' said Jaz.

We positioned ourselves round the room like the Stations of the Cross.

'So the reason we're here,' said David, compère for the

afternoon, 'is to talk through how you move forward from this – from this. Whether or not you decide you want to stay together, or part, we want to provide an opportunity for you both to have your say. So you know where you stand.'

Ian's face was set and pinched with acceptance, but Jaz sprang up out of her seat, immediately on the defensive. 'I thought we were just here to discuss access rights,' she said, looking from one of us to the other. 'I'm sorry, that's the only reason I'm here. Not for any kind of reconciliation. Mum?'

'Well,' I said. 'It can't do any harm. Since you're here.'

Can't it, said the expression on her face.

'Please,' said Ian. 'Please, Jaz, just let me talk to you.'

I wondered what the three of us looked like, poised on the edge of hope, while we waited for her to deliver her verdict.

David said: 'Don't you want the chance to tell Ian exactly what he's put you through? Don't you think he should hear it?'

Her face worked as she considered. After a few moments, she sat, but grudgingly. 'He knows,' she said.

'I don't believe he does,' said David. 'Not really. Only you can tell him that. Isn't there anything you want to ask him?'

When she didn't reply, he carried on.

'My plan was to create a safe forum, if you like. To let each of you speak for two minutes, uninterrupted, and say what you feel most needs saying. And have us here for back-up.'

Let each of you speak? I was thinking. It sounds like bloody speed-dating. She'll never buy that. Any second now, she's going to swear in his face.

'Neither of you must interrupt the other,' he said. 'That's essential. The person speaking has the floor, but for two minutes only. That should mean the most important things rise to the top – all the rest of it, you can deal with in your own time. But it's the most productive starting-point, trust me.'

To my utter amazement, she did.

'So you mean, get him to face up to what he's done.'

'I have faced—' Ian began, but David waved his hand.

'Just give it a shot.'

Something passed between them, which Jaz missed because she'd closed her eyes and was pulling her hands through her hair. I knew she was gearing up for an outburst. David had no idea what he was about to unleash.

'Jaz?'

'Is it my "go", then?'

'It is.'

'Right,' she began, her hands still busy. 'Right. OK, OK. I can't *get* why you did it. I mean, I *can't get* it. What in God's name did you think you were doing? When you had everything you wanted, I can't— Was she pretty? Was she worth it? Was she a *good fuck*? Because, you know, everything's ruined now, everything's gone, you've thrown everything away so I fucking hope she was worth it, and I swear to God if I ever *ever* meet that bitch I'll tear her fucking face off, then we'll see how she does stealing other people's husbands, sad fucking *cow* who can't get a proper boyfriend of her own.

'Did you not think? Did you not stop for one minute and think about me? About Matty? Everything we've been through together, that time you had those chest pains and you thought you were fucking dying, and I was running you up to hospital and you were practically making your fucking will in the car. And when I told you I was pregnant, and you *cried* because you were so blown away by it, and you said how you'd never truly been happy till you met me.

'And I could understand it – no, I couldn't understand it, but I could maybe get my head round it more if it was definitely just the once, just a complete one-off, but *how do I know?* Oh, I know what you *said*, but that counts for nothing, does it? Fucking damage limitation's all you're concerned with now.

Trouble is, as soon as you start lying to people, they stop trusting you, yeah? I'll never be able to believe another fucking thing you say. Any time you're late home, any time you're – anywhere. How could you not have thought that through? And me and Matty, and everything we had – how could you have blanked it? Was she so fucking fantastic that *the whole of the rest of your life went out of your head?*'

Ian had his fist against his mouth, and at that point he took his knuckles away and made as if to speak, but Jaz carried on.

'Do you not think *I've* had offers? Look at me. Look at me! Men are always coming on to me. That bloke at the garden centre who delivered the planters, I virtually had to push him out the door, he left his number and everything. The guy at the garage with the earring, he always chats me up. I could have an affair tomorrow if I wanted. But I wouldn't. See, that's the difference. I took my wedding vows seriously.'

'*I* did,' Ian began. 'It's—'

David's hand came up, warning. 'Let her finish.'

For a moment Jaz sat with her head bowed, hands clasped in her lap. Then she said in a flat, soft voice, 'I can talk for ever, but it won't change anything. You've ruined us. We can never go back. You know that, don't you? It's over, and it's your fault.'

After that there was a horrible silence. I could hear my heart thudding in my ears, so loud it must have been audible to everyone else.

'Can I speak now?' said Ian.

Jaz shrugged. 'I've nothing more to say.'

'Go on,' said David.

Ian shifted, cleared his throat, ran his hand across his brow. 'I'm not sure I can do this,' he said at last.

'Oh, get on with it,' said Jaz.

He held his palms upwards, defeated.

'I've gone over and over it in my mind, all the time you

wouldn't speak to me. Sitting there in the car with you, trying to hold it all back, and now I don't know where to begin. What can I say?'

'Sorry would be a start.'

'Of *course* I'm sorry!' The words exploded out of him. 'How could you think anything else! Sorry? There's not one minute goes past, not one second when I don't wish like mad it hadn't happened. I know I've done wrong! I know how hurt you are! God, if I could turn the clock back, I would do anything, anything for it not to—'

'That makes two of us, then.'

'—been trying and trying for weeks to apologise and make things right again but you wouldn't let me.'

'Because what is there you can say, Ian? How can you possibly make it OK again? That's what I've been telling you.'

'Then I might as well give up now.'

It was shocking to see this white-faced young man staring at Jaz with his jaw clenched and his breathing fast. A stranger in my house.

'No,' said Jaz. 'I want to hear anyway. *Explain to me* what you thought you were doing. I want to hear *every* detail, *every* step. I have to hear it.'

Oh, love, I thought. You don't.

Ian swallowed. 'It was nothing. It meant nothing. She was nothing. She is nothing.'

'So *why?*'

'Because. Because. What it was – she – it's hard to know how to—'

'Jesus!'

'Let him speak, Jasmine.' David twisted at his cuff. 'Two minutes. You had your time, now let him.'

'Fuck your two minutes,' muttered Jaz, but David ignored her.

'I will explain,' said Ian. 'But I can't do it in front of everyone. It has to be in private.'

I was on my feet in an instant, ready to leave them to it. David, though, stayed where he was. 'As long as you get your say.'

When no one spoke, he stood up, unfastened his watch and handed it to Jaz.

'Here,' he said. 'You'll need this. It's got a second hand.'

I couldn't believe the boldness of the gesture, but she took it from him.

We left the room as swiftly as we could, and closed the door behind us.

From the kitchen we could see Laverne hanging out her washing, and further down the garden, the top of Josh's head. I guessed by Matty's shrieks that the remote-controlled jeep was still in play.

David came to stand next to me at the window.

Without looking at him I said: 'It really is no good pushing Jaz into anything. If she feels cornered, she becomes very unpredictable. Softly softly catchee monkey, it has to be with her. She's been that way pretty much since she was a girl.'

He nodded. 'And my son's always been – what do they call certain metals? – ductile. Does as he's told. Just as well, given the circumstances of his upbringing.'

A sudden breeze flapped Laverne's sheets. I watched the surface of my pond shiver and tried to picture Ian as a boy.

'Has he told you why, yet?'

'Why this other woman?'

'Yes.'

'Not really.'

'Have you asked?'

'Of course. But it's difficult for him. I'm not sure he can

articulate it properly. I suspect simple opportunity played a part—'

'For God's sake! Are all men like that?' I snapped.

David moved away from me and sat down at the table. 'Well, I was never unfaithful to my wife, if that's what you mean.'

Bloody hell. 'I didn't mean you, I wasn't thinking of you. The way it came out was wrong.'

'Forget it. Really. I think we're all pretty wound up, aren't we? How about putting the kettle on? I could do with a very strong coffee.'

It was good to be given an everyday task. As I got the cups down, fetched out teaspoons, filled the sugar bowl, I tried to listen for any sounds from the living room. If Jaz and Ian were arguing, their voices would carry. But there was nothing. I flicked the water on to boil.

'Busy lady.' David pointed at the wall calendar hanging up on the larder door.

'You don't have to tell me.'

'Beavers is for, remind me?'

'Six-to-eights. Cubs eight to ten. Scouts after that.'

'Are you an Akela, then, or whatever they call it?'

'No, just general dogsbody. Orange squash-pourer, provider of fairy cakes, that sort of lark. They have so many rules now about adult-to-child ratios. I step in when they need an extra body.'

'Woggle at the ready?'

'I don't qualify for a woggle.'

'Bad luck. How did you get involved? Jaz wasn't a Beaver, was she?'

'Can you imagine Jaz joining any sort of organised brigade? No, it was the lad next door.' I came over and set the mugs down in front of him, and that's when I saw he was smirking.

'Well, actually, the joke's on you, David Reid, because these days girls can join Beavers if they want to. It's equal rights.'

'What – and boys Brownies?'

'I suppose so. Though I'm not sure there's a vast take-up.'

'Strange times we live in.' He lifted his coffee to sip, and paused.

'What?' I prompted him.

'Occasionally I have trouble negotiating this modern world of ours. I don't know if you ever feel that way, Carol.'

Just lately, all the time, I thought. David, there are mornings I wake up and I hardly dare get out of bed for fear of what the day holds. But I could tell he was trying to keep it light, so I said: 'Josh next door's always having to explain things to me. He comes out with all this stuff, and I'm sitting there trying to make sense of it. Once he said he was having a Wii for his birthday and I almost crashed the car. Because when words change their meaning, no one tells you, do they? They should have it on public information films, stop you getting yourself into bother. Mind you, at least I never went round calling people a wanker like my mother used to do. She thought it was a pet term, like "little tinker".'

'Good God. What did she say when you told her?'

'We never dared. The shock would have killed her.'

David drank his coffee and we both strained our ears for the sound of shouting. The longer this lull went on, we were thinking, the more hopeful it was.

'I do worry about what sort of world Matty's growing up into, though,' I said. 'When I was young – and I know that makes me sound about ninety – people knew where they were, somehow. The lines were drawn and you hadn't to cross them, and everyone benefited from that. Or so it seems to me.'

'I agree.'

'There are too many choices these days. I think that's at the root of it. People think they want choice, but if they have too much it can make life over-complicated. And then they're always looking over their shoulder, thinking should they have done this or that, and comparing other folk with where they are, what they've got. Which makes them dissatisfied and restless. Sometimes it's good just to be told what to do.'

'Well, it's human instinct to strive for freedom,' said David. 'But I know what you're saying. Somewhere there's a golden land between PC madness and the bad old days of forelock-tugging and trial by community.'

'I think we had it. I think that was our youth.'

There followed a silence which, under different circumstances, might have been companionable, but we were both too keyed up. I opened my mouth to speak – not sure what I would have said – but as I did so I saw something through the window that made me turn and look out. I was just in time to see my clothes prop, swayed by a powerful blast of wind, slide away from the washing line and fall with a metallic clatter across the pond. The top section struck a plastic planter which would normally have been stable enough, only I'd propped it up on a couple of bricks so the rim showed above the tops of the reeds. The planter toppled sideways, and lodged against a stone pot, spilling soil into the water.

'Timber,' said David, following my gaze.

All my mind could see for a few seconds was a sequence where it was Matty beneath the pole. If Matty had been in the garden then, if he'd been playing in the reeds just there . . . I stood and stared at the spot.

'Are you all right, Carol? I don't think there's too much damage. Shall we go and see?'

I took myself over to the door and opened it. The air was fresh and clean on my face, but the vision lingered.

'Do you want a hand?' asked David.

'No. I'll just go and right that planter. Won't be a mo.'

As soon as I was outside, my hair whipped around my face and my blouse flapped against my sides. The leaves of Laverne's aspen shimmered above the fence like fish scales. I picked my way across the long lawn and walked round the path to where the damage was. When I got close I could see the planter had cracked at the rim, creating a lip through which dark compost trickled, but was otherwise intact. No stems were broken, no flowers had come off. So I bent down and pulled the pot upright, patted the lobelias in securely, then set it back on its bricks. Then I knelt to sweep up the crumbs of earth. The water in front of me was cloudy with a film of particles across the surface, but that would soon break up.

I stood again and looked back at the house. Through the patio doors I could see Jaz and Ian; I didn't mean to spy, but I couldn't help myself. Jaz I made out fairly easily. She'd changed seats, and was now opposite the fireplace. I couldn't see Ian at all. Suddenly he moved and I realised he was crouched at Jaz's feet, like a man about to propose. They were too far away for me to make out any detail.

My chest went tight with hope and anxiety. So much hung on this afternoon, more than I thought I could bear. I flicked my gaze across to Laverne's, but her lawn was now deserted and her windows were dark. I knew they sat in the front to watch TV, and that's probably where Matty had gone. Back in my kitchen, David got up and began to pace about, his hand to his ear, his head cocked. Man on mobile. All of them seemed very far away. I knew I ought to go in, but I couldn't do it. Instead I stepped up to the fence and leaned against it, not caring about mildew marks or splinters.

'Come on, love,' I whispered. 'Come on, Jaz. Move it forward. Be brave.'

The light was changing around me, the afternoon turning

towards evening, and everything in the garden seemed very sharp and clear: the rags of dandelion leaves at my feet, the shrivelled heads of last year's lilac, the yellow-brown knuckles on the horsetail stalks. Once Jaz built a den in this section, resting the back panel of a wardrobe against the post and incorporating the side of the shed as one wall. I remembered her ferrying picnic cutlery and paper plates across the grass, and later having a major sulk at me because I'd said she couldn't use one of my pillows outside. It didn't feel like that long ago, but it was almost two decades.

Which made me think of what David and I had been discussing, about our generation having had the best of it, and that started a series of images falling like dominoes. Grass-sledging on an old door down Latimer's Bank; Eileen secretly drawing faces on the bananas in the school Harvest display; a yellow skirt of mine with white ric rac braid round the hem; Phil in his first work suit, a brown creation with huge lapels. I thought of the first time Phil asked me out, how he'd leaned against our gate at Pincroft whistling 'Maggie May'. How had I got here, to this point? Standing in my own garden, afraid to go in. And I wondered what David's youth had been like in comparison, and whether he'd always been so self-assured, and how we'd have got along if we'd known each other then. I was just trying to imagine what his wife might have been like, when the scene in the living room changed.

David took his hand away from his ear and looked round, as though distracted by a noise. Seconds later, Jaz was on her feet, Ian leaning sharply backwards to get out of the way and then he was up too, and both of them were waving their arms. I saw David slide his hand into his pocket, glance towards the living-room door and then turn to face the garden, searching for me.

I came out from the shelter of the fence and hurried back along the path. As I drew nearer I could make out Jaz's face; it had that chiselled look she gets when she's beyond all that's rational, and my heart sank. Ian had his back to me by then, but his gestures looked like pleading ones.

I wrenched at the door handle and slipped back inside the kitchen. There was no need to say anything. David shook his head at me and we both stood there listening to the row. After a while he walked across and put his hand on my shoulder, and the gesture brought tears to my eyes.

'Should we go through?' he said. 'I think we should go through.' Then he looked down at my face. 'Oh, Carol,' he said, and I let myself fall towards him to be held, just for a second.

That's when the living-room door burst open and Jaz flew in.

'Get him out!' she was shouting. 'Get him out of here! Get him out of this house!'

'Right, now, come on, calm down. There's nothing to be gained by all this shouting,' David began, letting me loose. I saw his chin go up assertively, and thought even through the chaos, Here's a man who's used to people listening to him. But I knew that tone wouldn't work with Jaz.

'Hey, love,' I said.

'Get him out!'

Ian appeared behind her. 'I didn't mean it like that,' he was saying. 'Please, Jaz, you know that's not what I meant.'

'*Get him out!*' She put her hands over her ears and screwed her eyes shut.

'Let's all take a short break,' said David.

'No,' I said. 'I'm sorry, David, that won't do it.'

'What, then?'

'I think Ian had better go. For now. We can re-group later.'

'Please, oh, God,' said Ian, though it wasn't clear who he was addressing. It wrung me out to hear him.

I went to put my arms round Jaz and she was stiff as a board. 'Sorry,' I mouthed to the others.

David stood for a few seconds, then nodded at his son. 'Get your coat.'

They shuffled round us into the hallway, David steering Ian as though he was dealing with an invalid. Over the top of Jaz's head I watched the two men, one tall and skinny, the other slightly shorter and thicker-set, and it reminded me of a war film I'd caught on TV a week ago, where the Captain led his shattered men to safety. David hauled their coats off the newel post and opened the front door. I was waiting for him to turn and say goodbye, but he didn't.

CHAPTER 10

Photograph 337, Album Three

Location: the hallway, Sunnybank, Shropshire

Taken by: Carol

Subject: Jaz, the evening she turns fourteen, with Nat. Carol's driven them to Manchester and back, because this is the birthday treat Jaz requested months ago. She wanted to go clothes shopping with her best friend, asked for no presents but money.

Initially the girls' plan is to go alone, on the train, but Carol puts her foot down. It's too far, they're too young. 'Quicker if you go by car,' she says. 'More time for the shops.'

A good argument, that, and the girls concede the point. It's not like they have to go round with her. Mrs Morgan can look in Lakeland or something, while they buzz off and have fun.

When they get to the Arndale, though, it becomes clear that Nat at least wants to stick by Carol's side. 'What do you think of this, Mrs Morgan?' she keeps saying, riffling through one clothes rail after another. 'Do you like that?' Carol can't see any of the garments suiting either of them: a baby pink cardigan with pom poms at the neck; tweed jodhpurs; a fringed velvet cap. Meanwhile Jaz casts longing looks across the atrium and sighs loudly.

When at last Jaz says, 'Are you coming, or what?' Nat claims to have period pain, and says that she must go somewhere she can sit down. Carol spots her cue. 'We'll meet you in River Island at twelve,' she tells her daughter. Then she takes Nat to a café, installs her behind a hot chocolate, and asks her what's going on.

Nat's sulky little mouth turns down even further.

'Come on,' says Carol, trying not to be irritated.

'She hates me and I don't know what to do,' says Nat.

'She doesn't hate you,' says Carol.

'She does,' says Nat.

It transpires that the casting list went up yesterday for the school play, and Nat's been the bearer of bad news. Jaz is not to be Eliza, nor even Mrs Higgins or Mrs Pearce. She's an Ascot lady – one of the crowd, merely.

'Did you get a bigger part than her?' asks Carol. But no, that's not it. Nat isn't even in the play.

'She really, really wanted to be Eliza,' says Nat. 'I think she's cross with me because I was the one who told her.'

'But that wouldn't make sense,' says Carol.

Nat gives her a look that says, Boy, you can be thick at times.

'Well. She'll get over it. Don't fret. You're her best friend,' says Carol.

'The problem is, I like Jaz more than she likes me,' says Nat, with a rare flash of perception.

'Nonsense,' lies Carol.

On the drive home, the atmosphere is better. Her lap laden with carrier bags, Jaz is starting to thaw. By the time they're on the motorway, it's grins all round. Carol glances from time to time in the mirror. Every day, it seems, her daughter becomes another degree less fathomable.

*

We'd taken a jigsaw with us this time to keep Matty occupied: coloured dogs that fit into matching slots on a board. Each dog had a wooden peg through its middle and an expression of injured surprise on its face.

I put Matty down on the carpet, Jaz unloaded his kit, and the nursing assistant cranked Dad's bed up into a sitting position.

'Now then, how are you?' I said, bending to kiss him. His cheek was cool and dry, slightly stubbly.

The nurse was ahead of me. 'He's had some disturbed nights lately so we've been letting him lie in. He missed his shave this week.'

'I can do it,' I said.

Jaz gave me a funny look. 'You're going to shave Grandad?'

'It's no bother. I've done it before.'

Eew, said her expression. I ignored it.

'Jaz has come to see you, Dad. And she's brought Matty. We think he might be cutting a tooth.'

Matty sat on the carpet, gnawing hard at one of the wooden dogs and drooling onto his T-shirt.

'Yeah, great timing, Matts,' said Jaz. 'Just what I need at the moment.'

In the locker next to Dad's bed I located his electric razor and some moisturizer.

'I don't know how you come here week after week,' Jaz had said on the way in.

'I come to see your grandad.'

'I know. But it's so depressing. The place, I mean.'

'Not really.'

The razor buzzed in my fingers and I turned Dad's face gently towards me. 'Just tidying you up,' I told him. 'Hold still.'

Close to, I could see all the damage that age does: the liver spots, the detail of loose skin over bone, the criss-cross of lines under his eyes. There was a little cyst on his upper lid, and his eyebrows were shaggy and needing a trim. A huge sense of protectiveness welled up in my chest, and I wanted to hug him to me. Jaz's presence held me back, though. When the razor made contact with his chin he flinched. I made a soothing sound, and slowly moved the foil up and down, around the moulding of his face.

'When you were little,' I said over my shoulder, 'Grandad let you make a perfume shop in his shed. Do you remember, Jaz?'

'No.'

'He saved you all his jam jars, cleared a shelf and helped you make labels.'

'Perfume?'

'Out of rose petals. He let you take half his best roses. You used to mash them up in water.'

'Oh, yeah.'

When I turned round, she was stretched out on the floor next to Matty, twirling a wooden dog by its peg.

'And you used to sell them to us for twenty pence a jar.'

'Yeah, they used to go all stinky in a day or two. I never learned, it was always a disappointment. I'd go, "Smell this beautiful scent" – then *ugh*.'

I smiled at her. Underneath my fingers, Dad shuddered.

'You used to spend hours together, you and your grandad. Hours and hours, nattering away. I think there were things you'd tell him that you wouldn't tell me or your dad.'

Jaz rolled over and sat up. 'What was Grandma like? I don't really remember her.'

A shrew, I thought. That's the word you'd use. Critical, negative, pessimistic. Must have made Dad's life grim. Didn't do much for mine either.

'She was very fond of you,' I said. Which was getting on for the truth. Once we'd gone to see her in the convalescent home and without even a word she'd taken toddler Jaz off into the grounds, leaving Dad and me sitting by the bed like fools for half an hour. Certainly she'd been more tolerant of Jaz than she ever was of us.

'Did Grandad miss her when she died?'

'He was devastated.'

I shifted round so I could get at Dad's other side. He blinked mildly at me, as though he knew I was there to do him a service even if he wasn't sure what that service was. 'Soon have you looking tip-top,' I told him.

'Can he hear you, though?' asked Jaz.

'Of course he can.'

She looked at me pityingly. Meanwhile Matty had been ferrying fistfuls of gravel from the yucca and was using them to fill the slots in his jigsaw, crouching intently. Small white stones trickled from his grasp and bounce-scattered across the floor.

Jaz turned back and assessed the scope of the operation. Then she pushed her hair back behind her ears and joined in, smoothing out the piles of gravel with her finger for him, patting them into place, picking at the ones that had bedded down in the carpet fibres. It was nice to watch, their two heads bobbing next to each other.

When all the holes were filled to his satisfaction, Matty began trying to force each dog on top. His small fingers pressed against the varnish so hard the skin turned white. Getting no result, he swapped dogs and pushed again. 'Gone,' he said. 'Gone, gone.'

'Will they not go in?' I said. 'Naughty doggies.'

'Gone!' He lifted up the jigsaw piece and banged it down.

'Nanna'll help,' I said, switching the shaver off. Jaz shook her head.

'Let him work it out for himself, Mum.'

Matty slammed the board a few more times, then drew his

arm back and flung his dog across the room. It landed near my feet, so I reached down and rescued it. 'Bad dog,' I said.

But when I raised my head, Matty was picking at the stones with his index finger and pushing them away, out of the hole. Jaz reached over and took the dog off me, and put it down next to him. When the slot was clear, he tried again, only with the wrong dog. I could see his frustration mounting and it was twisting me up inside.

'Matty,' I began.

'Look,' announced Jaz in the tone of a children's TV presenter. 'Look who's coming.' And she walked the right dog, the blue dog, along the edge of the board and onto his hand. His frown disappeared instantly, and where I'd have held the piece ready for him to slot in, she just passed it across, then waited till he'd worked out which was the right way round and we could give him a cheer.

'You're very good with him,' I said. Jaz shrugged. I was thinking, If only my mother had had a tenth of that patience.

Dad cleared his throat suddenly, then leaned forward as if to get a better view of his great-grandson. I got up off the bed and went to put the shaver away, keeping my eyes on him all the time. It seemed that, at any minute, he would speak.

'Ta,' said Matty. 'Ta, doggy.'

Jaz said: 'It's trying to give him the attention of two people, you know?' She handed another piece over.

'Grandad's watching you,' I said. 'Matty, can you wave at Great-Grandad? Say "hiya".'

'Hiya.'

'Because I don't think Ian's really sorry,' she went on. 'Sorry he's been caught, that's all. That's what I told him: "If you were bothered about your wife and child, you'd never have done it in the first place".'

I stroked Matty's head, for comfort.

'What gets me, Mum, is how he tried to make it sound like I had something to do with it.'

'I'm sure he didn't exactly mean that—'

'You weren't there!'

'All I'm saying is, some men aren't very good at coping when children are young. They can feel shut out. Maybe that's what he was—'

'So instead they go and jump on the first bit of skirt that comes their way.'

'I'm not saying it's right, I'm not making excuses for him.'

'Not much.'

A memory of Phil with his head in his hands, sitting on the stairs, weeping.

'I'm really not, Jaz. Only trying to explain what might have gone through his mind.'

'As though his *mind* had anything to do with it,' she snapped, pushing the jigsaw away and struggling to her feet.

'Will you try talking to him again? David would come over.'

'Oh, I'm quite sure he would,' she said in a tone I didn't much like. 'No, that's it. In fact, all Ian's speech-making did was make it clearer to me. I'm definitely getting a divorce. Definitely. It's over.'

I glanced across at Dad to see if anything had registered. He looked anxious, but probably not more than usual. I'd talk to him some more about Jaz next time, when I was on my own. Reassure him, explain.

'So,' I said cautiously. 'How are you going to arrange things with Matty?'

She didn't acknowledge me in any way. I might as well not have spoken. I could feel the fury sparking off her.

The sunburst clock ticked on, and we sat there watching Matty trying to force a green dog into a white hole, three adults playing mute: Dad because he couldn't speak, Jaz because she wouldn't, and me because I didn't dare.

The bouquet was waiting for me when I got home. It was propped against the front door, which meant Jaz spotted it immediately.

'What's that?' she said, even though it was perfectly obvious.

I got out of the car and hurried over to see. The card was inside a miniature envelope; on an instinct I whipped it out and stuck it in my pocket. The plastic holder I dropped deftly behind a bush. Jaz didn't see because she was checking Matty's straps.

'My God,' she said, when she got close. 'I bet those cost a bit.'

'Yes,' I said. I turned the key and stepped into the hall.

'Who are they from?'

'I don't know,' I said truthfully.

'Is there no card?'

'Can't see one. Are you having a drink?'

She was peering around the sides of the bouquet. Any minute now, I thought, she's going to stick her hands inside and begin parting the stems.

Eventually she gave up. 'No, I won't, thanks, because if I leave it any later Matty'll have his nap too late on and then I won't be able to get him off at bedtime.'

'OK, then. Well, drive safely and I'll see you Wednesday.'

'Yeah.' She paused in the doorway. 'It's not Dad, after a reconciliation, is it?'

I smiled. 'The flowers? Could be.'

She huffed, and left.

I walked through to the kitchen, holding the flowers ahead of me like an Olympic torch. Vases were in the base unit next to the cooker, so I laid the bouquet in the sink and squatted down to search. All my mother's crockery was stashed in here: her big blue and white serving dishes, her Lustreware tea set, her pressed glass bowls, and at the very back, her Crown Devon vases. I drew out the tallest, a pale blue ribbed funnel, and as I did so I could hear Phil go, *You're turning this house into Pincroft, that's what you're doing.* Because he'd hated the antimacassars with their embroidered peonies, and the uranium glass dressing-table set, and the ebony brush and mirror set that hung in the hallway. 'This old tat,' he used to say. Left to himself we'd have had a palace of vinyl and brushed steel.

I put everything back carefully in its proper place, and carried the vase over to the drainer. Then I set about unravelling the cellophane. Little sachet of plant food to make up, stem bases to cut or split, and all the time I still had my coat on and the card was burning a hole in the pocket. Dorothy Wynne's grand-daughter, the flowers might be from, although I'd already had a thank you card after the business with little Libby. Or Moira, as a pick-me-up because she knew I was having a difficult time. I positioned the gypsophila and ferns, and fed each bloom in one by one: yellow dahlias, yellow and white asters, a lily, white carnations. I coaxed them into place, then stepped back to consider the effect. Finally I topped up the water level and slid the vase onto the windowsill. Only then did I reach into my pockets and bring out the card.

My turn to apologise, I think. Onwards and upwards. David. X

I was touched by this little act of thoughtfulness. We'd not spoken since the fall-out – I'd wanted to ring, but hadn't dared in case he somehow blamed me for what had happened. But perhaps he now understood how little control I had over Jaz.

Relief made me suddenly exhausted, and I had to sit down. A bouquet of flowers. What would Phil think if he came round with the lawnmower and saw them? He'd be shocked to find they were from a man, that was certain. His ex-wife didn't have boyfriends. No subterfuge, either; I really didn't. When the girls at the gym joked or moaned about their partners, I laughed or frowned along with them. When they turned their attention to my love-life I always responded straight away with another question. Amazing how easy it is to divert someone straight back onto the topic of themselves. Jaz (drunk) asked me once why I'd never dated after Phil and, unable to break the habit of a lifetime, I'd gone, 'Would you like me to?' 'No,' she'd said. 'Too complicated. Too weird.' And that was the topic closed. But it wasn't Jaz who stopped me from dating, or even Phil. It was me.

I used to pick up magazines packed with true-life stories suggesting lovers were waiting to ambush you on every corner. *Crash Course in Romance – how a bump in the car led to a ring on my finger! He came to fix my burglar alarm – now it's wedding bells I'm hearing!* And probably if you put yourself about a bit, as my mother would say, you would find someone who wasn't revolting.

I wasn't in bad shape. Nor did I move in a world entirely of women. Men came into the shop sometimes, occasionally eyed me up. There was the haberdasher, Gavin, who used to flirt with me a little; he was nice, but he was married. Launce, who ran the photography class, had made several comments that might have been taken as overtures, but he was a lot older than me and anyway, it's possible he was only being friendly. One time I'd been asked out for a drink by Dorothy Wynne's gardener, a sharp-nosed Celt with sandy lashes and a bulging Adam's apple, not my type at all. So that had made me wary for a while of engaging in any ordinary polite chat, because the embarrassment of rejecting even virtual strangers was too distressing. I hate upsetting people.

But you did have to want to get out there, throw yourself into the hurly-burly. I found that hard. Even when we were teenagers, Eileen would be walking up to boys and chatting like it was no bother, while I'd be observing from a safe distance. 'Stop studying the ground all the time,' she'd say to me sometimes. 'Put your head up. Smile.' So I did, and look who I caught.

Now I found myself thinking about fluff-haired Derek, the first boy I ever kissed, how he danced with me at Pamela Martin's fourteenth birthday party, and how nothing had come of it afterwards because he was too shy to seek me out and I was too shy to put myself in his way. I remembered the brief crush I'd had on Tom Street, school football captain and future head boy, after he mended my locker door for me and commented how tidy I kept my books. But it was Phil, always Phil hanging about on the edges of my teenage consciousness, so that even when I was going out with Peter Robbins, who was decent and bright and not bad-looking, I couldn't help but keep a watch on Phil and secretly rejoice when he broke up with Margaret Hodgkiss.

For our first date he took me to the motorway bridge – it sounds so dull but it wasn't – and we watched traffic and talked. I remember saying to him, 'You're more serious when you're on your own.' I don't know what he said back, but I do recall him taking off my scarf and dangling it over the parapet, and laughing at my protests. I thought I'd die of happiness.

I could see him now, perched on our coping stones, swinging his legs. Mum never liked him but then, she liked nobody. Dad kept his mouth shut. *It's this other woman*, said Eileen, from thirty years ago. *That's who you should be angry with*.

On the windowsill, my flowers shone.

CHAPTER 11

Photograph 39, Album One

Location: Longleat Manor, Wiltshire

Taken by: Bob

Subject: the Knot Garden. Although the spectacular colours here won't show up on black and white film, he'll remember them, he thinks.

It's been a grand day out so far, in his new Austin 30 with its cream wheel trims, its rounded rear windscreen, the smart blue and black dashboard. The kind of car you want to take on a decent run. 'And what makes you think I've got time to swan off on a great long trip?' was Frieda's response when he first suggested the drive, but she's come anyway.

Inside, the house was like nothing you could dream of: great long galleries hung with tapestries, a staircase like the one Vivien Leigh fell down in Gone With the Wind, a twenty-seat table, ceilings so elaborately decorated it hurts your neck to take in all the detail. 'Have you seen?' he keeps asking Frieda. He's like a boy in his enthusiasm. 'Think of the dusting,' she says, shuddering. But he doesn't let that put him off his stride. What riches, what grandeur. It's overwhelming, the idea that anyone could live here, day to day.

Now they're out in the grounds and he's imagining what it must be like to be a lord. 'Who would you have wanted to be, if you could be anyone in history?' he asks Frieda.

'A man,' she says.

'What man?' he says.

'Any man,' she replies, and strides off, leaving him among the flowers. What's that supposed to mean? He's a patient bloke, but there are times he could go and sit in the driver's seat and lean his head against the Austin's horn.

Perhaps she'll be happier when the baby arrives. God help them both if she isn't.

We took the Beavers down to Blakemere Moss every year for orienteering and mapwork practice, but it meant an afternoon preparing the ground. This was my fourth year tying ribbons to saplings and laying twigs on the grass to make arrow shapes; the first time I'd ever carried out the task assisted by David and Matty.

The afternoon was damp and cool. By evening there would be a mist over the lake.

'Were you a Girl Scout?' asked David.

'Nope. My best friend spat on Brownies and Guides, so I never pursued it. Were you ever a Cub?'

He shook his head. 'I was a school prefect, briefly. Till I got demoted. Look, I'll do the ribbons if you like. It's easier for me to reach.'

'No, you hang onto Matty for me. I can't tie them very high or the Beavers won't be able to spot them.'

On the end of his toddler reins my grandson strained after ducks, water, freedom. I cleared a space of leaves till the soil showed, and aligned my lengths of wood so they pointed down the right path.

I said, 'It worries me she has no pattern, no model for a good marriage.'

David reached out a hand to help me up. 'For that matter, neither does Ian. It wasn't something either you or I chose, or can go back and change. Shouldering extra blame's not going to help anyone. I'm sure you did your best.'

'I tried.'

'Well, then. And Ian wasn't without maternal figures when he was growing up. He was very close to my sister at one time, before she moved to the States. I've had partners he's been fond of. Not so much Jacky, they never really hit it off, but some of the others. He still gets birthday cards from a couple. Here, let me hold that while you sort out your ribbon.' He took the clipboard from me and brought the map into focus, squinting. 'We're going round as far as the car park?'

'That's right.'

Matty pulled towards the lake, attracted by the swaying bulrush heads. I snapped a length of juncus for him and put it into his hand, and he was instantly satisfied.

'Does Ian get on well with – your new girlfriend?' I ventured.

'She isn't really a girlfriend, and they've not met,' said David. 'Did your flowers last?'

'Flowers? Oh, ages. In fact, I only threw the last ones away yesterday.'

'It's a decent florist. I've used them a few times.'

My spirits dipped a little. No woman likes to feel she's part of a bulk order.

We moved on, Matty stumbling between us on the ridgy mud. His frog wellies were already caked. They'd need sluicing before I handed them back.

'How's Ian managing?'

David clasped the reins more tightly and frowned. 'Doesn't talk much. Stays up late because he can't sleep, watches TV till the small hours. He's been very forgetful, forgot his coat one day, his briefcase this morning. Lost his watch last week and couldn't remember where he'd left it. He was like that after his mother died. Without being overdramatic, I think I can say my son's in real distress. But you perhaps wouldn't pick up on those things if you didn't know him. He's like me in a lot of ways. Doesn't make a show of his feelings. Jaz is like you?'

'God, no. She's just herself.'

For a while we walked in silence. The sky above the treeline was milky-blank and the vegetation on the far bank washed out and pale. We were coming to the timber bridge where the cotton grass grew; once Jaz had turned over a chunk of dead wood on this stretch and found a clutch of baby newts huddled underneath. When she'd touched them, they'd lain inert, like rubber animals. She wanted to take them home but I'd stood my ground that time. I didn't want their tiny amphibian deaths on my conscience.

'We'd to come to the Moss every few weeks when Jaz was a girl,' I said, sliding my secateurs into my pocket. 'For picnics, all sorts. Jaz used to love scrambling around and investigating.'

'Ian used to like Delamere Forest. We went camping there on a couple of occasions.'

I couldn't stop myself. 'You, in a tent?'

'Why ever not?'

'You're always so smart. I can't imagine you roughing it. This is the first time I've seen you not wearing a suit.'

David looked at me in mild surprise, then down at his jeans and walking boots. 'I'm sure it isn't.'

'It is. You think: the wedding, Matty's naming ceremony, the two or three meals we met up for to celebrate the engagement and make arrangements for the reception. I'm only saying, it's not a criticism.'

'Oh good.'

'Hang on, I need to post another marker.'

I spooled out more ribbon and clipped it to the right length.

The tree I'd lighted on was a rowan with thin, shivering leaves. In the autumn, Jaz used to pick the berries and wear them like earrings.

'We really don't know each other very well, do we?' said David from behind me.

'I know we're of the same mind. I know we both want to help.'

When I turned he was standing under a silver birch, his grey hair slightly dishevelled and the hems of his jeans flecked with mud, while my grandson – *his* grandson – poked at a puddle with his length of reed.

'Ian's desperate to see Matty. This situation can't go on indefinitely.'

'No, I know. She just needs a little bit of space. It's only till she's come to terms—'

'How long will that be, though, Carol?' At the lake's end a flock of gulls took off, slopping waves against the banks, disturbing the peace. 'I haven't told Ian where I am this afternoon. I did think about bringing him, just to meet up for half an hour, but . . .' He let the sentence hang.

I fixed my gaze on a ripple and followed it to the shore where ghost-Jaz crouched, skimming stone after stone across the water.

'So the Hungarian, right, he's explaining these three states of matter, yeah? How you've got your solids, your liquids and your gas.' Josh's voice was full of enthusiasm as I negotiated the Blakemere roundabout.

'Uh-huh. I know about those.'

'Yeah, and he's talking about how the molecules are packed together, and then he drags out this swivel chair he always sits on, and he goes: "*This is a chair.*" And straight away the boy he really hates, he stands up and starts applauding.'

'Ouch.'

'It was brilliant, 'cause after a second or two some of the others did the same, and soon the whole class was on their feet, clapping. All clapping the Hungarian's genius in being able to correctly identify a piece of furniture.'

'How did he react?'

'Aw, he just totally lost it. His head exploded. There were literally brains everywhere.'

'What, literally?' I indicated right and moved into the outside lane, ready for the traffic lights. 'Was the boy all right, though?' I said while we waited for green. 'Because the Hungarian can be vicious, can't he?'

Josh shrugged. 'It was worth it. It was a blast.'

'When I was at school we had a foreign teacher who could never keep control. Mr de Silva, his name was. Taught music. Don't know what he was doing in Bolton. The boys used to make his life hell.'

'What did they do?'

'Well, we had our singing in the hall, and it was a room with huge floor-length curtains down one side. The boys used to spend half of every lesson hiding behind these curtains. They'd wait till he turned to the piano, and then they'd sneak across, one by one, till there was hardly anyone left singing, just the girls. Mr de Silva must have noticed but I suppose he was too frightened to tackle us. Poor man. You'd see all these shoes sticking out from under the hem.'

'Smart.'

'Not that I'm giving you ideas.'

We pulled onto the main road; another minute and we'd be at the school.

'Can you let me out here?' Josh said suddenly.

'Here?'

'There's someone I need to talk to.'

I took my eyes off the road for a second to glance across at him, and he was leaning forward urgently. When I scanned up and down the pavement, the only likely people I could see were a pair of girls far up ahead.

'Ah,' I said.

'So if you could?'

'All right. Hang on.'

He was pawing at the door even as I was pulling in.

'Man with a mission,' I said, smiling.

'Something like that.' He reached for his bag.

'Have a nice day.'

'I won't.'

He set off walking fast. It wouldn't be fair to spy on him, but I let myself watch for twenty paces. His chin was set, his bag swung as he strode into the brightness of a new school day, and his loping, vulnerable gait reminded me painfully of Ian.

Which might have been what tipped me into action.

Matty concentrated as his father slotted two pieces of blue track together and hitched them to the existing layout. Thomas the Tank Engine's route would take him past the fire-place, under the coffee-table, across the carpet to the display cabinet and then alongside the radiator, where there was a junction that would either bring him back round to the hearth or up against a buffer. A plastic tunnel lay on its back like a giant green woodlouse, and next to Ian's feet was a polythene box of die-cast vehicles, ready for dispersal. Matty held the train.

'This is not taking sides. This is not condoning what he's done. I can't stress enough how important it is that Jaz does-n't get to hear about it,' I said to David, who was standing with me in the living-room doorway.

'I know. It's very good of you.'

Our eyes met and I could see at once he knew the score: if Ian was allowed to see his son, he was less likely to make some gesture motivated by spite. Desperate people sometimes did desperate things. The arrangement was about self-preservation, not charity.

That said, it felt nice to watch them together.

'Don't they have some great toys nowadays?' I said, as Ian took Matty's finger and showed him how to push the start lever.

'I'll say. I had a Hornby 00 gauge when I was a boy, but not till I was a lot older. This stuff's good. Chunky. Solid.'

'I got the metal ones at a boot sale, thought I'd been very clever but they're the wrong scale, of course. I'm always doing things like that.'

'You do very well, as far as I can see,' said David.

The train shirred past our feet. 'Watch out, Thomas!' I called after it.

'Gordon,' corrected the men in unison.

'Gordon's an LNER A3. Thomas is a Brighton Line E2,' added David helpfully.

At the opposite corner of the room, Matty piled cars, a bus and a steamroller onto the track, then sat back to wait for the crash.

'Catastrophe, that's what he enjoys best,' I said, as my grandson rocked himself with anticipation.

'Not that we had a lot of toys back then,' said David. 'We used to spend most of our time outdoors. Up trees, building dens, down the canal, wherever we fancied. I'd go out in a morning and I wouldn't come back for hours. We were never bored, I'll tell you.'

'You couldn't do that now, though.'

'Why not? Ian used to.'

'Did he?'

'Of course. I couldn't be watching him every minute of the day.'

The Gordon-train rounded the corner, trundled into the tunnel, emerged, and smashed into the roadblock. Matty's hands flew to his cheeks in mock horror. 'Uh-oh,' he said. The engine lay on its side, pistons working busily. 'Uh-oh!'

'Emergency,' cried Ian, and leaned over to fish an ambulance out of the box. Their heads bent together.

I thought I might feel less complicit if I took myself into another room.

'Let's leave them to it, shall we?' I said, detaching myself from the doorframe and stepping backwards into the hall. 'Come through. We'll swap news.'

David settled himself at the kitchen table and folded his hands like a man about to say grace.

'So, any movement at all from Jasmine yet?'

I flicked on the kettle and shook my head. 'But it's good she hasn't mentioned solicitors or anything like that for a bit. I think she's keeping her options open.'

'I'm quite sure she is,' replied David, rather acidly, and I realised how I'd sounded.

'What I mean is, if she doesn't want to start legal proceedings, then it must be because she doesn't think the marriage is necessarily over. Which is good. At the moment she seems to want to keep the status quo.'

'All right for her.'

'I do appreciate that.' The kettle clicked off, and I turned away from him to pour the water. 'It's not nice going behind your daughter's back, you know.'

Steam rose up around my face in a hot flush.

'Carol?' said Ian from the hallway. 'Carol, where do you keep Matty's changing stuff?'

'In his room, under the cot. But look, I'll do it.'

'No, you're fine. Stay where you are.' Ian was through the stair gate before I could argue.

I slotted the kettle back onto its stand and brought the cups across. 'He's good that way, isn't he? A real hands-on dad.'

When he's allowed to be, said David's expression.

The sun came out and lit up the kitchen. Twenty feet from the kitchen window, Mrs Wynne's cat leaped onto our fence and began to pick its way along the top.

'Phil was useless, nappy-wise. He never soiled his fingers with anything so basic.'

David shrugged. 'Different days, though, weren't they? I never changed a nappy either. Then again, I had my share of mopping up bodily fluids later on, with Jeanette.'

'Yes, of course.'

Ian thumped back down with the changing mat under his arm and disappeared into the lounge.

'He is a good father,' said David. 'Whatever else he's done.'

I had a sudden memory of Bolton Central Library as it was when I was a child, and me weaving between the rows of towering shelves to find Dad. His face lighting up when he saw me, holding his hand out for the book I was carrying. *Now, what have you got there?*

'I do think children need a father figure.'

'Glad to hear you say so.'

'It's true. Mine had more to do with bringing me up than my mother ever did.'

'How was that? Was she ill?'

'No, just nowty. You know, peevish, perpetually bad-tempered. Don't get me wrong, she did all the practical side, the washing and the meals. But it was Dad who made the time. He was marvellous with Jaz when she was little. Nowadays it's obviously different, because of his—'

'Watch out, gas masks at the ready, folks.' Ian was standing in the doorway swinging a nappy sack on his finger. 'Where do you want this, Carol?'

'Straight outside, black bin. Thanks.'

When he'd gone, David said, 'How often do you see your father?'

'I usually go Sunday mornings. The year he first went into Willowbrook I visited most evenings, but as time went on he got, I don't know, lost in himself. And it's hard to sit there, watching him decline.'

'I imagine it is.'

'So now it's once a week, and my evenings are spent at the pool or the Scout hut or the gym.'

'Ah, yes, your women's gym.' He raised his eyebrows. 'And what goes on there?'

'What do you think goes on? We do circuits—'

'Just women?'

'Just women.'

'I couldn't join, then?'

'I wouldn't have thought so.'

'That's discrimination.'

'Not really. It's not as though you're denied the opportunity to exercise somewhere else. Anyway, if you were prepared to stick on a pink leotard, we might have you.'

The back door flew open and Ian blundered in. 'I don't know what that child's been eating,' he complained, positioning himself at the sink and squirting soap into his palm. 'You could strip paint with the fumes.'

From the next room we could hear the sound of engine clashing with engine.

'The joys of fatherhood,' I nearly said. But just in time I realised I hadn't the confidence to make that sort of joke. We weren't on those terms any longer, probably never would be again.

Something else he'd fractured with his infidelity.

CHAPTER 12

Photograph: newspaper clipping, loose between the pages of The Marvellous Stories of Jesus *from the bureau, Sunny-bank*

Location: Tannerside church hall

Taken by: the Wigan Observer

Subject: Carol, aged about ten, sits with her mother and six other women at a decorator's table covered in 1,200 palm crosses. Every single one has been hand-made; Carol thinks she could construct a palm cross in her sleep. The hallway at Pincroft has been full of bundles of unsplit reeds that need separating, trimming and folding to make a loopy, top-heavy crucifix. Palm reeds dry your fingers and leave the skin powdery, a sensation Carol hates, though it's satisfying to watch the pile of squashy crosses grow. She likes to arrange them by size, compare the biggest with the smallest. 'Why can't we ask people to keep the ones they had last year?' she enquires of her mother. 'Because you can't,' snaps Frieda. 'Because it's about renewal,' explains the vicar. Carol's crosses will end up in hospices and old folk's homes, as well as with parishioners like bow-legged Mrs Greenhalgh. For the next twelve months those wispy tokens will be tucked behind calendars or picture-

frames, pressed into Bibles, or drawing-pinned to chimney-breasts. It's a pleasing thought.

Meanwhile Frieda surveys the table, her Passiontide labours complete, and hums to herself. Lent's the time of year she likes best, that period of contemplation and denial before the brashness of Easter. Her favourite hymns deal with blood, thorns, decay, scaffolds, toil, chariots of wrath, encircling gloom and Herod.

It occurs to Carol that her mother would probably like a full-size cross of her own; would bang in three of the nails herself.

After David and Ian had gone, I put Matty down for his nap, cleared away the train track, then went and lay on my own bed for a while. The house felt very empty. It reminded me of that first week Jaz left for Leeds and how I'd kept every radio in the house turned on, singing along to the music, answering the presenters back. Not that I ever saw a huge amount of Jaz in those days, even when she lived in the bedroom next door to mine. I'd hear her music, though, and smell her incense; her clothes were in the washing basket and her little pots in the fridge. All those years of nagging people to clear up after themselves, and suddenly tidiness equalled absence. The coat hooks by the front door laid bare after a lifetime undercover, the newel post naked at last. I was able to stand in my own hallway and hear the tap dripping in the kitchen, Laverne's wind chimes on the back porch, my own breath.

And without warning, my memory flicked to Phil, and the week of his leaving. I could see him now, standing in the kitchen with his car keys in his hand, while his suitcases waited at the bottom of the stairs. *Please, I'm so sorry. Can we not talk it through one more time?* Me, still in my slippers, commanding him from my threshold with the towering strength of the righteous.

He'd gone straight from me to Penny, and he'd been there ever since. Not so sorry after all, then.

A glow of outrage started up in my chest as I remembered snippets from afterwards: the call from the ironmongers telling me my wallpaper was in, when in fact Phil had placed the order for Penny; replying to all the Phil-and-Carol Christmas cards that year; discovering Mrs Wynne had told everyone it was Phil who'd left me. The wearying, wearying round of explanation, for months afterwards. Fielding other people's embarrassment and, worse, their pity.

Damn him to hell and back. Eight years gone, and he still had the ability to wind me up.

On the bedside table Matty's monitor made a rustling sound, and over the airwaves I heard him sigh. Then more silence.

I slowed my breathing deliberately, relaxed my muscles, and found myself wondering about David's not-girlfriend. At first I could only conjure up Jacky, complete with wedding hat. But then I thought of that advert for Sandals holiday resorts, and the mature couple who run through the waves, and I thought, Yes, that'll be her. Superior, upgraded, glossy. The sort of woman you'd never find travelling with a coachload of Beavers, singing 'A sailor went to sea sea sea'.

There it came again: Phil's face as I shut the door on him – his face the first time I asked him who Penny was – his face as Jaz got in the car to go to Nat's for a sleepover and I turned to him on the doorstep and said, 'We need to talk.'

Then the bell rang for real, and Matty woke and started crying and I ran to get him and staggered downstairs with my hair still messed up from the pillow and it was the man himself, bloody Phil at the bloody door.

We stood and stared at each other.

'You!' I said.

'I've got your lawnmower,' he said. 'What? What have I done now?'

I let him in anyway.

When he'd carried the lawnmower through to the shed he stood for a while on the patio, considering. Meanwhile I strapped Matty into his high chair, warmed a bowl of mash and mince and watched through the kitchen window as my ex-husband squatted down by the pond and poked at the reeds, got to his feet, strolled to the fence and peered into Laverne's garden. I was on the verge of going out to ask what the hell he thought he was doing when he started back up the path. But even then he seemed to be studying the paving slabs as he went, pausing to nudge with his toe at some unevenness, pressing down a bit of moss further on.

Finally he reached the back door.

'When you've quite finished,' I said.

'You've a slate missing off your roof.'

'Yes,' I said, though it was news to me.

'By the chimney.'

'I know.'

'Best get it seen to while the weather's fine.' He saw my expression. 'All right, I'm only trying to be helpful.'

'If you want to help, you can supervise your grandson while I clear away.'

'Okey-dokey.' He settled himself at the table, grinning. I passed over the bowl and Phil set it down on the tray. 'Chow-time, old chap.'

Matty looked at him indifferently, then picked up his spoon and began to bite the handle end.

'And here's his drink,' I said, holding out the beaker.

'Lucky Matty.' Phil looked hopefully in the direction of the kettle, but I ignored him.

'Don't let him bang it around or the lid comes off.'

'No, Miss.'

'And pull his bib back down, will you? It's all round his throat.' I turned away and began to tidy round the sink.

'So,' I heard him say, 'everything all right with you?'

'As much as it can be,' I said. Stupid question.

Matty gave a little yelp that turned into a giggle. When I looked round, Phil was pulling some kind of comedy face. Dinner sat untouched.

'Oops,' he said. 'Come on, Matt, let's get this show on the road.' He guided the spoon into the food and loaded it up.

'Matty can do that himself. I just need you to supervise.' I went back to wiping down the drainer.

'Any sign of Jaz and Ian getting themselves sorted?'

'Not yet.'

Just for a second I imagined telling him exactly who'd been here an hour before, what secret deals I'd been working.

'Oh well, probably best leave them to it. They're adults.'

'Yes.'

'But you're OK in yourself?'

'Why wouldn't I be?'

'Jesus, Carol, I'm only asking.'

'Watch your language,' I said. 'Little pitchers, big ears.'

The waggling zip pull on Phil's pocket had caught Matty's attention and he'd stopped eating. I put my dishcloth down, ready to take over.

'It's all right, I can manage,' said Phil. 'Come on, lad, chop chop.'

When he failed to get any reaction, he took the spoon himself and started making energetic scooping movements with it. Any minute now, I thought, he's going to pretend to eat it himself. And yes, there he was, smacking his lips half an inch above the spoon end with the hyperactive glee of a children's entertainer.

'Marcel Marceau would be proud.'

'I've got his interest, though.' Without warning Phil opened his mouth wide, bared his teeth, and lunged at the bowl, snapping his jaws. 'Mr Crocodile's after your stew.'

'He doesn't like it. Phil, look, you're frightening him.'

'Rubbish. He's laughing.'

'That's fear.'

As if to make some sort of statement, Matty took the spoon back and dropped it over the side.

'I'll get it,' said Phil. He bent down, reached in between the metal legs of the high chair, got a purchase on the smeary spoon handle, and retreated. Only, in levering himself back up again, he caught the tray with his shoulder and tipped it up. The bowl of cold mash slid backwards, caught against the lip, flipped up and emptied itself down Matty's front, before slipping off his lap and bouncing onto the lino.

'Oh, for *goodness* sake.'

'Give us a break, Carol. I'm doing my best.'

That's half the trouble, I nearly said. Even your best is bloody useless.

I picked up the roll of kitchen towel and started to unravel it. *You're just not comfortable in the role of Grandad, are you?* went my head. *Like you weren't comfortable in the role of Dad.*

'I'll get Matty down for you, shall I?'

'No. Leave him there till I've wiped this mess off the floor. And mind your feet; you're treading in it.'

You were nervous of Jaz, I told him silently, from the word go, and the bigger she got, the worse it became. And your approach to nerves is to go into joker mode, whether it's appropriate or not. I can still remember passing that girl in the hall at one of Jaz's birthday parties, and her saying, 'Mr Morgan's weird.' And I'd gone in and there you were, prancing round the table, wearing false teeth made out of orange peel and a party ring as a monocle. The only people laughing were the mums.

The stew had splashed further than I could have imagined. There was a great streak of it up the cupboard door below the sink, and blobs of pale mash across the tiles as far as the cooker.

And don't get me started on Mr Sock; you never knew when a joke was over. Asking her friends to park their broomsticks by the door, calling Natalie 'Miss Sunshine' to her face. That time Nat turned up crying and you asked if it was because she'd bought the wrong shade of nail polish again. Trust me, they didn't see the funny side. No one 'lightened up'.

Phil had sat down again, and Matty was throwing himself from side to side with a violence that made me glad the high chair had wide legs. I placed the bowl in the sink and turned on the tap. 'Get some spaghetti hoops out of the cupboard, will you, while I sponge his trousers. We'll start again.'

For a few minutes it was almost like old times, buzzing about the kitchen, getting in each other's way. Phil always did want to open the cutlery drawer at the exact same moment I was reaching over it to the toaster. But now he was asking questions all the time: 'The whole tin? Is a teaspoon OK? Does his cup need a wipe?' Then, as I was chopping toast into strips, he said, 'Penny's not been well.'

I tried not to pause, to keep the knife going while I considered how on earth to respond. Your ex-husband confides that his new partner is feeling under the weather. Do you a) punch the air and say *Serves the bitch right!* b) give him the long, cool look of someone who doesn't give a damn, or c) express polite sympathy. I carried on chopping, even though the toast fingers were now of julienne dimensions. What did he mean, 'not well'? Were we talking a nasty cold, or cancer? If I stood here biting the inside of my cheek and said absolutely nothing, would he elaborate?

Then the phone rang next to me, and the knife skittered out of my grasp and twirled across the work surface.

'Excuse me,' I said, and snatched up the receiver.

It was Jaz.

'Mum?'

'Yes. Hang on while I—' The back door was ajar and I slipped through it, closing it behind me, leaving Phil to play Grandad. The air on the patio was balmy. A wood pigeon cooed from the top of the shed. 'Everything all right, love?'

'Yeah, all it was, would you mind if I picked up Matty a bit late? This document's taking me longer than I thought. There's loads of legal jargon in it I keep having to look up.'

'No bother. Give me a call when you're near finishing and I'll bob him over. What's that I can hear in the background, by the way?'

'Tchaikovsky Piano Concerto. It helps me concentrate. Why?'

I smiled, even though she couldn't see me. 'I remember when it was nothing but thumping rock music with you. Thud thud thud through the floor.'

'I've always liked classical.'

'Have you?'

'Yeah.'

A skein of geese pulled across the sky, and I flew with them for a moment.

'Have you heard from Ian?' she said.

'No. Have you?'

A snort. 'Nothing. It's like he's not interested. Not interested in his own child. Can you believe it, after all that fuss?'

'Your dad's here,' I blurted.

'What's he want?'

125

'I don't think he knows himself. Look, I've got to go, Jaz. I left him in charge and he's bound to be making a hash of things. Lord knows what kind of a mess I'll find when I go back in.'

I pressed End Call and stepped back inside. The high chair was empty, Matty's bowl of spaghetti untouched.

'Phil? Phil?'

I hurried through to the living room. And there they were, Matty lying across the changing mat Ian had left out, bare legs kicking, and Phil unfurling a clean nappy with the flourish of a magician.

'What are you doing?'

'What's it look like? You were busy, Mr Stinky here needed sorting.'

'But you've never changed a nappy in your life.'

'I used to do Jaz's.'

'You didn't.'

'I bloody did, Carol. Christ, you've got a selective memory.'

'Watch your language,' I said, staring at the way he hoisted Matty's hips, slid the nappy under, pulled the side tabs clear, wrapped them neatly round the front.

'The old one's over there,' he said. 'I don't know where you want it putting.'

Which goes to show, you can be wrong about people, even those you think you know inside out.

CHAPTER 13

Photograph 279, Album Two

Location: Chester Zoo

Taken by: Carol

Subject: Jaz, eleven, stands in front of a wire-link fence, a toy snake draped round her neck. Phil's half-in, half-out of the photograph, which happens to be a good representation of how he is with the family these days. Earlier he tried to enliven the trip by breaking suddenly into a sprint, waving his arms and crying, 'They're loose! They're loose!'

After the panic has subsided, he is invited to the manager's office to explain himself. There is no explanation for Phil, thinks Carol. She has only recently trained him out of shouting, 'I've won!' every time he visits a cash machine, and writing For smuggling diamonds *on all her chequebook stubs. Really, it wears you down.*

So Phil skulks on the periphery of the picture, neither use nor ornament. Nobody takes any notice of him, that's the trouble; nobody understands his sense of humour. Well, there is one person he can make laugh, but she's not here.

*

'Sometimes,' I confided to Josh as we came into the outskirts of town, 'when I'm on a short journey, I get this mad impulse to keep going and not stop, drive and drive, and see where the road takes me.'

'Mum comes out with stuff like that,' he said.

'Maybe all mothers feel the same way.'

'Not just mums. If I could drive . . .'

'Another couple of years and you'll be old enough to learn.'

'Yeah, right, like Mum's ever going to let me loose behind a steering wheel.'

I knew what he meant: I couldn't picture it either.

'If I could,' he went on, 'I'd get on a plane this afternoon. If I was old enough, and I had a passport. And a stack of money.'

'And your mother would have a nervous breakdown. We'd be sweeping up the pieces even before you'd got to the departure lounge.'

'Yeah.' He picked at the skin around his thumbnail. 'Best stay at home and practise staring at the wallpaper.'

There were so many activities Laverne vetoed: she didn't want Josh travelling fifteen miles to spend the day in Chester on his own, or surfing the net unsupervised, wearing low-slung jeans, sticking posters in his room, listening to music with unsound lyrics, watching the catchphrase comedy he needed to be in the social loop. Laverne's list of prohibiteds was long and broad-ranging. She'd have had him in short trousers if she could.

'Well. It's hard being a mum,' I said non-committally.

'Harder being a teenager.'

'I expect it is these days, yes.'

He reached over the seat for his bag. 'My stop.'

'Here again? You want to walk?'

'Yup.'

'If you insist. I shan't ask.'

'Very wise.' Josh reached for the door handle.

'Have a nice day.'

'I won't.'

A burst of laughter greeted me as I walked in through the gym door. Every machine on the circuit was busy, the room was bright and the music punching. Gwen-the-instructor stood in the middle with her hand over her mouth, feigning shock. 'You wouldn't,' she was saying to Pauline. 'You wouldn't really.'

'I would,' said Pauline. 'And afterwards I wouldn't throw it in a hedge neither. I'd stick it in the mincer. Try sewing *that* back on.'

More laughter. I stuck my car keys and water bottle in the corner and came across to join the girls.

'Margaret's nearly finished,' Gwen told me. 'She'll be off in a sec.'

Change stations now, went the CD player. Margaret stepped off her board and headed for the water cooler, and I took her place.

On the machine opposite, Frances swung her shins backwards and forwards. 'If my husband was trying new things in bed, buying me flowers for no reason and taking more care with his appearance, then, to be honest, I wouldn't care if he was playing away. It'd be worth it.'

Gwen filled me in. 'We're talking about the Tell-Tale Signs your husband's having an affair.'

'I've been reading this article,' said Pauline.

'Yeah. If you tick more than four out of ten, chances are he's up to no good.'

'Problem is,' said Aud, pulling on the bars next to me, 'he can leave no tracks at all. Mine didn't. I hadn't a clue. Not a clue. No funny phone calls, no hiding his credit-card bills. It was because she was at work, it was all so easy for him.'

'How did you find out?'

'He told me. He said he was going, and why. I think he expected me to plead with him to stay. But I just said, "OK then, bugger off." You should've seen his face.'

'Weren't you upset?' said Gwen.

'I was shocked. It was a shock that he'd been lying to me, and to be on my own after so long. But you get used to it, and my sister, same thing had happened to her, so it wasn't too bad. Once, you know, I'd had time to come round.' (*Change stations now*, said the CD.) 'And I lost a stone in weight with the worry, so every cloud has a silver lining.'

'You go, girl,' said Pauline. We were all smiling as we moved round, all nodding our support, and I thought: I could confide if I wanted to. I could tell them how I had no idea Phil was seeing anyone the first time, because you don't expect that kind of behaviour early on in a marriage, especially not when your own parents have been so solidly faithful you never had to think about it. It didn't occur to me he might lie, that he might be going somewhere other than where he said. It had taken Mavis Pearson, Phil's boss's secretary, pulling me to one side at their Christmas dinner. Her emerald blouse, her coral lipstick so bright it was offensive. *I can't stand by and watch it going on, a young girl like you.*

'So it's been good in the long run,' Aud was saying.

'I still miss mine,' said a grey-haired woman whose name I wasn't sure of, though I saw her every week.

'Yeah?'

'I do. Even though it was me who finished it, and it's getting on for twelve years. My daughter, she's in her thirties and she still talks about us getting back together. I say to her, "Why should it matter? You've left home".'

'You can please yourself when you live alone, though, can't you?' said Gwen. (*Change stations now*, went the CD.)

The grey-haired woman climbed off her machine, frowning. 'I know it's fashionable to say you're fine on your own, but I hate it, if I'm being honest. I'm not lonely, I've plenty of friends. But if you go to – oh, say, a party or some do like that – when you get home, there's no one to compare notes with. There's no one to ask, "What did you think of her?" and "Wasn't it funny when such and such happened?". Do you know what I mean?' She stood there, outside the circuit, while we pumped our limbs sympathetically.

Gwen turned to me. 'You don't mind, do you, Carol?'

'What, being on my own?'

'Yeah.'

I let myself think for a moment before I answered, dragging hard on the bars above me and exhaling noisily. Yes, it was better to be alone than with a man like Phil, and his stupid games and continual excuses that ground you down, and it had been like switching a light on when he finally went; I was giddy for days afterwards. And Jaz had gone, 'What took you so long, Mum?' And I'd said, 'I was waiting till you went to college,' and she'd said, 'Well, you needn't have.' Which felt like a slap in the face at the time, but I didn't dwell. Three last-chances he'd had, and he'd blown them all. That's enough for anyone.

'I don't mind it. I'm not often *on* my own. Matty stays over Saturday nights, plus I have him Wednesday afternoons, and I'm at the shop every morning. Evenings I'm here or swimming or Beavers or something else. I don't know how I'd cope with a man on top.'

'Ooh, a man on top!'

I realised what I'd said. 'Honestly, you lot.'

'She means, she doesn't know how she'd fit a man in,' chuckled Pauline.

Now move away from your stations and check your heart rate, said the CD. *Three, two, one – go.*

We stood for ten seconds like mannequins, fingers on throats.

'Everyone OK?' asked Gwen when we'd finished.

'Mine's a little high,' I said.

'You know the best cure for a broken heart,' broke in Sheila from the far end of the room. 'Go out and get laid.'

Shrieks of mirth.

'It's whether you can find someone half-decent, though,' said Aud.

'Oh, I don't let that stand in my way. Use it or lose it, that's my motto.'

'We have noticed,' said Pauline.

'Yeah, well.' Sheila shook her hair back out of her face. 'Get out there, I say, make the most of yourself. Have some fun. You're a long time dead.'

'Thought for the day, ladies,' said Gwen.

Some of us are fine as we are, I wanted to say, but that would have broken the mood. So I just smiled and held my tongue. The music changed to 'Dancing Queen'.

It was my turn for the punchball next.

At least when you're single you can have all your things where you want them.

When Phil lived here it was a house of motoring magazines – stacks of them in the downstairs cloakroom, by the bed, next to the sofa, flooding out of the shoe cupboard every time you opened the doors. His piles of copper were another irritation. I was forever emptying the hollows of ornaments, sweeping coins from the edges of tables, shelves and mantelpieces. The space beneath the sideboard he used for housing not one but three knackered old pairs of slippers; refused to be trained out of the habit. So no matter how scrupulously I tidied the lounge, that area always looked a mess. Then there was his shaving equipment: chargers and spare foils left on the bedroom floor to be trodden on, capsules of gel and bottles of balm and oil spread across sink, bath end, windowsill.

But best of all was when he took his clothes away, and hey presto, I had a whole wardrobe to myself and all the drawers I wanted. Over the years I'd managed to fill them up again: a hanging rail, the shelf above it, the space below, a huge oak press that had been Mum's, and two slide-under-the-bed plastic cases full of clothes.

So it was all the more mystifying that, this afternoon, there was suddenly nothing in the room that suited me. Not one item. It was as though a stranger – conservative, uninspiring – had broken into the house while I was at work, and planted her outfits in place of mine.

I picked up a suede-front cardigan and held it to the light. Decent quality, well looked-after, practical, comfortable, there wasn't anything wrong with it. There was nothing wrong with the four pairs of jeans or the six pairs of cords, the chunky sweaters, the row of white blouses, the black evening tops, my dark jackets. True, there wasn't a lot of colour here – only really my blue going-out skirt, my red wedding suit, and a turquoise patterned dress I'd not worn for over twenty years but was too fond of to throw out. Yet, till today, this collection had functioned perfectly well as a working wardrobe.

Now not even my old favourites felt right. All about me sat heaps of alien clothes with me in the middle, wondering who I'd turned into.

I checked myself in the dressing-table mirror again. No doubt about it, the new haircut was at the root of the problem. Since Wednesday I was flickier, choppier, highlighted and properly coloured, as opposed to home-dyed in twenty minutes while I caught up on the hoovering or sorted my knicker drawer. I'd gone to bed worrying I'd hate my new hair in the morning, dreamed all night about my teeth dropping out, but then, when I got up, the style had fallen into place with a light brush. She'd told me it was low-maintenance, the girl in the salon. 'Takes years off you, too,' she said. And it did, I couldn't argue, only it somehow made me feel all exposed as well. My head no longer matched my body.

A memory of something that had never been popped into my mind: Jaz and me in a café in town, chatting happily, bags of shopping around our chair legs. It shouldn't have been an unreasonable scenario. Other women did these things, mums and daughters together. I thought, We could go round the precinct next week; she could give me advice, I could treat her to something new. Then I remembered how stroppy she'd been on the phone last time we'd spoken. And anyway, who'd look after Matty while we were trailing round the changing rooms? Not Ian, for sure. (A real memory: Jaz at fifteen disappearing into a shop called Scruffy Herbert's, telling me *on no account* to come in after her; me standing in the doorway like a fool while youths in Doc Martens pushed past, knocking my Wallace and Gromit shopping bag.)

I glanced down at my pile of also-wrong shoes. Next to my navy courts was a *Woman's Weekly* back page showing an advert for a locket, one of those collectibles you have to pay for by instalments. *To a precious daughter* was engraved on the gold outside, then, when you opened it, *The day you were born I was truly blessed. Celebrate the special bond that only a mother and daughter can appreciate*, urged the text below. *Imagine her delight when she unwraps this unique gift*. Imagine her falling about laughing, more like.

I kicked the magazine under the bed, sending one of my courts skidding after it. Then I lay back on the duvet and contemplated the ceiling rose for a while. If I turned my head I'd be able to see, above the mirror, the picture Jaz drew for me one Mother's Day when she was about nine. *To Mum*, it said. *I love you*. X X X X X X, the faded felt-tip elephant holding a bunch of flowers in its trunk. Which made me think of some of the presents she'd given me over the years: how she'd scoured the internet to replace the Sylvac bowl I loved but broke; the shoebox she decorated herself with silver-sprayed lace and pressed flowers; the Joanna Trollope novel she'd queued for an hour to get signed.

One of those optical illusions, my daughter was: two black faces in profile or was it one white vase, and you never could see both together at the same time.

CHAPTER 14

Photograph 414, Album Three

Location: Paignton, summer of 1999

Taken by: Eileen

*Subject: The sun shines strongly on Carol (oatmeal sundress)
and Jaz (thick grey cardigan). They are squashed into the carriage of a miniature train that carts visitors from one side of the
zoo to the other. Jaz isn't bothering to smile for the camera and
neither, for once, is Carol. Her thoughts are too full of last
night's events.*

*Eileen began it that first evening, mysteriously buying four
ice creams, and then passing one to a shabby drunk sitting on
the beach steps. 'Well, why not?' she declares gaily. Carol can
think of several responses, but daren't voice any of them. It
could be the medication that's making her so high, but then
Eileen's always had a tendency to make the sweeping gesture.*

*Of course, every time they go down after that, he's there
again and they have to repeat the exercise. Once Eileen adds
a cone of chips into the bargain. 'Ketchup,' says the tramp.
Not 'Thank you,' Carol notes. She can just imagine what Phil
would have to say and wishes, fleetingly, he were on holiday
with them. 'It might not be the kindest thing,' she says to*

Eileen later. 'Like feeding those stray cats in Portugal. What will he do when we leave?'

The situation resolves itself when, on the penultimate after-noon of the holiday, the drunk man collapses in front of them like a pole-axed heifer. Crack! goes his head against the concrete steps. 'Quick,' says Eileen, reaching for her mobile. 'Make sure he doesn't swallow his tongue.' I'm not putting my fingers in there, Carol thinks, but she does run over to check his airway. He's shivering and his teeth are chattering, despite the day's heat. If only she had something to throw over him, a blanket or a coat, but all she has on is her strappy dress; Eileen's no better, in her shorts and Aertex top. How lucky, then, that Jaz has her thick cardigan (even if she has worn it all week in the face of stifling heat and commonsense). Before her daughter can argue, Carol has whipped it off her shoulders and thrown it down.

'Oh, heavens,' says Eileen, her attention diverted momen-tarily from the prostrate tramp. 'Carol, whatever are those marks all over Jaz's arms?'

The rockery at the far end of the pond had been there for as long as we'd lived in the house, and I'd never liked it. To me, a garden's for living, flourishing plants, not lumps of stone. It hadn't helped that my thyme had disappeared, and though I'd replaced it twice, the new shoots hadn't taken. Then the heather had become diseased so that meant another bare patch. There was a bindweed infestation coming up one side and now, while the rest of the garden bloomed, the rockery just looked like something mid-moult.

I'd asked Laverne if I could employ Josh to help dismantle it, and she'd immediately volunteered his time for free. I hadn't argued. Instead, Josh and I had come to a private arrangement, involving the minimum wage and my lemon-rind cake. Here he came with the pick, thunking it into the earth and levering away energetically. Under his long-sleeved T-shirt his shoulders were becoming bulky with muscle; only in the western world did we call a fifteen-year-old a child. Yet at the same time it was astonishing he'd so lately been a little boy, whizzing Hot-Wheels cars off the front step and building slug traps. As we worked, I saw again a tiny Jaz toddling along the path; on her first bike riding circuits round the lawn. It felt like all my married life was recorded in this garden.

An hour into the job, the plants had been grubbed up, and the top rocks removed and wheeled down to the scrubby space behind the shed. We still had the sides to deal with and the soil to shift, but it was clear we'd be done before the end of the day.

'Make sure you bend your knees when you lift,' I warned as we hoisted an extra-large slab between us. 'I don't want to have to cart you home in that barrow.'

Josh shook his head. 'All teenagers' spines are made of elastic, didn't you know? We're indestructible, we are.'

Together we inched our way crab-wise towards the bottom fence.

'If we were shifting rocks on the moon,' Josh said, 'we could carry them on our fingertips. We could boot them along like footballs.'

'I remember a man playing golf on the moon.'

'For real?'

'And his friend threw a javelin. It went miles. Are you ready to let go?'

Josh nodded, and the stone thudded onto the turf between our feet. At the same moment I looked up and Jaz was standing by the back door.

'I did ring the bell,' she called, letting go of Matty's hand.

I came forward and held out my arms for my grandson, but

he veered off towards the flowerbed by the fence, after something he'd spied there. Jaz walked up to the blasted rockery and inspected our work.

'Ooh, nice gloves,' she said, tipping her head at Josh. 'Very *floral*.' He coloured immediately.

'They're mine, as you know,' I said. 'He borrowed them to protect his fingers.'

'If you say so.' She poked the soil with her toe. 'Looks like a bomb's gone off here. God, so many worms. Don't let Matty see them.'

Josh pulled off the offending gloves and dropped them in the barrow. He hitched up his trousers nervously.

'Everything all right?' I asked her.

Jaz shrugged. Over her shoulder I watched Matty fish a rubber ball out from the leaves, then start across to us, holding the ball out in front of him. When he got near he held the ball not to me or his mum, but to Josh.

'Oh no, mustn't interrupt the worker,' said Jaz, swiping the ball from Matty's hands.

'Actually,' said Josh, 'I might have to go.'

'So soon? How's school? Getting all gold stars, I hope. Have you got lots of friends? What's your favourite subject? I'm guessing it's not sport. Computers? Maths?'

'He got all As and Bs last year,' I said.

'Oh, jolly good. Mind you, exams are easier than when I was at school.'

'You're only twenty-seven, love.'

'Yeah, but the pass mark gets lowered every year. They were probably twice as hard when I did them.'

Is that why it took you two goes to get your A-levels? I could have said. But that wouldn't have been fair. Or wise.

'I'm trying to think who he reminds me of,' she continued, putting her index finger against her chin.

'Come on,' I said to Josh. 'You can rinse your boots off under the outside tap. I've put the money next to the kettle for you.'

He dithered for a second, then re-hitched his trousers and set off across the lawn.

'Aled Jones,' Jaz shouted after him. 'That's who you look like. Stick a ruff round your neck and you'd be the spit.'

'Leave him alone,' I said, taking the ball from her and passing it back to Matty. 'And hush.'

'What? What have I said? He's a dork, anyway.'

I bent to prise out one of the smaller stones. 'No, he isn't. Why are you being so mean? He's a nice boy.'

'Same thing. A bit of teasing'll do him good. He needs toughening up.'

'He'll get there.'

'I pity him if he doesn't. You can be too soft on people, you know.'

'Like I'm too soft on you?' I said under my breath.

Perhaps she heard me, perhaps she didn't.

'Your hair.'

The stone came loose and I stood up. 'I wasn't sure you'd noticed.'

'God, yeah. I've been considering it. It suits you. It's a shock, because you never change, do you? But, yeah. What prompted the chop?'

'An impulse. *Ten Years Younger*. Who knows?' I set off with the stone towards the shed, and Jaz followed me.

'I used to help you in the garden, didn't I?' she said.

The rock dropped from my hands and I turned round to look at her. 'Oh, Jaz. You aren't jealous, are you? Is that why you chased him away?'

'Course not. I just wanted to talk to you on your own.'

'Oh?'

'Don't get your hopes up. It's nothing new, you've heard it

all before. Only, everything's really bad today, really bad. Like when it first happened. It's like, your anger kind of holds you together for so long, keeps you running, and then all at once you come crashing down?'

I nodded.

'How did you stand it, Mum, being on your own?'

She wasn't after an answer, which was lucky because I didn't have one. 'Here,' I said, reaching over for my spade, and she took the shaft in both fists as though it was a weapon.

'It's not that I want him back,' she said, 'but that doesn't stop me from feeling shit. I've not been sleeping. Everything goes round and round and round in my head till I have to get up even if it's two, three, four in the morning. Sometimes I catch myself talking to Ian out loud, as if he's in the room with me. I can't concentrate on work or anything, keep forgetting stuff. The worst is, I get so I think I'm coming out of it, and then I have a day like this one where I literally can't stand to be in the house on my own. Before I came here, I thought I was going mad. When's it going to get better, Mum? *Will* it get better?'

It was her eyes that worried me. I thought I recognised that look from before.

'Oh, love.' I was pulling off my gloves to hug her when my mobile went. Jaz swore again. 'I'll let it ring,' I said.

'No, go on,' she said. 'You might as well get it.'

So I picked up.

'Hello?' said David's voice. 'Carol? Have I called at a bad time?'

I stood by the sink and watched Jaz through the window. She'd moved to the edge of the pond to throw little pieces of grass and leaves on the water. Matty was still poking around the bottom of the hedge.

'We were just dismantling the rockery.' Guilt had me almost panting.

'And what had the rockery done to offend you?'

'Been a damn mess for years and years. It was when the heather disappeared it began to look really awful. The problem with heather is it tends to spread out and then die in the middle.'

'I know how it feels.'

On Jaz's right was a cherry tree we'd planted over the hamster. I thought of the morning she'd come in from burying him and I'd made her eggy bread and she'd been too sad to eat it. The more parenthood goes on, the more you realise how little you can put right.

'The reason I called,' David was saying, 'is to check whether Wednesday's still OK. You weren't sure, remember? But I could do with getting it in the diary. Ian can take a flexi-day. We could come over after lunch, if that suited.'

'It's fine. I can always give you a ring at the last minute if the situation changes.'

'You can, but please don't. Cancel at the last minute, I mean.' I could hear his breathing down the line. 'You've no idea what these visits mean to Ian.'

'Who was that?' said Jaz, as soon as I stepped through the back door.

I'd meant to lie but I couldn't; not about that, anyway. 'Your father-in-law.'

Her face fell. 'What's he ringing for?'

'For a chat. A chat with me, Jaz. To me.'

I must have overstressed that last bit, because her expression changed to one of puzzlement, then alarm.

'He's a nice man,' I continued, my blood thumping. 'We were talking about gardening.'

Yes, and I was born yesterday, she was clearly thinking. 'Well, I'd rather you didn't see him at the moment.'

'I'm not "seeing" him.'

'Being in contact, whatever. It feels like you're ganging up on me.'

'Don't be ridiculous. I like him, that's all. He's sensible to talk to.' Not a posturing idiot like your father, I could have added.

'I don't like it,' she said. 'Next time you speak to him, tell him from me he can fuck off.'

'Jaz!' I whipped round to see if Matty had heard, but he'd moved to the top of the garden and was digging with a stick near the drain. When I turned back she'd sat down on the grass with her shoulders slumped and her hair hanging. Part of me longed to shake her, to say, *We could all give up, love. Snap out of it, shape yourself.* But the stronger urge was to comfort.

I settled myself next to her.

'Look, Jaz, will you not reconsider?'

Her head came up, sulky and puzzled.

'I'm asking you straight out: please, please think about a reconciliation with Ian. You're so down, you're going to make yourself ill. I know what it's like, the aftermath—'

'How dare you!' she cried, jerking into life. 'What kind of a mother are you to suggest that?'

'One who wants the best for you. For Matty.'

'What, and you think going crawling back to a man who's got zero respect for me is "the best"? That the best thing for Matty is to grow up in a household where the parents loathe each other? I had to do that, and it was hell.'

I struggled to be gentle with her. 'You say that when you look back now, but at the time, you know, you were perfectly OK. You were, Jaz. You're seeing it from an adult's perspective.'

'What fucking planet were you on? How can you say that?

Were you *blind*? Or are you deliberately misremembering because that suits you?'

'I know that when you were older, just before your dad and I split up—'

'What about that time I saw him with Penny in town and I came home practically in tears? How can you not remember that?' She was wild-eyed now, and flushed.

'You did come home upset once – I think you were about twelve? But that was because you'd had a row with Nat.'

'Yes: *over Dad*. We'd argued because she'd told me Penny was *his mistress* and I didn't believe her.'

'You didn't tell me that.'

'I thought you knew! You *did* know. He'd been screwing her for years!'

'I knew about Penny, yes, but not why you were upset. You didn't say.'

'Did you ever ask, Mum? Did you *ever* stop to ask me?'

We were staring at each other then, completely absorbed, so I don't know exactly how it happened. I heard a single terrific splash, no other sound, and when I turned, the water in the pond was slopping the banks and Matty wasn't by the drain-pipe any more.

It's not deep, my pond, but Matty's not very tall.

Before I'd struggled to my feet, Jaz had jumped up, thundered onto the plank bridge, scrambled down into the water, and was bending and feeling with her hands. In another second she'd hauled him out, streaming. 'Help me!' she shouted, because he was heavy and slippery and she was weighed down by her own sodden clothes. Her face was distorted, her mouth pulled down in an awful grimace, and her T-shirt was sticking to her skin in shiny folds. The ends of her hair were fused with moisture. At that moment I was completely terrified of her. But I lunged forward and took my grandson, who was writhing and retching, into my arms, and laid him on the grass. I felt the cold stain of him spreading across my blouse.

Jaz hauled herself onto the bank and bent over him. Matty's fair arms were marked with mud and strands of blanketweed; spots of duckweed clung to his cheek. Though I knew it wasn't important right now, I was desperate to wipe them away, to reclaim him from that nasty water.

'We'll get him in the bath,' I said.

She shot me this look, then went back to crouching over him, running her hands over his hair and chafing his fingers. The whole business, from Matty falling in till now, probably took less than a minute, but I knew I'd be re-playing it for the rest of my life.

Matty curled his body round, retched again, and began to howl. Jaz gathered him up and hugged him to her. 'Shhh, shhh,' she said. Their pose was like an old-fashioned painting, *Mother and Sick Child*.

'Let's get him inside,' I said, but they were a closed unit.

With difficulty I stood up – my legs were like rubber – and said, 'I'll start a bath running. He'll be frozen.'

'I *told* you to get it filled in when he was born! Told you!' She tried to shake wet strands of hair off her face but they wouldn't budge. 'Go and call the Health Centre. Tell them he might have inhaled some water. I want him checking over. I'll dry him off, I'll see to him.'

I hovered for a second. 'You're all right,' I said. 'You're all right, sweetheart.'

Matty just yelled harder.

'*Mum*,' Jaz said.

Behind her, the dark water was still churning with cloudy sediment like a collapsing universe. I ran to do as I was told.

CHAPTER 15

Photograph 419, Album Four

Location: Blakemere Moss, Nantwich

Taken by: Carol

Subject: a winter landscape – frozen water, bleached banks, stark trees, featureless sky. The only colour comes from the red light in the corner, which at first looks like a sunset. In fact it is chemical discoloration, caused by Carol leaving the film in the camera too long. It's been a pig of a year (losing Eileen to cancer, Dad's diagnosis, Jaz dropping out, hormones shutting up shop) and she hasn't felt like recording much of it. If ever there was a picture that summed up a moment, it's this.

By the time I told Josh about it on Monday morning, the pond incident was beginning to sound not nearly so bad.

'Of course he was upset, but once we'd got him dry, once Jaz had talked to the doctor and he'd given the OK, we went to the Gingerbread Playbarn afterwards and let Matty loose in the ball pit.'

'I used to love those places.'

'They're great, aren't they? Kids can hurl themselves about for hours and nobody minds.'

'Yeah, but I don't qualify any longer. The curse of soma-totropin.'

'The curse of what?'

Josh stretched his legs as far as he could into the cramped space of the Micra's foot well. 'Human growth hormone. The Hungarian was banging on about it last week.'

'And how is our Hungarian? Still picking on that boy?'

He shook his head. 'Had a nasty incident with a sports bag, brought him right down.'

'What happened?'

'He likes to kick our bags out the way, if we leave them between the benches type of thing. He doesn't bend down and shift them, or tell us to, oh no. He just gets his toe in. Biff. Splinter.'

'Is he allowed to do that?'

Josh shrugged. 'We're supposed to stick our bags in the lockers outside, but nobody does because then your stuff goes walkabout. So someone had the idea to fill an old one with bricks, yeah, and plant it in the aisle. The Hungarian, he comes swooping down like a rugby player and gives it an almighty boot – *crunch*. Bones splintering, blood all over his sock, probably. It was excellent. We were killing ourselves.'

'Good God. What did he do?'

'Limped off in agony.'

'Didn't you get into trouble?'

'He didn't want to lose face, did he? Like, if he'd started unzipping the bag and shouting at us, he'd just have looked even more of a wazz than he already did.' Josh must have seen my expression. 'He totally deserved it. Wish it had been his kneecaps.'

'When I was at school,' I said, 'one trick we did was we used to zap each other with compass points.'

'What? Like, stab each other?'

'*No.*' I braked to let a bus pull out in front of me. 'Static electricity. There was this section of nylon carpet outside the Head's office, and if you shuffled your feet and then held out your compass point-first, you could give someone an electric shock. Sparks and all. It nipped, actually.'

'Cool.'

'I don't know who first discovered it, but every Year would pass it onto the kids below. We used to have battles there, although it was risky, what with the Head being just the other side of the door. My friend Eileen was particularly gifted in that department. And my ex-husband.'

'Expelliarmus!'

'Pretty much. Do you still use compasses these days?'

'Yup.'

We were coming to the lay-by where he liked to be let out these days. 'Well,' I said, 'don't let on it was me who told you.'

Josh mimed a compass-point electrocution. 'You may feel a little prick.'

'Have a nice day.'

He dragged his sports kit over the head-rest. 'I won't.'

The door slammed and he loped away.

A stream of lorries and buses kept me stationary, then the traffic came to a halt altogether. I stopped indicating, and put the handbrake back on. Images of Matty floating face down and lifeless in the water immediately covered my vision, and I had to wind down the window and breathe in some cold air to clear my head. 'I'll see about filling in the pond straight away,' I'd promised Jaz. To be fair, she hadn't gone on about it. She hadn't needed to. 'You know, when he's round here, I never take my eyes off him.' That had been the last thing I'd said to her. My eyes welled.

This was no good. Tissues, I needed tissues, and to pull myself together. Ridiculous to churn myself up about what might have been. There was nothing useful in the glove box, or in the door pockets, so I groped behind the passenger seat for the storage compartment there. All I could feel was the packet of wet-wipes I always kept handy for Matty. I unclipped my seat belt and turned to hunt properly, and that's when I saw the plastic bag on the floor, half-hidden under the front seat. I knew without opening it what was inside: Josh's football boots, which he needed today.

Could I still catch him? Forty minutes till I had to open the shop, so I wasn't in a desperate hurry. I wiped my eyes on my cuff, re-buckled my belt, indicated and pulled out into the traffic once more, cruising as slowly as I dared. Luckily it was all stop-start along this stretch anyway, with the crossing by the school and the roundabout up ahead. I crawled past the billboard advertising Thorn Valley Golf Club, past the bus shelter, then the ambulance station, all the while trying to work out how far he could have got during the time I was sitting in the lay-by.

Without warning Josh shot across the road two cars in front of me, straight out into the traffic, like a fugitive in a cop show. He actually jumped over the end of someone's bonnet. Brakes squealed and someone bibbed their horn. I only got a glimpse of his progress because a van was in the way, but after a few awful seconds I saw him reach the far pavement, running.

I'd hardly had time to register that when three other figures appeared in pursuit, dodging crazily between vehicles, swinging sports bags. I had an impression of flying shirts, a white face with the mouth open shouting something I couldn't hear, before they were gone too. Car horns were blaring, and a man in the opposite carriageway had wound down his window to lean out and curse. His lips were making shapes: *Fucking yobs. What the fuck do you think you're doing?*

And I sat there in my Micra, with those football boots on my front seat, not knowing what to do.

'What happened next?' said David, putting his mug down on the table and frowning.

I let my gaze shift to the far end of the room where Ian and Matty were building Duplo towers on the carpet. It had been raining heavily all day, and we had the lights on against the gloom. A stream of water fell from the middle of the gutter where the course was blocked, or damaged: another job I needed to sort out.

'There was a space of about a minute for me to make up my mind,' I told him. 'I thought, I could carry on up to the round-about, come back on myself, and then either drive on to work, or make a left turn into the school car park. And that's what I did, stop at the school. Because I couldn't just go off and leave things, could I?'

David gave a very slight shrug.

'No, I couldn't. I'd have been thinking about him all day, worrying. With me being the one to drop him off, it felt like my responsibility. And I'm very fond of the lad.'

'I've gathered.'

'So I managed to find the main entrance, and it's not easy because it's such a big building, and all the while I was look-ing around to see if I could spot him but I couldn't. There were, I don't know, hundreds of children milling about, not always looking where they were going. I got to the secretary's desk but she was on the phone and I had to stand there and wait, all these kids streaming past me, laughing and yelling, and they're so loud I could barely think what I wanted to say. Then she finished the call, but there was another woman in front of me.

'By the time she'd been dealt with, the place was quietening down. I told the secretary I had Josh's boots and I needed to give them to him, and she looked up what room he was in and nabbed a lad going past to take me up there. Just as well she did because I'd never have found my way otherwise. I said to the boy, "It's like a rabbit warren, isn't it?" But he said you got used to it.

'He showed me to a classroom and left me there, and I peeped through the glass and I could see Josh at the back, putting his books out on the table. He seemed all right. So I knocked on the door and the teacher, he was only young himself, said to come in, and I held the bag up and asked if I could have a word with Josh. I thought when Josh saw me he might get up and come over, and I could talk to him outside, in private. But he stayed where he was.'

David had this expression on his face as if to say, 'I know how this story's going to end.'

'I took the bag over and said, "Here's your boots," and he just went, "Thanks." I was trying to catch his eye but he wouldn't look at me. I couldn't stand there for ever, so I said, "OK?" And he said, "*Fine*." Like that, quite determined. There was nothing I could do without making a fuss, although I did toy with the idea of speaking to the teacher. Then I thought I'd better have a chat with Josh first.'

'What you don't want to do is make the situation worse,' said David.

'No, that's what I was worried about. I haven't mentioned it to his mum yet for the same reason. She's hyper at the best of times.'

'And what's Josh got to say on the matter?'

Over by the window, Matty's tower leaned, toppled, and scattered itself widely across the floor. 'Uh-oh,' he said. 'Cash!' Ian reached across and ruffled his hair.

'I asked him this morning. He says it was nothing. Does it

sound like nothing to you? Do you think he's being bullied? Should I tell Laverne? He is lying, isn't he?'

'Almost certainly he's lying,' said David, swilling his coffee round in its mug. 'But I don't think you should interfere. Not yet, anyway.'

'It's not interfering, it's helping someone who I think's in trouble.'

'Boys have chased other boys since time began, Carol. It's what they do.'

'Across busy roads, in front of cars? Imagine if – And then, I've been thinking: sometimes he tells me about this pupil the teacher picks on, and I think it's him. He tells it as though it's another boy, but it's him, I'm sure of it. So that teacher needs to be dealt with, because he's inflaming the situation, he's giving the bullies licence. It's abuse.'

David drained his cup and set it down decisively.

'Wouldn't you say you've got enough on your plate just at the moment?'

All the fight and the fury went out of me, and I sagged. 'You mean with the pond.'

I had no idea why I kept telling everyone about it. Laverne and Mrs Wynne, Moira and several customers at The Olive, the girls down the gym and the man who called for the Betterware catalogue had all been treated to the story of how I nearly drowned my grandson. I'd even gone so far as to ring Phil and pour out the tale to him.

'To be honest,' said David. 'I was thinking more—'

'The next time you come, it'll be filled in, I promise. I've contacted a landscaping firm, and I'm going to have a word with the Ahernes at the back because they've got a pond and they could take my newts.'

'I don't think you need go that far, Carol.' David stood up and wandered over to the French window. Rain was running down the other side in torrents, creating a weird light, blurring the shapes into each other so that my garden was a fluid landscape of unnatural greens.

'Oh, I do, I do. It'll break my heart to get rid of it, but I can't take the risk.'

'Steel mesh would fix it.' David turned and bent to intercept Matty who was about to collide with his legs. He lifted his grandson off the ground, brought him round to face Ian, then propelled him back the way he'd come, in one neat action.

'You mean a fence?' I asked.

'No. A flat grid over the top. I've installed them in a couple of properties. There are regs about gauge, it's got to be rigid and secure. But I can give you the name of a company who'll fit you one. You don't have to lose your pond unless you want to.'

'Really?' The news lifted my spirits hugely. 'And they're definitely safe that way?'

'RoSPA recommended.'

I thought again of the day Ian dug out my pond, how delighted I'd been then.

'You've a solution for everything, haven't you?'

'No, not quite everything. But a pond's nothing. Ponds can be sorted, like *that*.' He clicked his fingers, then we both looked at each other for a long bleak moment.

Over in the corner, father and son were sorting bricks into piles of different colours, or trying to. Matty was just making piles.

I said: 'Would you believe I'd planned a picnic for this afternoon?'

'Ah.'

'Although Matty would probably like it, splashing about in a downpour. Toddlers do.'

'Well, middle-aged people don't. Anyway, you don't want to spoil your new hairdo.'

I put my hand up to my fringe self-consciously.

'It's very nice,' he said. 'Here's an idea: couldn't you spread a picnic blanket out on the floor in here? Children don't really care what you do as long as you're doing it with them.'

'Doesn't it get wearing, being so brilliant all the time?'

David rewarded me with a thin smile. 'Actually, it's a trick I remember Jeanette pulling once when Ian was little. Do you want a hand putting your sausage rolls out?'

We left Matty and Ian now making a snake or a wall or a lying-down tower, and went into the kitchen to plate up.

Which is how Phil came to find us half an hour later: kneeling round one of my mother's tray cloths, sipping from plastic beakers, while Matty crumbled breadsticks down his front.

I read the look on Ian's face as the bell rang, and rang again. 'She's in Manchester all day,' I said, as I scrambled to my feet. 'She'd an appointment at the university.'

The men exchanged glances. I hurried out into the hall.

'Carol?' said Phil when I opened the door, as though there was some doubt in his mind as to my identity. Water was dripping from the porch down the back of his coat; beyond him the street was a haze of rain.

'What do you want?' I asked, hanging onto the doorframe and blocking the entrance.

'I was passing. You seemed upset.'

'When?'

'On the phone.'

'No.'

'You were. About the pond, and Matty.'

'I'm fine.'

'Oh. Well. Good. I've a present for him, anyway.' Phil jiggled a plastic carrier at me.

Perhaps Matty had heard his name, because a few seconds later he appeared at my side. 'Gappa,' he said.

'Hello, mate,' said Phil, and squatted down so he was at Matty's level. 'Fancy seeing you. Now, what do you think I've got in this bag, eh? Shall I come in and show you?'

I stepped back to allow him a foot of space.

'Yeah?' he said, straightening up again. 'Hey, Matt, what's in the bag?'

Zero response.

'What do you reckon? An elephant? A bus?'

'Oh, for goodness' sake.'

Matty had already lost interest and was wandering over towards the stair gate, so I took the bag off Phil and investigated for myself.

It was a cardboard box with the Lego symbol on the tab. Little pieces shifted inside as I turned it over. The front showed a red robot shooting death rays out of its fingers.

'Bionicle,' said Phil. 'Let him see.'

'No.'

'What?'

'It's not suitable. It's too old.'

Phil gritted his teeth in exasperation. 'You can build it *for him*, Carol. I know he can't manage the construction on his own, but every lad likes a robot.'

'Yes, but it's got small parts. See? *Not suitable for children under 36 months. Choking hazard.*'

'They only say that to cover themselves. Look at what Jaz had to play with when she was little. Your button tin, for one. Beads, plastic figures, pebbles. She never came to any harm, did she?'

'That was when she was older. I'll put it away for him, Phil.'

Now Matty came toddling back over, reaching up to grasp Phil's trouser leg. 'Gappa,' he said again.

'I might have known there'd be something wrong with it,' said Phil. 'My present. I'd have put money on that.'

'You know, you're the one—' I began, but the box slipped out of my hand and fell with a thunk and a rattle onto the carpet. Phil waited till I bent to retrieve it, then took the opportunity to slip past with Matty. 'Oh, hang on, it's not really convenient,' I called after him, but too late because he was standing in the entrance to the living room with his mouth open.

'Carol?'

'It's all right,' I said, even though it wasn't, not by a long chalk.

David stood up as if he was meeting a client, and stretched out his hand. 'Phil.'

'Is Jaz here?'

'No, she's working today,' I said, feeling my face grow hot.

'. . . dropped by,' mumbled Ian in the background.

'We're having a picnic,' went on David.

'Ta,' said Matty, passing up a cherry tomato. Phil took it from him and stared at it.

David gave up on the handshake and sat down again. 'Help yourself,' he said. 'I can recommend the Dairylea.'

I watched Phil dither on the spot, the back of his coat still stained by the rain, and I could tell exactly what was going through his head.

'How's business?' said David. 'This banking thing affecting you at all?'

'Not really,' said Phil. 'Jaz is working, you say, Carol?'

I nodded.

He turned back to David. 'So . . .'

'I came to see my grandson,' said David. 'Incidentally, I think we may have solved the pond problem. Do you want to tell him, Carol?'

Although Phil, as the only man standing, should have had the advantage, he was the one out of place and awkward. He cleared his throat, turned his gaze to Ian. One adulterer to another, I was thinking. David's the only decent one among you. For a few seconds I let myself run a little fantasy: Phil and David locked in physical combat, brawling across the remains of the picnic so that beakers spilled over, fairy cakes were squashed, my mother's ornaments trembled in the display cabinet.

Then Matty, picking his way across the tray cloth, trod on a plate, lost his balance and fell over. He struck his head on the arm of the sofa and began to cry. I started forwards, but Ian was already pulling him onto his lap, shushing and stroking.

Phil's hand was on my arm.

'Come into the kitchen, you,' he said. 'I need a word.'

The light coming in through the window was that golden, pre-sunset type that should make you feel relaxed. Perhaps Dad was relaxed. How was I to know? They'd shifted his chair forward so he could see out of the window, but as the sun dipped lower he'd become dazzled, so I'd turned him side-on. One cheek and ear was gilded, like an angel's.

'Mrs Wynne's granddaughter's not so good,' I said.

In the corridor outside I could hear shouting, and then a nurse's voice, calm and upbeat.

'You remember when her little girl had that fit? Well, Libby's all right, but they don't know if the baby's growing properly. Mrs Wynne says she's got to go in for some tests.' I stretched my fingers out into the shaft of light. 'Which is obviously worrying. When I think about it now, Jaz had an easy pregnancy, didn't she?'

It wasn't my day to be there, but I'd been sitting at home and suddenly I needed to see my dad. Now I was here, I still felt restless and undone.

The glass on the sunburst clock bulged, as if there was too much time inside it, and the earth rolled us towards night. Someone's walking frame tap-tapped along the corridor.

'I just wish I knew,' I said, forgetting the fiction that he could hear, that he could understand, that I'd get any response; forgetting it all and talking to myself. 'Am I doing the right thing? Letting them into my house, going behind her back? She's my daughter.'

You're playing a fucking dangerous game, I heard Phil say again.

'Who should I be supporting here? Who counts the most, Matty, or Jaz?'

Under Dad's eye a nerve flickered, a momentary spasm. That was all. Nothing more.

CHAPTER 16

Photograph: unnumbered, loose inside an old Bunny-Bons toffee tin, the shed, Sunnybank.

Location: outside Jaz's university hall of residence, Leeds

Taken by: Tomasz Ramzinski

Subject: Jaz and her father stand with their backs against the wall, as if they're about to be shot. Phil has his arms folded and Jaz is biting her nails. To Jaz's left, some boy inside the building squashes his face against the window in a grotesque leer.

This has been a disaster of a day.

Phil's intention was to drive his girlfriend, Penny, over to Leeds so she could meet Jaz properly. But on the way there, he apparently said something wrong – he's not sure what – and before he knew it, Pen was accusing him of all sorts. Not taking the relationship seriously, not committing, being ashamed of her, not earning enough money, taking no interest in soft furnishings. After a while he stopped listening. The upshot was, she sat in the car while he went to see his daughter on his own.

Jaz seems OK, as far as he can tell. Has a boyfriend, has a girlfriend, likes her tutor, isn't living in squalor. He'd say *she's a bit restless, a bit impatient, but maybe that's just with him. Hasn't she always found him irritating?*

Then the boyfriend makes an appearance, and she loses interest in her dad altogether.

Before Phil leaves, he gets the boyfriend – very full of himself, that one – to take a photo. It would be nice to show the picture to Carol; she worries about Jaz being away from home. That he can never do, though. She'd winkle out the details of the trip in no time. For all he's a practised adulterer, he's a lousy liar.

I'd come off the machines and was doing my stretches when Sheila bounced into the gym. (Poor Sheila, whose grandchildren were growing up on the other side of the world.) She clocked in at the computer, looked across, and saw me.

'You drive a blue Micra, don't you?' she said.

My heart sank. 'What's up? Have I been pranged?'

'Not exactly.'

I cut the stretches short, picked up my keys and hurried outside to see.

My car was parked in its usual spot, unharmed, except that tied round the driver's-side wing mirror was a silver helium balloon. It strained and twisted on its string, flashing in the sunlight.

'Looks like someone's got an admirer,' said Sheila behind me.

'Looks like someone's playing silly beggars,' I said.

I walked around and started picking at the knot. It wasn't very secure and soon came loose under my fingernails. I teased out the loop, pulled the tail free and the balloon jerked, jerked again, then floated upwards, off to God knows where. A fraction of a second too late, I realised I could have kept it for Matty.

*

'You know about Monday?' said Laverne over the fence as I was attempting to skim duckweed off my pond.

'Josh not needing a lift? Yes, he reminded me. And it's two weeks, isn't it?'

'That's right.'

'Is he looking forward to his work experience?'

'Yes – well – I don't know. Why he chose the cottage hospital, all those ill people, when he could have gone in a nice clean office.'

'I should imagine he'll be good with the patients, though. Is that what he wants to do when he leaves school? Nursing, something in that line?'

Laverne pursed her lips doubtfully. 'I'm not sure. I don't want to think about it. My little boy, growing up too fast. I've no idea what to do about his birthday, either, that's coming up next month. He's at a funny age. You haven't any suggestions, have you?'

'For his party or his present?'

'Both.' She tilted her head back and looked at the sky, as if inspiration might be writ there. 'It sounds silly to say it about your own son, but – he's strange, in some ways. I don't feel I know him that well.'

'It doesn't sound silly at all,' I said, then wondered whether I'd come across as rude. 'What I mean is, just because someone's part of your family doesn't mean you're privy to their deepest thoughts. It used to be a struggle to buy for Jaz. In the end we just gave her money, and that always went down well.'

'Oh, I'm not giving him *money*,' she said, as though I'd suggested parcelling up some crack cocaine. 'He's got to have a proper present.'

I tried to imagine what might make it onto Laverne's approved list. A book? A non-violent video? 'How about one of those "experience days" where they get to drive a rally car?'

She shuddered. 'Not that.'

'Or zookeeper for a day? Dorothy Wynne's chiropodist did that, said it was amazing. Josh likes animals, doesn't he? And he could invite a few friends to meet him at the zoo after-wards.'

'I'm not . . .' Her face grew vague. 'His friends . . . It's a part of his life that . . . Look, Carol, does he ever talk to you about school? I know you chat in the car.'

The truth was, Josh wasn't talking to me at the moment. Nowadays we mainly sat in silence on the drive to school. The most response I'd had lately was when I told him the story of how Eileen and I had covered our maths books in foil and then flashed them in the eyes of the teacher all lesson long, but even then he was only briefly interested.

'I thought he might have let something slip,' she said. 'To you.'

'What about?'

'I don't know.' She was looking straight at me now, her stringy neck at full stretch, her eyes too wide. I thought of a programme I'd seen about parents who have their kids micro-chipped, and who put up hidden cameras to spy on their childminders. Then I remembered Josh running into the road. What he needed for his birthday were self-defence lessons and a Kevlar vest.

'I think there's something going on. Sometimes he – You would tell me,' she said, 'if you knew there was something wrong?'

The moment teetered on its edge.

'Wouldn't you?'

It was the pause that undid me.

I was actually in bed when the phone went. Not asleep, but settled and wound-down with the lights low. Chilled, as Jaz would say. Then this jaunty blast of music, jerking me into wakefulness. It wasn't the landline, either, it was my mobile, which meant I had to get up, switch on the main light, and hunt the thing down.

'Seriously, though,' went Phil's tinny little voice, as though we'd been in the middle of a conversation, 'I don't think you should be having him round.'

'What?'

'I've been thinking about road signs. You know.'

'No.'

'Those flashing boards that tell you to slow down.'

'Are you drunk, Phil? You sound drunk.'

'A bit.'

I retreated to the bed and climbed back in, pulling the duvet up around myself for decency. 'Where's Penny?'

'Not here.'

Why else would you be calling me so late, I nearly said. 'She's not in hospital, is she?'

'God, why do you say that?' Phil sounded frightened.

'You told me she wasn't well.'

'Oh, no, she's fine. She's, no, she's. Gone to a friend's. Anyway, we're not talking about her.'

'Look, Phil, what do you want?'

There was some scuffly noise and heavy breathing; perhaps he'd dropped the phone. I was on the point of giving up when he spoke again.

'It's bothering me. If you keep having Ian round, Jaz'll find out and then there'll be hell to pay.'

I made myself count to five before I replied.

'So you said, Phil. But if I block him from seeing his son, there'll be trouble from a different direction, trust me. And when I've tried to negotiate between them, that's been disastrous too. Far as I can tell, I'm between a rock and a hard place and another rock.'

'He's not threatened you, has he? Stuck-up bastard. Because if he has—'

'It's not like that. But Ian has rights, and if Jaz ignores them—'

'We can't start telling her what to do or she'll get shirty with us as well.'

'You think I don't know that? For God's sake!'

'I don't have an answer,' said Phil.

'So what's new?'

'Carol, I—'

'Stirring things up, to no purpose! As if you're in any position to adopt the moral high ground. And stop tying balloons to my car, stupid bloody carry-on. And stop calling me when your girlfriend's away. And get my shed cleared out. Why don't you *ever* do anything *useful*?'

I switched the phone off.

Might as well get up and make a drink, do some stretches, maybe sort out some bills. There was no chance of getting a good night's sleep now.

When I'm in a particularly self-destructive mood, I get out the photograph of Penny. No one knows I have it, not even Jaz, and she actually took the damn thing.

It was one afternoon when Phil had dropped by with some message or other (this was after the divorce, when we were supposed to be square and sorted), and Penny was in the car. He told me. 'Pen's outside,' he said. I don't know if he was expecting me to ask her in. I'm ashamed to admit this, but my immediate response was to stalk across and jerk the curtains closed. Then, of course, we'd been plunged into ridiculous gloom. I ought to have taken him through to the kitchen, only that felt like defeat, so whatever it was we needed to talk about we did in semi-darkness, like those ex-cons on TV whose faces have been hidden to protect their identities. I'd been aware of Jaz crashing about upstairs, but my mind had been on other things. Then, when Phil had gone, she came down and showed me what was on my own digital camera: a bored-looking, pudding-faced blonde gazing out of a car window. That was the first time I'd laid eyes on my husband's mistress.

I could have seen her before, if I'd wanted. I'm sure I could have found all kinds of evidence over the years, had I looked for it. I could have hung around near the office, or hired someone to trail her and make a report. Some wives do that, collect files of information; their way of coping. My energy's always gone into blotting Penny out.

Nevertheless some fragments of unwanted information have slipped through. She wears contact lenses; her brother's a nurse; she has to use special shampoo or she gets eczema; she has a mild London accent; her dad once served Dick Emery a tank-full of petrol; she's never wanted children; she's an immoral, unsisterly witch.

I ought to have deleted the picture at once – two presses of a button and it would have gone for ever. But instead I put the camera to one side, waited till Jaz was out one evening, and printed a copy. I wiped the image off the camera, then sat and held the photograph in my hands for an age, just looking at it. This is her? I kept thinking. *This?* Penny's mouth was one of those too-small smug ones, her cheeks plump and going to jowl. Her hair hung to shoulder length, in no particular style. Difficult to tell much about her figure or clothes, but she looked wider than I was, and lumpier. Like me, she was middle-aged. That was all. A completely unremarkable woman.

I remember laughing, at first, in disbelief. Mistresses were supposed to be glamorous and young and willowy. I imagined saying to Phil, *God, is she truly the best you could manage? You junked your marriage for THIS?* After a while I put the photo down, went to my bedroom and, with trembling hands, redid my hair and make-up, as though I was getting ready for the date of my life.

For half an hour after that, I'd been high as a kite. Then, without any warning I was sobbing without restraint, the way I hadn't let go in years. Within minutes my face was a slimy mess, my breath juddering uncontrollably. It felt as though every single tear I'd held back, every spurt of rage I'd stifled over the years was now rushing out of me in a torrent, a huge outpouring that I was physically incapable of stopping.

I have no idea how long this session lasted, but finally I think I just ran out of steam. That was the last occasion I cried over Phil. By the time Jaz came home I'd showered and blow-dried my hair, rubbed on my night cream, and was sitting watching *Blackadder II* in my dressing-gown. 'Everything OK?' she'd asked me. 'Fine,' I'd told her.

I keep meaning to get rid of Penny's photo: burn it, or post it through the floorboards so that, in years to come, strangers will go searching for wires or pipes and find this fragment of an evening's self-harm under a layer of dust and mouse dirt. It's what she deserves. And yet I can't quite bring myself to let the picture go. So it lives in my bureau, face down at the back of the drawer, and whenever I need to stick a knife into myself, out comes Penny again.

I'm well aware I shouldn't, but it's not as if I actually cut myself, the way some women do. The way my daughter did.

CHAPTER 17

Photograph 404, Album Three

Location: a Little Chef car park, half way between Sunnybank and Leeds University

Taken by: Carol

Subject: Jaz leaning against the bonnet of Phil's car. She looks cross, but that's only because she's trying to hide her nerves. Behind her, the boot and half the back seat are crammed with the gear she thinks she will need for her first term.

Phil is not in the picture, even though he is the one doing the driving. As a now officially ex-husband, he shouldn't be on the scene at all, except that Carol's car is suddenly kaput and there seems no other way, at such short notice, of transporting Jaz's goods and chattels across the country. Penny has magnanimously agreed it is OK.

Never have fifty miles seemed so far.

At the previous stop, Carol had to go in search of Phil; found him standing by the side of the road wearing his old fluorescent jacket and holding Jaz's hairdryer to simulate a police speed trap. 'Bloody hilarious watching them slam their brakes on,' was his explanation.

'Why does Dad have to be such a prick?' mutters Jaz, below Phil's hearing, and both women snigger miserably together. It is the one bright spot in a long, long journey.

The kitchen of the Scout hut always smelled of powder paint because it also served as the art storage area. Over the worktop where I was now slicing bread rolls hung a string of papier-maché-covered balloons; both windowsills were jammed with unpainted clay candleholders. Before I'd been able to get at the fridge, I'd had to shift a full-size post box built of corrugated card.

On the other side of the steel serving shutter, the gang show was in full swing. Rows of parents, grandparents and Scout- and Cub-siblings were being entertained by various ropey acts, prior to a sing-along and buffet. One of the mums was supposed to be helping me with the catering, but she hadn't shown. All the leaders were out the front, supervising.

'Two big piles of rolls, one cheese spread and one chocolate, and bugger healthy eating,' Akela had told me. There was also squash to make up and tins of cakes and biscuits to unpack. 'I'm really sorry I can't stay,' she said. 'Another pair of hands would have been useful, wouldn't it?'

Snatches of the show filtered through as I worked. 'Let the audience see your card,' I heard as I punctured the foil on a jar of Nutella. 'Pass me my magic cloth, Wolverine.' The butter had gone hard and I had to beat it with a fork before it was any good. I thought of my mother whisking egg whites by hand and how red and furious her face would turn before she'd finished. 'Was this your card?' the magician cried. 'Oh, hang on.'

Which is when the back door opened and David walked in. I almost dropped my fork in shock.

'Is something wrong?' was my immediate question.

'No.'

'Why are you here?'

'I was passing. I wanted to see you.'

'How did you know where I was?'

'You said yesterday, on the phone.'

His appearance, unannounced and out of context, flustered me and I lost track of where I was up to and knocked over my jar.

'Are you busy?' he said as I scrabbled about.

I raised my eyebrows at the piles of food.

'OK, I'll rephrase that: would you like some help while I'm here?'

'Were you really "just passing"?'

'No.'

'So what is it? Has something happened with Ian or Jaz?'

'Not that I'm aware of, and I only saw Ian half an hour ago. No, I was just at a loose end and I wanted to see you. Should it be so strange?'

You're fooling no one, I thought. Something's rattled you. You've had a row with Ian and you needed a refuge, let everything simmer down. I could just tell.

'All right,' I said. 'Since you're offering, you're more than welcome. Hang your coat up over there and wash your hands. I need those cake tins unpacking, and what's in them arranging on the foil platters in the corner. We've probably got about fifteen minutes till the end of the show and I've not even started on drinks yet.'

David followed my instructions, rolled up his shirt-sleeves and set about plating-up. Skull-jarring music thumped through the wall from next door. 'What in God's name's that?' he asked, peering through the slots between the shutters.

'Charlie Blunt break-dancing. It's all right, he'll be finished in another thirty seconds.'

'You sat through rehearsals?'

'God, no, they do all their rehearsing at home. But I know because he used to do exactly the same act before he became a Cub, while he was still a Beaver.'

I sawed into bread at top speed, careless of the skin between my finger and thumb.

'How did you get into all this in the first place, Carol?'

'The Boy Scout thing? Gosh, well, Sal Vaughan, the original Dove – not this new one who I don't really know yet – was a friend of Laverne's. I started helping Beavers when Josh was in the pack, and stayed on after he left. But I sometimes get drafted in for Cub and Scout dos as well, hence tonight.'

'And you do this for no pay?'

I drew the back of my hand across my brow in a gesture of martyrdom. 'Actually, the ones who deserve medals are the pack leaders who turn up every week and have to organise all the events and be responsible. I just potter in the background.'

The thumping bass stopped at last, to be replaced after a pause by a halting violin solo. David prised the lid off another tin.

'Ah, yet more fairy cakes. How many are we feeding? Five thousand, is it?'

'You have no idea how much these lads can get through at a sitting. It's devastation. They hold competitions to see who can stuff the most in their mouth at once.'

'Does that come under badgework?'

'Scoffers Award.'

A little grin appeared on David's face.

'What?' I said.

'This vast acreage of food. Reminds me of the birthday parties Jeanette used to throw when Ian was small. She always over-catered, always we'd be eating leftovers for a week afterwards.'

'Well, you do. I did, with Jaz.'

'It was like a competition: the table had to be crammed. Hedgehogs out of Matchmakers, jelly goldfish.'

I said, 'How long were you married?'

'Eleven years. Though we met three years before that. She was a secretary in my father's office. I came back from London, and there she was.' His brow furrowed at the memory.

'Was she ill a long time?'

'About two years, from first diagnosis.'

'It must have been hard.'

'Yes.'

'I'm sorry,' I said, as the violin scraped to a conclusion.

David shook his head. 'I'll say what no one else is entitled to: it's twenty years ago, and life moves on. At the time she died I never thought it would, but it does and thank God for it.'

I watched as he carried on laying out cakes to some precise and careful pattern of his own devising. He looked so comfortable with himself, this man in his fifties, with his expensive shirt and sleek haircut, that it was impossible to imagine him young and vulnerable. Twenty years ago, when I was trying to work out whether to dismantle my marriage or not.

The sandwiches finished, I put the butter away and shook the crumbs into the sink. I was about to move the conversation on by asking about work when a Cub on the other side of the screen shouted, 'Hey, mums and dads, want a great family day out, with fun and thrills for all ages?'

'Yeah,' someone yelled back gamely.

There was a brief pause, some whispering, and a giggle.

'Then come to – shurrup, stop it, Tom – come to Knickerworld! The country's only pants-based theme park. Yes, we've got it all at *Knicker*world.'

The audience tittered. David raised his eyebrows at me.

'They write the script themselves,' I said.

'Evidently.'

'*There's millions of knickers all under one roof,*' sang the Cub.

'Kids,' called another one. 'Come and ride in our giant Y-fronts! See our display of famous people's kecks! Marvel at the history of undercrackers in our award-winning museum! And don't forget to pick up some souvenir grundies in the gift shop.'

'Because you're worth it.'

'Try on a selection of smalls from other countries, including porcupine pants, termite trunks, bumblebee boxers and shark-skin Speedos.'

'Knickerworld, the best of both worlds.'

After every line there was shrill laughter, which quickly began to affect the performers themselves. The routine continued, but with gaps of increasing duration where the boys were struck voiceless, convulsed with the hilarity of their own jokes.

'Visit our fabulous café and sample shreddies with a difference—'

'*Maybe she's born with it, maybe it's underpants.*'

'See royal golden pants.'

'*Here come the pants—*'

'And our special room of record-breaking pants.'

'*The pants effect.*'

'– including the smelliest –'

'*The pants of your life.*'

'– your mum's –'

'– big hairy pants –'

The sketch dissolved into helpless sniggering, and Akela took charge. 'Thank you, Robbie and Max, for that very interesting sketch. I'm sure we'll all be saving up to go to, er, Knickerworld in the near future.'

I could hear several boys having what sounded like asthma attacks.

'Easily amused, aren't they?' said David.

'God, yes. Anything at all to do with undercarriages.'

'. . . the part where we ask the families to join in,' Akela was saying, 'as a way of showing their appreciation for the boys' hard work. So if I could ask Martin . . .'

'Quick,' I said, 'we've got about five minutes to sort the drinks.'

While David tore open the polythene wrapper and released the cups, I poured a couple of inches of undiluted juice into an empty gallon container and held the neck under the cold tap. Through the wall came the jolly sound of audience participation.

'There were snakes, snakes, big as garden rakes,
In the store, in the store.'

Once the squash was made up, we started a production line. David held each cup at the base to stop it falling over, and I filled it as far as the plastic crimps.

'In the quartermaster's store.'

After about the first ten we got into a rhythm. 'Anyway, what about you?' said David.

'What about me?'

'Where are you up to?'

'In what way?'

'With your life. The past. Anything.'

'There were gulls, gulls, pecking on your skull.'

My mind at once emptied itself. All I could dredge up at that instant was a random image, a night over thirty years ago, back at Pincroft, trying to write my wedding list during a power cut. When the electricity came on afterwards, my mother found that one of the candles had burned a black spot on the underside of the shelf above and the only person she could blame for it was herself.

'There's nothing to tell,' I said. 'I am who I am: Jaz's mum, Matty's grandma.'

'And?'

'*Akela, Akela, Snogging with a sailor.*'

'I don't know what you mean, David. I'm fifty-two, I'm divorced. I work in a gift shop. I like photography and gardening, I'm a member of a women's gym – you already know all this.'

'You're telling me your CV. What about *you?*'

'*My eyes are dim, I cannot see*
I have not brought my specs with me
I have not brought my specs with me.'

The song dissolved into screams and whoops and clapping. And then the shutter went up a fraction and Charlie Blunt's face peered underneath. 'Akela says are you ready for us?'

'We are,' I said, with the sense of someone who's had a narrow escape, though I couldn't have told you what from.

The hall was hot and full and a sea of green sweatshirts. Scouts came forward to take the plates and offer them round; the drinks were serve-yourself.

'Are you finished here, or do you have to stick around?' asked David.

'My work here is done. Someone else can wash up.'

The boys were giddy with post-performance relief, high and naughty and fun. I looked out across the rows of chairs and saw parents I recognised, children I'd watched grow up. Martin Clark, a Venture Scout in his last term at school, I'd known since he was a shy ten-year-old with a speech impediment; now he was six feet tall and comfortable playing guitar in front of forty people. I felt my throat tighten at this glow of youth before me. All that energy and promise and clear skin.

'Do you fancy a drink, then?' said David.

I let him lead me back through the kitchen and out of the rear entrance into the car park.

'Where's your Micra?' he asked.

'I walked. It's only twenty minutes.'

He came round to open the passenger door of his Audi. I'd forgotten such courtesies. Inside it was clean and polished, no wet wipes on the floor or muddy marks on the seats. No sweet wrappers in the coin compartment.

'Where shall we go?'

'The Lion's nice.'

'I don't know where that is.'

'Top of the High Street. I'll direct you. Although we're not going anywhere just yet.' In front of us a Saab waited for an ancient Citroën to complete a twelve-point turn. 'Why he doesn't back out . . .'

I wound the window down and breathed in the spring evening.

'How's, you know, your girlfriend who isn't your girlfriend?' I said.

For a few seconds he didn't answer. I thought he was concentrating on the Citroën.

'David?'

'I'm not seeing her any more.'

'Oh. Oh, I'm sorry.'

'I told her this evening.'

So that was why he'd been after my company. As I'd guessed, not for its own pleasure, but because he needed cheering up. Only I'd picked the wrong source of upset. I weighed the thought, decided it was OK; we all require the distraction of the ordinary at times of emotional crisis. 'You should have said.'

'Well.'

'Was it horrible? I'm really sorry.'

'Bloody awful, actually, but it had to be done. And now it's finished.'

I pictured him in some grand hotel foyer speaking urgently with a woman who looked like the model on the Golden Age skin cream ads. Then I thought, Why am I imagining him in a hotel? They'd have been in David's house, or round at hers. I wondered whether she'd cried or shouted, or just been incredibly cool. 'Did she have an idea?'

'She claimed she didn't. I wish I'd never— But I did.'

The Citroën flung itself at the gate-post, stopped with a fraction of an inch to spare.

'Rotten for you,' I said inadequately, 'on top of everything else.'

'No, really, a relief. For me. It's not been – she's not – she wasn't—'

In my imagination I saw the Baroness from *The Sound of Music* flick her cigarette towards Maria.

'I knew something was up, as soon as you came in.'

'There you go, then.'

'As long as you're not too . . . Because whatever the circumstances, these things are always a bit upsetting. You might not realise till later what it's taken out of you.'

'I was sick of the complications, if you want to know,' he said abruptly.

The door of the Scout hut opened and a man walked out onto the steps. I saw the flare of a lighter, then, a beat later, drifting smoke. Midges danced round the security light above. Further off, the orange glow of halogen showed through the horse chestnut trees and there was the sickle moon coming up, like an illustration from one of Matty's bedtime books.

Sick of the complications. Complications. The word snagged. *A complicated friend.* Lurch-jerk went the Citroën, backwards and forwards. *Ian hasn't met her.* I remembered the furtive way David had held his shoulders, pacing about my kitchen with his mobile to his ear. *Not really a girlfriend.*

The Citroën shot forward into the open street, and at the same moment, something clicked together in my brain.

'My God,' I said, 'she was married.'

'Well. Yes.'

'You were having an affair with her!'

'I appreciate it's not ideal. That's why I finished it.'

'Not ideal? *Not ideal?*' I stared across at his handsome, serious face, trying to read what I'd missed there. His forehead was creased with dismay.

'All right,' he said. 'I can see why you'd be upset. What you have to say to yourself, though, is, she's an adult, making her own choices, and you don't know the background, and I thought long and hard before I got involved. I'm not about to wreck anyone's marriage. Very much not.'

'Excuse me,' I said. 'If I could speak from the other side. You obviously have no idea.'

'It was insensitive of me to tell you. I should never have said anything.'

'No, no, I'm glad you did.'

'I wouldn't lie to you, Carol. I could have lied, but I chose not to. But you don't know her, it's not as if they're friends of yours. No one's been hurt, because no one knows.'

'That's not the point.'

David gripped the steering wheel. 'Look, I'd *never* have cheated on Jeanette, I've told you that already. Never.'

'And yet you're encouraging this woman to. Bloody funny set of morals.'

'It happened. I didn't plan it, I didn't look for it. It was just – an interaction,' he said.

'God Almighty, I've heard it called some things! "Interaction"? I'll tell you what it is. It's lies and disrespect and deceit and humiliation. It's shoddy and low. No wonder Ian's like he is.' I reached for the door handle.

'Where are you going?'

'Home.' I climbed back out into the car park.

'If I can just—'

'For God's sake! I thought you were one of the decent ones,' I said, and slammed the door against his explanations.

CHAPTER 18

Photograph: clipping inside a wartime edition of Housewife *magazine, marking an article called 'Nerves: The Enemy of Youth and Good Looks'. From Carol's bureau, Sunnybank.*

Location: the foot of Tannerside Brow, Bolton

Taken by: the Wigan Observer, *November 1968*

Subject: New Bypass Open At Last, *says the headline. Despite the promise of sleet, the morning's turned out fine and brisk and every shadow on the tarmac is sharp. Not even British weather can get in the way of progress today. Carol's dad stands shoulder to shoulder with the County Surveyor and Bridgemaster and the mayoral consort, in front of a line of traffic cones. On the other side of the picture, the mayor poses with scissors agape.*

Bob White is here in his capacity as councillor. He is proud of the bypass, proud of his village and of the contribution he and his fellows make to it. Because what a piece of work this is! The area of the new carriageway alone is 37,400 square yards. The total amount of pitching used was 14,000 tons, and before that they laid down 13,500 tons of broken stone and 800 tons of cement. 19,400 cubic yards they had to excavate, in total. Numbers like those make an ordinary man feel nothing's impossible.

He's proud, too, of his recent promotion to foreman at work, and of his new Austin 1100 in coffee and cream. He's proud of his daughter, who'll be reading the second of the Nine Lessons at the school carol service. Even Frieda's managed to be pleased at that bit of news.

When they've packed up here, he'll go back to the council offices for a celebratory sherry, and then it's on to Millie Pharaoh's for a cup of tea, a chat about the old days, and a spell upstairs. Nearly two years have passed since her husband died, eight months since they started with this other arrangement. There's no harm in it, so long as nobody knows.

There are so many things in life just now to be grateful for.

I've never been a fan of Good Fridays. There's always an unsettling and gloomy atmosphere to them, especially when it gets to that dead hour, mid-afternoon. Which I suppose, when you think about it, there ought to be: Jesus had a lot more to contend with than running low on milk and the shops being shut.

In between rain showers I'd been trying to set up an Easter-egg hunt for Matty, because Jaz was going away for the weekend with Nat. I'd offered to keep Matty with me so she could let her hair down for once, have some fun, but she'd got all defensive. 'Of course I'm taking him with me, Mum. Why wouldn't I? It's Easter and I want to be with him. Don't know what kind of a mother you think I am.'

So we were making like it was Sunday, and although Jaz didn't know it, some of the eggs outside were Ian's, delivered to my doorstep while I was at work.

The sun emerged thinly as I was lifting Matty from his high chair, so I parked him by the back door and grabbed the little bucket.

'He's too young,' said Jaz, shaking her head. 'He won't understand what he's supposed to do.'

'I'll help him,' I said. 'You know what an egg is, don't you, Matty?'

'Look,' he said, pointing at the window to where the water was dripping off the top sill. 'Uh-oh.'

'It's only spitting, hardly even that. Here, hold the bucket.'

I knelt to zip his coat. Jaz came round to tie the strings on his hood.

'OK, love?' I said.

'I think I am, yeah.' She smiled, and an indescribable relief washed over me. As we stood up together, I couldn't resist reaching out and drawing her in for a hug. For about five seconds she let me hold her, then she pulled away. 'It's a better day today, Mum,' she said.

'Good.'

'It has to come round eventually, doesn't it?'

'It does.' Though there'll be times you feel as if you've gone back to square one, I thought.

Meanwhile, Matty flapped his arms and pushed against me. I stepped aside and opened the door, and he shot out onto the soggy lawn. 'Your bucket,' I called after him.

'Watch out for that bloody pond,' said Jaz behind me.

I caught up with Matty and tried to hand him the bucket, but he wasn't having any. Two collared doves were stalking about under the feeder like a pair of wind-up toys, and those were what he wanted.

'Can you see any eggs?'

The doves cringed and took off. Matty came to a halt.

'Whatever's under this bush?' I said, for all the world like someone who'd not been crouched next to it ten minutes before. 'Look!'

His eyes swivelled to me for a second, then away again.

'Here's one,' I said, holding it up for him. The sun caught the foil in a brilliant flash, and at last he was interested. He tottered forward. 'Pop it in here, and we'll find some more.'

Matty took the egg, came up to the bucket and peered over the rim. 'Let it go, sweetheart,' I said, and after some hesitation, he did. *Thunk* it went against the bottom of the bucket.

I hooked the handle back over my arm, then steered him in the direction of the fence where my stone squirrel balanced another egg in the V between its tail and its back. This time Matty spotted the prize unaided.

See, Jaz? I thought. I knew she'd be at the window, keeping an eye on us, but that was all right. Matty and I, we were fine, we were blitzing it. So much we had in store over the next few years: treasure hunts, the Science Museum, pantomimes and nature trails, growing seeds, sharing books, constructing a runway for Santa out of tea-lights. My heart contracted with anticipation.

On his way back to me, Matty paused to check out a scrap of orange netting from around an old fat-ball, then lighted on a length of cane, left over from when I'd staked out my sweet peas last year. I rattled the bucket but it failed to register. There's no getting between a boy and his stick.

'Come on,' I said loudly. 'Quick, before the jackdaws get them.'

A few drops of rain speckled my face and within half a minute, the surface of the pond was a mass of radiating circles, the leaves on the bushes quivering again.

'I can see something shiny by the shed. What do you think it might be?'

Matty came forward like a midget king, still clutching his cane and egg, and allowed me to adjust his hood.

'Bucky, Nanna,' he said, and I lowered it for him.

I led him up the other side of the garden where we collected two more eggs.

'How many have we got? Shall we count?' I said, but the shower was getting heavier. Jaz appeared at the door.

'Don't get him soaked,' she called out.

'It's not cold, and he's got spare socks upstairs. Anyway, we're nearly done.'

I'd set the last egg, a larger one, on top of a stone mushroom, and wedged it in place with a couple of brick shards. As soon as Matty saw it, he ran across and began whacking the mushroom with his stick.

'Hoy, stop that,' shouted Jaz.

'He's all right,' I said. Raindrops fizzed on the paving stones around my feet. 'Come on, Matty, grab that big one and let's go back in.'

He turned, but in the wrong direction, and ran off down the garden once more. My grandson may only be small, but he can shift when he wants to. Jaz and I exchanged glances, then she launched herself out of the door after him, while I nipped round the other way with the idea of heading him off. Waves of rain were sweeping across the lawn, and Jaz had no coat on.

Matty got as far as the shed, tripped over his own cane, rolled against the compost heap, righted himself and turned to grin at us. I had one of those moments where your brain goes into camera mode and you know you've captured the scene for ever: his slightly bowed stance as he prepared to take flight again, the highlights on his cheeks, tiny white teeth against the pinkness of his new gums, his miniature thumb against the knobbled cane. There were grass clippings all down the back of one leg. His eyes were slits of mischief.

'You little tinker,' I said. I held my arms open, but he went instead to his mother, and she picked him right up and whirled him round. I could hear him shrieking with excitement, even above the thrumming water.

By now, Jaz was very wet. Shining drops swelled at the ends

of her hair, and her eye make-up was smudged where she'd wiped her face with her sleeve. 'Good heavens, the state of you,' I said as I drew near. 'Give him to me, and run and get yourself inside.'

'I think it's too late for that, Mum.' She was laughing, and Matty was laughing. I took his hand and she held onto the other, and we swung him between us in giant bounds back towards the house.

'What a team, though,' I said, raising my face to the rain and closing my eyes. I imagined how we'd look from above, an aerial view of the three of us, a twisting string of family moving across a green rectangle. I wished I could've had a photograph of that.

When we got inside, I told Jaz she could borrow one of my tops while I changed Matty's footwear. True to form, it was my brand new purple blouse she came down in, a bath towel wrapped round her head. Even like that, she looked lovely.

She pulled at the cuffs, appraising. 'This is nice.'

'No need to sound surprised,' I said.

The television had been playing to itself all the while. Now it showed a man in a white dinner jacket bursting through a giant illuminated mouth onto a stage full of showgirls.

'What on earth's this?'

'How should I know?' said Jaz, dropping the magazine back onto the cushion. She came round and settled herself on the sofa next to Matty, who was lying on his side with his thumb between his lips.

The man in the white jacket raised a silver-topped cane, and H-E-R-O-D appeared above him, spelled out in lights. He wore a white carnation in his lapel, and his bow tie matched his hanky. His hair was slicked back, immaculate.

'Huh.' She nodded at the screen. 'You know who he reminds me of?'

'Don't say it.'

'But he does. Look at him. Look at the way he's kitted out.'

'David does not dress like that.'

'I didn't say he did. I said I was reminded of him.'

The showgirls began a dance routine, their pink dresses shimmering, their diamond collars winking with every gesture.

'You don't still see him, do you, Mum?'

'No,' I said, which was, coincidentally, now the truth.

'Good,' she said. 'Because I was beginning to wonder.'

'Wonder what?'

'You *know*.' Herod jumped onto a grand piano. 'You used to do this funny little smirk whenever you mentioned him. You did. Yes, you did. But there's no way you two would get together, is there?'

'Of course not,' I said.

'It would pretty much be incest. Plus he's such an upper-class twit.'

'He isn't really. Not that.'

'See, you're doing it again. Stop sticking up for him, will you? He's a nob, and his son's a bastard. Just because he's got money, he thinks he's better than us.'

'I don't think that's true, Jaz.' But even as I said it, I was thinking, Why am I bothering to defend him?

'The way he speaks, that thing he does with his eyebrows. So smug. Do you remember how he had to have the last word at the wedding?'

'Only because your dad forgot to toast you at the end of his speech.' (And say how beautiful you looked, or express any kind of confidence in the match.) 'He was too busy telling jokes. Someone had to step in and deliver the line.'

'What about afterwards, when he said Dad ought to have been working the clubs?'

'Yes, all right. That was probably below the belt.'

Our doorbell rang as Herod backed away up the stage, ranting.

'Not that any of it matters now.' I got to my feet. Through the window I could see Josh standing under the porch, and I was glad because it was weeks since I'd had a proper chance to talk to him, what with his work experience and then the school breaking up for the holidays. He was clutching a plastic bag in his hand: Laverne's Easter exchange, that would be. You get into these customs and then it's hard to know when to draw a line under them. I'd always bought a chocolate egg for Josh when he was little, so she started buying one for Matty, and here today was her six-foot son, still the recipient of a Thornton's bunny for which he would be made to write a thank you card. *Oh, for God's sake, knock it on the head*, I imagined Phil saying.

I opened the front door, all smiles. Josh was flushed and breathing hard, as though he'd been running.

'Hello!' I said gaily. 'Enjoying the break? How was work experience? I've got something for you, if you give me a minute.'

'Here,' he said, and thrust out his fist with the bag in it.

'Oh, for me? Well, for Matty. That's lovely, tell your mother thanks. And I've got, hang on a sec, I thought I left yours—'

'Jesus! Take it, will you?' he snapped. And before I could react, he'd hurled the bag past me, into the hall, where it knocked into a bowl of grape hyacinths I'd put on the telephone table ready to take to Dad.

'Oh,' I squeaked in shock.

The bowl had been shunted to the edge but not tipped off. One of the stems looked to be snapped.

When I turned back to the door, Josh was already striding away. Instinct told me not to call after him. Instead I watched him go, my hands on my cheeks, my heart thumping. In my head I heard myself telling Laverne how I thought he wasn't happy at school, remembered that worried crease between her eyebrows, and I knew, I knew exactly what I'd done. 'Oh, Josh,' I said under my breath. 'Oh hell.'

Back in the lounge the TV was still going, but Herod had been replaced by Roly Mo. 'We turned over,' she said. 'Who was it?'

'Josh.' I was almost too shaken to speak the name.

Jaz pulled a face. 'Doughboy? I don't know why he doesn't just move in here. Anyway,' she went on, 'what I was saying was, if you did start seeing David, it would make things impossible for me. With Matty, for one. I wouldn't want to be leaving Matty in a house where David might turn up. Do you understand what I'm saying, Mum?'

I sat down on the sofa next to them, and it felt as though I'd crawled onto an island in the middle of a stormy sea. Every day as a grandmother seemed to bring new anxieties, new traps for me to fall into. Even choosing Matty's egg had been a trial – Jaz might complain it was too big, not ethical, contained E numbers, should have been something else entirely, e.g. an educational toy. Three nights before, and unable to sleep, I'd texted Phil to check again he'd keep his mouth shut about Ian. Even when he'd replied (*No wy dnt wrry*) I couldn't damp down my small-hours terror.

I looked across at Jaz, her hair still spiky from the rain, the yoke of my purple blouse marked with damp smears. She was nodding her head to Roly Mo's song, humming, terrifying in her unconcern.

The rain dried up, and in the end it was such a beautiful evening we took the baby monitor out onto the patio and opened a bottle of wine there.

'What time do you want wakening tomorrow?' I asked her.

'We have to be at Nat's for half-nine, so, eightish.'

'I'll get Matty ready for you.'

We were gearing up to have one of those amazing pink and blue sunsets. I pulled my garden chair closer to hers, and we sat and watched the clouds slowly change colour. For a long time neither of us spoke. A robin was singing from the cypress tree, and the breeze brought us faint snatches of Laverne's piano music. The scent of grass and lilac and flowering currant mingled in a green tang.

I pointed with the toe of my shoe. 'All along the edge of that bed are the tulips Matty helped plant last autumn.'

'Yeah?'

'Well, I held him while he dropped a few bulbs in the right place. They should be coming into flower any day now, I must remember to show him.'

'I'd take that cane off him first.'

'It's locked in the shed.'

'Very wise.'

The lights on the monitor stayed still, and we drank our wine.

'Do you remember that time you put in all those bulbs for me, when I'd broken my arm?' I said. 'You were such a help. I taught you how to load the washer and use the grill, all sorts. You kept us ticking over. I'd never have managed otherwise.'

Jaz leaned back and crossed her ankles. 'You do know, Mum, you're always on about when I was little?'

'Am I?'

'Yup. You bloody live down Memory Lane, you do, it's your permanent address. I wish you wouldn't, sometimes.'

'Why?'

'Because I sometimes feel you only liked me when I was younger.'

'Don't be ridiculous,' I said.

She smoothed the hair from out of her eyes. It was hard to tell how serious she was being. 'You're not telling me you've always felt exactly the same way about me all the way through my life?'

For a moment, I was thrown.

'Of course it changes,' I said, after a few seconds' thought. 'But it's the same, as well. Like a tree going through different seasons; it's always a tree.'

'So I'm a tree, now?'

'No, not you. Us.'

'If you say so.'

A bee dithered through the forget-me-nots at the edge of the pond like a fat woman rooting through jumble.

I said: 'You know that time you were at Leeds?'

'Do you mean during, or after?'

'After, I suppose. When you were poorly.' I paused to let her protest, but she didn't, so I carried on. 'The way you are now, upset – it's not like it was then, is it? You wouldn't let things get so bad again without telling me?'

'No.'

'Because then, you were away from home, on your own. You didn't have the support.'

'I know, that's why I came back. It did help. Eventually.'

I let that last word finish resonating before I spoke again.

'What happened at Leeds, Jaz? You never really told me.'

'I drank too much, I blew my grant on clothes and music. Like students do.'

'Drugs?'

'Never.'

'Honestly?'

'Oh, well, yeah, a bit, at school.'

'I *knew* it.' That drifting-away look she'd worn all the way through Year Twelve, the skulking about and moods.

'Truly, Mum, nothing since the Sixth Form, and only half a dozen roll-ups even then. No big deal. I wouldn't be telling you now if it was. This is, like, ten years ago. What were *you* doing ten years ago?'

Still putting up with my marriage, just. I took her point.

The sky turned pinker, and I poured us more wine.

'I got involved with someone off my course and he let me down, that was all,' she said in a rush. 'And I totally wasn't expecting it, and he told people our private stuff, which was shit, and . . . I just didn't deal with it very well.'

'Oh, love,' I said. 'I wish you'd told me at the time. I thought it must be something—' Something worse, I was thinking, though I didn't dare say it. A broken heart? After all the hoo-ha, that was it? But at the same time I was overwhelmed with relief that it turned out to be such an ordinary kind of tragedy, and that she'd confided at last.

'Funny,' she went on, 'I thought it was such a big deal back then, the end of the world, yeah? And now, against everything that's happened lately, it's a blip. I don't know why I got myself into such a state about it. I should have learned my lesson.'

'How do you mean?'

'That it's obviously me. Obviously I'm destined to fuck up when it comes to men, and that was the warning shot. Or maybe it's not my fault, maybe they're all like that, and it's simply a matter of *when* they cheat on you. They're all bastards, aren't they?'

She sounded so hopeless I couldn't bear it.

'Not all, love. Look at your grandad. Nearly fifty years he was with your grandma.'

'Maybe fidelity's gone out of fashion, then,' she snapped.

I put my glass down and reached across the gap for her hand. 'Listen. Think about this: whatever happens with Ian,

you've got Matty out of it. Same as I had you, when my marriage ended.'

Jaz gave a wan smile. 'A great consolation, was I?'

'Yes,' I said, squeezing her fingers earnestly. 'You were.'

Reeds bent in the breeze, stirring the water's surface. The
memory of Josh's outburst came on me like a pain and I swivelled my mind away.

'I just, I get so frightened, Mum.'

'I know.'

'Sometimes I wish I was little again.'

I wish that too, I thought. We all knew where we were in
those days.

'Once upon a time,' I said. 'There was a pig called Grunt.'

'God, no, spare us the Grunt stories.'

'Poor Grunt.'

'Poor Grunt nothing. I've got a story for you: once upon a
time there was a woman who got bloody everything wrong in
her life.'

'Oh, Jaz, you haven't. You've got so much ahead of you.'

'I was talking about you,' she said, laughing. I can't tell you
what a good sound it was.

'You, young lady, are sailing very close to the wind,' I said.

'So ground me,' she said.

'You're not too big to put over my knee,' I said.

When the business with Ian was sorted out, whichever way
it went, I could start again with her. Without Phil to distract
me, I could be the kind of mother I always meant to be. A me
of the future waved down from the monorail at Chester Zoo,
my face flanked by Matty and Jaz.

My second chance, it was going to be. This time, I'd make
good.

CHAPTER 19

Photograph: web print-out, tucked inside a copy of La Symphonie Pastorale *from a box in the loft, Sunnybank*

Location: the Adler-Tate lecture theatre, Modern Languages Department, Leeds University

Taken by: Dr López Covas

Subject: Dr Nick Page posing for his Staff Profile entry. His smile is broad and chipper, though, in truth, this appointment isn't working out quite as he imagined. There are changes he's keen to make, but it's too soon and anyway, he's not senior enough. Still, early days. The second term's bound to be easier.

On the plus side, he's already identified a particularly bright first-year student who looks as though she might prove interesting. Jasmine Morgan, her name is. Dark and troubled, bright and brittle. Those are the kind of students he likes.

Nothing draws him more than a knotty problem, a contradiction.

I had Radio 3 on while I took out the old bedding plants and put in new. Radio 2 was airing an outraged phone-in, and on 4 it was the news, an endless pageant of human suffering, incompetence and doom. I found some piano music that suited the bright day, and I was just about to see off a cockchafer grub with my trowel when the announcer said, 'La Berceuse, from Fauré's Dolly Suite'. Then the opening notes started and it was like an electric shock down my spine: instantly I was by the fire at Pincroft again, shunting around some lead farm animals that had been my dad's. Mum was ironing, there was a wooden maiden draped with pillowcases and underslips, and in the corner, the big radiogram playing the theme tune to Listen With Mother. And as I crouched by that planter, trowel-edge poised, I swear I could still smell the hot cloth steaming, and the beeswax polish my mother always used. It was a scene of perfect security and calm.

The loss bloomed inside me, taking my breath for a moment, so that I had to get up and walk about for a while. Mum may not always have been a ray of sunshine, but there's comfort to be had in normality, I imagined telling Dad. Except that he wasn't there any more either. I knew that, really.

A noise from next door brought me out of it. Whatever would Laverne say if she came out and found me like this? How would I explain myself? Ridiculous to be upset at fifty-two because you're no longer a child. But there I was.

When I got back to the cockchafer, he'd spied his chance and burrowed away. I dabbed my eyes on the hem of my blouse, and carried on planting.

Lying awake that night, I tried to envisage how Jaz might sum up her childhood. I'd worked so hard to make her days sunny, surely her memories would be positive ones.

If she was here with me now, I'd tell her how vital it is to keep hold of those moments from the past, because they make up who you are. 'That's why Grandad's so lost,' I'd say. 'That's why I take all these photos. You have to hang onto the good times to see you through the bad. Happy memories make a happy person.'

And she'd go, 'Don't be so simple, Mum. You can't *choose* what you remember.'

And I'd say, 'Yes, you can. You just have to make an effort.'

'Dad couldn't come, he says he's sorry,' Ian announced as I took his coat. 'He's got a meeting.'

Ah, I thought. So that's how the land lies. How much had David told him about our last evening together? Ian didn't seem embarrassed by the message.

As soon as he saw his dad, Matty hurled himself across the living room. 'Hey, it's the Mattster!' said Ian, picking him up and swinging him round. I took myself into the kitchen and left them to it. One of the most important skills of being a grandparent is knowing when to melt away.

After a few minutes I returned with a tray of coffee, biscuits and squash.

'Where's Jaz today?' said Ian, as he always did.

'Gone to the university again to have a look at some reference books. Some of those specialist dictionaries cost hundreds, apparently. She can't afford to buy them, so she saves up her vocab queries—'

'She's been getting cash from me every week,' said Ian. 'She's not going short.'

'I never said she was.' I put the tray down carefully.

Ian had knelt down and dragged out the box of plastic rail track. Now he began to hunt through it, separating straight and curved pieces into bundles. At his side, Matty dug around and unearthed random lengths which he thrust in Ian's face. 'Here y'are,' he kept saying. 'Here y'are.'

'I think anyway she's coming round to the idea of sorting out access,' I said.

About time, said Ian's expression.

They made a simple circuit together – Ian constructed, Matty sabotaged, Ian repaired – and set a tunnel over one side.

'What you need now is some trains,' I said.

'Have a look in my jacket pocket, Carol, while I put this bridge together,' said Ian.

I went over to the chair, rummaged, and found a brand new engine, still in its packaging.

'Well, Matty,' I said. 'Look at this! What's this one called?'

'It's Diesel Ten,' said Ian.

'He doesn't look very friendly.'

'That's because he's a baddie. You've got to have baddies.'

'Have you?' I passed it across and Ian set to extracting it from the box.

'There's a battery in the other pocket,' he said.

'I'll say I bought it. If Jaz asks, I mean. Otherwise, obviously, I shan't say anything.' I felt myself blush as I handed him the battery. 'How is your dad?'

'Fine. He's been looking into the legal position. Where I stand.'

The phone started to ring.

'Well. Like I was saying, we might not have to do this much longer,' I said to him over my shoulder.

It was Phil calling. 'I can bring you some steel mesh to go over the pond,' he said. 'I've found someone who does sheets of it. Be a lot less expensive than getting a firm in.'

'Not now,' I told him, too sharply.

'Why? Who's there?'

My delay told him all he needed to know.

'It's not David and Ian, is it? Bloody hell, Carol, you've not got them round again?'

'Ian's here, yes,' I said. 'Not David. Look, I'll call you tonight. It's good about the mesh. Thanks.' And I put the phone down.

'I think there's someone at your back door,' said Ian. 'Someone's knocking.'

So I went through to the kitchen to find Dorothy Wynne's granddaughter Alice rapping on the pane.

'Does Matty want a sunflower?' she said when I opened up. 'Libby's grown a whole bunch of seedlings and we thought Matty might like a couple, you know, to have a race with.'

'That's great. Yes, he'd love that, thanks. Is Libby here?'

'Granny's keeping an eye. Libs is having a nap; she was up in the night, twice, and then she's been so crabby all morning. Let sleeping kids lie, I say. We're all worn out with her.'

'And how are you? How many weeks is it now?'

'Nearly thirty one.' Alice ran her hand over her huge belly.

'You're keeping well?'

Something flickered across her face 'Pretty much. They say I'm on the big side for my dates.'

'Perhaps you're further on than you thought.'

'No, it's not that. There's more fluid than there should be, or something.' She shook her head. 'I don't know. I'm trying not to think about it, 'cause there's nothing I can do. Keeping my feet up, counting the kicks. There's a lot of kicking going on.'

'Well then. I'm sure it'll be fine,' I said, trying a reassuring smile. 'And Libby's OK?'

'She's great, yeah. No time to sit and worry while Libs is around!'

As Alice waddled back down the side of the house, I thought of the last months of my own pregnancy with Jaz, and the nightmares I'd been plagued with. Even now, so many years on, I could remember scenes from them. The fear starts before your children are even born, and it never, ever lets up. That's something nobody tells you till it's too late.

In the living room, Matty was staging more crashes and Ian

was building an extension to the circuit so as to use a set of points he'd discovered.

'My neighbour's granddaughter,' I said.

'Uh-huh.' He carried on slotting sections together.

I found myself glancing at the clock, calculating how long it would be before the visit was up. Still another hour and forty minutes. It definitely wasn't as easy with David missing from the scene. Say what you liked about him, he made things flow.

I turned on the TV for some background noise and it was the news, with a story about a divorced father who'd abducted his children and killed them, before shooting himself. Hastily I flicked through the channels till I found CBeebies, and picked up my coffee, which was now cold.

'Actually, would you mind turning it off, Carol?' said Ian.

The heat rose to my cheeks again. 'Oh, all right. Sorry. Why?'

'Because the time I get with my son is too precious to waste. I want to be able to play with him, properly play with him, and I can't do that if he's gawping at *64 Zoo Lane*.'

My mouth fell open with a mixture of dismay and outrage. I don't have to do this, you know, I could have said. I don't have to have you in my house, behind my daughter's back, with all the hideous stress and guilt that costs me. You should be damn grateful I'm letting you across the threshold at all, my lad, never mind dictating.

Fortunately the doorbell went before I could say any of this, so I simply handed the remote over and went to see who it was.

Laverne. 'Hi,' she said, from the step. Which isn't usual for her; she normally trots straight in.

'Everything OK?' I asked.

'I just wanted to let you know.' She tossed her hair back and clasped her hands in front of her. Even in her casual moments she moves like a dancer. 'Just wanted to say, Carol, term starts on Monday—'

'Yes, I've got it on my calendar. Josh all ready, is he?'

'He, well, he won't be needing a lift in. So you don't have to bother.'

'Is he poorly?'

She gave an awkward little smile. 'He's, no, we've had a chat and he wants to start going on the bus. I mean, it's time, probably. He's at that age.'

Behind me I could hear Matty squealing, and Ian's voice saying over and over, 'No, you don't.'

'That's fine,' I said quickly. 'Yes, of course. No problem.'

'Because it'll be easier for you in the mornings.'

'It will, though it's never been a bother, Laverne.'

'And we're so grateful for all the years you've done it.'

'It's been a pleasure. He's a smashing lad.'

'I wouldn't want you to think we didn't appreciate it.'

'No, really, it's been great.'

As I closed the door I thought, How desperate must Josh be not to come in my car with me any more? The realisation set up a horrible pressure against my breastbone. I wanted to run straight away to their house, apologise, explain that I was only trying to help when I confided in Laverne about the bullying. Because it's what they always say to do: tell someone. She could go down the school now and sort it, and everything would be all right. *Yeah, same as we did with Jaz?* came Phil's sarcastic voice. *I warned you not to get involved*, added David in my head.

Back in the lounge, Ian had the cushions off the sofa and Matty was rolling about on them.

'Sorry,' I said, out of habit. 'It's like Paddy's market here today.'

'No, I'm sorry,' said Ian. 'I shouldn't have, you know, the TV thing. Anyway, I'm going to take him outside. Have a kick-about while it's fine.'

He didn't invite me to join them, and I didn't ask. I sat myself near the window and watched Ian's big hands close round his son's small body, Matty squeaking and wriggling and jerking his short legs as he was lifted in the air. It was a different approach from mine and Jaz's. Rougher, more direct. Lads and dads. And I felt a sudden rush of vindication. If Jaz walked in here now and saw them, I'd simply say, 'This is why they need to be together. Look. Look at Matty's face.'

When they'd gone out, I went and sat in the bay and had five minutes with my eyes closed. Jaz materialised in the chair opposite, as she'd been when she was recovering from her depression, dull-eyed and subdued. *I've always given you trouble, haven't I?* Oh, I told her silently, but you were worth it, in spite of everything. *Honestly?* Then came Eileen's voice: *Raising Jaz has been like swimming upstream all the way; that's what you told me.*

Another, younger Jaz interrupted, swinging through the door: *Hey, Mum, why did the hedgehog cross the road?*

For all the grief with Phil, if I could have snapped my fingers and gone back in time, I would have done. I'd have given anything at that moment to see Jaz when she was little, have that period of my life over again. *Guess what*, said a newly pregnant Jaz. *They gave me a copy of the scan. Do you want to see?*

Before I'd even thought about it, I was out of that chair and kneeling on the carpet, peering at the shelf below the window, looking for my past.

Just before I got married I'd gathered up all the photographs I could find lying around Pincroft. Some were in a biscuit tin in the back bedroom wardrobe, there were a few loose in the bureau, I had my own little cache I kept in my jewellery box. But when I flicked through, there seemed to be a lot of gaps.

'Where are the rest?' I said to my mother. 'Oh, we've never bothered much,' she'd replied. 'We're not a family who takes photographs.' A fact which became self-evident when I began to go through them properly. 'Did you even have a wedding album?' I said. 'Oh yes, we've got one of those,' she said. 'It's in the back room somewhere. Don't ask me to go searching for it.'

In the final count there'd been a couple of dozen of me/us, a few odd ones of my parents from when they were younger, plus a set of very small black and white holiday snaps of castles, mountains, swans, piers, coaching inns, formal gardens, etc. These became my first collection, pasted into a modest ring-bound album with stripy vinyl covers. I don't know why it felt so important to draw the family history together like this, but it did. 'Don't you mind me taking them away?' I'd asked. 'If you want them, love, you have them,' said Dad. 'No,' said Mum.

My next album was bigger, with a hessian front; it began with Early Marriage and ended with Jaz on her first day at secondary school. The camera we owned back then had been Phil's, but after some pestering I'd got him to show me how to use it so that, by the middle of this collection, probably three-quarters of the pictures had been snapped by me. Which was good, because Phil was a careless photographer who regularly missed people's feet off, forgot to prime the flash, let the strap flop over the shutter at the last minute. He never composed a background in his life. Often I had to load the film for him because his fingers weren't patient enough to guide the tiny plastic spokes into the celluloid slots. Finally I got my own Instamatic, and from then on I was official family photographer. I became the person who decided which memories to keep, and which to discard.

My fingers moved along the bookshelf, touching spines for the pleasure of ownership. Here was album five, a posh job in burgundy velvet covers, and pretty much every one of its pages devoted to Matty. Number four – gilt-edged navy leather – was mostly experimental stuff from when I did my evening classes: studies of my father's hands; light through different types of leaves; still-life sequences where I kept changing the shutter speed. I was proud of that collection. It came out of a bad time, but I'd made good.

The album I most needed to look at right now, though, was number three, charting Jaz's older years. I wasn't sure whether Ian had ever seen it. He might be interested. We might all be able to look at it together sometime in the future, when all this was sorted.

The first picture, which I'd stuck onto the inside cover, was a portrait I'd taken of her when she was about twelve. We'd gone to a local folly and climbed a tower there. Then I'd asked her to lean her arm on the stone windowsill and look out across the countryside as though she was lost in thought. Corny, I know, but it made a lovely shot; the skin in particular was amazing. *And this was pre-digital, so there was no enhancement going on*, I imagined telling Ian.

On the next page was a Christmas scene, Jaz and Eileen dancing a waltz across our lounge, both of them wearing false moustaches. 'I've told you about Eileen,' I'd say to Ian. 'My best friend. Jaz's unofficial aunty.' *Among my many other accomplishments*, went Eileen. I flipped the pages.

Dad's birthday: Jaz, Phil and Dad sitting round the table and holding up glasses of wine (Pomagne for Jaz).

Calais: Jaz sitting at a wrought-iron table, sipping a bottle of grenadine through a straw. Phil next to her wearing a child's beach bucket on his head and making a Tommy Cooper gesture with his hands.

Jaz and Phil perched on a flint wall, squinting in the sunshine. Jaz's long limbs are milk-white; Phil is boiled pink.

Jaz dressed as Marceline for a school production of *Le Mariage de Figaro*.

The back page of the school prospectus, showing Jaz in the library with her head bowed over a copy of *Das Beste*.

Jaz and me on the patio, soaking up the sun on the last afternoon before she left for Leeds.

Rare close-up of Jaz without make-up, eyes cast down modestly.

The back inside cover of the album had a pocket for negatives, and in there was a folded newspaper clipping: *Missing Girl Found*. I didn't need to take that one out and look at it because it was burned on my memory.

These albums are my most precious possessions, I imagined telling Ian. *I couldn't put a price on them. They're the first things I'd grab if the house was on fire.*

After Matty, said Ian.

Obviously after Matty. I'd throw myself into an inferno to save Matty. And I saw myself battering down a door – no, running up a burning staircase – no, stumbling through a smoke-filled bedroom, calling his name.

The sound of a diesel engine faded in on the other side of the window; swelled, throbbed, then went ominously dead. As I pushed myself up off the carpet to see who it was had pulled into our drive, a car door slammed.

Jaz's car.

For a split second, all I could do was stare in horror.

Then I was staggering to my feet and throwing myself down the hall towards the back door.

CHAPTER 20

Photograph 256, Album Two

Location: the garden, Sunnybank

Taken by: Carol

*Subject: A close-up of seven-year-old Jaz grinning, sans two
of her top teeth. Her hair is in bunches and her lashes are
impossibly long. It is about this age people start to recommend
child-modelling agencies.*

*The teeth have been having adventures all of their own.
The first popped out while they were in the car, and promptly
fell down the hole at the base of the seat belt. Carol has to ask
Phil for his flexible claw and torch (it's lucky he knows his way
round that shed, because she certainly doesn't). The second
tooth gets mislaid by an idiot dinner lady and is never found,
but Carol pretends, by substituting the first in its place, to have
discovered it lodged in the front pocket of Jaz's school bag. The
third Jaz loses herself, but it turns up in the lining of her coat,
a barely detectable lump in the hem. 'Why are they so damn
small?' asks Phil, as though there's something personal and
deliberate about Jaz's dental dimensions.*

*The fourth tooth makes it unscathed to the pillow, but
Carol, distracted by a bad marital row, forgets and is woken*

in the morning by howls of outrage as Jaz unwraps the hanky to find the tooth and nothing but the tooth. 'I expect the fairy was called away to a molar emergency,' says Carol, and gives her double-pay the night after.

She's heard recently that some parents leave trails of glitter across the windowsill, make footprints by poking dolls into plant pots, leave gifts of new toothbrushes and certificates and stickers. Well then, Jaz shall have it all. There is nothing Carol won't do to make her daughter's childhood as secure and magical as it can be.

The minute or so Jaz spent hammering on the door was enough for me to get out the back and warn Ian.

All I had to say was her name. His face went rigid and he just stood there, holding the football between his hands while Matty reached up and pawed at it. I thought, Oh God, he's going to argue, he's going to face her out.

'Where's your car?' I hissed at him.

'Round the back of Rydal Avenue. There wasn't room when I—'

'Then she doesn't know for certain you're here,' I said. I was still holding onto the shred of hope that if I got him off the premises, we could bluff our way out. 'Please, Ian, oh, please, go. For me.'

My distress outfaced him, I think. He glanced quickly round the garden as if assessing where he might hide, like some lover in a farce, and I heard him swear under his breath. Then he took off, running at the fence and vaulting it easily. He landed heavily, then righted himself, pelted across Laverne's lawn and disappeared round the side of her house. Immediately I hoisted Matty up into my arms, and hurried back through to let Jaz in.

*

It was Penny who was my undoing. Once again.

She'd heard Phil talking to me on the phone, caught the gist of the conversation, taken herself straight upstairs and called Jaz.

'Why would she *do* that?' I asked Phil later.

'Jealous,' he said.

The irony of that nearly killed me.

'Where is he?' shouted Jaz, bursting in the second I unfastened the door.

'Matty's here,' I said.

She stormed past me and into the lounge. Matty was wriggling to be put down, so I lowered him to the floor and he tottered after Jaz. But she took no notice, almost knocking him over as she doubled back. I watched her grab the newel and swing herself round, her knuckles white. She wrenched open the stair-gate, then her feet were pounding up the steps, and after a moment, I heard doors slamming against walls.

'Come on,' I said to Matty. 'Let's get you some juice.' And I walked him to the kitchen.

I ran the tap to get the water cold and reached for his beaker, at which point Jaz dashed past us, yanked open the back door and threw herself out onto the patio. I carried on making Matty's drink, counting down the last few seconds of calm.

'I know he's been here,' she cried as she came back in. 'I know what you've been up to.'

So here I was, in the scenario I'd never dared rehearse for fear of bringing it on. As Jaz stood and looked at me I thought, I've got to decide, here and now, to lie. Once I'm committed, that's it. 'You don't mean Ian, do you?' I said, as neutrally as I could.

'Of course I bloody mean Ian. Where is he? Where *is* he?'

I snapped the lid on the beaker and passed it down to Matty, who was clinging to my skirt. He refused to take it off me, so I stuck it on the corner of the table, then leaned myself against the sink unit to try and stop my legs shaking.

'He's here,' she said again.

'No, he isn't.'

Jaz seemed uncertain for a moment. She's not used to me lying, and she was probably considering her source, weighing my truth against Penny's. But her eyes were still wild.

'I promise you, Ian isn't here.'

Her hands went to her scalp and she started pulling at her hair. She was breathing very fast. 'If I find he has been.'

'Well, he hasn't. I don't know who's put the idea into your head, but you need to calm down. You're upsetting Matty and you're doing yourself no good. Listen, I'll put some milk on and I'll make us a Horlicks, then you can talk about what's upsetting you.' I managed a weak smile. 'After I've changed someone's nappy, anyway.'

I detached myself from the sink and steered Matty past her, towards the hallway.

'If he's been here—' she said again, menacingly.

Once I was round the corner, my legs nearly gave way. I steadied myself on the back of a chair while my grandson tugged at cushion tassels. 'Come here,' I said to him, and to my surprise he left the tassels at once and edged round till he was up against me. I bent down and held him very tight. 'Nanna loves you, you know,' I said into his hair. *You have no idea how much. There aren't the words to describe it.*

He began to wriggle, but I held on another few seconds.

'I hate Ian,' said Jaz from close behind me. 'It's like a suffocating sensation when I think about him, like I can't breathe. Do you know what I mean?'

I nodded, then let Matty go.

'I couldn't bear the thought of him sneaking round here.'

'Well, I don't know where you got the idea from.'

The changing mat was in the far corner along with the nappies, bags, wipes, cream. I got Matty laid down and commenced removing his trousers.

'Someone rang me,' she said.

'What?'

Jaz looked sheepish. 'Someone. All right. You can guess who.'

For a few seconds, I couldn't. Not for seven years has Penny had any contact with me, made any kind of approach. She took my husband; why would she need to do more?

'Pen said she'd overheard Dad talking to you about it,' Jaz went on.

'So Penny rang you?'

'Yeah.'

'She overheard us talking? She's never been here, how could she?'

'On the phone.'

As understanding dawned, I thought I'd burst into flames with the horror of it. My skin grew hot and my heart banged against my ribs as I pictured Penny hovering on the stairs, ears strained. What had I said? What had Phil said? Oh dear God, dear God.

'I know,' Jaz was saying. 'I should have thought. The woman's a bitch, she'd claim anything to make trouble, wouldn't she?'

Dimly I was aware of Matty rolling and kicking his naked legs against the plastic mat, clean nappies scattering.

'But you get a call like that – You can understand why I came haring round, can't you, Mum? Just the thought.'

I wanted to cry out, run upstairs and shut the bedroom door and howl. Matty, taking advantage of my distracted state, squirmed some more and sent the Sudocrem pot rolling towards the hearth. I bent and placed my hands on his waist to calm him down, and because I needed to hide my face from Jaz till I got myself under control.

'She's a nasty piece of work,' I said, my voice coming out strangled and high.

'It is such a bloody mess, though. All of it. Like, you've made a massive mess of your life and now mine's gone the same way, and they're kind of rebounding off each other.'

I said nothing to that.

'See, I know I'll have to let Ian see Matty at some point, I'm not stupid. But he can bloody well wait on me, till I'm ready, and I'm not ready yet, Mum. I still wake at night thinking of what he did, and replay that bloody text message, and it all sits on my shoulders and weighs me down. I'm never free of it. I can never forget. Some days I'm so depressed I could— But he'll not win, I shan't let him bring me right down. No one's ever going to hurt me like that again.'

I carried on cleaning my grandson, bagging up his nappy, pushing a new one under his hips.

'So he can wait, because he deserves to be kept waiting; he needs to know how it feels to have everything ripped from under you.'

If Jaz would only go, it might be all right. I could close the front door, draw the curtains and have a good furious weep, I could be back in control. From there, we could maybe move the access thing forward so I was never in this position again. I'd sit down and think about a better way. But for now I was wrung out and distressed, and I needed to be on my own.

'I suppose what I mean is, he needs to be hurt before he can understand what he's done.'

'Could you get the Sudocrem for me, love,' I said.

She walked over towards the fireplace. 'See, Matty's the only power I have over him now.'

I reached for Matty's trousers and began feeding his feet through the elasticated bottoms. 'That's not true, Jaz. He loves you.'

'Fuck you.'

'Jaz,' I said urgently. 'Matty's listening.'

'*Fuck you.*'

The trousers had caught under the back fold of the new nappy, but they came free at last and I pulled them up. Then I turned round.

Jaz was holding the jacket Ian had hung on the back of the chair.

We stared at each other for the longest moment.

'Fuck you both,' she said.

If I thought I'd seen Jaz angry before, I was wrong. She seemed to tower above us, raging, a cyclone of furious abuse. You came out of me, I thought as she flailed her arms and yelled. I nursed you on my lap. 'How could you?' she was screaming. 'Behind my back! You lied! I knew something was going on! Whose side are you on? I thought I could trust you!' And I remembered a doctor once asking, the time Jaz was ill, had I noticed how she seemed to direct her emotions inwards rather than outwards. And I hadn't noticed that, no, and I wondered what he'd say if he were here now.

'How many times?' she went on. 'How many lies have you told me? Sneaking behind my back. And to think I was bothered about you seeing David; Jesus! I suppose it was him who fucking talked you into this set-up. It was, wasn't it? I can tell by your face. Jesus fucking wept. What kind of mother are you? Interfering, making me look a bloody fool. This is *worse* than what Ian did. Has he been laughing at me? Have all three of you been? How could you *do* it, Mum? How could you set up something like that after all I've been through. How could you even let him in the house?' I'd have attempted a reply if she'd paused to draw breath, only she didn't. 'I should have expected this,' she shouted, 'this betrayal. After all, it's what my whole life's been about, hasn't it?'

And even though my chief urge was to throw myself at her feet and grovel for forgiveness, at the back of my mind I was thinking, Oh, stop being so melodramatic. I noticed Matty had crawled across to the bay and was twisting himself up in the curtain, and I longed to go over and cuddle him but I didn't dare move. If she'd let me speak I could've explained to her about damage limitation and being frightened of what Ian might do, but she just kept on and on at top volume, like someone blasting a cold water hose directly at me so that my chief instinct was to put my hands up and cover my face.

'I might have expected it,' she said. 'I should have known, because when have you ever, ever stuck up for me? Never, that's when. Not once. When I came home from Leeds you treated me like a bloody nuisance, a hypochondriac—'

'I know, and I apologised for that.'

'You never stuck up for me against the teachers, or when—'

'I did!'

'—those girls were having a go at me.'

'I went in and spoke to the Head.'

'Yeah, and accepted what she said without question, rolled over and took it because you always bloody do.'

'You wouldn't tell me what it was about!'

'I tried to talk to you, but you weren't interested.'

'When? That's not true, I'd always make time for you!'

'You were going to some charity thing. I was following you round the house trying to speak to you and all you were bothered about was the fact that your stupid fucking Stetson wouldn't fit.'

'I don't remember that.'

'Yes, you do. You had to borrow a load of line-dancing gear off Moira. I wanted to talk to you that night and you didn't have time for me.'

'I didn't know! How was I supposed to know?'

'The trouble with you is, you think everyone should just "put up with it and make the best," of whatever's happening, and that's why Dad kept cheating on you, because you never fought back: you just let him walk all over you.'

'That's not fair. I did it for you as much as anyone.'

'Yeah, well, thanks for nothing.' Jaz turned her head, perhaps to check on Matty, and saw my albums out on the floor. 'And as for these!' She aimed a kick at the nearest one, and my stomach flipped over. 'Happy fucking Families.'

'Don't,' I said.

'Your precious bloody photos. Your version of the past. Not mine! Not the truth! Papering over the fucking cracks. Tell you what, I'm going to start an album of my own that tells the real story. 'Cause all these are one great big *lie*, and I'm sick of lies. I've had a lifetime's-worth of them.'

She dropped to her haunches and scowled at the open page. I thought for one awful minute she was going to start ripping the album apart but instead she pointed furiously. 'Look at this one here. Solange bloody Moreau. You let her get away with murder, coming down in the night to watch TV, turning her nose up at everything you put on her plate then raiding the cupboards when she felt like it. Telling me off if I so much as held a fork wrong, like I was about five. You ruined that visit for me. She knew she could do exactly what she liked and you'd say nothing.'

'She was a guest. She was a long way from home.'

'She used to laugh at you, did you know? Behind your back. She thought you were such a pushover. You know she was a thief? That she shoplifted a whole load of stuff? Ooh, but you thought she was Little Girl Lost, away from her mummy. You were pathetic.'

'I didn't know.'

'You'd never have taken any notice if I'd told you.'

'That's not true.'

Over in the corner, Matty was still clinging to the curtain, rolling himself against the wall in a way that made my heart cringe. Jaz whipped the pages over, rewinding, and stabbed at some other crime.

'That fucking red Fiesta. Remember when you first got it and you drove me round to Penny's house and we sat across the street for an hour?'

'I never did that.'

'Oh, yes, you did. You think I'm too young to remember. You bought me a necklace made of sweets. In fact, you had this bag with you, kept bringing stuff out of it, comics and plastic crap. To keep me quiet. You'd come prepared, as ever.'

In all conscience I had forgotten, till she said.

'And this, Seaworld – my birthday treat, supposedly. All smiley smiley in front of the shark tank, but you were in a foul mood with Dad and you wouldn't talk to him. Wouldn't have a proper row with him and get it out in the open, oh no. Sulked and poisoned the day.'

'I wasn't sulking,' I said. 'I was upset and trying to keep myself together. It was very difficult for me sometimes.'

'You think I don't know what it's like to have a husband who screws around? Remember? Except I *deal with it*. I don't *close my eyes and pretend it's not happening*.'

This inventory of all my failings as a parent: I never realised they'd been catalogued so carefully. Somewhere on the edge of my consciousness a voice was saying, 'But you *haven't* been dealing with it, Jaz. That's why I've had to step in.' I didn't dare say that out loud, though. My instinct's always been to appease. I was made that way.

I said: 'You were always the most important thing in my life; always. No question. I put up with your dad because I thought it was best for you.'

'Which is a lie. You were too scared to do anything about it.'

'Because I didn't want to break up the home. I didn't want your childhood disrupted like poor Natalie's. You're only remembering the bad moments. Most of the time we were fine, you had everything you could wish for, and you know, actually for years it worked. Dad and I did care about each other, despite—'

'Oh yeah, it looks like it.' She stood up again and tossed her hair back, and I got a good look at her face. It was white and furious. 'No *wonder* I've never been able to hold down a relationship, the twisted model I grew up with. No wonder I picked a man who let me down. You *taught me* to make bad choices. You fucked up my childhood, and now I'm trying to get myself back on track, you're *interfering and lying and fucking everything up again!*'

Jaz scooped up the nearest album and heaved it at the wall. I heard the spine crack, felt the thud through my feet as the album hit the carpet. Pages fanned messily out like a broken bird's wing.

'That's what I think of your version!' she cried. 'I don't know whose life this is meant to be in here, but it's not mine.'

'Please, love, I'm sorry about Ian. I'm so sorry. I was trying—'

'Too late! Too *fucking* late! Don't you see what you've done? I can never trust you again. At least it's clear what I should do now: I'm not letting you *anywhere near* Matty in future. You're not *fit*. Half-drowning him, standing there while he falls in the pond, letting complete bastards in the house, and all lies lies lies. You'd probably have let Ian take him off abroad, you'd probably be packing his fucking suitcase for him. Who knows what you're capable of? Standing up in court and testifying against me, I wouldn't be surprised. You're not right and you're certainly not fit to be in charge of a grandchild. Oh no. You've shown me where you stand, you've made your choices.'

'Listen, I would never – all it was – I was—'

There was actual spittle on her bottom lip, I noticed.

'No! No excuses! I've had enough of them. I can't believe a word you say any more, so I'm not listening. You take a good look at your grandson, Mum, because I'll tell you now, you're never going to see him again. Ever. That's it. Finished. This farce is over.'

Then she stalked over to the corner where Matty sat rocking, picked him up as though he were a parcel and carried him out of the front door.

Car doors slammed, the engine revved furiously, then they were gone. I don't believe she even paused to strap him into his child seat.

After a moment or two, I staggered into the hall and sank down onto the bottom step. The cold bar of the stair-gate frame dug into my side. I felt as though all my bones had been unjointed.

If I was thinking anything, it was, Let her go, let her have her tantrum, get it out of her system. Give her space before you do anything else.

Which was a mistake, as it turned out, because it gave her time to run.

CHAPTER 21

Photograph 502, Album 5

Location: The Countess hospital, Chester

Taken by: Carol

Subject: Matty aged 6 hours, asleep in his crib under a waffle blanket.

Photograph: 505

Location: the Countess Hospital

Taken by: Carol

Subject: as above, but from close.

Photograph: 512

Location: the Countess Hospital

Taken by: Carol

Subject: the information card above Matty's head showing his name, sex, DOB, birth weight, length, circumference of head.

Photograph 544

Location: Jaz and Ian's lounge

Taken by: Carol

Subject: Matty, four days old, lying on the sofa in a stripy Babygro.

Photograph 585

Location: Jaz and Ian's kitchen

Taken by: Carol

Subject: Matty, one week old, in his car seat, asleep.

Photograph 600

Location: Jaz's bathroom

Taken by: Carol

Subject: Jaz bends over the baby bath, supporting Matty's upper body and head with one hand, and swilling water with the other. Matty is crying.

Photograph 616

Location: Carol's lounge

Taken by: Ian

Subject: Carol stands in the bay window, cradling two-week-old Matty. Her expression is one of ecstasy.

They had a beautiful day for it. Akela was supervising from the canal bank, while Brown Owl, stationed on the bridge above, had charge of the plastic ducks. One of the Beavers had been given the honour of blowing the whistle to start the race. The tow path was packed with spectators.

'Little one not with you today?' asked Dove, pushing past with her clipboard.

I shook my head. 'I did buy him a duck, because he has a set of them in his bath, and I thought he'd like to see them all together.'

But she was gone, headed for the finishing line to adjudicate there. 'Who's got my net?' I heard her shout.

Families milled around. I saw a toddler straining at his reins, a group of older kids poking with a stick at something in the water, two teenage girls strolling hip to hip. There were prams and balloons and ice creams and bunting and a whole lot of flesh on show. Uniformed Scouts and Guides were taking round baskets of raffle tickets. It should have been a perfect afternoon.

The whistle went and there was an extended splashing as Akela tipped the ducks over the parapet. Those nearby yelped and stepped back, laughing and brushing at their clothes. I noticed Alice resting against the wooden arms of the lock gate, and Libby next to her. I hoped they wouldn't see me. I wished I'd never come.

Because I'd been so intent on not pursuing Jaz, on giving her space to come round, it had taken me a couple of days to realise she was gone. I'd thought it was a bad sign Ian hadn't been in touch. When I plucked up the courage to ring him, he told me he'd been waiting on silence, like me.

So she hadn't even paused to blast him out, I thought. Just upped and left. That's how angry she was.

I'd driven over, and the house had been shut up. A neighbour saw me peering through the back window, said Jaz had given him four or five pot plants because she was 'going away and they'd only die if she left them where they were'. Did he know where she was headed? No, he didn't. Of course he didn't. So I'd gone back home and got my emergency key, the key she'd made me swear never to show Ian even though it was his dad's house, and I let myself in.

The first thing I'd done was dash upstairs and check Matty's cot, only to find it stripped. Coming back downstairs, I clocked the pile of post peeping out from behind the door curtain. Even from the hall I could see the kitchen was spookily tidy, no piles of shoes on the mat, no plates to put away. Last, I visited the lounge, stepping over folders of notes and foreign language books. One dictionary was under the table, as though it had been kicked. I'd retrieved it and laid it on the windowsill. The whole place had felt as though it was holding its breath.

Mums and grandmas jostled against me as the crowd moved slowly along the path, following the movement of the ducks. I cast my eye over the bobbing fleet of yellow plastic, wondering which was Matty's, and was crippled suddenly by a fear so intense I could have collapsed there and then on the grass.

'Watch the lady,' someone said behind me, and a split second afterwards I felt a solid warm mass knock into my calves. When I looked down it was a girl about Matty's age, not much older, wearing a sunhat that had fallen over her eyes. 'Sorry,' said the grey-haired woman who was steering her, and she flashed me one of those grandma-to-grandma smiles. It was like a knife in the heart. I had to get away from this tide of cheer.

The tow path being so narrow and the crowd so big, there was almost nowhere for me to go, but I managed to sidestep into the hedge, and from there ease my way back to the wall of the lock-keeper's cottage. Alice and Libby were catching up fast, and I knew I couldn't cope with the encounter. Between the cottage and its breezeblock garage there was a narrow alleyway, what my mother would have called a ginnel, so I slipped quickly into that. This is someone's private property! I was thinking. What in God's name are you doing, Carol? But it didn't stop me. I just kept going.

I emerged round the back of the cottage to face a long, immaculate garden, full of ornaments and add-ons. Stone animals eyed my progress; gravel had never crunched so loud. I dodged a miniature wheelbarrow, hurried past a picture window and started down the path that ran along the side of the lawn, searching for a gate out onto the cinder track.

Almost at once I heard the sound of a top-floor sash being pushed up. I half-turned, lost my balance and stumbled into a bed of lavender.

'Hoy, you!' a man's voice called.

The normal me would have stopped, faced him, and apologised sincerely for trespassing. That wasn't a consideration for now, though. I didn't even bother framing the words.

Instead I charged on through his plants, snapping red hot pokers and lupins and foxgloves like I'd never cared for flowers in my life. Clouds of pollen rose up around me, spider webs wiped themselves across my bare forearms.

'What the hell do you think you're doing?' he shouted.

There was no gate, and the picket fence was too high to stride over unaided. In the corner, though, I could see a stone bench that I thought I might use as a leg-up.

'This is *not* a public right of way. I'm sick of it. I'm calling the police.'

I reached the seat, hoisted up my skirt, climbed on, and jumped forward.

'Bloody sick of it! If there's any damage, you're paying for it, lady!'

He was still yelling as I landed with a thud in the dirt. My ankle went over and I grazed the palm of my hand, but I managed not to go sprawling. When I looked around, the immediate stretch of lane was deserted – no one to identify me or confirm my criminal activity – so I began to hobble between the ruts in the direction of the main road. I didn't look back. Just let him come after me, just let him.

At the end of the track was the A41. I emerged from between the hedges of the lane into a roar of traffic, big lorries thundering past at sixty so you could feel the suck and beat of air from them on your face. My car was parked round the side of the Horse and Jockey; I could see it 300 yards down the hill. I could go home now, if I wanted. Did I want to go home? I didn't know, couldn't think. Another tanker shot past me, whipping my hair about my face. In the gap which followed, I launched myself into the road, limping as fast as I could. A car horn sounded. I was past caring.

Inside the pub it was cool and almost empty, the calm before the duck race finished and everyone piled back. I decided I'd use the loo, splash cold water on my face while I pulled myself together. It was what my mother used to do to calm herself. The number of times I stood in public toilets watching her bend over the sink, wrists offered up to the tap. Sometimes she'd finish by pulling out her Yardley's cologne stick and rubbing it across her temples. 'This is what it's like, being a woman,' she once said to me. 'You'll find out.'

When my face was dry again, I went into a cubicle and locked the door. I put the toilet lid down and sat, listening to the pipes gurgle and the hum of cars through the open window.

'If she's taken Matty without telling me,' Ian had said, 'it's abduction.'

I'd put on this fake no-nonsense tone, even though inside I was panicking.

'Don't be dramatic. She was upset, she needed a break, that's all.'

'Where? Has she been in touch with you?'

'Not yet, but she will.'

Ian had sworn at me, and then David came on. 'Look, do you know where Matty is, or not?'

'I've a good idea,' I lied, outrageously. 'Give her two or three weeks' space, let her calm down, then I'll go up and see her and bring him back.'

'What if she won't let you?'

'I'm his grandmother.'

'And do you know how much that counts for in law?' said David. 'You might as well be the postman or the butcher.'

'I know how her mind works. I'll talk her round.'

'The way you did before, Carol?'

'Give me this chance. You know what she's like when you corner her.'

Seconds ticked by while he considered.

'I understand that,' he said at last, and I thought how strange it was that David seemed to have more of a handle on Jaz than her own father did. 'OK, you win. For now. I'll talk to Ian about it. But come back to me soon. Otherwise—'

He didn't need to complete the threat.

Ever since that call, I'd been living a strung-out life, vibrating between hope and terror, and in no state to tell which was more realistic. I ached, ached for Matty's weight on my lap, the feel of his palm against mine, the scent of his hair. All last night I'd been kept awake by two voices running through my head. My own – *What if she doesn't come back?* – and Eileen's, reciting over and over some line of poetry we'd had to learn at school – *And Lycius' arms were empty of delight.* 'I only ever wanted to help,' I said to Jaz, in my head. 'You know I'd never take sides against you. You and Matty are the world.' But even an imaginary Jaz wouldn't answer me.

I thought of the little rituals Matty and I had going: giving three kisses at bedtime; the Dalmatian-spot towel he used for his bath and how he loved to be rolled up in it; breakfast porridge in his farmyard animals bowl; playing growly tigers through the bars of the stair-gate. And for no reason at all there came to me an image of Dad and Jaz standing in his garden shed, tightening something into a vice – I swear I could smell the oil and rust. (A pictureframe, was he helping her make? A hamster ladder?)

That was all gone now: that was the past and you expected to lose it. It was a sadness you were prepared for. But what I couldn't bear was the thought that I might lose the future, too. Because that's what Matty was, that sense of life continuing, the sense that, however old and decrepit you felt, however many of your peers got ill – or died – there was this new generation carrying it on, and carrying it on for you. A new set of hopes, a job well done, your own small impact on the world secured. And someone, too, who'd look up to you, who always had the time to spend on nothing much and was delighted to spend it with you. Children and grandparents are such a natural fit.

I don't know how long I sat in the gloom like that, trying to articulate, to no one at all, what Matty meant. Then suddenly I heard a swing door thump open. Someone walked into the toilets, clearing their throat, and when I came to myself I was staring at the crinoline lady logo on the hygiene bags, and half-recalling that same motif embroidered on a traycloth of my mother's.

'Carol? Carol?'

My name registered like a shock. I stood up unsteadily, held the wall for a few seconds, then shot the bolt back.

Dove was standing by the sink, waving an envelope at me. 'You've won!' she was saying.

'Won what?'

'The duck race. We've been looking everywhere for you. We thought you'd gone home, but your neighbour said your car was still here. So I thought, I'll just pop and check . . . It's fifty pounds!'

She held out the envelope and I took it. *Number 169: Matty Reid (via Carol Morgan)*, it said on the front. Someone had drawn a smiling duck in the top right-hand corner.

'Fifty pounds,' said Dove again. I suppose she was waiting for a more dramatic response.

'Thanks.'

'I bet you can't believe it. We had nearly three hundred ducks, you know. Fantastic support. A really good turn-out. And this weather, can you believe it? What a shame Matty isn't here. He'd have loved it. He'd have been cheering.'

'Yes.'

Her eyes scanned my face. Just go, I was thinking. Leave me alone.

'First prize, eh?' she said. 'Fantastic. All those toys you can buy him.'

'Yes.'

She gave up on me and half-turned away. *Should've seen her reaction*, she'd tell the others later. *Never even cracked a smile, can you believe it? Fifty quid!*

'Anyway,' she said, 'you've obviously got the lucky touch this week, haven't you? Lucky Granny.'

I waited till the door hissed shut behind her.

'Looks like it,' I said.

Natalie was currently living back at her mum's, a Seventies semi on the Bowbrook Estate where every street was named after a bird. 'Skylark Rise! Like there were ever skylarks anywhere near there,' I remembered saying to Phil once. 'Oh, there were, apparently,' he'd said. 'All up that side of the town was fields. Some woman at work was telling me.'

Some Woman at Work: it was months before I cottoned on. Now I never walked along this road without thinking of Penny. It had become another area her existence had polluted.

I'd called ahead to say I was coming, so I knew Nat would be in, she couldn't pretend she wasn't. Her small face showed briefly at the window, and I thought what a hard look she'd always had about her, even as a child. Now she was twenty-seven, and her features had settled into a scowl. All the highlighting and tanning beds and nail polish in the world couldn't offset her vinegar soul.

'I don't know where she is,' were her first words as she opened the door. 'I told you that on the phone.'

'Yes, I'd love a coffee,' I said brightly, stepping forward so she had no choice but to let me across the threshold.

Nat frowned, grudging. 'OK. It'll have to be a quick one. I've to be back at work at two.'

I took myself through to their lounge and waited for her to make the drinks. I wanted a minute to get my head straight.

Last time I ruined everything by losing my temper. It had been Phil who'd got the information out of her, in the end.

Phil who'd grabbed my arm as I went to slap her. Twelve years ago I'd sat in this same room, on this same cream leather sofa, under that David Shepherd print of lion cubs, desperate to know where on God's earth my daughter was.

Nat came in with one cup only and put it on the coffee-table next to me. 'You tried ringing her?'

Of course I've bloody tried ringing her. What kind of an idiot do you take me for?

'Yes,' I said. 'There's no answer. I've left messages. Has she been in touch with you?'

'No.'

'And she didn't speak to you before she took off?'

'No.' Nat perched herself on the arm of the chair opposite. 'I know you won't believe me.'

Can you blame me?

The ghosts of before shifted through the room. Skinny Nat in her school uniform, her shrew of a mother standing by the telephone with her arms folded. Me, shouting in their faces.

'She's a grown woman,' said Nat. 'It's not the same.'

'No, I know that.'

Last time Jaz had been intercepted at Lancaster services on the M6, having cadged a lift with a lorry driver. She'd told him she was eighteen. Thank God he'd been a decent sort, who'd called as soon as he realised something wasn't right. Daughters of his own, he had. But before that, Nat had let slip Jaz was headed north. Why north? Nat didn't know, or said she didn't. Jaz would never tell.

'Do you think,' I said, 'she might have gone in the same direction?'

Nat shrugged.

I tried again. 'When you last spoke, was there anything she said, any clue she might have given about her plans? Did she tell you about Ian?'

'What about him?'

'Me letting him see Matty at my house.'

'Oh, that, yeah.' She let her gaze drift over to the window.

So, I thought, she did speak to you before she went. You bloody little liar, Natalie Gardiner. I took a deep breath.

'What did she say?'

'She was really pissed off. Like, really really. I've never seen her as . . . Jesus, she was mad. With you, mostly.'

'I was trying to help, Nat.'

'Yeah,' she said. 'I know you were.'

That unexpected sympathy made my eyes prick with tears. 'I was worried about Ian. That he might retaliate. You hear stories in the news.'

She nodded.

'At the very least, David was talking about involving the courts. And if Jaz doesn't come back soon—'

'He could get shitty.'

'Which is the last thing Jaz needs right now. So can you see what I was trying to do, Nat?'

I thought I had her on my side for a moment. She squinted at me, as if considering. 'You shouldn't have done it behind her back, though.'

'I know.'

The room blurred.

'I'm sorry,' I said, wiping at my eyes with my knuckle. 'Only I miss her. I miss Matty. I just want to know where they are. I know I've messed up, I know I should have stuck up for her more, and she's been saying about how she hated me staying married to her dad. I had no idea. Did you know, did she ever tell you? She didn't tell me. At least, I don't think she did. What I thought was, if I let Ian come round a couple of times, it would keep him sweet, stop him getting too resentful while he waited for her to get herself together. It would take the pressure off. She wouldn't move an inch, you know, wouldn't even talk to him. I couldn't sit by and do nothing, could I? All my life, I've been trying to do the right thing and it's never good enough. Whatever I do, turns out I should have done the opposite. I must have been a really bad mother. Sometimes I think I might as well not have tried.' My voice was thick with self-pity. 'I just want them back, how it was, together. That's all I want.'

'Tell you something,' said Nat, as I attempted to fish out a hanky from my sleeve, 'I'm never having any fucking children. Seems like one big fucking load of grief to me.'

When I'd dabbed my face dry and looked up, she was watching me with what might have been pity, or boredom.

'Please,' I said. 'I'm begging you. If you know anything.'

There followed a long moment where Nat stared up at the ceiling, down at the carpet, and finally settled her gaze on the lion picture above my head.

'She could be in Leeds.'

'Leeds?'

'There's a guy.'

'Who?' I never knew any of the boys she dated then. 'What's he called?'

'Not sure.'

'Did she say she was going to see him?'

'No. She mentioned him a few times.'

'And he's still in Leeds?'

'He might be.' Nat was twisting a strand of hair round and round her finger. 'I don't know for definite. It's just, like I said, she was talking about him before she went.'

'What did she say?'

'I can't remember.'

The urge to rise up, grab her by the shoulders and shake her till her teeth rattled was tremendous. At the same time, my mind was racing ahead. Where did Jaz keep her address book? Might she have left it behind?

'Nat, is there anything else I need to know? Anything at all, *please*. Do you think he's all right, this man? Is Jaz safe?'

She gave a nervous sort of giggle. 'I don't know him. She might not be there, anyway. I've told you all I can.'

I thought I'd better go before I slapped her again.

On the doorstep, she said to me: 'Sorry. It must be shit.'

'Yes,' I said. 'It is.'

I walked to the end of the road, counted thirty, then retraced my steps. This time, instead of marching up the front path, I slipped down the side of the house and round the back. I ducked under the kitchen window, then crouched down behind the door. Gingerly I rose and peered through the glass. The kitchen was empty.

I pressed the handle down by degrees, pushed, and the door gave. I opened it as stealthily as I could, holding my breath, hearing nothing over the pounding of my heart. Then I stepped inside.

'—your fucking mother,' I heard Nat say, from the lounge. 'Oh, going on at me, you know.'

I went faint.

'No,' she said. '*No.* No, I *didn't.*'

A pause.

'Well, where *are* you?'

Slam slam slam slam went the blood in my ears.

'No, I won't. I *won't.* I promise.'

I moved forwards.

'Suit yourself,' said Nat hotly. 'But I'm not having—' That was when she turned round and saw me in the doorway.

'Oh, fuck,' she said, taking the mobile away from her cheek.

'Give it to me!' I shouted. 'Give it to me!'

I don't know whether it was fear or spite made her drop the

phone, but the next second I was scrabbling across the carpet for it. My hands were shaking so badly, and the thing was so bloody tiny, I could barely pick it up.

At last I managed to jam the speaker against my ear. 'Jaz? Jaz? Are you there? Jaz?' All the concentration I had was focused on that moment, as if I could conjure my daughter's voice by sheer force of will. My eyes were screwed tight shut, and my shoulders hunched away from Nat, blocking her out. 'Jaz, please,' I said into the silence.

I stood that way for what seemed like a long time.

When I opened my eyes, Nat was picking up her car keys from the table, and the phone was dead in my hands.

CHAPTER 22

Photograph: unnumbered, wedged between pages 40 and 41 of La Symphonie Pastorale, *in a box in the loft, Sunnybank*

Location: Hunger Hills, Horsforth, Leeds

Taken by: Stephanie Page

Subject: a group of students in hiking gear pose at the base of a huge oak tree. Jaz is on the extreme right, in borrowed boots, borrowed socks, borrowed cagoule. Next to her stands Dr Nick Page, the youngest tutor in the department and a man who has not yet quite sorted out his staff-pupil boundaries. A hearty man, a muscular Christian, mens sana in corpore sano *is his motto and he likes to encourage these academic young people out of the library (or the bar, or bed) and up a hillside once in a while. Luckily, his wife enjoys this sort of caper too.*

'Having fun?' Mrs Page asks Jaz as the group begins to move apart. 'Yes,' says Jaz, and finds, to her surprise, it's true. Up here, on this high ground, the situation with Tomasz doesn't seem quite so serious, though she knows that every step of the descent will bring it back into focus.

But maybe it will work itself out. There must be something she can do to get Tomasz all to herself. The fresh air is help-

*ing to clear her head, and she thinks she might be on the verge
of a plan.*

*She hitches up her rucksack and sets off down the track. Dr
Page soon falls in next to her.*

*'Let me tell you,' he says eagerly, 'how this place got its
name.'*

You know the sensation when you bite down with an amalgam
filling against tinfoil? That's how I felt all the time now, only
from inside my chest: a poisonous, sick fizzing of nerves below
my ribcage. Food lodged in my throat; trying to get to sleep was
like sprawling on jagged stone. When I watched TV or read,
nothing went in. I'd have liked to go to the gym, see the girls,
but I couldn't face them. My own fault. I'd made Matty the
centre of so many stories, it was the first question people asked.
How's your grandson? And what could I say? 'My daughter's so
disgusted with me that she's taken him away and I don't know
where he is. Yes, I'm that bad a parent.' Shame layered on grief
layered on fear layered on anger. I didn't know what to do with
myself.

If Jaz had been taking photographs for her unhappy album,
she'd have had a field day. Daft Carol getting to the supermarket checkout and finding six pots of Splat in her basket,
when there's no one now to eat them; rooting like a madwoman through her bag at two in the morning to check again
for non-existent phone messages; eating toast over the sink
because she can't bear to get a plate from the cupboard where
Matty's cup and dish are kept; driving straight into the back of
a 4 × 4 and crumpling her bonnet to buggery.

And now I was on this train to Leeds. When Jaz was at the
university, I used to drive up, but my head being the way it was,
I didn't trust myself not to have an accident. Aside from the
prang, I'd had two near-misses in the previous three days. So

the train was safer, but on the other hand it meant there was nothing to do but stare out of the window and think. The magazine I'd bought at the station was no go: first headline in it turned out to be *My Ex Stole Our Daughters*. I rolled it up and stuck it in the bin between the seats.

We flicked past rows of terraces that reminded me of Bolton, and housing estates that made me think of Nat. Sometimes in the gardens there were ride-on toys, or climbing frames, or swings. A group of children waved from a cycle track. Look, Matty! I wanted to say. A stadium! A weir! Rabbits! Narrowboats! The loss of him was a solid space sitting in the carriage with me, and outside it, and all around, in everything.

When I'd gone back to Jaz's, the first thing I'd done was run upstairs and check the cot again. I knew it would still be stripped, but I had to see anyway. The times I'd stood listening to Matty's wind-up night light, watching for his eyes to close. I fought the temptation to put it on – to drop the cot side, kneel with my cheek against the bare mattress – and instead turned and walked across the landing, into Jaz's bedroom.

The train jolted, bringing me out of myself. In front of me a red-headed woman about my age was struggling through the inter-connecting door with a hot drink in each hand and a large bag over the crook of one arm. She paused to hitch up the bag and, as she did so, the doors started to slide shut. I thought that, like lift doors, they'd spring apart when they encountered the least resistance, but these swept on, thumping hard into her shoulder. She stumbled against the wall and winced. But then she quickly righted herself to carry on down the aisle, her spine straight, flicking her eyes away from my gaze in a way I knew meant, *This is not how life treats me. That was not a representative scene. I'm really not the kind of person who spends her time being humiliated and pushed about. Stop looking.*

We plunged into a tunnel, and all I could see through the window was my own anxious reflection. Let me say, I would never normally have gone into Jaz's bedroom without being asked, or searched through her dressing-table drawers or the bottom of the wardrobe or under her bed. I'm not that kind of a mother. All through her teens she'd kept a candy-striped hat box full of private bits and pieces – love letters, diaries, that sort of caper – and I'd never so much as run a duster across the lid. But the shelf by the phone had been empty, her address book gone, so where else could I look? I remembered a Filofax with a pair of lips on the cover that she'd still been using in her first year at Leeds. I thought, if I could locate that, I might be in with a chance.

The train came out into daylight again, and the memory of Phil's voice: *Oh, come on, you know Jaz. She likes to make a statement. She'll be back. Try not to get so worked up.* As he'd been speaking, I'd glanced out of the kitchen door and seen Matty's tulips, straight and bright like a row of scarlet soldiers. How long would it be before the petals dropped? Would he get to see them? Would he be back playing in my garden next week, next month, never? I said to Phil, 'It *feels* bad. She was livid with me, you've no idea. You don't understand Jaz the way I do.' 'So you're always telling me,' he'd said.

In the Filofax I'd found just two Leeds addresses: a crossed-out one for her personal tutor, a man I dimly remembered meeting once while she was showing me round the union, and one for a Sam Barnett. Not a name that rang any bells, but then Jaz had kept her university life strictly private and she was rarely at home, even in the holidays. Every week I'd written to her or rung, but all I ever had in return was a handful of texts and the occasional request to send up something she'd forgotten. She'd pass on odd incidents – there was this boy who played his guitar on the roof, there was this girl who got drunk and fell down the faculty stairs – and sometimes let slip names or nicknames, but never the same one twice. Bright enquiries only made her clam up. 'She was that way at school,' Phil had said. 'Just be grateful she's settled. Don't keep digging.' It's hard when they're not around to keep an eye on, though.

The Sam address had been updated twice, which seemed hopeful. I'd written it down, and placed the book back in the hat box, wiping my fingermarks off the lid guiltily. As though that would make any difference.

The carriage door opened again and a young woman walked through with a boy of about seven or eight. She was holding him by the shoulders, a light, protective contact to steady him as we rocked from side to side. I wanted to put out my hand to touch him as well, but that would have looked mad. My limbs twitched uselessly. Huge smooth fields flashed by, one after another, and a line of pylons, and a scrapyard and a lake, and Phil's voice came again: *Try not to get so worked up.* Then my own voice, snapping down the phone line: *Oh, it must be marvellous not to care.* His hurt silence. My parting shot: *And while you're at it, you can tell Penny to piss off.*

'She already has,' he'd said. 'She walked out six days ago.'

The red-headed woman blundered past me again, a coffee stain down her blouse. She saw me looking, smiled slightly and raised her eyebrows in a gesture of complicity. *This tricky world, eh?*

I turned my face away. I wasn't like her, I wasn't a victim.

I was going to find my daughter and put things right.

'You're a girl,' I said, staring at the person who called herself Sam Barnett. The boy-toddler she was holding shifted on her hip. Her free hand was on the door, ready to close it in my face.

'Uh huh.'

I looked round to see if my taxi was still there, but it had gone. The terraced street stretched empty.

'Do you mind telling me who you are?' she said.

This woman could almost have been Jaz's sister. Her face was rounder, and her eyes had an oriental look about them, but her hair and colouring were the same. The likeness made me shiver. Jaz would never have worn slippers with tracksuit bottoms and a shirt with sauce stains at the cuff, though.

'Carol Morgan. I'm looking for my daughter,' I said.

The child whimpered and squirmed. 'Jesus,' she said under her breath.

'I think you used to know her?'

'Now's not very—'

'I won't keep you. I only want to know she's OK.'

Sam let the boy slide down her body onto the tiled floor, where he sat leaning against her, whining. 'Sorry, who are we talking about, here?'

'Jaz Morgan. Jasmine. You were at university together.'

'Jaz? Yeah. God. Sheesh.'

'Do you know where she is?'

She shook her head. 'No, no idea. Haven't spoken to her for ages; you're asking the wrong person. You should've rung, saved yourself a journey.'

Except, I could have said, when your daughter won't even answer the phone to you, your best bet is to turn up without warning and try and catch her out. I needed to come and walk these streets between Hyde Park and Headingly anyway, just in case she was magically there, simply because, once upon a time, she had been.

'I'm looking for a man she used to know.'

'Can't help you. That was all years ago. Another life. And like I said, now isn't a good time.' She nodded down at the boy.

'We've only just got back from the doctor's; I've had no sleep for two nights.'

'What's the matter with him?' I said quickly, as her hand tightened on the door.

Both of us peered at the child, who was now lolling his head from side to side and breathing noisily through his mouth. His cheeks were bright red.

'The doctor says it's a virus. He said we have to let it run its course. There's all sorts of bugs going round. Do you reckon he's teething?'

'I don't know. Could be.'

'He won't eat, won't play, can't seem to drop off. It's completely fucking knackering.'

'When exactly did you last speak to Jaz?' I said, dropping to my haunches so I could take a better look.

'I told you; I haven't talked to her for about, ooh, three years. We kept in touch a bit after she left, but it petered out.'

'You were her friend?'

'Sort of. But then—'

Without warning, the child leaned forward and vomited onto the doorstep. Milky drool spattered across the grey stone next to me.

'Oh, shit,' she said. She took a step forward and I knew she was preparing to draw him inside and close the door on me.

'Hang on a minute,' I said. I lifted the hair up on his forehead because I thought I'd glimpsed something there. 'What did the doctor say again?'

'A virus. Why?'

'Can we take him inside and get his T-shirt off?'

I must have frightened her, because she didn't hesitate.

The house was tidier than I'd imagined, and the décor modern, plain and light. Even so, the back room was poky and I had to bring him up to the window to see properly. Sam sat him on the table and peeled off his top while I hunted my reading glasses out of my handbag. You could tell he was poorly because he barely protested.

'How old is he?' I asked.

'Two next month. He's had a lot of ear infections, we're always up at the surgery with him. You get so you think, I don't want to bother them again. But then, when it's night time and he's burning up . . .'

I put my palms to the butter-soft skin of his chest. Then I checked under his fringe again. 'See that?' I said, pointing above his eyebrow.

There was a tiny clear blister marking the fair skin.

'My God,' she said. 'What is it?'

'Chickenpox, I think.'

'I thought that was red spots?'

The child twisted away from us, and we caught sight of his back. 'Like those?'

There weren't many, just three or four, like flea bites.

Sam frowned. 'When I had it, I was absolutely covered. I remember.'

'It can vary. Jaz had hardly any at all.'

'Should I try that glass test thing?'

'You can if you want to.'

She poked one of the spots with her finger experimentally. The redness vanished for a second, then flushed back.

'So what do you do for chickenpox?'

'There isn't really anything, other than ride it out. Oh, cut his nails as short as you can so he doesn't scratch himself into a nasty mess. And keep him cool, don't cover him up with thick blankets. Have you any calamine lotion?'

'No.'

'Don't worry, you can get it in any chemist. Sudocrem'll do in the meantime.'

'And the being sick?'

I shrugged. 'Toddlers do tend to, for no special reason. But if you're at all concerned, get him back to the doctor's. They won't mind. It's better than worrying all night.'

She sat down heavily, then she slid the boy towards her and onto her lap. Both of them looked exhausted. 'Are you a health visitor or something?'

'Just a grandma who's seen lots of cases of chickenpox over the years.'

'Well, if that's all it is . . . Sometimes he seems to go from one infection to another with no pause in between. And there's no one to ask.'

'Your mum?'

'Lives in Spain. Too busy having a good time to bother with grandchildren.' Her eyelids closed. 'I'd make a cup of tea if I had the energy.'

'Stay there,' I said.

When I came back, she'd laid him out on the sofa, and he looked to be almost asleep. His long lashes quivered against his cheeks, and he kept making long, juddery sighs. Up and down his little chest went, his fingers curled and relaxed. What would she say if I reached down and stroked his hair?

'You seem like a nice woman,' she said suddenly. 'I don't know why Jaz always had such a downer on you.'

'Me neither. Look, Sam, are you absolutely sure you can't help me? I really could do with a lead.'

The boy's breathing seemed to fill the room.

She said, 'You'd better let me have your story. Then maybe we'll take it from there.'

'OK, well, I should tell you now,' she said when I'd finished. 'Jaz and I had a – a fall-out. I was pretty pissed off at the time.

I'm sorry about her marriage. If it's any consolation, though, I think she can look after herself.'

'Do you?' I wondered what version of Jaz she'd known.

'God, yeah. She's got a core of steel.'

'Why did she drop out of the course?'

'Didn't she tell you?'

'No.' I felt foolish saying it. 'We didn't even realise she had dropped out, at first. It's not like school, where the teachers ring the parents and send out letters if anything's wrong.' The whole thing was conducted in private, between the university and Jaz. Data protection, I was told when I phoned the department. She was an adult, it was her business, and nothing to do with me. Unless she wanted to involve me, which she didn't.

'Didn't she mention my name at all?'

I struggled to remember. 'I don't think so. I mean, not especially. She used to come at me with a whole list, all funny-sounding nick-names. Slothy was one, and there was another called Meat. She shared a house in the second year with two Zoology students, I do know that, but she was only with them a term.'

Flashback to Jaz that Christmas before she left Leeds, slouching over her plate. I was furious that I'd gone to the trouble of cooking a proper dinner for the two of us, and then she wouldn't eat it. *Nothing I do is ever good enough*, I'd said to her.

'She was supposed to share with me,' said Sam. 'Me and Tomasz. We were – friends. It's complicated.'

'I might have heard her mention Tom.'

'You would have.'

'He was her boyfriend?'

Sam's eyes were dark and clouded. 'He was my boyfriend. Then he was hers, then he was mine again. Although it wasn't as clear as that. It wasn't like anyone drew a line, you know?

Sometimes it was this, sometimes that. Mainly we were friends. That was when it was best. Brilliant, actually.'

'Sounds complicated.'

'It wasn't, though, that was the thing. We just hung around together. Went up Majestyks or Heaven and Hell or the Union; best time of my life, really.'

'Until?'

She looked away. 'It was tricky to keep the balance going long-term. We dated other people, me and Jaz, but never anyone serious. I think we both really loved Tomasz. I think secretly we were each hoping he'd choose us and that the other one would be OK with it. Like that was ever going to come off. I'm sure he found the whole situation . . . you know. Two women, mad for him.

'Jaz had a lot of little flings, and there was this one guy, Andy, I went out with a few times. She set us up, then kept pushing us together, even though I wasn't totally sold on the idea. I knew what she was up to. But Andy was too . . . he wasn't Tomasz, basically. I finished with him to get back with Tomasz—'

'Was Jaz going out with Tomasz then?'

'Like I said, it was a sort of fluid situation. I suppose they were closer at that point. Well, obviously . . .' She gave a funny sort of laugh.

'And Jaz was upset?'

'She was OK with it. It had happened before. What you have to realise is, it was like we were playing some stupid game of tennis, with Tomasz as the ball. I think she assumed she'd get him back, but she wasn't that serious, you know? We were all still going round together. Having a laugh.'

Sam shifted in her chair. A worry line had formed between her brows.

'This,' she went on, 'is where it gets tricky. The other guy I'd been seeing, Andy, he came round to the house and gave me this big speech about love, how we were meant to be together and stuff. He got himself in a total state. Now I look back, I can see he wasn't balanced – he was ill, really, but I didn't pick up on the clues. And then it was coming up to the end of term, and we were supposed to be doing exams, and that's when he killed himself.'

'Good God,' I said.

Against the ordinariness of this pale, neat living room came scenes I'd caught on television: a figure climbing over a railway bridge; a washbasin spattered with blood; a young man's body sprawled across a bed.

'An overdose,' she said, cutting into my thoughts. 'He'd tried it before, when he was in the sixth form. There wasn't a note. Some people are wired that way, it's no one's fault. It wasn't my fault I didn't want to go out with him, was it? Was it?'

'No.' My mouth was very dry. 'And Jaz? Was she involved at all?'

Sam ignored me. 'There was an inquest, obviously. Have you ever been to one of those? Fucking awful. Like a court. Fucking big room. But they said no one was to blame.'

'Did Jaz go?'

'No. I had to. I had to stand up in public and tell them what he'd been like. His parents were there – I had to do all that on my own.'

So much of my daughter's life that I knew nothing about. It was as though a huge gong had been struck inside my head and was reverberating, on and on.

'It must have been awful for you,' I said.

'Yeah, it fucking was. Talking like this – you think something's in the past and then it all comes back.'

'I can imagine,' I said carefully, 'you must feel, even if it's nothing to do with you, a sense of guilt.'

'It wasn't my fault. They said.'

'No, it wasn't. But nevertheless, very distressing for every-one involved.'

'I didn't last much longer than Jaz, you know. One more term and I was back at my mum's. At the time I just wanted to get away. Then I meet someone, get married and find myself here again. There's irony for you.'

'So do you think that's why Jaz became ill? Do you think she was affected by what happened to this boy?'

Sam raised her head and looked at me directly. A bitter tri-umph gleamed in her eyes.

'I reckon that was probably more to do with the abortion,' she said.

CHAPTER 23

Photograph: unnumbered, stuffed down the back of the immersion heater, Sunnybank

Location: Bar Coda, the Student Union, Leeds

Taken by: Tomasz

Subject: Jaz and Sam lean in together, grinning. Sam has her arm round Jaz's neck, and there is a good deal of bare shoulder and décolleté on view. 'Go on,' urges Tomasz, 'kiss her.' Which one is he addressing? In practical terms, it doesn't matter. Jaz lays her head against Sam's neck because she doesn't want to snog a girl, even for Tomasz. He says he's drunk, but she's been watching him and she thinks otherwise.

'Mmm, my mate,' says Sam, swaying slightly. All at once Jaz is desperate to remove Sam's clammy arm from against her skin. She wants to escape this hot loud room, break out into the panoramic night, and run and run. But that would mean leaving the other two on their own.

It's not the evening any of them have been hoping for.

I sat holding Dad's limp hand and told him all about it.

'How could she not have confided in me? How could I not have known? If she'd come to me, I could have helped, we could have talked it through. She didn't need to have got rid of the baby; I could have supported her. Surely she didn't think I'd be angry with her. *Would* I have been angry with her?'

Dad blinked.

'I wouldn't, would I? I might have said she'd been a bit silly, but I wouldn't have gone on about it. If she'd come home and announced, "Mum, I'm pregnant",' I paused for a moment to construct the scene, trying to imagine myself saying, 'There there, not to worry, we'll see you through.' How likely would that response have been? To have held my tongue about how hard she'd worked to get to university, or how we'd all strug-gled to get her through those re-takes, or the cash Phil and I had scraped together to start her off? Would I really have been able to pretend unalloyed delight?

Then I thought of Matty, newborn, and what a rush of love I'd felt when I'd held him. That faint prickle of remembered lactation as I held him against my breasts, the endless mar-velling at his miniature perfection. Feeling almost drowned in the weight of pride, responsibility and privilege. All that lost to me, to us both: it was an intolerable thought.

Eh, our little Jaz, I heard Dad saying, from across time.

'But I'm speaking from the other side of experience,' I said to him. 'I know now what it's like to be a grandma. That wouldn't have been the case if she'd come to me when she was only twenty-one. I was just a mother then, and that would have made all the difference. Having a grandchild around puts, I don't know, a layer of tolerance between you somehow. Perhaps it's because you're speaking more on a level with each other. You're both mums, so you've a better understanding. Or she's grown up, or you've understood that she's grown up. I can't pin down exactly why, but it alters things right down to the core. So, obviously, I wouldn't have felt the same about a pregnancy as I do now.'

We were all different people back then, love, said Dad.

'See, what counselling did she have, that's what I want to know. Where did she go to have it done? Was he around for her, this Tomasz? God, if he was here now—'

Sam had been infuriatingly short on detail. Yes, the baby was Tomasz's; yes, she thought he might have taken Jaz to the clinic but she didn't know if he'd stayed or not. 'We'd all kind of fallen out by then,' she said. As though they'd been kids having some stupid spat, instead of adults dealing with a matter of life or death. 'Have you got his address?' I'd asked her. 'No,' she said, 'I've no idea where he is.' 'Do you think there's any chance Jaz might be with him now?' I said. 'I wouldn't have thought so,' she'd said. Then she'd turned away from me deliberately and bent over her sleeping boy. She'd done the damage. The discussion was closed.

I squeezed Dad's fingers in mine. 'I need to see this man who hurt Jaz,' I said.

Why?

'Because she might be with him. And because I need to understand her more. No wonder she was angry when she came home. I thought it was with me. But if I'd known. If only I'd known, Dad.'

I couldn't have told you what was bothering me the most: the loss of a baby who I could only conjure in the form of Matty; the idea of Jaz, hurt and lonely and going through such an ordeal on her own; guilt at the way I'd treated her when she dropped out; resentment that by keeping silent, she'd put me in that position. Fear that I knew my daughter so little.

The door opened suddenly and one of the care assistants came in holding a pair of hair clippers. 'Oh!' she said. 'It's so quiet in here I thought he was on his own. Sorry.'

I struggled to come out of my thoughts. Had I not been speaking aloud?

'We're—' I started, but she'd already gone, closing the door softly.

Dad shivered. I kept hold of his hand.

I don't know how much longer we sat like that, talking to each other in silence.

Phil was, as usual, more pragmatic.

'Plenty of girls have abortions. Thousands every year. It's a standard medical procedure, perfectly safe, perfectly legal. Don't get yourself in a state about it, Carol.'

He knelt by the pond, retractable tape measure in one hand, squared paper in the other, a pencil stuck behind his ear. Out of nowhere had come this baking hot day; even the pale grey paving slabs were dazzling.

'But why didn't she tell me?'

Phil paused in his calculations and looked at me, his eyebrows raised.

'Oh, don't start,' I said.

'All I was going to say is, she doesn't like a fuss. She knew she'd messed up and didn't need you to ram it home.'

'I would *never* have told her she'd "messed up". How could you think I'd say such a thing?'

He sighed, took out his pencil and began to mark points on the sheet.

'I know Jaz,' I went on, 'and I know she couldn't have gone through an abortion without being emotionally scarred by it, never mind the physical side. And for her to have faced it on her own – that's what gets me, Phil. I was sitting at home in ignorance while she was going through hell.'

'You were sorting your dad out, as I remember,' he said grimly. 'And there was – Well, you had a few things on your mind that year.'

'Eileen,' I said, to stop him mentioning the divorce.

'Yes, Eileen.'

Insects skated across the surface of the pond inside sliding rings of light.

Phil said: 'Do you not think Jaz might have been keeping schtum to protect you?'

'I wouldn't have thought so. She doesn't operate like that. Oh, God, where did I go wrong, Phil? When she was little we got on really well. Even when she became a teenager it wasn't so bad—'

'Only because you let her have her own way and a bag to put it in.'

'I did not.'

He shrugged, pulled out a length of tape. 'OK.'

'But when she hit nineteen, twenty, I was the devil incarnate. You weren't there to see, but I tell you, I couldn't do a thing right. If I said "good morning" to her, she'd bristle like I'd sworn in her face.'

'I wouldn't take it personally,' said Phil. 'She always dismissed *me* as a fool.' And for a second he looked so forlorn I could almost have gone across and put my arms round him.

He sighed, scrambled stiffly to his feet and then stood looking at me.

'Are you all right?' I said.

'Trying to remember if I've any four-inch staples in the shed.'

I was still imagining what would have happened if I had walked up and touched him.

'Six-inch would do it, but I don't want to go any bigger than that.'

'Don't ask me,' I said. 'No one but you knows their way round that place. One day I'll drag everything out and make a bonfire.'

'I do hope you're joking, Carol.'

'Or alternatively, you could get on and clear it like you've promised so many times.'

'And then every time you needed a job doing, I'd have to bring all my tools round with me. Do you want me to fit this grid over your pond, or not?'

We weren't comfortable enough with each other for this kind of banter. *You moved out of this house, you should have taken all your stuff with you*, my head was going. *Sticking your foot in the door, that's what it amounts to. God knows why I've put up with it all these years.*

Ungrateful cow, he was thinking; I could see it in his face.

I waved a hand in a vague sort of 'have it your own way' gesture, and he disappeared into the shed.

It was much cooler in the kitchen, but I still stood with the cold tap running over my wrists. Tomasz Ramzinski had been easy to track down via Friends Reunited, and then the phone book. But again, I wasn't going to risk calling first.

'Are you sure you want to pursue this?' Phil had said when I first told him. 'If she's not there, you'll have wasted your time, got all wound up for nothing. If she is, she'll be that pissed off with you.'

I hated him for being right, but I didn't seem able to help myself. 'I'll talk her round,' I'd said. 'She's not going to climb out of the back window and run off, is she? Maybe I could just see Matty for a little while. Get my fix.' Give Phil his due, he'd let that comment lie.

When he emerged from the shed, shielding his eyes against the sun, I went out with a glass of water.

'Here,' I said. 'You don't want to get a headache.'

'Ta.' He took it from me, and nodded towards a clump of glyceria. 'I'm going to need to drill some holes around the edge. That all right? It shouldn't affect your liner or anything.'

When I didn't reply, he knelt back down at the pond's edge

and started counting squares on his diagram. His lips moved in silent calculation.

I said: 'I can't believe you're taking it all so calmly.'

'Taking what?'

'Jaz going off with Matty. What she said to me. Anyone would think you didn't care.'

Phil stopped dead and put down his drawing. 'Never say that, Carol. Never say that again.'

He went back to marking his diagram.

'I'm sorry,' I said lamely. 'You just don't seem to get worked up the way I do.'

'Look,' he said, tucking his pencil behind his ear again, 'how about I go down to Bristol with you? You don't want to be messing about on trains; let me drive you. It'll be moral support. Someone to chat to.'

I thought of Sam's face, that tight half-smile as she realised the impact of what she was delivering. Watching me as I struggled to take everything in. It would have been good to have had someone with me that day. Even Phil.

'Well,' I said.

'I could tell you about Pen on the way,' he added carelessly.

You can take a running jump, I thought. I snatched up his almost empty glass and flung the dregs onto the dusty flagstones where they left a dark-blotched trail, like a nursery painting of a caterpillar. 'You come,' I said, 'on condition you don't say a word about her. I don't want to hear her name. I don't want to know.'

'I thought you'd want—'

'Your problem, nothing to do with me any more, Phil. That was me in another life.'

All those times I'd prayed she'd bugger off and leave us. At first so he'd stay, then that he'd come back to me, and finally that he'd show up just so I could tell him to get lost. Now, like so many events you desperately wish for, the nothingness when it arrived was staggering.

'You come with me because you're Jaz's dad, yes?'

He dropped his gaze. 'She might still ring or text. You never know.'

'She won't.'

'I'll see you Saturday, then,' he said, and turned away again to study his figures, his bent back towards me.

I'd no intention of telling David, but it came out anyway.

'I came to ask whether there was any news,' he said, walking into my hallway with a clipboard in one hand and calculator in the other. As if the last time I'd seen him I hadn't slammed a car door in his face.

'What are those for?' I asked.

'I thought I'd measure your pond so we could price up a grid. Might as well get something useful done.'

'Oh,' I said, 'Phil's seeing to it.'

'He's getting professionals in?'

'No, he's fitting something himself.'

David pressed his lips together disapprovingly.

I said, 'He's checked the gauge, it's the proper stuff. If it doesn't look a hundred per cent safe in the finish, I'll take it up and start again.'

'OK.' He pocketed the calculator, laid the clipboard on the windowsill, and sat down. 'So, have you heard from Jasmine yet?'

The stand-by lines I'd rehearsed dissolved from my memory and I found myself mouthing like a fish.

'That'll be a no, then.'

'I did go – she wasn't where I thought she was. But probably—' I began. He interrupted me.

'Look, Carol, I'm here to fight Ian's corner. My son needs to see his child. There's no argument about that. But I'm also on your side, the side that wants Jasmine and Ian talking again, even if it's only to engineer an amicable and fair break-up plan with minimum damage to all parties. So you have to be straight with me. It's really important that you are.'

The open concern on his face made me feel shabby. 'I didn't set out to deceive you.'

He waved his hand. 'Let's just re-cap. You don't know where Matty is right at this moment. That's the state of play, isn't it?'

'Yes, but there's a man . . .'

David raised his eyebrows.

'. . . an old friend, lives in Bristol. It's possible she might be staying with him. I'm going down tomorrow.'

'And you think Jasmine will be there?'

'I don't know. I can't get her to answer my calls. There's a good chance.'

He gave me a searching look. 'You're going tomorrow?'

'First thing.'

'Ring me when you get down there.'

'Soon as I know anything. I promise.'

He stood up. 'Well. I'll report back to Ian. What can I say, except I hope for everyone's sake she's there.'

Before he stepped through the front door, I slid my keys off the hall table, snapped Jaz's spare key off the fob and, without explanation, fumbled it into his hand. He pocketed it without comment or fuss; I can't tell you how grateful I was for that.

The evening was another warm one, so I went round opening upstairs windows to let some air through. In the back bedroom that had once been Jaz's, I unhooked the latch and leaned out over the garden. The light was fading and fine textures were more or less gone, but I could still make out distinct colours and shapes. House martins gabbled under the eaves somewhere near, and traffic passed distantly. Then, overlaying these sounds, came a strange, light, repetitive thumping from the direction of Laverne's. It was one of those noises you don't notice at first, like a tap dripping – and then when you do, you can't hear anything else. *Thunk, du-dum. Thunk, du-dum.*

I craned to see what it was. Funny she wasn't out herself, because it must be driving her mad, what with her artistic nature. *Thunk, du-dum.* After thirty seconds there was a lull, and a football rolled into view across their lawn. Josh appeared, slouching after it, bending and scooping. As he turned he raised his face in my direction, but he didn't acknowledge me. He walked back out of sight with the ball under his arm, and then the noise started again. Kick, hit-bounce. Kick, hit-bounce. A troubled boy booting a football against brick in the gathering dark, his mother inside, registering each sulky resonance. *Fuck you all, fuck you all.*

I closed the window against the sound, and went downstairs to turn on the TV.

CHAPTER 24

Photograph 122, Album Two

Location: woodland, Alnwick, 1976

Taken by: Carol

Subject: Phil, wearing a maroon velvet jacket, sitting astride a tree trunk and pretending he's on a horse.

Earlier that afternoon, he made the mistake of asking why she looked so down when they're supposed to be on holiday and enjoying themselves.

Out it all pours, how she's thought over and over she was pregnant then found she wasn't, how she might never have children, how she's failed as a wife. 'If I don't have children, I think I'll die,' she says melodramatically.

'Rubbish,' he says, ruffling her hair. 'We've not been married five minutes.'

Over a year, thinks Carol. Long enough.

But Phil doesn't seem the slightest bit concerned that he might be hitched to a barren woman. Instead he starts talking about his so-called super-sperm, demonic white tadpoles that wear little cloaks and have magical powers. 'They're waiting,' he says, 'for that special egg. An everyday egg won't do. It's got to be a top-grade one. Nothing but the best.' He mimes the sperm's wiggly journey, acts their expressions as they search and reject, and search again. He gives them the voice of David Niven in A Matter of Life and Death.

Then he takes her in his arms and puts his lips to hers. The clouds scud over their heads and the grass quivers around them.

This is what he's good at: when she leans on him, when she lets him be the man.

I put on old clothes for travelling, then swapped them for something smarter, then changed back into old again. Bristol was a long way. I was standing in front of the mirror, wondering how I wanted to look when I met the man who'd wrecked my daughter's head, when the doorbell rang.

To my surprise, it was David.

'I'm going out,' I said.

'I know. That's why I'm here.'

It took me a moment before I understood. 'You want to come with me?'

'If you'll let me, I'd like to drive you down. It's a good three hours and I know your car's still crimped. I'd wait outside when we got there. I wouldn't interfere – that's very much not my agenda – or I'd come in with you, if that's what you wanted. Whatever suited you. I'd just like to be involved.'

I said, 'Phil's taking me.'

'I see.'

'Sorry,' I said. 'I should have mentioned it. But thanks ever so much for coming round.'

'All right. But you will give me a ring when you get there? To let me know what's . . .' He trailed off, frowning. 'Can you hear music? Or am I hallucinating?'

He was right, it was my mobile. By the time I'd hunted it down, the screen was displaying Missed Call, but I knew it was

Phil. I left David where he stood, took myself into the kitchen and rang straight back.

'Ah, Carol,' said Phil. 'I am still coming round, but I might be a bit late. Something's happened.'

'Something?'

There was shouting in the background, a woman's voice.

'Pen's here. She wants— *No, it isn't. Wait. Wait! There's no need!*' I heard him mutter an aside, then his voice became loud again. 'I didn't know she was coming. She wants to pick up some stuff.'

'Phil, I need to get down there.'

'Yeah, I'll be with you, soon as I've got rid of her.'

'Fine,' I said crisply.

'Don't be like that.'

'I'm not being like anything. Obviously there are still things you need to sort out. Don't bother coming over, I'm setting off now.'

And I clicked the phone closed.

I came back out into the hall where David was writing something on my telephone pad. 'I was going to see myself out,' he said.

'If it's three hours to Bristol,' I said to him, 'we'd better get going, hadn't we?'

The first part of the drive was completed in silence. My head was all Phil, all anger and humiliation and disappointment and images of bloody Penny, bloody bloody Pen, jowly cow blundering into my life, buggering everything up again and again and again! God, I hated her.

Two feet away from David I sat and stewed in my own thick fog of loathing; when that began to disperse, I remembered where we were going, and then it was fear enveloped me instead. I sat clutching the seat belt, trying to work out how I'd cope if we got there and there was no Matty, no Jaz, and why should she be there? This was a longer-than-long shot, I was only setting myself up for a fall. I tried not to imagine her opening the door to me, Matty behind her, peeping round her legs. I tried not to imagine my grandson tottering forward for a hug, me lifting him up and squeezing him to my chest, his hair against my cheek, his hot smooth skin brushing my lips as I kissed him and kissed him. And the more I strained to banish the pictures, the clearer they became till they were as sharp as real memories.

David was saying something. It was like someone speaking to you from the poolside when your head's underwater: '—if you get car sick. Wind the window down if you need it.'

'I'm fine,' I snapped. I felt as though his interruption had foiled an actual reunion. When I glanced across, his expression was completely neutral. Was it just a front? Was he, secretly, as churned up as me? Why did he have to call me out of myself like that? Now I was wrong-footed, on top of everything else. The miles were rolling away under us and I wasn't prepared. 'Sorry, I'm a bit tense.'

'Or we can have the radio on if you want background noise.' He pushed a button on his dashboard, and something busy and classical came out of the speakers.

'No, thanks.'

He switched the music off. We covered another silent mile.

'Who are we going to see, exactly?'

'Oh. Her ex, sort of. Although she's not been in touch with him since she was married, her friend told me.'

'And what do we know about him?'

'Only that Jaz dated him at university, and that it was quite serious. The break-up was what started her illness, I think.'

I wasn't going to tell David about the abortion. No one was hearing that.

I said, 'I suppose Ian's in a state.'

'He's pretty wound up, yes. Though still very aware that whatever Jaz is up to, he started the whole business. That's holding him down at the moment. I don't know how long for.'

'Does he know about today?'

'He's had to go into work.'

'On a Saturday?'

'Some kind of project crisis that won't wait. No point dragging him away from that, stressing him out over what might be a wild-goose chase. I'll tell him when I get home,' said David, as if there were nothing to debate about such a strategy. Imagine having offspring who respected your opinion like that, who assumed you knew what you were doing, who were prepared to put their life into your hands.

By the outskirts of Birmingham, the traffic had grown much heavier. We passed huge, thundering lorries with wheel arches as high as my head. The landscape on either side was hoardings and warehouses and factories and banks of transformers. Wires criss-crossed the skyline.

I said, 'One thing I've realised, I don't know my son-in-law at all. Not even slightly.'

'If it's any consolation, I think he took us all by surprise.'

Here came a truck with a yellow digger on the back, but I had no one to point it out to.

'When you look back, though, can you see where the affair came from?'

David was silent for a long while. I thought he'd decided not to answer, or perhaps he'd shaken his head and I'd not seen. The traffic became mesmerising if you gazed at it for too long.

Suddenly he said, 'What you have to understand about Ian is, he has absolutely no self-confidence.'

'I can't believe that,' I said. 'His background. His education.'

'You're confusing confidence with being well turned-out, polite, nicely spoken. It's not the same thing, Carol. I've trained Ian over the years to come across as relatively easy with himself, but it's a veneer. I don't know how far even Jasmine appreciates that, for all the time they've spent together. She may not. He's become adept at disguise.'

I found myself staring at a row of grey and beige tower blocks, imagining myself transported there, my own face to the window, watching the distant cars.

'Do you think it comes down to having a difficult childhood? Losing his mum?'

'Oh, it started before that. Long before. When Ian was born, there were babies in cribs either side who lay like dolls and never made a murmur. Ian was fretful from the minute he came out; I could almost have told you then we'd have trouble at nursery, and starting school, and changing classes, and that every little setback would be a crisis. In a sense he didn't cope too badly with Jeanette dying, in that his life then was one drama after another, so that just became one more to deal with. I did my best, under the circumstances.

'He calmed down as he got older, grew a thicker skin, learned the social graces. I'd say he enjoyed certainly the sixth form and university. Barring a couple of hiccups.

'Then he married your daughter, a woman – let's be frank – in a completely different league from anyone else he's ever dated. Not that he'd had many girlfriends to begin with.'

'Surely if he felt like that, he'd have hung onto Jaz all the more tightly?'

'Why do some women who've had a violent upbringing go on to choose a violent partner? Or girls whose mothers had them too young fall pregnant themselves before they're able to cope with a baby? Why do people drink too much, or take harmful drugs, or get themselves repeatedly into debt? We all come with a self-destruct button, Carol, it's just that some of us are better at resisting than others. My guess is that when this woman threw herself at him, flattery scrambled his brains. The boost to his confidence eclipsed everything else. Even, momentarily, his love for Jasmine and Matty.'

Excuse-lines from Phil echoed in the back of my mind: *You and Jaz make me feel the odd one out. Sometimes I think I'm invisible to you. It's like I come last in this house.*

'I hope you're not suggesting Jaz is to blame?' I said. 'It's not her fault she's beautiful. You know, he's had *nothing* but kindness off our family.'

'It's not an excuse,' said David. 'Just an attempt at explanation. Anyway, I could be wrong. He doesn't speak to me about it. By the way,' he nodded at the plaster across my knuckles, 'what happened to your hand?'

'Oh. Silly accident.'

'Argument with a cheese-grater?'

'Not exactly.'

To tell him, or not. He waited while I decided, and it was knowing I didn't have to say any more that made me want to.

'God, it's so stupid. I punched a wall.'

'And why did you do that?'

'I don't know. I had this mad moment last night where suddenly I didn't know what to do with myself, I just needed to thump something. I hope that doesn't sound too disturbed.'

'Can I suggest a cushion next time?'

In spite of everything, he made me smile. 'It's not me. I don't do things like that. Unless I'm someone different from who I thought I was.'

'That's always possible.'

We were out of the city now and into countryside. The pressure in the car was less somehow, even though every revolution of the wheels brought me closer to Jaz, or to her absence.

'A month after Jeanette died,' said David, 'I tried to dig up a tree root in the garden. That was idiotic of me, because really it needed experts in with proper equipment. But I wasn't bothered about that, I just wanted to attack something. I used a pick and a spade and I went at it non-stop for two hours, and by the end I'd taken all the skin off the palms of both hands. They were so bad I had to go up to the surgery to have them dressed. I couldn't drive for a week.'

'Oh, God.'

'Time moves on. This too shall pass. It will, Carol.'

Much later, as we were getting ready to come off the motorway, I realised there was something else I needed to get off my chest.

'I feel as though I should say sorry.'

'What for?'

'Shouting at you. What I said about, you know.' *No wonder Ian's like he is.*

'You feel you should, but you don't especially want to?'

I blushed. 'That's about it, yes. It seemed important at the time. Now, compared with everything else that's happened – And it wasn't really my business anyway. And I should have let you have your say. Those are the bits I'm sorry for.'

'A selective apology.' He rubbed his wrist strap, stretched his shoulders back in his seat. 'Well, you were selectively right, if it's any consolation. Not about all of it; you don't know the details and I'm not prepared to share those because it would mean breaking a promise. Although, if anyone would have understood, it would have been you.'

'I don't want to hear.'

But I was thinking about those stories you read in magazines: people with partners who were very badly disabled or ill, open marriages, marriages where one person simply didn't want sex and the other had been left stranded. Perhaps it was one of these he was talking about. Perhaps not. Perhaps you could never ever justify that kind of deceit.

He said, 'I hope you know me well enough by now to appreciate I'm not wholly devoid of morals. There were special circumstances. It wasn't a bad thing I was doing, at least I didn't think it was when it started, but I ended it because it didn't sit right with me. I got drawn in against my better judgement. The way it began, I thought I couldn't say no without hurting someone I thought a lot of . . . No, I've already said too much.'

'Let's leave it there, then,' I said.

'Let's,' he said.

At last I sat back and let my mind drift. Ian showing me the picture of the pram he'd marked in the catalogue. Ian opening their fridge and counting up the jars of cling peach pieces Jaz had stockpiled to satisfy her pregnancy cravings. Jaz lifting up her skirt and showing me the veins in her legs. Jaz unfolding the kick chart that the midwife had given her, the little blocks shaded with ink that meant the baby was alive. Meeting Ian at the entrance to the maternity ward, neither of us able to shape a coherent sentence. Laughing at Phil because he brought in a packet of make-up remover tissues instead of baby wipes. The way Ian leaned protectively over Jaz to shield her when she was breastfeeding. Her expression as the wedding car drove off. Ian sitting next to Dad's bed, reading him articles from the local paper. Ian reading to Matty at bedtime and putting on a high-pitched voice for a mouse. Matty standing up in his cot, pointing at a teddy he'd thrown onto the floor. Six-week-old Matty strapped into his baby carrier, asleep on Ian's back. Matty asleep on my sofa, while I sat by him and watched over him.

'It's saying junction nineteen.' David nodded at the satnav screen. 'So the next one.'

I pulled down the mirror to check my lipstick. Behind me on the back seat Jacky materialised, wedding hat and all. She became the Baroness, who became Penny. *You're nothing, any of you*, I told them, pushing the mirror back up and vanishing them with a flip.

When I looked out of the window, we were crossing the estuary, into Bristol.

CHAPTER 25

Photograph 468, Album Four

Location: the back garden, Sunnybank

Taken by: Carol

Subject: Jaz and Ian, the week before their wedding. Jaz is throwing her head back at something Ian's said, and he's smiling because he's pleased he's made her laugh, and oh, the look of love in his eyes.

Clifton turned out to be a place of Georgian terraces set on hills. As we cruised along, counting off street names, I turned my head this way and that, hoping against sanity to catch a glimpse of Jaz and Matty. Was that Spar one she'd been in, buying milk, bread, bananas for Matty? Every young woman we passed had me leaning forward, eyes screwed up for maximum focus. If I could have conjured her through mere wanting, she'd have been there in an instant.

'We're here,' said David as we turned down a lane of tall pastel houses. 'Are you all right?'

I'd had my eyes closed for a moment, praying. 'Not really.'

'Shall I walk you across?'

'No, I'll be fine. Watch for me, though.'

'Of course.' He reached across and opened the door for me.

Tomasz won't be in, I thought. He'll still be at work or with friends or in town or whatever it is young men do these days. The desperation to see Jaz and Matty again was like the heel of a hand pressing against my throat. Let them be there, I thought. I'll do anything. Then: He won't be in, he won't be in. These games we play with fate, as if we have any control over anything.

The building that had looked smart from a distance was shabbier when you got close up, the lawn scraggy and full of weeds. Multiple buzzers and name tags revealed flats, not a single house. I pressed *Ramzinski*, and waited.

He was in. The door opened and a broad, good-looking blond man in an open-necked shirt hung onto the doorframe. 'Yeah?' he said. An excited sports commentary boomed somewhere behind him.

The words were sticky in my mouth. 'Is Jasmine in?'

His look told me she wasn't.

'You are Tomasz Ramzinski?'

'Yeah.'

'I'm looking for Jaz Morgan.'

'*Jaz*? She isn't here. Why would she be?'

'I'm her mother.' Knowing David was across the road, looking out for me, made me braver. 'Has she been in touch? Do you know where she is?'

'No, no idea. Don't know. Sorry, I can't help you.' He started to close the door.

'Could I come in for just a minute?'

Tomasz looked doubtful.

'Just for a minute, please. I won't keep you. I'm really desperate.'

He backed off enough for me to step up and inside, and we stood in the open hallway, eyeing each other.

'I'll be blunt,' I said. 'My daughter's missing and I'm concerned over her whereabouts.'

'Shit,' he said, with a nod at sympathy. Behind him, the high ceiling was cracked between the coving and picture rail, and there was dust on the skirting, old flyers littering the floor tiles.

'I know you were . . . involved at one point. When did you last speak to her?'

He shrugged. 'Not for ages. Since she was going to get married. We used to email, but then she met this guy and it stopped. Nothing since then. We're talking, I dunno, maybe three years. When you say missing, is it, like, you should go to the police or something?'

I shook my head quickly. 'We had a row. I only want to find her and say sorry. Know she's OK. She has a little boy. My grandson.'

'Shit,' he said again.

'Have you any idea at all where she might be?'

'Nope.'

'You can't think of anyone she might have gone to? Anyone from Leeds? Anyone you used to email about?'

He folded his muscular arms and leaned against the grubby wall. 'God, I don't know. She used to hang about with a girl called Sam, ages back; no idea where she is, though.'

'I know where Sam is.'

All at once I had his attention. He detached himself from the wall and let his arms drop to his sides. 'Yeah? Holy fuck, where?'

'She didn't go far. Headingly.'

'No way! She left – did she come back, then?'

'Evidently.'

'Aw, for real?' He grinned and shook his head at the marvellous irony. 'She doing all right?'

'Yes, she's fine. She has a baby. But what I need to know is—'

'A kid? No way.'

'A little boy, yes. She seemed to be doing fine. But what I—'

'How did you know where to find her?'

'In my daughter's address book.'

'What? Jaz had her address? All that time?' Tomasz's expression changed to one of disbelief. 'Fucking hell. So when I was emailing her and Sam got mentioned and she said she didn't know – Fuck. Do you know it? Can you remember the house number and the street?'

I took a step forward. 'What can you tell me about my daughter? What don't I know that might help me find her?'

His lips puckered round half-formed words as he weighed up the deal.

'Come up,' he said.

What I saw first as I walked into his flat was a huge black and white photograph. It hung above the marble mantel, dominating the room: Tomasz, during a game of rugby, mid-pass. His fair hair flicked out as he turned to grasp the ball, and his jaw was set, the cords in his neck standing out. The thighs were rounded, straining against his shorts, and his boots dug into mud, a sliding pivot before his blurred team mates. It was a moment beautifully captured; when your own muscles react in sympathy, that's a good action shot. He saw me looking, and smiled briefly. He just likes the photo because it's of himself, I thought.

The rest of the room was decently furnished, but messy. He'd spread all the sections of a weekend newspaper across the floor, and there was a plate of crumbs beside it. Golf clubs leaned against the chimney-breast and a series of trophies lined the mantelpiece. The rest of the clutter was mainly magazines and mugs and items of clothing. The sweater draped over the back of the chair was surely a woman's.

Tomasz muted the widescreen TV while I sat on the edge of his man-size sofa.

'So how was she?' he said. 'Is she married?'

For a mad second I thought he meant Jaz. 'I'll give you Sam's address and you can see for yourself,' I said coldly, struggling to contain my temper.

He was scrabbling for a pen almost before I'd finished the sentence.

'I can't believe Jaz never let on they were still in touch. I can't believe she kept it from me.' Then he paused, Biro in hand. 'Actually, yeah, I can.'

I said: 'You must know you hurt my daughter very much.'

'We split up. People do. It's shit, but there you go.'

I was imagining myself unsheathing one of his golf clubs and swinging it full pelt against his TV screen, his portrait, his pretty face. 'Sam told me about the abortion.'

He looked sick then.

'What can I say?'

'You can tell me why you didn't give her the support she needed. Why didn't you go with her?'

'Where to?'

'The clinic. It was your baby.'

'She didn't want me to.'

'I find that hard to believe,' I said. I watched his neck grow pinker, his eyes flick away from me.

'She went with her personal tutor. That's who she wanted.'

'Jaz wasn't on her own, then?'

'No. She stayed with him and his wife afterwards.'

'What: in his house?'

'Yeah.'

'How long for?'

'A couple of days.'

'What was his name? Where did he live?'

'Dunno. Can't remember.'

I hate you, I thought. I hate you so much it's all I can do not to leap up and attack you. 'How was she?'

'OK.'

'OK? You're telling me that my daughter went through an operation as traumatic as that and she was *perfectly fine* with it?'

He shook his head in irritation. 'I'm not saying it was nothing! I mean, it wasn't something she'd have chosen to go through, obviously, but she really wasn't that cut up about it. I think she saw it as something she had to get done. Like, like going to the dentist.' He saw my face, forestalled me. 'Just, don't, yeah? Don't even say it. You might not want to hear all this, Mrs Morgan, but it's how it was, that's how it was for her. I was there, I saw. I fucking saw, right? She was strung out and pissed off, but she wasn't running round in tears.'

'Some people show grief in different ways!'

'Sure, but – honestly, Jaz wasn't that affected.'

'So not affected she had a breakdown when she came home.'

'Did she?' He looked properly taken aback then. 'Shit. She never said. I didn't know that.'

'Well, you wouldn't, would you? I presume you didn't bother contacting her in those months after she left Leeds, or you'd have known.'

Tomasz shifted, and hooked his thumbs defensively in his jeans pockets.

'Look, don't try and pin that on me. None of us were in touch at that time. I don't know what Sam told you, but the three of us got blown apart. It all just went – it was a fucking mess. Jaz didn't want to see me. Boy, did she not want to see me. Then Sam disappeared off the map. Then I start getting emails from Jaz again, then a couple of years down the line she meets this bloke she wants to marry and I'm dropped again. Seems to me like she was the one calling the shots. Took me all my time just to keep up with her.'

'Then why was she so desperately upset? Why did she lie in bed for weeks and need me to help get her up and dressed every day as though she was some kind of invalid? Tell me that!'

As I sat looking up at him, trembling with rage, he only shook his head pityingly. 'You really don't get your daughter at all, do you?' Then he walked away from me so he was standing in front of the hearth, underneath his own vast image.

'It was Andy Spicer dying,' he said. 'Did Sam fill you in on that stuff?'

'But that wasn't Jaz's fault!'

'Not that Sam knew, really, not the whole story. I'll tell you why Jaz was wrecked over it: because she thought she was responsible.'

I tried again to protest, but he spoke right over me, his tone low and dangerous.

'And she was responsible, in a way. Those two, her and Sam, teasing him and drawing him in. Big old joke that was. Then – and this is the bit Sam doesn't know, God help her – Jaz went round to his flat and spun him this lie about how Sam really did love him, and if he went back and crawled to her, she'd be his for the taking. Totally set the poor bastard up. 'Cause he was like, he was really into her – into Sam, I mean. Then afterwards, the two of them were laughing about him to his face. *To his face*, Mrs Morgan. Within his hearing, anyway.'

'They didn't know he was going to—'

'No, none of us did. None of us did.' His face creased up in disgust. I could only guess what scenes he was playing out in his head.

'And you didn't tell anyone about what Jaz had said to this boy?'

'For fuck's sake, it was enough of a mess!'

I was floundering, trying to imagine why she'd have done something so cruel. Whatever I didn't understand about her, I knew she was never like that. It must have been Sam's fault, or Tomasz's, or maybe she thought this Andy really did stand a chance. His parents standing in a courtroom to hear how he died. Maybe the whole tale was all lies, from start to finish.

'Did Jaz love you very much?' I heard myself say.

Tomasz exhaled raggedly, the breath of someone struggling to contain themselves in the face of unbelievable provocation, and for a moment I experienced a flicker of fear. But then he shrugged and half-turned away towards his row of shiny trophies. He said, 'We were really young, everything was weird – you could never tell who was being serious.'

Did you love her? I wanted to ask, but I didn't dare. I think I knew the answer.

'Anyway, that's all there is,' he said, facing me again, straightening his back aggressively. 'I've told you everything I can think of, whether you like it or not. Can I have Sam's address now?'

Your version, I thought, that's what you've told me. I took the pad of paper he'd placed on the sofa arm and scribbled something down off the top of my head. There was no way I was letting him near Sam's little boy. I'd have liked to tear the page out, screw it into a tight ball and throw it at him, but I was afraid that once I gave full vent, I'd not be able to stop. The moment I'd put my pen down, Tomasz lunged and snatched the pad off me, scanning it greedily.

'Are you sure this is right?' he snapped.

'Quite sure.'

I wondered whether he could tell I was lying, and what he might do to me if he guessed.

'Good. Get out, then.'

I stood up, and tottered towards the door.

'Oh, and Mrs Morgan,' I heard him say behind me. 'One last thing. When you leave here, yeah, go to the end of the street, turn left, and then *fuck off out of my life.*'

'Drive,' I said to David as I closed the car door. He revved the engine the way they do in cop shows, and the car shot forward.

'Where?' he said.

I didn't answer.

We travelled through wide and gracious streets that took us gradually upwards. On another day it would have been pleasant to look out at the cream-coloured houses with their balconies and hanging baskets, the shops with their striped awnings, but my vision was all poisoned with Tomasz.

After a few minutes, David pulled in under a line of trees, braked, and switched off the engine. 'Come here,' he said, turning in his seat. I leaned across and he gathered me in against his chest.

'She wasn't there,' he said.

'No.'

'Have you found out where they are?'

'No.'

'Do you want to tell me what happened?'

'I can't, not all of it. He's a horrible man. Let me just—'

His grip tightened. 'I'm sorry, Carol.'

'For Ian, you mean.'

'For all of us. For you.'

He went on holding me, and I imagined a pair of satellite

beams coming down, one on our car and one fixing Jaz wherever she was, like a mathematical compass. All it came down to was two points on a map; a simple straight line could connect us, if only I had that knowledge. Sometimes it's the straightforwardness of a situation that drives you mad.

CHAPTER 26

Photograph 632, Album Five

Location: Carol's sofa

Taken by: Laverne

Subject: baby Matty, swaddled like a papoose, lying across Carol's lap with his eyes closed in blissful sleep. Everyone is sagging with relief because the marathon crying session's finally over. 'You've certainly got the magic touch, Carol,' Laverne says as she squints through the viewfinder. 'Oh yes, Grandma knows best,' says Dorothy Wynne.

*   At the edge of the shot you can see Jaz's hand reaching across to reclaim him.*

When the call came next day it was David, not Ian.

'What was his reaction?' I asked fearfully.

'I need to see you, to explain,' he said. 'Are you in this afternoon?'

'Helping at the County Show. Akela's dad's been rushed into hospital, and they're an adult short to oversee the hot drinks.'

'And you can't get out of it?'

'I promised, they're expecting me.'

'I'll see you there, then.'

Which is why he found me with my ear against a tea urn, trying to listen for sounds of bubbling. 'I don't know whether this is working,' I explained. 'How long do you think it takes to boil something this size?'

David touched the side lightly with his fingertips. 'When did you switch it on?'

'Half an hour ago.'

'Should be on the way by now.'

'That's what I thought.'

Boys in green sweatshirts buzzed around the tables shaking out paper cloths, setting down sugar bowls, unstacking chairs in a scene of cheery industry.

'And the generator's working?' David was saying.

'Definitely. Can't you hear it?'

He left the urn and followed the lead to the back of the tent while I made up two big containers of orange squash. A minute later he was back.

'I've pressed the re-set button. It should be fine now,' he said. 'Is there anything else I can do to speed things up here? When can you get away?'

'Soon as Dove gets here, but she was having a replacement windscreen fitted this morning so she can't come till that's finished.'

'It really is all go, isn't it?'

'Chaos in every area.' And I thought of the clearing I'd been doing at two that morning, unable to sleep and so turning out more of the accumulated junk of the last eight years.

Charlie Blunt appeared at my elbow with a column of shrink-wrapped plastic cups he couldn't open. While I was wrestling with that, two Cubs larking about burst a full bag of sugar over the grass.

'I'll go and have a wander,' said David, 'come back when

you're less rushed. You need to give your full attention to what I've got to tell you.'

As he walked away, I felt the panic begin to unstring me again.

He was waiting by the birds of prey tent opposite. I came up by his side, and we watched a falconer trying to coax a buzzard off his glove and onto a perch. The bird kept baulking and flapping its wings, but the man persisted until at last the buzzard settled where he wanted it. Then it sat, swivelling its head in a way that made me feel ashamed for looking.

'Ian's making an appointment with a solicitor first thing,' said David. 'I think it's time. I feel that if she'd had any intention of getting back with him, she'd have been in contact.'

'We don't know that for sure.'

'Some men would have been to the police by now.'

'Ian wouldn't do that.'

'He's talked about it. I've told him to wait.'

I couldn't help marvelling once again at the level of influence David held over his son.

'But if the situation carries on much longer, Carol—'

'I know.'

'So he'll get an application for contact in place, and the moment Jasmine reappears, we can start it moving through the courts.'

What if she still blocks him? I was thinking. But David was ahead of me.

'If the application's approved,' he went on, 'and I can't see any reason why it wouldn't be, then she'll have to comply. Breaking the terms of a contact order can be serious. Ultimately, you can go to prison for it.'

'Oh my God.'

'I don't mean to frighten you, I'm just saying, that's the law.

Fathers' rights. Ian's rights.' He patted my shoulder in what I assumed was an attempt to reassure.

'I wish she'd just come home!' I burst out.

Some of the birds shifted on their perches, talons flexing nervously.

'She'll have to, sooner or later. There's too much needs attention. Her books, her work, Ian says half her clothes are still in the wardrobe. There are people she'd need to notify, health visitors and such. Even if you don't know exactly where she is right now, Carol, she hasn't vanished into the ether.'

'She'd leave clothes, she wouldn't be bothered about coming back for them. Not if she's decided to keep away.'

'I agree if she was on her own she might be able to melt into the crowds, but she's got Matty with her. He has no passport, he'll need registering with a doctor if she settles for any length of time. We know Jasmine's car registration. When her savings run out she'll have to start using cash machines, and then we can check the joint bank statements.' David counted off each point on his fingers. 'It might take a little while, but we'd find her.'

He took my arm and began to lead me back from the pen, away from the tents and people, towards the boundary of the field. As we drew near the hawthorn hedge he said, 'And look at it this way, Carol: once a proper framework's in place, it'll be easier for them to talk to each other.'

'Jaz hates being told what to do, though.'

'It wouldn't be a case of that. I'm talking about a formal dialogue, Jasmine working with a solicitor to draw up terms and responses she approves.'

'So the marriage is over.'

His pause told me all I needed to know.

'But even if they divorce, they can still work as a team for Matty. I believe Jasmine will do that, when it comes to the crunch. Don't you?'

'I want to say yes.'

Soon the showground would be open. Marshalls in fluorescent jackets stalked between the stands, reeled out cables, consulted clipboards, spoke into two-way radios. The public would stream in: hundreds of families enjoying a sunny day, with no idea how lucky they were.

'There's one thing I need to ask you,' I went on. 'You know what you said once, about me being like the postman or the butcher?'

David looked puzzled.

'You said,' I went on, 'that if I tried to get access to Matty, I'd have no chance because I had no legal rights. Was that it, or did I misunderstand? Because I was thinking, maybe *I* could apply for a contact order as well, if necessary.'

He was looking puzzled. 'You? A contact order?'

'She was pretty cross with me before she went.'

'Not so cross she'd block you from seeing Matty.'

I'm never letting you near him again, I heard her say. *You just can't be trusted, can you?* 'I only want to make sure where I stand.'

'What exactly did she say to you, Carol? Did she say she wouldn't let you see him?'

Over the rustling of the trees I could hear the megaphone squawking a way off, and someone playing 'Heaven is a Place on Earth'. I said, 'She came out with a lot of things, the way you do when you've had a shock. When she comes home, we can talk it through. But I thought it was as well to know the legal position. That's all.'

We began to walk along the edge of the field. It felt pleasant to match his pace, to be physically close to someone bigger and stronger than myself, who smelled of good aftershave and who knew where he was going.

'A couple of years back,' he said, 'I was on a train to

London. There was a lad, a youth, swearing into his phone, legs sprawling out in the aisle so everyone who went past had to step over them. The carriage was packed and the language wasn't nice. No one said anything for a while; you know what people are like. But then he started playing thumping music with offensive lyrics, very aggressive. An elderly man in the seat behind him stood up, looked over and asked him politely to turn it down or put his headphones on. The boy ignored him, so the man's friend, also in his sixties or seventies, I'd guess, stood up and repeated the request. This time, the response was a volley of abuse and the volume cranked up.'

'What did you do?' I was waiting for some tale of heroism on his part: how David, the voice of confident reason, saved the day.

'Nothing, to my shame. The boy was a few rows down from me, and I was busy working on my laptop. I suppose I decided it wasn't my problem.'

'Well,' I said, 'people get knifed for interfering these days. So what happened?'

'The two old men started singing.'

'Singing?'

'That's right. I hadn't realised before, but they were part of a group, some choir or other. When I looked properly, the carriage was full of white-haired men in blue blazers – on their way to a performance, I assume, or back from one. These two struck up with "Bye Bye Blackbird", and within a few bars there were twenty, thirty doing all the descants. It was loud, too. *A capella* can be deafening at close quarters. They completely drowned out the boy. By the time they'd got to the third verse, he'd gathered his stuff together and stomped off to another section of the train. We never saw him for the rest of the journey.'

As David had been speaking, I was seeing it unfold, watching the delighted expressions spread from seat to seat, hearing the swelling chords, feeling the buzz that comes from being united. 'Oh, I love that song. My dad used to sing it when he was working in the garden.'

'After they'd finished, everyone broke into a round of applause, so they launched into "The Black Hills of Dakota", and then "If I Had a Hammer". Other passengers were joining in. The whole atmosphere was like a carnival. I've never forgotten it.' David was staring into the middle distance thoughtfully. 'The shift in who controlled that carriage was amazing.'

'And?'

'It taught me a lesson. I suppose what I'm coming round to is that you mustn't ever think you're powerless. You should never sit back and assume there's no hope. If it comes to it that you do need to fight for Matty, I'll be right behind you; we'll work together, and whatever's ahead, we'll give it our best shot. Yes?'

The gates ahead of us had opened and people were streaming onto the field.

'Do you want to know something terrible?' I said. 'There are moments I think I hate my own daughter. She was such a lovely baby, I had control of her then. I suppose you think I'm awful for saying that.'

'Not awful, just honest.'

'Does it all boil down to power, in the end? All the relationships we ever have, is that what they're about?'

'You need a drink,' he said. 'So do I. Let's go find one.'

'Life is a Roller Coaster' sang the Tannoy as we picked our way forward.

I shouldn't have worn a skirt and mules, or I should have chosen a different place to go walking. Last time I'd been down the public footpath by the old railway bridge had been with

Matty, early spring, when the grass and weeds were still short. We'd watched a jackdaw pulling a tuft of wool off barbed wire, and Matty had found a pile of ash from a bonfire and paddled around in it till his shoes went grey.

Now, coming towards the end of summer, the track was waist-high nettles and sticky burr and thistles, and my calves and shins were striped with welts. It was madness to keep going, but I did, stamping down the taller stalks so they snapped and lay prone. Every one of them felt my wrath. Ten times I'd tried phoning Jaz this evening, all the while knowing I'd get the same recorded message, but unable to stop myself.

'The difference is,' David had explained, 'Ian's name is on the birth certificate. Yours isn't. It's a crucial difference, in law.'

'But all the hundreds of hours I've spent with Matty, all the love I've given him. That counts for nothing?'

I didn't believe him, but afterwards he'd helped me Google the facts. Thirteen and a half million grandparents there were in the UK, providing a massive 60 per cent of all the country's childcare. Without our input, the job market would collapse and families go under, lose their houses, fall apart. If grandparents ever chose to go on strike, there'd be economic crisis.

And that was only looking at cold finance. What about the emotional stability we gave our grandchildren? The continuous sense of who they were, where they'd come from? We were the ones with time to spend, and experience. We held the family stories. We were the ones who passed on the great secrets of their parents' youth: that their mum was once a naughty girl, or their dad a frightened little boy. It was from us the very young often had their first exposure to disability, learning how to work round a physical restriction with practical good humour.

The love we gave was different, too: less judgemental, unclouded. Some of us had got it wrong with our own kids, but we knew the way forward now and were determined to make good. All this we did willingly and for free.

Yet if Jaz did ban me from seeing Matty, I wouldn't have a leg to stand on.

Theoretically, as David said, I could try for a contact order, but to do that I'd first have to approach the court and request permission to apply for one. Like having to ask for a key to a cupboard in which was locked the key to your door. Throughout the legal proceedings, the onus would be on me to prove I had a meaningful relationship with my grandson (even though I worked five days a week and only had him in my spare time and had once nearly drowned him). Matty, my very best advocate, would be able to contribute nothing.

I'd read that, in the end, the vast majority of applications by grandparents were unsuccessful, and even where they won, the order for access was often ignored. The whole process would involve officials and reports and standing up in court, and would last for months, and cost a small fortune. And there were a million others like me, denied contact with the people they most loved in the world. The unfairness of it beggared belief.

A shadow fell across the field in front of me, and I looked up. Against the summer evening sky a red balloon drifted, clean and bright, like an illustration from a children's book. 'Look', I longed to say to Matty. 'Give them a wave!'

The balloon was rising steadily as I watched, the basket suspended like a matchbox underneath. Then the flame shot up, orange against the blue, and I thought, How amazing that a tiny jet of fire can raise that huge structure hundreds of feet. Incredible. For a few moments I was up there with them, out of myself and carried along.

I head Eileen's voice: *If you had the chance to see into your own future, would you take it?* God, I would! We'd had a weekend at Blackpool, just after I was married – her, me, Phil – and she'd been eyeing up the clairvoyants' caravans along the sea-front. 'No,' I'd said, in answer to her question. She'd laughed at me and called me a coward. Later that night, and drunk, she'd laid half a chicken pie on the top step of a caravan. 'Let's see if Gypsy Romana predicts *that* when she comes skipping out tomorrow morning.' 'Like they sleep in their vans,' Phil had scoffed, and they'd had a bit of a fight. She never did have a reading, though, for all her talk.

The balloon passed over the allotments, and on towards town. Ahead of me the track ended in a stile, but so lost in nettles I knew I'd never stand a chance of getting near. I'd gone as far as I could. The light was changing, and it was time to go home.

On the way back towards the bridge, I began toying with the idea of ringing Jaz again. Part of me knew this was not the way, that she hated any kind of pursuit. Then again, if I didn't try, would she realise how desperately I was missing her? Maybe, in the end, I'd wear her down. Maybe I'd catch her at a mellow moment, if she had any mellow moments these days. All of a sudden, a hot flare engulfed me at the injustice, the sheer cruelty of her behaviour. *She used to cut her arms, you know*, I imagined telling a courtroom. *There's a history of insta-bility. He'd be much better off with me.*

The next second I was shaking the picture away, appalled.

'If you want an exchange of confessions,' David had said, 'then listen to this: when Jeanette died, I was relieved. I loved her, I would have gone to the ends of the earth for her, but the truth was I was weary of the months of pain and suffering and the broken nights and the visitors trooping through the house and the sense of death hanging over all of us, stringing us out. Now, does that make you think any less of me?'

I was shaken out of memory by a sudden, violent shout coming from somewhere near the bridge. 'You FUCK-ing wanker!' a girl yelled, her voice ripping across the evening. 'You *fuck*ing dickhead.'

The atmosphere of the evening changed at once. Suddenly I saw myself as I was: a lone middle-aged woman more than a mile from the nearest house and without a mobile phone. A figure shot out from under the arch, then ran back under, laughing. There was more calling, more swearing, the clatter of pebbles against stone.

'I'll *fuck*ing kill you for that! Tosser.'

I hesitated, considering whether to go forward or stay where I was. You heard about these gangs, and what they got up to. There were always stories in the paper. A man near us had literally been frightened to death by a bunch of youths; they hadn't even needed to lay a finger on him.

'You stupid fucking *prick*!'

No, better keep going. I needed to pass them to get back to the main road. If they came out and saw me, if they started shouting at me, what I'd do would be feign deafness. They wanted you to talk back, so I wouldn't give them the satisfaction. Dumbness was my best defence.

'Oi, stop! STOP!'

Was that to me? I made myself look straight ahead, my pace fast but steady. Turning back wasn't an option; the path was too overgrown. I could walk out into the middle of the field, but that would only make me more conspicuous, and if they did spot me it would be obvious what I was doing, which would attract comment in itself. Mad sandal-shod woman, flattening crops.

Best to stick with it, and hope. The path went up and over the top of the bridge, so provided these kids stayed where they were, I had no need to cross their line of vision. I risked a quick glance to the side. No sign of anyone.

'You utter fucking twat,' said the girl again.

'I can make a match burn twice,' I heard a boy say.

'Fuck off.'

More laughter, and a whoop. It was impossible to tell how many of them there were, or how old. I moved my steps away from the centre of the path, where the grit crunched, onto the muffled grass.

'That was my hair,' whined the girl.

'Aw, kiss it better.' There was a burst of tinny music, and someone threw what might have been a coloured plastic lighter out onto the grass.

I visualised David's train carriage, the blue-suited white-haired men standing to defeat the forces of yobbism. Where was a passing *a capella* group when you needed one? A memory flashed on me of Dad humming while he shaved in the kitchen, his mirror propped on the eye-level grill pan and a dish of water on the cold gas ring. Black and white tiles, the kitchenette with the fold-down front and built-in shopping reminder. When I was safe and small and knew what lay in front of me each day.

'Give it us back, you little shit!'

And David's voice went, *Get a grip, Carol. This is a public footpath and you have every right to be here, just as much as who-ever it is howling and cursing under the arch. Look, they probably won't come out, and even if they do, why should they be interested in you? You're not hassling them. You're quite clearly walking away, minding your own business. Forget what you've read in the news-papers; they have to scare to sell. Kids being noisy in a deserted spot isn't the crime of the century. They're not harming anyone. Just keep going. Put your shoulders back. Steady your breathing.*

In my mind, Dad still hummed 'Bye Bye Blackbird', haunt-ingly. I slowed my pace to match the rhythm of the song, and lifted my chin. It did help, a bit.

At the start of the bridge rise, a track strewn with litter

branched off down the bank and, as I passed it, a boy wandered out from under the arch, scanning the ground. I watched him nervously out of the corner of my eye. There was something familiar about the back of his head.

'Give it up,' called the girl. 'It was knackered anyway.'

The boy lifted his head to shout back, and caught sight of me standing above him. I saw his lips form the word *fuck*. Josh.

'Oh my God,' continued the girl. 'See this, will you?'

Josh and I carried on staring at each other.

'I've got a text from Vic. Oh my God. Oh my God.'

Do not speak, his eyes said. *Do not go home and mention this to my mum. I don't know you and you don't know me. You owe me. Shut it.* At the same time I was taking all this in, I was thinking, He's done something to his fringe since I last saw him, it's made his face look squarer. Is that a cigarette between his fingers? Where does Laverne think he is tonight? Drama group?

'Hoy, Joshy. Come see this.'

He gave me a tiny shake of the head, just as the girl wandered out. I turned and began to walk quickly away.

'I don't fucking believe her. If she fucking thinks I'm taking any notice . . .' The girl's sentence trailed off. 'What you looking at? Who was that?'

The balloon was a red football vanishing behind far-off trees.

'No one,' I heard him say. 'It wasn't anybody.'

CHAPTER 27

Photograph 217, Album Two

Location: James House Hospice, Worsley, Manchester

Taken by: Carol

Subject: Jaz, six, is sitting on a slatted white bench, holding on to her grandma's elbow crutch. Behind her, an impressive wisteria drapes its loaded arms over the stonework of the rear wall. The hospice manager is a keen horticulturalist himself, and knows the value of a well-kept garden for those in need of earthly balm. No one crosses these soft and level lawns without feeling a degree better. A blackbird sings each evening in the conifer, as if by arrangement, and worms send up their inoffensive casts between the patients' feet. Peonies bud, bloom, drop and seed by the path; tiny nymphs squirm across the surface of the bird bath. If Carol and her mother could make any kind of peace, it would be here.

And they do find something like it, in that Carol's so far managed not to ask anything provocative – why did you have children if you didn't want them, for instance – and Frieda's refrained from making any final sour quips. It's the best that could be hoped for.

During this particular visit, her mother consents to sit outside

286

for quarter of an hour. Once she's made it to the bench, Jaz
climbs up alongside her and asks her what it's like to be dying.
You'd think Frieda would be offended, but she takes the ques-
tion in her stride. It may be that she's too tired to object.

'Don't they favour each other?' observes Bob.

'No,' says Carol, appalled.

'I meant the eyes, round the eyes,' he says. 'I've never
really noticed before.'

Carol looks, but won't see. Four to six weeks, the doctor's
said, so it makes no odds anyway.

So there we were, working alongside each other like the married
couple we used to be. Phil was unwrapping Rawlbolts on the
patio, and I was turning out kitchen drawers and cupboards and
attempting to rationalise the contents. Like that married couple,
we were holding an icy, singing silence between us that had us
both clattering about and clearing our throats just for the relief of
sound. Fit the grid and bugger off, I was thinking. I could hear his
thoughts, too, clamouring back: Bloody hell, I come round here
to help her out and she acts like she's the one doing *me* a favour.
The quarrels where no one speaks are always the noisiest.

After a while I put the radio on, and tried to follow a discussion about the European Union.

Meanwhile I pulled out tea towels still in their wrapping,
icing-bag nozzles, yet more of my mother's embroidered cloths.
Three hand-whisks, it turned out I owned – not including the
K beater for a defunct Kenwood Chef – plus four incomplete
canteens of cutlery, and a set of unused American measuring
cups. As I peeled away old lining paper, David's voice floated
in over the rest: *Why did you stay so long with Phil?*

The question, spoken in the dim back room of a country
pub, had caught me off-guard. 'For Jaz,' I'd said, as I always did.
'I thought the disruption would be too damaging for her.'

'That must have taken a lot of strength.'

'Except now Jaz claims I stayed out of cowardice, and that I ruined her childhood because I was scared to strike out on my own.'

'Wouldn't she have been disturbed if you'd split up?'

'Probably. She didn't want me to change my name after the divorce; how's that for inconsistency?'

'Had you intended to?'

'I wasn't sure. I didn't want Jaz and me not to match. And I didn't want to go backwards, to be Carol White again. Hobson's choice, really. They should let you have a special divorce name that you choose. A naming party, you could have, a special dinner or something.'

David had said that was a good idea, and then we'd just sat for ages, listening to the blare and clatter of the fruit machine round the corner, sipping our drinks. A different kind of not-talking.

The kitchen door banging against the wall made me jump.

'For God's sake!' I said.

Phil looked guilty, then irritated. 'You want a new stopper,' he said, glancing at the floor. 'You'll end up with a hole in your plaster otherwise.'

'No, because no one else flings the door open like you.'

'Two minutes of a job to screw one in.'

'I don't need one!'

We glared at each other.

This is not your house! Screw a bloody stopper in your own floor!
Jesus wept, woman, I was only making a suggestion.

'What do you want, anyway?' I said ungraciously.

'A slash,' he said, and pushed past me.

I carried on with the clearing, piling up crockery into sets.

As he came back down the stairs I could hear him whistling 'Tie a Yellow Ribbon'. Its jauntiness, and the sheer tactlessness of his choice, infuriated me beyond sanity.

'I don't think you're remotely bothered about Matty,' I snapped.

Phil's step faltered in the doorway. 'Eh?'

'You don't love Matty as much as I do, and that's the reason you're not concerned.'

He closed his eyes. 'Don't start, Carol.'

'Well, you can't do,' I said, my fingers tightening on one of my mother's Coalport plates. 'Otherwise you'd be as upset as me. Wouldn't you? *Wouldn't you?*'

'Look,' he said, 'how many times do I have to repeat myself? I love my grandson and I'll be glad when he comes home.'

'You think she'll bring him back?'

'Of course she will.'

'And let us see him?'

'I expect so.'

'"Expect so"? Dear God, have you no feelings at all?'

He put his palm to his forehead. 'I meant she will do. Jesus. You take her too seriously. You give her too much power over you.'

'That's because she *has* power!' I cried, flinging the plate downwards so it smashed onto the floor. The impact was startling. Shards of white china shot across the tiles in all directions.

'Jesus wept, Carol,' he said. 'Listen to me. I'll say it for the last time: I love Matty. Right?' I gripped the edge of the table, trembling. 'I'm just maybe not as obsessed with him as you are.'

'I'm NOT obsessed!'

'You've seen a lot of him, had him round two, three times a week—'

'Which makes it harder.'

'So, like, you've had a good run—'

I threw a second plate and it exploded into the jamb near his feet, making him jerk with shock. 'Shit. There was no need for that.'

'Had a good run? Had a *good run*?' I yelled.

'I didn't mean – oh, I don't know what I meant. Only, you're always on about him. Always. But the bottom line is, he's not your child.'

'He's my *grandson*! If it wasn't for me, he wouldn't *exist*!'

'That still doesn't make him yours.'

Images whirled around my head of Matty, me, Jaz. I thought of the early days when I'd watched her trying to breastfeed, and how I'd tried so hard not to show disappointment when she gave up at three months. I remembered him taking his first steps and not telling her because I wanted her to think they happened when she was there, and how I had to pretend surprise when she showed me his first tooth breaking through the gum. Stocking up with the very particular brand of baby food she wanted him to have, taking off the cot bumper because she said it might make him over-heat. Doing as I was told, to the letter, on every occasion. 'You talk as though I'm one of these interfering types who flout their daughter's rules and constantly tell them where they're going wrong. I've never done that. I never would.'

'It's more subtle than that, Carol. You, you act as if he's yours.'

'But—' I floundered for a moment. 'Don't all grandparents feel that way? It's a special bond, it's like *double* the family tie. That's why Matty's so special: he's mine, and mine again.'

When I looked up, Phil's eyes were roving over the mess of splinters that fanned out across the floor.

'Oh,' I said, 'this is pointless. I can see you don't get it at all. But then, why should you? You were a bloody awful dad, so why should you be any better at being a grandad?'

Accusation crackled between us. Snatches of past rows needled back through the airwaves, as though the house had absorbed and kept them inside its walls, waiting for a fresh bout of fighting. Suddenly the desire to hurt Phil overwhelmed any sense of the damage I might do to myself. Even when you think everything's been said about a break-up, it's amazing how much more can be dredged to the surface by a burst of real temper. Here came the rest of it, unstoppable:

'If you'd been a better father to Jaz, I bet you this situation would never have happened. She wouldn't have grown up so resentful, she'd have chosen a better husband, we'd have been a normal, stable family.'

'Jaz is just Jaz; she is who she is. Same as your mother was just your mother. You're not being fair.'

'What's fairness got to do with anything? When was fairness ever a factor in our marriage?' I saw again Mavis Pearson, that bright green blouse, her coral lipstick mouth making sympathetic shapes at me, and felt the hot prickle that comes from realising you're an object of someone's pity. 'Twenty-four years of shambles and lies; what a bloody waste of everyone's time!'

'So why did you stay, Carol?'

'I don't bloody know. Because when you want to believe someone, you do. I kept thinking it would peter out, you'd come to your senses. But you didn't.'

He was shaking his head as if he couldn't fathom things either.

'I mean, why *her*?' I'd rehearsed the question a thousand times, but never spoken it out loud because it sounded too humiliating. Now, though, I felt I had nothing to lose. '*Why her*? What in God's name makes you prefer *her* to me?'

'I don't. Not now. Not for a long time.'

'You did; of course you did. You made a choice.'

'It wasn't as simple as that. I got, I don't know, tangled up.'

'See, I can understand a slip, a one-off, like Ian made. But to go back to her, and keep going back when you said you wouldn't, and the lies are worse than the infidelity, they hurt a hell of a lot more. And everything you could have wanted was here. God, when you think of how some wives are.'

'I couldn't seem to get myself out of it.'

'You didn't want to.'

'I did. It was difficult. She wasn't—'

'Wasn't what?' I hissed.

'She wasn't strong like you are. You always got on with things. She fell apart every time I tried to finish. She couldn't cope. She needed me.'

I couldn't believe my ears. '*We* needed you! Jaz and I. Your *family*.'

'She used to threaten suicide, all sorts.'

'And you fell for it.'

'She's not—'

'Not what?'

'Stable,' he said, avoiding my gaze. 'Well, you know, don't you? Ringing Jaz up. She's very jealous, very unpredictable. She does stuff, and then she's sorry afterwards.'

'And this is the woman you chose over me?' I caught sight of my face in the glass of the oven door and I hardly recognised myself. 'So what you're saying here is, my mistake was to behave too well? I was too dignified and contained? That if I'd thrown myself down on the floor, wailing and carrying on like a lunatic, you'd have stayed? Bloody hell, Phil. Have you any idea what you've just said?' I took a step towards him, and he flinched. 'You know what? Don't *ever* let her come round here because I will kill her.'

'I've not seen you like this before,' he said in a small voice.

Before I could say any more, a tower of Worcester tea cups I'd stacked earlier toppled over, and two fell off the edge of the table and broke.

'Fuck you,' I heard myself say. Then I sat down and covered my face with my hands. I wasn't crying, I just needed to block him out for a moment.

'What if I told you,' he said cautiously, 'that she really had gone this time. For good.'

I kept my hands where they were and spoke between my fingers.

'You say what you *want* to be true.'

Now I sensed him come forward, heard him pull the chair out from under the other side of the table and sit down.

'This time it's different, Carol: I told her to go. She's taken all her gear.'

'Yeah yeah.'

'Come round and see.'

'The day hell freezes over.'

'I haven't even a washing machine.'

'You're confusing me with someone who gives a damn.'

Faint thudding rap music was coming from Laverne's. Through the open back door I could hear a lawnmower doing the last cut of the season. Opposite me, Phil sighed noisily.

'I don't know what I can say.'

'Best keep it shut, then. You've done enough damage.'

'Carol, I always loved you. I still do. It just got complicated. I painted myself into a corner.'

'Stop, please.'

'I'm sorry.'

'I'm damn sure you are.'

'If you ever took me back—'

'I said, stop it.'

He shifted on his chair and cleared his throat.

'Well. Whatever – whatever *we* are, I'm still Jaz's dad and I'm still Matty's grandad, and I'll do what I can to help you get them back. I'm fitting this grid so if you have to go to court, you can say you've taken safety measures, yeah? . . . I'm doing my best.'

When I took my fingers away from my eyes, he was bowed over the table. 'God,' he said, 'I wouldn't mind, but I've been that fucking miserable.'

It was the line I'd waited nearly all my married life to hear. I pictured him sitting alone in his empty flat, the walls marked with the shape of departed furniture, the carpets dented and unhoovered. Excellent. Served him right.

'Anyway,' he said lamely. 'It's a fucking mess, in't it?'

The rap music from Laverne's rose in volume.

'I'd best get on and finish the grid.' He pushed the chair back, got to his feet and lumbered out.

There I sat between my trembling towers of china. Outside, the drill began to whine again.

In the end I went and fetched a dustpan and brush, and began to sweep up the shards of my marriage.

'Do you mind if I ask you something?' said David as we strolled back down the High Street together one quiet Sunday afternoon. Once again he had charge of my clipboard; this time we were taking photographs of town landmarks for the Beavers' Local History Hunt.

I snapped my lens cap over the shutter.

'Go on.'

'Do you think I'm too controlling, Carol?'

The question took me by surprise. 'Controlling?'

'A controlling person.'

'In what way?'

'With Ian.'

'Whatever's made you say that?'

'It's something he came out with yesterday evening.'

I waited for more, but he obviously felt he'd given me enough, that any more detail was superfluous.

We walked on a few paces while I thought about what he'd said. In one sense it was deeply flattering he trusted me to answer a question like that, a question which admitted a vulnerability I hadn't seen before. But at the same time I was alarmed because I wasn't at all sure what to say. *Was* David too controlling a father? I had no idea. Not from where I stood, certainly. No, no, he wasn't. In fact, the more I considered, the crosser I felt on his behalf.

'You're not, no,' I said. 'And I hope you stuck up for yourself.'

'I told him it was nonsense.'

'Good. What was his reaction?'

David shrugged. 'Hard to tell; he didn't say a great deal after that. He's fine today. I was just interested in your take.'

We walked on past the card shop with its oriel window and 1720 date stone, past Healey's café and the Civic Centre, till we were within sight of the Victorian arcade.

'I'm sure it's the stress talking, that's all. Ian's lashing out at you because you're around, you're available to be lashed out at.'

'Yes, it might be that.'

'Hey, don't you lose confidence, or we're all done for.' I smiled to show this was a joke, even though I kind of meant it. I'd come to rely on his mild brand of arrogance over the past weeks. Another ditherer like me on the case would have spelled disaster.

David gazed past me, down towards the precinct with its hanging baskets and new heritage-style litter bins. After a moment, I slid my arm through his, and the furrows on his brow eased a fraction. He looked down at my arm, and laughed ruefully.

'What?' I asked.

'Well, God help us, Carol, someone needs to pretend they know what they're doing,' he said.

CHAPTER 28

Photograph: unnumbered, from a page inside a pile of old newspapers at the bottom of Carol's cleaning cupboard

Location: the Long Room, Chester Race Course

Taken by: the Chester Chronicle

Subject: a crowd of people in evening dress, including Pippa Williams, her husband Lionel, and David, stand grouped around a signed football shirt donated by Wayne Rooney. The shirt is the star prize in the after-dinner charity auction, which they hope will raise in the region of £2,000 towards the Wirral and North Cheshire Prostate Cancer Group's Doppler Scanner appeal.

'It's the most common male cancer,' Pippa tells the reporter. 'Very treatable if caught early, so it's vital we raise public awareness.'

Lionel says nothing. Even before he became ill he wasn't the sort to stand up and give speeches. He simply watches from the sidelines, full of admiration. His wife's been a marvel, as tireless in the role of campaigner as she's been in nursing him. She could not have been more supportive, more loving. As yet they have not talked about how she'll manage when he's gone, but she seems so strong he can't imagine her not coping and that gives him some relief.

Pippa is not feeling strong at all. Two evenings before, she was sobbing in David's kitchen. 'It's so bloody awful, trying to put on a brave face. So exhausting. Never letting up. You must know what that's like.'

David does. He loves them both. He hates seeing his friends suffer like this. He puts his arms around her and lets her cry it all out against his shoulder.

'I need somewhere to come sometimes,' she says. 'Lionel mustn't see me like this.'

'Whatever I can do to help,' says David.

He feels her grip tighten around him, her hot breathing in his ear; then, hesitantly at first, her lips moving across the fresh-shaved skin of his neck.

He does not know how to push her away.

My parents' most important documents – the birth and wedding certificates, their old insurance policies and household receipts – were in an old briefcase under the spare bed. When someone dies, it's not always easy to know what to throw away and what to keep, and a lot of my mother's everyday bits and pieces had been bundled up and stowed away in odd corners. Over the years I'd disposed of a few items, a few pockets, as I came across them, but the bureau was where most of her things lived, and I'd forgotten what I'd stowed away in there.

In starting to clear it now I'd already unearthed a bag of hairnets, several dozen parish magazines, a sealed packet of triple-absorbent-super-mega-maxi Dr Whites, assorted cigarette cards, nine sachets of Atrixo, six cologne sticks used and unused, corn plasters, a felt corsage, her second-best purse, a giant bottle of Quink and a bundle of memorial service sheets. Rubbish, it was. Tat, junk. Why ever had we both given it house room?

Then there were her ancient magazines: *Housewife, Mother*

and Home, the *Homecraft Book,* all pushing a routine where every day your letterbox must be wiped free of fingerprints, the doorstep scrubbed, the porch swept; where every week all metal items and light bulbs had to be polished, lace mats rinsed and ironed, walls and ceilings brushed down. Where washing your clothes involved steeping, blueing and starching, and cleaning your fireplace required blacklead, methylated spirits and wax. *Use two dusters, one in each hand for speed,* one article advised. *Wallpaper can be rubbed clean with a simple flour-and-water dough. And why not hem old shirts and use them as kitchen towels? Or quilt worn towels into bath mats?* suggested another.

Thank God I was born when I was, I thought smugly. What a bloody dull existence it must have been.

A picture came to me of a future Jaz clearing out this house, and what she might find, and how she might assess me by the remnants of my life.

And then the bell rang.

'You're not moving, are you?' Laverne stared round the living room at the assorted boxes and bin bags, the emptied bureau and the dislocated drawers. Behind her, in the doorway, lurked Josh.

'No,' I said. 'Just having a clear-out.'

On the rug by my feet was strewn more evidence of my mother: piles of *Picture Post* and *Everybody's Magazine, Bairnswear* paper bags of half-used embroidery silks, bundles of cotton cloth cut into strips with pinking shears, packets of Coverax jam seals, a St Bruno's Flake tobacco tin of little horn buttons, a Keating's Powder pot containing twenty or thirty suspender clips. Old Sylko cotton reels, bright as the day Mum must have bought them, spilled out of a Coredoxa cigar box, along with several packets of Co-operative needles and a box of birthday cake candles. One large, scratched Coronation tin contained about two hundred recipe clippings, some of which obviously dated from the days of rationing. Cauliflower Fool, Spaghetti Mould, Semolina Soup.

Laverne frowned sympathetically. 'You haven't heard anything from Jaz, still?'

'No.'

'Well,' said Laverne, and stopped, because what comment can you make in such a situation that doesn't sound either trite or alarmist?

'Would Josh like a slice of lemon cake?' I said, more brightly than I felt.

He shook his head emphatically. 'I have to go in a minute.'

'He has to be at Healey's for eleven,' she said. 'I'm giving him a lift in. He's got an interview.'

'Not an interview, Mum.'

'Healey's coffee shop?' I asked.

'That's right,' said Laverne. 'They want more Saturday kitchen staff – waiters, washers up. I wasn't sure, because, you know, if he wants something, I can buy it for him – well, we can talk about it – but he thinks he should be earning.'

'Mum,' said Josh.

'So I said he could pop along and see, although I wasn't sure it would suit him. It's not a particularly pleasant job, is it? But I suppose they need to try these things for themselves.'

She turned a searching gaze on him, trying no doubt to imagine him in a steaming kitchen with a swearing chef. Self-conscious, Josh put his hand up to check his fringe. As he did so, the cuff of his shirt flopped open.

'Do your button up, at least,' said Laverne.

'Haven't got one.'

'Haven't you? You'll need to go and change, then.'

'I'll roll my sleeves up, it'll be fine.'

'No, it won't. Oh, see, Carol, he hasn't got a button on that one, either.'

'It doesn't matter,' he said. 'They won't care.'

'I'm not taking you like that. Go home and put your green shirt on.'

I could see the temper gathering on Josh's face. 'Hey,' I said. 'I've cotton and a threaded needle here, ready. There's buttons in that tobacco tin; I can have one sewn on before you've reached the top of your stairs.'

'It's both cuffs,' said Laverne.

'Then you do one and I'll do the other. Come on, Josh. Sit at the table and we'll have you sorted in two minutes. I promise.'

Jesus, he mouthed, but he went over and slumped down, wrists out in front of him like someone awaiting the application of thumbscrews. 'Eleven o' clock, I have to be there,' he muttered.

'Heaps of time yet,' I said, handing a needle to Laverne. She pulled a chair round and we positioned ourselves either side of him so there was no escape.

For half a minute there was just the movement of cloth being punctured and thread drawn tight. Then Laverne said: 'The reason I actually came round was, I heard some awful news this morning.'

I kept up my careful rhythm with the needle. Logic told me, if she had any information about my daughter and grandson, she'd have come straight out with it. In fact, she'd asked *me*, hadn't she? Even so, I felt the panic surge.

'What, Laverne? What is it?'

'Alice.'

'Alice?' Not Jaz.

'Dorothy Wynne's Alice.'

'Oh, yes. Sorry. Is she all right? Has she had the baby? I knew it must be any time soon.'

300

'She's had a little boy, but he's very poorly. There's something wrong. A disability of some sort, I'm not sure what exactly. It's serious, though, I do know that. Mrs Wynne caught me as I was wheeling the bin round. She's ever so upset. I said I'd tell you, save her having to.'

'God, that's awful. I am sorry. Is Alice all right?'

'Physically I think she's OK. It's the baby. And obviously she's very distressed, as you would be.'

Between us, Josh studied the table-top.

'The thing is,' Laverne was saying, 'you expect babies these days to be healthy, don't you? It never crosses your mind that anything might go wrong.'

It used to cross mine, I thought. Every day I was pregnant with Jaz, I scared myself stupid, imagining the worst. When she was born perfect, I couldn't believe it. And when, afterwards, we tried for another baby and it never happened, I didn't dare rail against fate in case what I already had was taken away from me. Did I ever worry for unborn Matty? No: somehow I always trusted he'd be all right. Jaz worried, though. She told me some nights she was wakened several times with bad dreams. Perhaps it's something to do with feeling another heartbeat beneath your ribs; that's enough to send anyone's mind off-balance.

'Joshy came out blue, with oxygen deprivation. They brought him round, but it was – I can't imagine what Alice must be going through, can you?'

'No,' I said.

'And she's so young, isn't she? It's such a lot for anyone, let alone – should we send a card? What do you say? Not congratulations. Or should we? I don't know.' She looked about for scissors, found none, wound the cotton round her finger and tugged. Then she sat back, her eyes searching my face.

'Let me have a word with Mrs Wynne,' I said. 'I suppose a

lot depends on how the baby's doing. You know, the long term.'

'However is she going to cope, though?'

'I don't know,' I said, and broke off the last piece of thread.

Released at last, Josh jerked his chair back and stood up. 'Great. Can we get going now, Mum?'

'In a minute,' she said. 'I'm sorry, Carol. He's been really stroppy lately – Oh, it's just so sad. Should we send some flowers?'

'Flowers would be good. Maybe some for Mrs Wynne, too.'

'You ask yourself why on earth these things have to happen to good people.' Laverne gazed round the room as though the answer might be lying somewhere among my piles of paper and junk. Then she sighed and stood up.

'Will you order the flowers?' she began, moving towards the door. But in squeezing past the edge of the table, she knocked off an ancient Kestos Nursing Brassière box. There was a sound like marbles clicking together, and a whole heap of miniature light bulbs spilled out onto the carpet.

Josh made a growling noise. 'Nice one, Mum.'

'Watch where you're treading,' I said hastily, imagining how tiny the glass splinters might be if any of the bulbs got crushed.

'Oh, heavens, Carol,' she said. 'What are they? I can barely see them. Josh, stick that light on, would you?'

'Leave them, I'll do it,' I said, conscious of her son loitering.

'No, it's all right, we're still early. We are, Josh.' Laverne bent down and began swishing her palms over the carpet. With extreme care I lowered myself onto my knees next to her and we hunted about blindly. 'Don't move your left foot,' she'd go. 'There's something glinting.' And I'd freeze, and she'd say, 'Oh no, it was a speck of glitter.' Or I'd say, 'Under the sofa end, near your hand. A bit further. A bit further.' They were like dolls' bulbs, and I wondered where they'd fitted and why the filaments were different colours and how many of them still worked. This was exactly why all the rubbish needed to go.

From somewhere above me Josh went, 'Is this Jaz?'

'Where?'

I scrambled to my feet at once, but he was only holding up a photograph.

He passed it to me and I peered into the picture, my heart contracting painfully. It was Jaz, aged about thirteen, almost unrecognisable with her round, unmade-up face and her hair in little plaits like dreadlocks. She was sitting with Nat on the steps of a shabby caravan, holding a bottle of Coke aloft as if she was offering up a toast. On her feet, which were stretched out in front of her, she sported a pair of men's boots, much too big for her.

'Where did you find it?'

'Here.' He pointed at a yellow Kodak envelope which I'd balanced on the back of the sofa. 'That one was stuck against another.'

I took the wedge of prints and flicked through them. They were ones I'd found when I was going through Dad's boxes in the shed, but I'd mislaid them in the panic over Libby. How had they ended up in the bureau? I lost all sorts these days. Here again were the frog, the toadstool, the horse, Nat astride a gate, but the shot Josh had asked about was new to me.

'She looks like a gypsy,' said Josh.

'You shouldn't go through people's personal things,' said Laverne, pulling herself upright and brushing at her jeans.

'It was out on top, I was only looking. Can we go now?'

'He means "thank you, Carol, for sewing my shirt",' said Laverne.

'Yeah, cheers.'

'Any time,' I said, and winked at him. I did get the tiniest of smiles back, so that was something.

After I'd seen them out I went back into the lounge, piled all my mother's belongings back into the bureau, and shut the door on them. Today was not the day for getting rid of the past.

CHAPTER 29

Photograph: loose inside a Cook Electric! *brochure at the bottom of the bureau, Sunnybank*

Location: Canterbury

Taken by: Reverend Pendlebury

Subject: the exterior of the cathedral, south-west aspect.

It's been a long journey, but worth it. Frieda had thought, on the coach, with the rest of the Mothers' Union, that she had another headache starting, but the pain vanishes once she's in the nave. The cathedral is blissfully cool, and dim. If everyone will just leave her alone, she'll be fine.

'How long are we going to be?' asks Carol, pulling down on Frieda's bag so the strap cuts into her shoulder.

'I don't know,' says Frieda.

'I need the toilet,' whines Carol.

So they have to go and look for the ladies', and as they hurry along the aisles, Frieda feels a flush starting, and when they get to the washrooms she realises she's left her cologne stick at home. 'Why didn't you go when we got off the bus?' she says to the cubicle door, but gets no answer.

By the time they make it back to the nave, she's incandescent with heat. Sliding into a pew, she lowers her burning brow to the back of her hand, and prays.

'The vicar says Jesus was born in a cellar,' Carol whispers suddenly in her ear, making her jump.

Frieda raises her head and Carol skips off.

After a while, the glow subsides. Other women, her friends, come and go without fuss. Kneelers sag under the weight of pious knees, sending up little spurts of dust into the light. Someone starts to play the organ quietly and the notes are like a thread of silver beads unravelling in her soul.

Partially restored, she stands and steps out into the aisle, which is when she sees her daughter spinning like a Dervish among the tombs in the Warrior Chapel. What does she think she's doing? People are looking.

'This is NOT a playground!' she snaps, and drags Carol outside to retch over the grass and her own shoes.

'Did you see the pelican?' asks Carol, when everything's come up.

Behind them, a woman exclaims with delight over some small feat of ordinariness her baby has just performed.

'There's a pelican in the window,' Carol continues. 'It's a symbol of the Redeemer, because it tears its own breast that the young may feed. A man told me. Wouldn't it die, though? And the babies starve? Joyce Whittle's rabbit ate its babies, did I tell you?'

Five minutes – five minutes' peace was all Frieda wanted.

'And Joyce says spiders eat each other. If you were a pelican, would you tear your own flesh? Say we had no food and we were starving to death, except we had one slice of bread between us, would you give it all to me?'

'Of course I would,' says Frieda. But Carol is picking at a scab on her knee and doesn't bother listening to the answer.

*

The last time I'd been round to David's house for dinner, it was Jacky who'd let us in. Jacky had shown us through, made us drinks, talked about wedding venues and hire cars and menus, while David stood by the grand fireplace, overseeing the discussion, master of this hall. 'Bloody lording it around,' Phil had said afterwards. And I'd replied, 'Get a taxi back to Penny's; you're drunk.'

Even though I knew Jacky was long gone, it's hard to shift the idea that places stay as they were when you last saw them, so I was still relieved when David answered the door.

'I did mean to tidy up,' he said.

A glance round his hallway showed only a pair of shoes on the parquet by the door and a folded sweater on the stairs. 'Get away. You should see my place at the moment. House Clearances R Us.'

He took my coat. 'There's a lot to be said for keeping busy. Ian's been stripping wallpaper.'

The large sitting room I remembered as a palette of calm, of pale lemon and white and oatmeal slub, where Jacky had placed a huge arrangement of lilies and gerbera on the table in front of the window, and set two or three of those church candles burning on the marble hearth. This evening there were none of these feminine traces, only papers spread across the table-top, a calculator and a receipt spike, and books and cups and whisky tumblers dotted about. 'Tax return,' he said. 'Demands a lot of surface area.'

'And I had you down as one of those types who lines up their pencils in order.'

'Think again,' he said.

While he was getting me a drink I walked around, taking in the detail. When Jacky was semi-resident, she'd streamlined this place so it was like a show home. Since then, the house had returned to what I guessed was its more normal

David-state, so instead of matching beige vases on the mantelpiece we had scissors and an iPod dock, a tube of Superglue, a glasses case. Towers of DVDs jostled his Art Deco clock; the Georgian slops bowl I'd admired now contained cufflinks and a bottle of tea tree oil.

And on the chimney breast, a selection of photographs I'd never seen before.

In the centre of the arrangement hung the largest picture, Ian the infant, lighter-haired and minus some teeth and with a face you'd almost have called chubby. Then, above that, primary school Ian, sporting a too-short trim and a wide, nervous grimace. Higher still was a sharper-featured Ian with imperfect teenage skin. They were glossy, well-framed images, yet there was something in the pitch of his eyebrows, or the apologetic hunch of his shoulders, that seemed to cancel out the smile every time. Even as late as his degree portrait, you could see the pinch of anxiety on his face. By the wedding, he'd managed to straighten his posture and relax his frown into the Ian I knew, or thought I knew. The wide eyes, the tightness of his lips, you'd just have put down to usual wedding-day jitters. Which, obviously, I did. I wanted him to be right so I made him right.

'My gallery,' said David, setting down two wine glasses. 'A work in progress.'

'They weren't up last time.'

'You've shamed me into sorting out my collection. Most of my photographs have been living loose in wallets or on my hard drive; it's about time I imposed some order.'

'I treasure my albums,' I said.

'I know you do.' He opened a drawer in the side of the table. 'Here. I have to finish up next door, but in the meantime, you might be interested in these.'

He pressed a wad of pictures into my hand, and left me.

It was an intimacy I'd not been expecting.

The top few were the older, smaller type of prints with a white border. David I was able to pick out immediately, even though he was in short trousers and had his hair in a side parting. A family posed against a holly hedge, then on a beach, by a bridge, outside a church: mother, father, two boys and an older girl. And as I looked at each scene, I had the curious sensation of standing between two doorways, with David's life playing out in front of me and my own somewhere behind my back. So when I studied his parents' large Victorian house, I was also seeing Tannerside's old vicarage and the garden parties where my mother served the teas, and the ancient grey pony they used to have giving rides round the lower lawn; and then I thought of Pincroft itself, one Deco semi in a street full of the same, and how we wore our ordinariness proudly, like a union badge. David's father, with his broad shoulders and confident, lifted chin, seemed to emphasise my dad's slight frame, while the mother, elegant in pencil skirt and plain blouse, showed me that even back then, women in their thirties didn't have to look two decades older, the way my mother had done.

There was a class photograph much like my own, except all the pupils were boys and the teacher's face a whole lot sterner. It took me a moment to locate David because now (at fifteen – sixteen?) he wore his hair combed forward in a mop top. His hands in his lap, his shoulders back, he stared moodily at the camera, looking exactly like the kind of student who'd have been made a prefect and then demoted shortly afterwards.

My laughter at the next batch brought David into the room again. 'OK,' he said, 'what's so hilarious?'

I pointed at the shot of him standing in front of a farm gate, his hair lapping his collar, sideburns adorning his cheeks. 'Tan jacket and a black polo neck? You look as though you're posing for an album cover.'

'Meanwhile you were dressing like Sandy Denny. Go on, admit it, you used to wear shawls and Indian shirts.'

'It was against the law not to in those days.'

The next picture was of a young woman standing on a canal tow-path. She was kitted out in jeans and a long coat and a crocheted hat, and carried a patchwork shoulder bag. 'She's pretty. Is this Jeanette?'

'No, pre-Jeanette. I was still in London then. The next one should be her.'

And there she was, his late wife, a fresh-faced brunette with bobbed hair, apple-cheeked and wide-hipped. Where her pinafore dress ended she had on maroon patent knee boots that reminded me of a pair I used to own myself. I don't know what I'd been expecting, but she still took me by surprise. 'Gosh, she's young,' I said.

'Twenty-one when I met her, twenty-four when we married.' He took the bundle of photos off me and began to move more swiftly through them. 'Some of these I used to have on display, and then I took them down. It became . . . It's not as if I need them to remember. You don't forget the things that have mattered, do you? But perhaps I should put one or two up again.'

I wondered whether Jacky had asked for them to be packed away. Or maybe David felt that when Ian left home, it was time to move on. Duty to the present balanced against duty to the past.

'This is our wedding . . . wedding . . . wedding again . . . reception, honeymoon – all these honeymoon. This is in Dumfries with my sister, at our mother's seventieth, my brother on his boat, Jeanette passing her driving test, Jeanette pregnant, Ian, Ian, Ian, Ian in his new uniform – he fell down the stairs the day that was taken and gave himself a bloody nose. This one's shortly after we discovered Jeanette was ill.'

We paused at a Christmas dinner scene. Ian was waving his

hands in the air, after some comic effect, while his mother clutched the stem of her wine glass and smiled at the camera. 'Did she know it was serious?'

'Oh yes.'

'Did Ian?'

'I thought he should be told, but Jeanette didn't agree. In the end I went against her. That was hard.'

'You're better being honest in these situations, even with children.'

David nodded. 'Thank you for saying that. I still believe it was the right course of action. Although my motivations were partly selfish, I confess.'

'In what way?'

'I appreciate this sounds terrible, but at the time I felt it wasn't fair of her to "escape" and leave me to deal with Ian. I know, it's a dreadful thing to admit. But I really truly believed she needed to shoulder some of his grief, not leave it all for me to mop up afterwards. He had questions I wouldn't have known how to answer. Do you understand? But that was cruel of me when she was so sick. I should have let her have her way.'

'No,' I said. 'I'm absolutely sure your instinct was correct. They needed to say a proper goodbye, didn't they? Ian would have been devastated if you'd denied him that.'

David only cleared his throat and flicked onto the next photo, but I knew for once I'd said just the right thing.

The next two dozen shots featured a succession of women. First it was a long-faced blonde who favoured ponytails and jeans, and who liked pub lunches and picnics and vintage car rallies. ('Susannah,' said David.) She gave way to a plump, dark woman, older than him, with a motherly face and a hair-style not unlike Jeanette's. In the first few pictures she was playing with Ian – beach cricket, hoisting him onto a tree branch, bike riding together – and I began to think perhaps she'd been a nanny, or even that this was the sister, put on weight. But no, because here they were dressed up to the nines and he had his arm around her, and her beaming smile told me this was not a sibling embrace. ('Fiona,' said David. 'A Scot.') Then there was a Sloaney type, frilled collars and navy V-necks, slightly pronounced chin, who'd shared a Christmas with them and at least one family holiday. ('Rachel,' said David.) Lastly we had Jacky, the lovely Jacky, immaculate even when she was crouched in between the geese and ducks by the Old Dee Bridge, holding a Value bread bag. Sometimes Sloaney Rachel appeared with them, and once or twice a fortysomething grey-blonde I recognised as Susannah, aged.

I wanted to say something like, 'Great, good for you,' or 'At least you weren't lonely,' or 'Well, life's for living,' but however I tried to frame my words I sounded trite or, worse, sarcastic. Luckily, David summed up for me.

'Yes, they were nice girls, and much-needed company at the time. Some of them are friends to this day.'

'But not Jacky.'

'Not Jacky.'

Or the other one, I thought.

He glanced at his watch. 'I need to go and stick some broc-coli on. Give me another five minutes.'

He took himself off again, leaving me to finish the photos alone.

From now on they were all of Ian: at a friend's wedding; pushing an elderly lady in a wheelchair; in sunglasses leaning against a white stone column; feeding a lamb; pointing at a tor; climbing into the basket of a hot air balloon; patting the roof of a blue Fiat Panda; waving from Chester city walls; in run-ning gear; in university cap and gown; holding the hand of a girl with an oversized forehead.

And lastly, with Jaz. They sat outside the Rocket at a wrought-iron table, eyes screwed up against the dazzle of the whitewashed walls. Jaz must have been working that day because she was wearing an apron, but they were never very busy there and staff often used to come and sit with customers for a chat. Ian was lifting up a chunky mug, and Jaz had her head on his shoulder. Behind them bloomed bright baskets of geraniums.

Even though I'd anticipated coming across such a picture, the sight of her still safe in the past brought on a pang of pure agony.

'Carol?' I heard David calling.

'Coming.'

Just before I set them down, I turned the prints over and riffled through them to check the backs. I don't know what I was hoping, or fearing, to find. Every one turned out to be unmarked; he'd added not a word of commentary or identification anywhere. But then, I thought, why should he? I never needed such prompts either. I always remembered exactly what had been happening in all of mine.

We sat in his kitchen to eat.

'This is nice,' I said, looking round me.

'Stew or kitchen?'

'Both.'

'Jacky used to say the kitchen was dated. I suppose it is, but I don't honestly care as long as everything's clean and works.'

'Quite right too.'

I wanted to say it was good he'd learned to cook, but I was worried that might come across as patronising. My head was still buzzing with his photographs, random scenes that I was struggling to place in their proper sequence. Which girlfriend had he liked the most? Who was it had ended each relationship, and under what circumstances? Had any of them broken his heart?

'OK, Carol?'

Worried he might somehow see inside my head, I caught at the first topic that floated past. 'Why did you get stripped of your school prefect badge?'

David let out a short, yelping laugh. 'How on earth did you know about that?'

'You told me. When we were walking with Matty on the Moss.'

'Did I? Good Lord. Now why would I have brought up that event, of all things?' He looked at me quizzically.

'Hey, if you don't want to tell me, say so. But of course, now I'm imagining all sorts—'

'I should make something up, then, something spectacular. It's going to be such a let-down.'

'Oh, get on with it.'

'If you really want to know, I was given the boot for helping produce a satirical magazine mocking the staff and governors.'

'Blimey. Like Oz?'

'Not like Oz at all. Nothing terribly bad, actually, but containing opinions which deviated somewhat from the official school line. Rude rather than libellous. The print quality was so poor I'm amazed anyone could decipher it. You know what it's like when you photocopy a photocopy of a photograph, especially when you've added a pair of horns.'

'Sounds fun.'

'It was a total rubbish. We thought we were being edgy, when in fact we were just being boorish. But I was already in trouble for smuggling out percussion instruments for our band to borrow.'

'Tambourine up the jumper?'

'Castanets down the trousers, something like that.'

'I didn't know you were in a band.'

'Yes, and we were pretty bloody awful at that, too. Six English grammar-school boys pretending to be Aphrodite's Child. We'd never have stood an actual gig. Anyway, the upshot was, I was suspended for three days and permanently demoted. I had to behave after that or I'd have been expelled. Even my father wouldn't have been able to save me.'

'I was always too scared to be naughty at school,' I said. 'Too scared and too unimaginative. Mrs Blind Obedience, I was.'

David clicked his tongue. 'There you go again, doing yourself down.'

'And what have you just been doing? The band was "awful", the magazine was "indecipherable".'

'Yes, but I was stating the truth.'

'So was I.'

We frowned at each other across the table.

'I still say you've a tendency to rubbish yourself unnecessarily. It's like a reflex response. You can't help yourself.'

'Do you charge by the hour?'

'I only meant, you're better than you think you are. There. Will that do? One day, perhaps, I'll learn to master the art of giving a straight compliment, and you'll master the art of accepting one.'

'Quits.'

'You're looking very nice this evening, Carol.'

'Thank you.'

I smiled into my stew, and fought down the urge to tell him my blouse had come from the Scope shop. Let him admire uninterrupted.

Evening wore on, the sky darkened. When we were both straining to see our plates in front of us, he got up and drew the blinds and switched on the lights. The gloom had been friendly, the brightness felt like an intrusion. 'Shall I leave the hall light on, and these ones off?' he asked.

I nodded. 'Though I should warn you, there's a risk I'll go to sleep.'

'I'll try and be more stimulating company for you.'

'It's the wine,' I said, 'not you. Anyway, you should take it as a compliment. You put me at my ease.'

'Likewise.'

The house was stiller than mine, I noticed; no noise from next door, no grumbling joists or musical pipework. Perhaps it had absorbed less drama into its walls over the years. I said, 'I wish we'd got to know each other better, sooner.'

David leaned forward and topped up my glass. 'It wasn't the right time.'

'No. I wish it wasn't the right time now, if you know what I mean.'

'Because of Jasmine and Ian.'

'But since we don't have a choice, I'm glad, for us. I'm drunk.'

'You're not.'

I am, I thought.

He made coffee, and I told him about Josh's find.

'I think Nat must have taken the photograph. They look like they're in a gypsy camp.'

'A gypsy camp?'

'When Jaz was about ten, some travellers set up on the field behind the surgery – not that it's a field now – but anyway, Jaz was fascinated. I think for two pins she'd have moved in with them. Phil had to ban her from going there, in the end. She was getting very intense.'

'In what way?'

'She seemed to feel we'd let her down. There was opposition, petitions and letters in the paper, but we weren't involved. I suppose she wanted us to pile in on the gypsies' side. Then the camp moved on, and we thought she'd forgotten about it. Five years later, she ran away; we never found out where she'd been headed. I've been turning it over in my mind all afternoon.'

'Do you think she might have joined up with some travellers?'

'God, I don't know. I'm grasping at straws.'

Jaz reading out snippets from *Local News and Views* in a loud, scandalised voice. Jaz in the courtyard of the Rocket, convinced she'd found the love of her life. All at once my mood plummeted, and I felt overwhelmed with despair.

'Oh, David, I miss them so much it's like being ill. There are some days I don't know what to do with myself. I'm angry with her, I'm angry with Ian, I'm sick of feeling anxious and churned up and frightened of a future I thought was going to bring us so much joy.

'And it's everywhere I turn, you know? Wall-to-wall grimness and suffering. My dad, stuck in that home with no idea who he is. Eileen gone; your wife. Good people! I heard this afternoon that my neighbour's grand-daughter's had a disabled baby. She's such a lovely girl and we were all thrilled for her when she told us she was expecting, and now she's sitting in intensive care not knowing what the next hour'll bring. I just thought, Is there anything that's safe to believe in? Why do we risk being optimistic, and getting close to people, and trying to do a bit of good in the world? What's the point of any of it? Because even if Jaz comes back, she and I are broken, her marriage is gone. It all comes to nothing. It all seems to turn bad eventually.'

He listened without interrupting. Then I heard the scrape of his chair, saw his shadow as he passed between me and the light, felt his touch on my arm.

Please don't claim everything's going to be fine, I prayed. *Don't make glib promises about things which aren't in your power. I don't think I could stand it if you did.*

'All I know, Carol, is, whatever's ahead, you're not on your own. I'll do whatever I practically can to support you. You do understand that?'

I gave a faint nod.

'It's the only certainty I can give you, truthfully.'

His hand fumbled for mine, and I clasped it hard.

'Listen, I have a proposition for you,' he went on.

'What?' I struggled to concentrate over the roar of my own emotion.

'Well, one contribution I could make is to supply funds – no, hear me out – to cover legal procedures, private investigators, whatever you need. I've hesitated to offer till now because of – dealings – at the wedding.'

'Oh, God. That.' Phil grumbling and muttering about passing on receipts, me making comments about Jacky's clothing budget. It made me wince to remember. 'I didn't mean to come across as ungrateful.'

'You didn't. Well, it's water under the bridge. But the point is, whatever you decide you need to do here, I don't want you to feel constrained by finances.'

'That's very generous. I can't take money from you, though.'

'It wouldn't be like that. Matty's my grandson too. It's in my interests to see him reunited with his family. All of his family, on both sides.'

If it would help get Jaz back, I'd have agreed to anything. 'I'll think about it,' I said. 'It's incredibly kind of you.'

'No strings.'

'No.'

'I mean, absolutely none.'

'OK.'

'Good. I wanted to be clear on that. It's a practical arrangement first and foremost, there's no payback, no one's in anyone's debt. A job needs doing, simply that. Because the other thing you need to be aware of . . .' David's face was strained, and for the first time ever, I thought I glimpsed his son in him '. . . I should probably say at this stage. It's possible I may have fallen a little bit in love with you. Do you think that's going to be a problem?'

Strange what rises to the surface of your mind at moments of crisis.

Once, when I was a little girl, my mother and I went on a day trip to somewhere with a cathedral. There are no photographs of this expedition, which I think might have been organised by the Mothers' Union, but I remember it vividly all the same. Not the name of the place, only details: the carved screens, the smell of the wood polish, the ice-smooth veiny columns, the clank of the grating underfoot. While my mother was fishing for loose change to donate, I tiptoed into a side chapel to stroke the carvings of dead knights. Ahead was a vast arched window, through which beams of coloured light slanted down, and the walls on either side of me glowed with embroidered flags. You could see why God chose to hang out here.

Looking above me, I was awed by the vast height of the ceiling, and the way the vaulting at the tops of the pillars seemed to draw together like crystal fans. The scale was humbling and exhilarating at the same time. A surge of excitement rose up in me, and I wanted to shout at the top of my voice (at least till I spotted my mother standing under the central tower, studying the information leaflets). So instead, overwhelmed by spiritual energy, I began to turn on the spot. I tipped my head back, focused on one of the painted bosses, spread my arms out wide, and revolved. I remember spinning faster and faster, till my surroundings were lost in a holy smudge. At the same moment, someone started to play the treble line to 'Jesu, Joy of Man's Desiring'. I was on the verge of being Taken Up.

My mother's voice jerked me out of it. I staggered and fell against a tomb, the scenery still whizzing past in nauseating feints. Closing my eyes made no difference. Nothing was stationary any more.

'I think I've had a religious experience,' I told her.

'You're confusing God with dizziness,' she said, and took me outside so she could tell me off properly.

I don't know why that memory came back so keenly now, unless it was to warn me how easy it is to confuse different sensations, especially when they're very strong. You can think you've received Divine Communion when, in fact, you're just giddy. You can think you've fallen in love when the truth is you're grateful, tired and lonely. *Not him, Mum, anyone but him*, said Jaz, in my head.

3.30 a.m. and I was still prowling round the house, unable to sleep. Couldn't find anything on the internet about imminent gypsy gatherings, except for the Stow Horse Fair – and that was still a month off. And what would I do if I went there? Walk round with a loud-hailer? I kept seeing David's face, the sad lines round his eyes. Thought of kissing Phil, that first time on the bridge as a teenager, and years later in the B&B where we stayed on honeymoon, those funny damp patches on the ceiling paper, and me trembling with nerves under the sheets in case the owners could hear us doing it.

'Not now,' I'd told David. Under the intensity of his gaze I'd felt almost hysterical. 'Everything's complicated. It's a weird, bad time.'

'I know. That's why you have to seize the day, though. Life's short.' He squeezed my fingers in time to the last two syllables.

'No. But it's—' *Everything*, I wanted to say. 'Too much. You're my friend.'

'And I can't be anything else?'

His face was so close I could have kissed him. I wanted to, dear God, I really did. My whole body was charged with longing and fear.

Instead I got up in a rush, stumbled into the hall, and without even picking up my coat, ran out of the house like some idiot schoolgirl.

I don't know who he thinks he is, went Phil.

Next time you speak to him, tell him from me he can fuck off – Jaz.

I've no time for all this love stuff – Eileen, in a deckchair, her eyes hidden behind sunglasses. *It's like dancing on a cliff edge.*

Dad's face as it used to be, animated and keen – *As long as you're happy, that's all that matters. Are you happy?*

These pre-dawn hours were like another dimension altogether. Every second could last an hour, you could live a lifetime in one night.

I wandered back over to the computer and shut it down. Then I started a bath running, and did some stretches while I waited. Would David be in bed still, or pacing round the house, like me? What was he doing at this exact moment? My mind whirred insanely. It's past four! I kept thinking. You've got till seven to get through. I'd have given the world to be able to flick an off-switch, blot everything out for even a couple of hours.

But then, if I'd been asleep, I'd never have heard the text come in.

CHAPTER 30

Photograph 180, Album Two

Location: the back garden, Sunnybank

Taken by: Carol

Subject: Jaz, strapped into her toddler reins, and swiping at a dandelion clock. Technically speaking, it's an excellent piece of composition, even though it's one of Carol's earliest attempts at portrait. She's captured Jaz's chubby profile, the anticipatory parting of her young lips as her open grasp bears down on the seed head. It's a perfect scene of summer.

Would you believe that, only the previous night, Jaz is at death's door? That she brews up a mysterious fever with such rapidity even Phil, dismisser of panic, is alarmed? The screaming doesn't help: high-pitched, unnatural, distressing beyond sanity. When she's still screaming at midnight, Phil tells Carol he's driving them up to the cottage hospital.

So they bundle her and her car seat into the night air, and almost immediately she settles. By the time they get to hospital, she's cooing and chattering like a normal three-year-old. The doctor lifts her onto the examination table and she giggles in his face.

On their way home, the radio starts to play Neil Young's

'Heart of Gold'. Phil pulls the car into a lay-by opposite the park and, with the engine still running, climbs out, unclips Jaz from her seat, and carries her onto the municipal lawns. Then he holds her against his chest, and begins to twirl round in a lop-sided waltz. The moon and stars behind them are picture-book-bright.

'Don't let her catch cold,' Carol shouts.

What is this strange, unpleasant sensation in the pit of her stomach? Surely it should be her job to dance with her daughter in the moonlight?

My instinct would have been to phone David, but after what he'd said, I couldn't bring myself to dial. I was too frightened.

I paced around for a couple of minutes, then I tried Phil. He was, after all, Jaz's dad, and I needed someone with me. When I got no response, I tried again. Eventually he answered, groggily.

'It's me,' I gushed. 'I know where Jaz is. She's sent me her address. Can you drive me there?'

There was a long silence. 'Carol?'

I said, 'Can you drive me to Harrogate?'

'When?'

'Now.'

'Jesus.'

I waited, listening for sounds to show he might be with someone, but there was nothing. No female voice asking what was going on.

'It's half past four in the morning,' he said. 'Can you give me time to have a coffee and some breakfast? If she's sent you her address, she's not going to be skipping off, is she? We can wait till it gets light, at least.' Probably he was twitching the curtain aside to look out, because there was a pause and I heard him swear under his breath. 'I need to look at an atlas, anyway.'

He turned up later than he said he would, by which time I was climbing the walls.

'You said six-thirty at the latest.'

'And it's six forty-three, Carol. Now tell me what's up.'

'In the car,' I said, pushing him out of the front door and slamming it behind us. How lucky, in the end, that I wasn't tied any more to taking Josh into school. Moira I could call on the way, ask her to open the shop. All that mattered was getting to my daughter.

Once we were on the road I read out the text. Just Jaz's name, and an address. No message.

'You tried to ring back?'

'Of course I bloody did.'

'No luck?'

'What do you think?'

'And it was her number?'

'Yes.'

The streetlamps flicked past as we sped down the dual carriageway.

I said, 'You don't think she's being held prisoner, do you?'

Phil snorted with laughter, which was annoying as hell and reassuring at the same time. 'Don't be daft.'

'We could ring the police, ask them to be on stand-by.'

'No, Carol.'

I glanced across, took in his grey-streaked hair, his sagging jawline, the creases round his eyes and mouth. Then I pulled down the sunshade mirror and studied my own tired face. I felt old and stupid and not up to the job. I wanted it to be David in the driving seat.

'You're shivering,' he said. 'There's a coat in the back if you want.'

'One of Pen's?'

His knuckles tightened on the steering wheel. 'For the last

time, she isn't around any more. How many times do I have to keep saying it?'

I scowled, and reached round for the overcoat.

'And there's a flask in the glove compartment. Help yourself,' he muttered.

'Tea? Coffee?'

'Brandy.'

We drove on under a grey, uncertain sky. All I could feel, as the miles clocked up, was terror: of Jaz not being there, or her being there but still not letting me see Matty, of her changing her mind and fleeing again, of her being in some terrible trouble. It seemed as though I'd spent all my life as a mother in a state of churning fear. Labour pain's nothing to what comes after. From the first moment you're pregnant, everyone seems to have a horror story to tell you. *They did a scan and found there was no head*, I remember overhearing someone in the shop say, and I had to go home early that day and had weeks of terrible nightmares. And the potential for pain starts even before you're pregnant, from the second you admit that you want a child. Moira tried for years, had miscarriage after miscarriage and all sorts of tests and humiliating procedures, and in the end had to learn to live without. I can't imagine what that must have been like. All I ever wanted was a baby.

And yet, when I got home from hospital with newborn Jaz, I remember looking at her and thinking, Dear God, I don't know what to do with her. That awful lurch when the idea that you truly have got an actual baby sinks in, and that what you've done, in having a child, is open yourself up forever to the worst hurt imaginable (and I saw again Jaz hauling Matty out of the water, his drenched clothes streaming and his face streaked with weed). There's no magic age where you can stop worrying, either, because after falling in ponds and meningitis and choking there's paedophiles and bullying and drugs and car crashes. Teenage boys getting knifed and shot, girls getting raped. I thought of Alice's little baby, pictured him lying in an incubator with a name tag round his tender ankle, and wondered how on earth she would bear it.

Having a child was like building a house on an unexploded bomb. At any moment, the possibility for devastation was part of your life. In some ways, Eileen had been clever to steer clear of it all.

'I'm not sure I can cope with this,' I said. We were coming onto the motorway, and Phil was looking away from me, over his shoulder.

'Course you can,' he said, flicking the indicator.

'I daren't let myself think Matty might be there, because if he's not, if it's like last time when I went down to Bristol—'

Lorries roared into line beside us, and behind us, and ahead. Danger was everywhere.

'Tell you who I was dreaming about when I got your call. You remember that chemistry teacher, the one with the lisp? God knows why she made an appearance after all these years.'

'I know what you're trying to do,' I said.

'In the dream she was really friendly, not like she was when we were at school. Mary bloody Whitehouse in a lab coat. God, she went ballistic over that chlorine gas business, didn't she? Absolutely livid. I got the cane for that.'

'You deserved it.'

'It wasn't me who didn't close the fume cupboard properly. That was her.'

'Yes, but you didn't have to fall off your stool and pretend you were choking to death, did you? Dribbling everywhere, jerking around. Even I thought you were a gonner.'

Phil grinned. 'Hey, do you remember that assembly when we

had that ex-pupil come to talk to us about how he'd won the war?'

'You got the cane for that as well,' I said. I could see him now, tie askew, making a dash across the playground to where the tall man with the military bearing stood conversing with the Headmaster. Phil had tagged the man on the arm, for all the world as though they were playing a game of chase, then run off shouting at the top of his voice, 'I'm cured! It's a miracle! I was blind and now I can see!'

'Grand days, eh?'

'If you say so.'

'They never did find out who added Hitler moustaches to all the photos in the entrance hall.'

'It's nothing to be proud of.'

'I seem to recall you finding it pretty funny at the time. In fact, didn't you and Eileen get a bit creative yourselves with the speech-day programmes at one point?' Phil raised an eyebrow at me, and my lips twitched, in spite of myself. It was nerves, though, that was all.

There were hold-ups on the M62. As the car slowed down, then halted, I gripped the handle of my bag so tight I left fingernail marks in the leather.

'I saw Edith Hilton last week,' said Phil. 'Coming out of Aldi.'

'Is she still alive?'

'Unless what I saw was a zombie.'

'Very amusing. I meant she must be getting on.'

He reached into the pocket between the seats, hooked out an elderly Polo and stuck it in his mouth. 'How long's Laverne been living next door? It's only about twelve years, and Edith would have been, what, sixty when she moved out? So she'll be in her seventies, that's all. Still a way to go before she's a contender for Britain's Oldest Woman.'

'Britain's Oldest Bag, more like.'

'You weren't fond of her, were you?' Clicky-click went the mint against his teeth.

'No. She was horrible to Jaz. Horrible full stop.'

'Do you remember that time you swapped all her flower bulbs for pickling onions?'

'You told me to.'

'Yeah. Good, wasn't it?'

The traffic started to move again. I thought of Edith Hilton peering suspiciously over the new green shoots in her border, bending to pinch the leaves and then sniffing her fingers, while Phil and I hooted with laughter from behind the front-room curtain. She'd had a son, a nasty piece of work, who complained about Jaz more or less constantly. Didn't like her climbing the tree in our garden because he thought she was spying on his mother; objected to the noise they made when Nat came round; claimed they were poking fun, when they were just giggling like young girls do. I always tried to be polite, but it wasn't easy. One time he banged on the door to moan they were playing their music with the window open and his mother didn't like it. I'd stood there on the step for five minutes, explaining it was a new birthday CD-player, and reassuring him it wouldn't happen again, and apologising for any disturbance. Then Phil had come up behind me and said to him, 'Tell you what, Norman: why don't you just fuck off?' and shut the door in his face. And that, astonishingly, was the last we'd heard of him. For all his failings as a husband, Phil sometimes hit the nail on the head.

'Poor woman, such trouble she had with her lawn,' he said now as we came onto the M60.

I looked sideways at him. 'Was that you?'

'Yup.'

'How?'

'Coca Cola. Kills the grass. Takes it ages to grow back properly. She went bonkers trying to work out what caused those lines. I saw her putting down fertilizer, extra turf, all sorts. Always those lines came back, though. What a mystery, eh?'

'Why didn't you tell me at the time?'

'I thought it would be more convincing if you were mystified too.'

At last he'd made me smile properly. 'Do you think there's any chance you'll ever grow up?'

'God, no.'

When we came off the motorway, there was another hold-up: some roadworks with a complicated three-way lights system and traffic backing up for miles.

'Keep calm,' he said. 'Have a Polo.'

'You know I hate them.'

'We used to play that car game with Murray mints, do you remember? Who could make their sweet last the longest. And we always let Jaz win because that way you got the maximum amount of peace. It chipped away another twenty minutes or so off a long journey.'

'What if that text's a wind-up, Phil?'

'It won't be. Try not to think about it. There's no mileage in getting yourself upset before we've even got there. Is there?'

'No,' I said reluctantly.

He switched the radio on, and twiddled the dial till he found 'Stuck in the Middle With You'. 'Hey, what about that time Natalie sat on the dolls'-house roof and the whole thing collapsed? All those bloody miniature spindles for the banisters; I was months putting them right. And I got Superglue on your mother's tablecloth, do you remember?'

I let him prattle on because it was easier than trying to shut him up. How he used to wind Jaz up by singing *Take my paw, I'm a hamster in paradise* whenever she cleaned Mojo out; how once, when we were courting, my mother had invited him to Sunday lunch and he'd choked spectacularly on a string of beef fat; that time he'd been changing on the beach in Fowey, larking about, and had overbalanced and given everyone a flash.

But as we came into the outskirts of Harrogate finally, even he went quiet. Only when Neil Young's 'Heart of Gold' came on the radio did he break the silence. 'Hey, do you remember when Jaz cooked up that massive temperature out of nowhere, and we had to do a midnight dash to hospital?'

'I do,' I said. I could recall the scene so clearly. 'The minute we walked through the door she was right as rain. Then, on the way home, you stopped the car and I took her out into the park and whirled her round. I was that relieved.'

Phil opened his mouth as if to speak, but then shook his head and stayed silent.

We were driving between rows of tall stone houses. In one of these, or something like it, Jaz and Matty were waiting for us.

'It wasn't all bad, was it?' said Phil, after a while.

'No.'

'I mean, we've history, haven't we?'

'Too much,' I said.

After that, neither of us spoke till we saw Soulton Street.

I'd printed out the directions from the computer, but now I came to look at the detail, one side had been cut off and some of it we were having to guess. The stone houses gave way to a modern estate, then to rows of semis like Sunnybank, then a council estate. Then we seemed to be passing through the edge of Harrogate and out into the countryside again. I was about to say I thought we must have gone wrong when I recognised a road number, and understood where we were. A couple more turnings, one, two, and the next one was us.

We found ourselves in a cul-de-sac flanked by terraced grey cottages, all with little porches and square front gardens, fields and moorland behind. Phil slowed the car to a crawl so I could peer at house numbers.

'It's on your side,' I said, swinging round in my seat to face him.

He was leaning forward, frowning, his lips drawn into a kind of snarl. It was the first evidence I'd seen that he might be under stress. 'Over there. That's Jaz's car,' he said.

I started to shake.

Within the next second my focus shifted to something moving just beyond the car in one of the gardens: a small white figure behind black railings. 'Matty', I tried to say, but only a whisper came out. Blindly I felt for the handle and pushed the door open even though the car was still moving, but my seat belt locked and held me back. I scrabbled for the release clip.

'Wait,' said Phil.

'There! Look!' I said.

He pulled up, and turned the engine off. 'What are you planning to do, Carol?'

It was as if he could read my mind. He looked into my eyes and saw the film play out: me running across the road, grabbing Matty, lifting him over the fence, dashing back to our getaway car with my grandson in my arms.

'No,' he said sternly.

'What's he doing out on his own? He's not safe.'

'There are railings all round, and a gate.'

'Who's keeping an eye on him, though?'

'The front door's open. Someone'll be watching out, trust me.'

It was impossible to see anything in the windows from this angle, bar reflections of the sky. The porch was empty.

331

'Take a moment or two,' said Phil, placing his hand on my arm. 'How are you going to do this? You want me to come over with you? You're not going to get hysterical, are you?'

'I'm not going to get hysterical, no. I just need to—' Again I felt for the handle. The physical urge to hold Matty was becoming overpowering, eclipsing even, for that moment, the risk of upsetting Jaz.

'I'll walk across with you. We'll put our heads round the door and see what happens.'

'Let me have a minute with him first.'

He sighed, then shook his head. 'You know, Jaz is my daughter too. I'd quite like to see she's OK.'

'You told me she was fine!'

'Carol. Calm down.' He took my wrists in his hands and held them, and I let my eyes close while I counted to ten. My breathing was too fast, my heart pounding. When I opened my eyes, Matty was still there. I shivered violently.

'Now,' I said. 'Please.'

'Come on, then.'

I climbed out, and Phil escorted me across the road as if I were an invalid. My legs were weak with nerves, and when I got to the railings I had to hold onto them for support. Matty was crouched on the lawn, two-handedly bashing some gourd-shaped object against the ground. His hair had grown, and he was wearing a cream-coloured outfit I hadn't seen before, with grass stains on the knees. So absorbed was he that he didn't look up till the gate creaked open.

'Hello,' I said, trying to keep my voice steady.

'Macca, Nanna, look,' he said, straightening up and holding out his gourd. In one swooping movement I reached down, lifted and pulled him tightly to me, nestling my face into his curls, and his weight and shape were such a blissful sensation against me I could have cried out. There's no feeling on earth like holding a child you love. It's a comfort beyond anything else, a crucial jigsaw piece slotted home. Matty smelled of shampoo and butter and soil and himself. I breathed him in, and thanked God.

Somewhere in the background I was aware of Phil shifting about; then I heard the sound of footsteps in the porch. I knew we only had seconds left, and I kept my eyes screwed shut.

And then Jaz's voice went, 'Jesus wept, *you*!' and the game was up.

CHAPTER 31

Photograph 155, Album Two

Location: the back garden, Sunnybank

Taken by: Carol

Subject: Eileen under the lilac tree, holding newborn Jaz. She looks so utterly absurd with a baby in her arms that, at first, Carol laughs out loud. Eileen wants to know what's so funny. Carol realises, in the nick of time, that the truth might not be diplomatic. 'I'm just a bit giddy,' she says instead. And because Carol has been high as a kite since the birth, manically so, Eileen accepts this explanation.

She does look bloody odd, though; there's no getting away from it.

I kept my face buried against my grandson, counting down the last few moments.

'Hey up,' said Phil.

When I mustered the courage to peep, Jaz was, astonishingly, in the process of embracing him. He looked caught out and embarrassed, and relieved. 'Dad!' she said. 'What are *you* doing here?'

'You sent a text.'

'No, I didn't.'

She moved over to me and I thought maybe I was going to get a hug too. But the outstretched arms were for Matty. Of course. It was all I could do not to cling onto him and fight her. A part of myself tore away with him, and I was left standing there, exposed and frightened.

'Jaz didn't send a text. I did.' A short man with a frank, pleasant face was advancing across the lawn towards Phil.

I waited for Jaz to explode with fury, but she just went, 'Oh! I should have known.'

'Well, someone had to.' He smiled at me as he shook Phil's hand. 'Nick Page, pleased to meet you. Shall we go in?'

I glanced at Phil. *I don't know, should we? Are you getting any of this?*

He gave a tiny shrug. At the same time, Nick Page took my elbow and began to draw me towards the door. As we walked, I was gaining the impression of someone who liked to act older than his years. In spite of the slightly receded hairline, he didn't look much past thirty-five. *Who is this guy? Do we know him? How should I be playing this?* said Phil's expression. *No idea,* I signalled back.

We funnelled through the porch straight into a wide, light room with cream walls and a bare wooden floor. Books filled almost every available horizontal space except for the mantelpiece, which had been used to display a collection of African masks and statuettes. Above the fireplace was a mirror with a blue and green mosaic frame, while near the opposite skirting board, a stone painted with a rainbow served as a doorstop. Hippy, I was thinking. Intellectual, middle-class. Everything here's ethically sourced and unprocessed; I'd seen rooms like this in the Sunday magazines. What a contrast from Sunnybank's chintz cushions and Beswick budgies. No china cabinets here, I'd be prepared to bet.

Indignation rose up in me. I was who I was, I'd done my best and if all Jaz valued in the end turned out to be a certain set of lifestyle trappings, then that was her failing, not mine. To come across the country to this man and seek shelter here, when the ones she'd left at home were beside themselves—

'What can I get you?' asked Nick, clasping his hands like a hearty waiter.

'Tea, please,' I said feebly.

'Tea,' echoed Phil.

Nick took himself off, leaving us to our awkwardness, and that's when I registered the little shrivelled palm cross tacked to the chimney breast.

'For God's sake, sit down,' said Jaz, and plonked herself on the large squashy sofa with Matty on her knee. At once he slid himself onto the cushion next to her, and reached up for me. He was still holding his gourd.

'What is it, love?' I asked, bending to see. My heart was thudding as though I'd swum ten lengths.

'African maracas,' replied Jaz. 'Nick spent some time in Kenya.'

Who is he? I wanted to ask, but didn't dare voice the question yet.

'Who is he?' said Phil.

Jaz laughed, as if we were being particularly dense. 'Nick Page. You do know him. Dr Page. When I was at Leeds? You met him, Mum.'

I thought about it, and tried to recall the detail: standing with Jaz in the Union building, being hailed by a man in a moss-green jacket. I couldn't have told you another thing about the encounter, though. *Yes, Jaz, I did meet him, for about ten seconds, more than six years ago. If I'd known you were going to run off with him, I'd have paid a sight more attention.* How much older than her was he, for a start? Wasn't it against the rules, or something? Could she possibly have stepped straight from Ian to an old fogey like this?

Then, in a rush of understanding, I heard Tomasz's voice once more: *She went to the clinic with her personal tutor.*

Back he came into the lounge, Dr Page, with a tray of cups and a bright smile for everyone. 'That's the kettle on,' he said, placing the cups on the coffee-table and settling himself on a carved stool by the fender. 'Now. I'm guessing there are probably lots of questions you'd like to ask.'

'I'll say,' growled Phil.

For God's sake, don't ruin it, I thought. I held onto Matty, who'd decided to study the bobbles on my jumper, and stroked his hair in an effort to calm myself.

'You're Jaz's teacher?' I said.

'I was.' They exchanged a smile that made my heart contract with jealousy. 'I had that privilege.'

Phil addressed Jaz. 'Have you been here all the time, then?'

'About a fortnight. I went to Whitby, first off.'

'*Whitby? Why?*'

'I felt like going to the seaside. We stayed in a hotel.'

'Who did?'

'Me and Matty. Who do you think?'

'What hotel was it?'

'Just a hotel, I dunno.'

I said, 'I wish you'd let me know where you were. It was – really difficult.' That was as much protest as I dared.

'Yeah.' Again she cast her eyes towards Dr Page. 'Sorry.'

'Nanna bag. Here y'are, Nanna,' said Matty, struggling to pull up the strap he was sitting on.

'Are you coming home, Jaz?'

At that moment, the door in the far corner was pushed open and a young woman walked in carrying a teapot. Her blonde hair fell forward as she put the pot down, a process that involved her bending at the knee rather than the waist, since she was heavily pregnant.

'This is my wife, Steph,' said Dr Page.

Oh thank God, I nearly said out loud. I don't know how Phil was feeling at that moment, but I could have whooped with relief. Now I knew for certain we weren't looking at a predatory tutor taking advantage of an ex-student; I wouldn't have to go back to David and Ian and break the news that Jaz had moved in with a new lover a hundred miles away, and field their outrage and dismay. Simply, Jaz had been with friends, people who knew her history and accepted her, who were in a position to offer practical help.

'Nice to meet you,' I said, meaning it.

'I must tell you,' she said. 'Jaz has been such a help to me these last two weeks.'

'She contacted me to ask if she could drop by for a chat, catch up on old times,' continued Dr Page. 'Then, when she got here . . . well, she ended up staying. Turns out there was quite a lot to talk about! Not that it's put us out in any way. As Steph says, she's actually been a tremendous help. Although we didn't know till yesterday that she hadn't told you where she was.'

'I was *going* to phone,' said Jaz, rolling her eyes as if she was fourteen again.

'Well, you don't need to now, do you? Mrs Morgan, your daughter and I had a very long discussion late last night.'

'You're telling me.'

'And I'd say she resolved quite a few issues that were troubling her. Is that a fair summary, Jaz?'

Another of those looks passed between them.

'Yeah, I'm feeling loads better,' she said. 'I've got a lot of stuff into perspective. Sometimes you have to, you know, get right away.'

'You certainly did that,' said Phil. 'Your mum—'

'Shh,' I said.

Dr Page nodded understandingly. 'So we've done a lot of talking, and a little bit of praying, and I think Jaz feels it might be time to come home.'

Jaz nodded. 'I'm much more straightened out. I'm in a better place now.'

I heard Phil snort under his breath. *A little bit of praying?* I was thinking. Is this the same person who told me not eighteen months ago that having a child christened was a form of bullying? Who as a teenager, for spite, once picked the cross off a hot cross bun before eating it? Then again, hadn't she begged me last Advent for my Nativity set, and put it on display in the front-room window? I closed my eyes and thought of us all gathered round the table for Christmas dinner. Dear God, that it might happen.

'When do you think you might be ready?' I asked.

'Oh, I reckon she's pretty much ready now,' said Dr Page. 'Is that right, Jaz? You could pop upstairs and pack your stuff while your mum and dad finish their tea. Then you can all set off home together. A merry convoy. Steph'll help you gather your bits and pieces. Leave Matty down here, eh?'

'Oh, I don't know. It feels a bit sudden. Maybe tomorrow, so I can sort a few more things.'

'Didn't we say last night that delay becomes, in the end, an additional burden?'

'Yeah, I know. I can see that. But it's still—'

'The truth is, you'll never be as ready as you are right now. You admitted that yourself, not twelve hours ago. Take control of the moment, eh?' He leaned forward encouragingly. 'I know you can do this, or I shouldn't ask you.'

She went like a lamb.

Once she was gone, he said, 'I'm sorry I couldn't let you

know earlier. We weren't aware of the full situation. But I want you to be clear, I didn't go behind her back in contacting you; she had said she would ring you within the next couple of days. I just felt it might be difficult for her to make the call, and I didn't want you worrying even a minute longer than necessary.'

'If we could have talked to you before we came up,' Phil began.

'Yes, I did consider that. But I decided, on balance, it would be better if she could explain to you herself, here. I didn't want to overstep my remit.' His manner was so candid, so disarming. All those years ago my daughter must have sat in his study, pouring out crisis after crisis: Tomasz, the boy who killed himself, a positive pregnancy test. This man and his wife drove her to the clinic and stayed with her till the abortion was done. Took her back home with them, tucked her up in bed, brought her painkillers and sanitary towels, mopped her tears. Things I should have done myself, but wasn't allowed. Gratitude struggled with jealousy, and shame.

'You were her *personal* tutor?' I asked carefully.

'I was.' He looked at me for a long moment. *Don't ask me what I've promised to keep confidential*, his eyes said.

'It was a damn shame she packed in her degree,' said Phil. 'That you couldn't have talked her round. Whatever the circumstances.'

Dr Page stepped across to the window and addressed himself to the far hills.

'She did what she felt she had to, at the time. I agree, it was a great shame she didn't complete her course. She was one of the best students in her year. But she's using her languages, and enjoying them – not every graduate can claim that. And you know, Steph and I are very fond of her.' After a pause, his focus came back to us and he smiled. 'I really do believe Jaz has turned an important corner these last few weeks. I know she'll want to talk a lot more when she gets home.'

'I suppose we should say thank you,' said Phil.

Dr Page spread his hands, like a vicar giving a blessing. 'You must have my number before you go.'

Damn right, said Phil's expression.

Matty lolled against me and drummed his heels against the sofa arm. 'Shh,' I said. He burrowed his face against my stomach, and it was as though we'd never been apart.

'Tell you what, let him take those maracas,' said Dr Page. 'He seems to have developed a fancy for them.'

Ten minutes later we were all back in the porch.

'Is it OK if I ring Ian? Or do you want to do it?' I asked Jaz. I'd been rehearsing the question all the while she was upstairs.

'Yeah, you do it.'

'You know, I had to give him the key.'

'Well, obviously.'

'Right.' I took in her pretty, heart-shaped face and my heart clenched with hope. 'Oh, you've had a proper fringe cut.'

'Have you only just noticed?' She shook her hair out of her eyes, and took hold of Matty by his coat sleeve.

We shuffled at Matty-speed towards the gate. Phil took the opportunity to slip his hand in mine and I didn't pull away. 'Come on,' he said, drawing me ahead. 'It's a long drive home.'

'What if she doesn't follow us?' I whispered. When I turned back, Dr Page had lifted open her car boot and was swinging cases and bags inside.

'She will.'

Together we walked across the street.

I'm glad you were with me today, I thought. But I didn't say the words out loud.

CHAPTER 32

Photograph: unnumbered, from Carol's wedding album

Location: round the back of St Stephen's C of E, Tannerside, Bolton

Taken by: Ribble Photographic Studios

Subject: Carol stands in full-length white, white-capped, with a bouquet of irises, freesia and roses. Although she is smiling, there's a slight clenching of the jaw that betrays the fact she's frozen, as cold as the granite memorial tablets beneath the soles of her inadequate slippers. Her feet are in pain. 'It's almost June,' she mutters to bridesmaid Eileen, 'but it's like crossing the Arctic. It's not what you expect.'

'Nothing ever is,' says Eileen. The wind whips through the weave of their thin silk gowns and the ribbons round Carol's veil tangle madly. 'I'll be as blue as my dress by the time this photographer's sorted,' adds Eileen.

Earlier, when they are trying to warm themselves in the ladies', Carol says: 'Don't let people boss you about when it's your turn. Have the wedding you want.'

'If I ever get married,' Eileen replies, 'which I doubt. I'm running away to Jamaica and doing it on the beach. In a white

bikini, to a Sean Connery lookalike, and we'll leave for our honeymoon on a jet ski.'

She's really weird today, thinks Carol. Jittery, distracted, near the edge. Snapped Phil's head off earlier over nothing. You wouldn't think she'd get so keyed up about being a brides-maid, at her age.

'Best avoid the bouquet, then,' says Carol archly. She's too full of her own happiness to care much anyway.

The first thing I noticed, on returning to Jaz and Ian's house, was that the gate had been replaced. An unpainted wooden one now hung from the hinges, while the old wrought-iron one lay flat on the lawn, grass poking up through the scrolls.

I paused on the step to listen. Some toy of Matty's sounded a klaxon repeatedly, and I could hear Ian's irritated tones over the top of it.

The door was on the latch so I knocked loudly, then let myself in.

It was the light that struck me. Where the hall used to be papered with a dark, embossed design, the walls were now a plain milk-coffee colour, and the woodwork gleaming white. The changes made the place seem much bigger, despite the stairs being once more cluttered with toys and washing and books. It was wonderful to see again Matty's plastic bits and pieces strewn about, though I noticed with a jolt that the wed-ding photo had been taken down from the wall.

'Then get someone in to *fix it!*' shouted Jaz from the top of the stairs. Which is when she saw me. 'Oh, Mum, hi. I was just sorting out Matty's stuff. I'll be with you in a minute.' She raised her voice unpleasantly. 'Ian, can you stick the kettle on?'

Ian emerged from the lounge. He rearranged his features into a smile, nodded a greeting and headed for the kitchen. I could guess what his face was doing once he'd turned his back on me.

I went to find Matty.

He was in the living room playing with one of those big multicoloured learning centres. The top section had a row of chunky talking buttons in various shapes, and the lower half was all farmyard animals that made the appropriate noises when you pressed them. Along the bottom was a flashing keyboard.

I lowered myself onto the carpet next to him and began to pick out the tune of 'Baa Baa Black Sheep', while my grandson provided a descant of moos and quacks. It was a bit of a racket, to be honest, but no one else was in the room.

Even though he'd only been away a season, Matty had changed. His development had leaped forward. He knew all sorts of new words, plus a fragment of a song I'd not taught him, with accompanying actions. He could negotiate my back step without needing his hand held. He could turn the pages of a book by himself and build a four-block tower out of bricks. Every time he stayed over we had a marathon bedtime reading session, and after I'd tucked him in I'd go up four or five times just to lean over his cot and look at him. For a week and a half I'd had the bitter pleasure of discovering what I'd missed. And all the while, in the background, I was aware of Jaz still poised to deliver our fates.

Here she came now, stropping into the room, her colour high. I snatched my hand away from the keyboard.

'Heating's playing up,' she said.

'Oh, love. You look tired.'

'Yeah, well.' She dropped onto the sofa. 'I'm not sleeping. No one is. Matty won't settle when I'm in the room and I seem to be waking at every little squeak or sniffle he makes. So the nights are pretty long, aren't they, old chap?'

'Why are you sleeping in there? Has he not been well?'

'Ian's got our bed,' she said.

I didn't know what to say to that.

Instead I told her about Moira's sister's mini-trampoline she was getting rid of, and did Matty want it. 'It's nearly new, it folds away, and it's got safety bars on the side. It's a decent one, ELC.'

'Great,' said Jaz flatly. 'Tell her thanks.'

I heard the back door judder open and shut, and assumed Ian had gone outside for something. But a few moments later, it was David who walked in on us. He must have left his shoes on the mat but he still wore his coat. From his gloved hand dangled a pair of secateurs.

'Carol!' He laid the secateurs on the chair arm by Jaz, and opened his arms for me. I started forward, then panicked. Jaz was watching me with eyes like flint. I faltered, took a few more steps till I was within his range, and submitted to a brief embrace.

'Nice to see you.' I pushed him away and stepped back.

'And you,' he said, frowning.

'How are you getting on?' Jaz asked him, pointedly moving the secateurs to the top of the bookcase where they'd be out of Matty's reach.

'I need a hacksaw, I've come in to ask for one.'

Jaz turned to me. 'We're taking out the elder tree by the kitchen window, Mum. It's making the room dark and rotting the sill outside. Cut out the *dead wood*.'

'I thought you said you were getting another loaf,' said Ian, coming in with a tray of mugs and setting it down. 'We've only crusts left. I can't do Matty toast with that.'

'Well, you know, I've had a few other jobs to do.'

I said, 'He's coming home with me in a minute. I can give him dinner.'

David was still standing in the corner, watching me. 'It's been a while since I've seen you, Carol.'

'Only a week,' I said, for Jaz's benefit.

'A fortnight,' he said. 'I thought we might have had a chance to catch up.'

'I've been really busy, I've not caught my breath yet.'

'It does seem to be all go.'

'Ian,' said Jaz, 'if you're going back into the kitchen, can you get Matty's coat off the hall radiator and stick it by the door, ready?'

He went out of the room, there was a pause, then he shouted back, 'It's not there.'

'What do you mean?'

'I mean it's not there.' His face reappeared round the jamb.

'I told you to take it out of the machine.'

'No, you didn't.'

'Yes, I did. Oh, for God's sake. I knew you weren't listening. Now it'll be wringing wet!'

She hauled herself up off the sofa, and as she bent her head I saw the blueish-grey skin under her lower lids.

Don't leave me alone with David! I wanted to shout, but she was already gone.

'Well,' he said.

Matty was prodding at the flashing lights on his board. I scrambled up stiffly, saying, 'It must be difficult for both of them—'

'Carol.'

'I'd better go help out, if you can keep an eye on this one.' Quickly I slid past him and into the hall.

'Carol?' he said behind me. 'Carol!' But I pretended not to hear.

Afterwards, he phoned. 'Let me come round and see you,' he said.

'Wait till we hear what's happening. Wait till Jaz makes her decision.'

'She's back home. She's made it.'

'I don't think she has.'

'Why won't you meet me, Carol?'

'Let's just wait,' I said.

Sometimes I'd get out the wedding album and look at his picture, one hand covering Jacky. If the photos had been loose, I'd have got the scissors and cut her off.

I don't know why I assumed she'd invited me to go shopping and have lunch, like a regular mum and grown-up daughter.

'I want you to come and see a flat with me,' Jaz said when I met her by the Civic Centre.

My hopes plummeted, there and then.

'Don't panic,' she continued. 'I'm not going far. But it'll be easier all round. Ian and I'll be able to talk to each other better if we have some space. At the moment it's just grim. The atmosphere's like you wouldn't believe. I've got to go or it'll do my head in.'

She took my bag for me, a small, unlooked-for kindness, and we began to walk up the High Street together.

'It's bound to be difficult at first,' I said, 'when you think what's gone on. I'm sure things'll get easier. Can you not give it a bit longer?'

'Nope. This isn't a snap decision, Mum, I've thought it through. It's the best way.'

'OK, well, how about you move in with me for a few weeks? And then that's saving you money, and you're not tied up in a contract or anything.'

'Thanks, but I want to go with the flat.' She smiled tightly at me. 'It's all right, you know, I'm not about to take off again.'

'I don't think I could bear it if you did, Jaz.'

I glimpsed our reflection in the butcher's window, caught the way she lowered her head guiltily.

'How will you afford it?' I said.

'Ian. Benefits. I'll work something out.'

'Does he know what you're planning?'

'Yes.'

'What does he think?'

'He agrees. It's been too much of a shock coming together again. And he's angry with me, so fucking angry, and I'm angry with him and we've so much to sort out but all we're doing is fighting. So I've told him it's our best chance.'

'Did you mean it?'

'Yeah, I do.'

We passed the shop where I bought my grandson's Moses basket and his first car seat. Behind the window a couple stooped to examine the mechanism on a collapsible pram.

'How's Matty with it all?'

Jaz shrugged. 'He was having a tantrum when I left. Didn't want to wear his shoes, wanted to keep his slippers on all day. I've left Ian dealing with it.'

'That's normal, coming up to two. You were a nightmare at that age. What are you doing for his birthday?'

'I'm not sure.'

'You could have some of his little friends round from nursery.'

'Maybe.'

Please be together for him, I wanted to say. *There's no better gift for a child.* 'I could bake some muffins.'

'Can't think that far ahead right now, Mum.'

We passed Boots, and Healey's café, and the side street that led down to Bark End and The Olive.

I said, 'See the pet shop across the road? That used to be Falkirk's, where we bought your first school uniform.

Do you remember? Gosh, you were a little scrap in those days.'

'Nick said you phoned him last week,' she said. 'Don't worry, he wouldn't tell me what you talked about. He never breaks a confidence.'

Bully for him, I thought. Saint Page. 'What do you reckon to him?' Phil had asked me on the drive back. 'Is he on the level or what?' 'I think he is on the level,' I'd replied. That didn't mean I had to like him, though.

'It was only to thank him again.'

'I don't mind you discussing me, Mum.'

What's he got that I haven't? I wanted to say. *How come you'll listen to him and not to me?* 'I expect he confirmed you'd had a terrible upbringing and everything that had happened to you was my fault.'

Jaz shook her head. 'He gave me a right bollocking, actually. In a nice way. He told me to grow up.'

'Oh,' I said.

'But he was fantastic with me. Not just letting me stay; more than that. The way he listens and just sort of suggests things subtly, so you can work out what you think without being hassled. Not telling you what to do, but, you know, guiding you. He's laid-back, *and* super-moral. It's difficult to explain. When I was at uni . . .'

'What?'

'He was very kind. He's been like a dad.'

'You've got a dad.'

'Yeah, right.' She pulled a sneery face.

'You never give him a chance,' I heard myself say. 'He cares a lot about you.'

Jaz raised her eyebrows, but she didn't say anything.

We reached the top of the High Street. 'Where do we go from here?' I asked.

'Down Overdale Road. It's near the Catholic church.'

A side of town I hadn't visited since the days of the divorce. This was the back of the library and the health centre, a row of Georgian buildings housing law firms and accountants. Makinson & Todd had been my solicitors. The brass plate was still up, and I wondered whether at this moment, a woman like me was sitting in Mr Todd's office, unpicking her marriage.

'David cares about you too,' I added recklessly, as we crossed to the opposite pavement.

'He can fuck off.'

'Jaz, if it wasn't for his intervention, Ian would have had the police after you.'

She sighed and swapped the bag to her other hand.

You don't seem to realise what a bloody dangerous game you were playing, or how I had to fight to keep you out of trouble, I wanted to shout at her. But before I could marshal the right words, she changed the subject.

'You've been moving stuff round.'

'Where?'

'Your house.'

'I've been having a clear-out.'

'It's good, it looks bigger.'

'It should do. I've been right through, taken eleven bags to the tip and five to the charity shop. There were still a load of your dad's car mags in the hall cupboard, plus all my mother's sewing patterns, balls and balls of dish-cloth yarn, parish magazines going back to the Seventies. Suddenly I have all this extra storage space. Just the shed to tackle. Although, I might leave that now.'

Now you're home, I meant.

We turned onto Overdale Road.

'Tell you what, Mum: I wish I could go through my head like that and drag out all the bad memories. Sort through and dump the rubbish. Why should I have to cart it round with me all my life?'

I guessed she was imagining Ian with the other woman, or recalling the night she found out, or the rows afterwards. Or maybe it was Tomasz she couldn't shake out of her mind, or Sam, or the boy who killed himself. Into my own consciousness came, unbidden, a memory of Dad standing in his living room, unable to tell me where he was and near to tears. I had no clever answers to offer my daughter.

Instead I said, 'Ian must be glad to have Matty back.'

Something softened in her face. 'Uh-huh.'

'And Matty pleased to see his daddy.'

'Yeah.'

'He must have missed him so much.'

'Don't push it, Mum,' she said, but without real heat. Then, 'Here we are. This is it.'

We were standing outside a large cream and orange Edwardian villa. 'Can we go in?'

'The estate agent's due any time now. What do you reckon so far?'

'Fine,' I said, trying not to look at the unloved square of lawn. 'It's a quiet road. I can't imagine the Catholics get very rowdy.'

She put down my bag and leaned against the coping stones. 'I meant to ask, are you free tomorrow afternoon?'

'Yes. Why? Do you want me to go look at another flat with you?'

'I need to see Grandad.'

To my shame, I almost said, *Why?* 'He's no better, there's no change in him.'

'I want to go anyway.'

'Come round when you're ready, then.'

'Should I bring Matty?'

I gave her a look, mock-despairing. 'What on earth do you think I'm going to say to that, hey?'

At least I got a proper smile out of her.

The day was fine, sharp and bright, and, as if in response, Dad seemed on better form than I'd seen him for a while. He was up in his chair, shaved and dressed, apparently watching the birds on the feeder outside his window. He didn't look up when we came in, but he hasn't done for nearly two years now. I know the way things are with him, though it doesn't stop me hoping.

'You're looking well,' I said, kissing his cheek. Jaz came in behind me with her changing bag in one hand and Matty's reins in the other, plus a carrier of toys and snacks to keep him entertained. I watched as she unpacked, laying out his Duplo first.

'He likes the stones in the yucca pot,' I said, but this time Matty only glanced at the corner, and settled down in the middle of the floor.

Meanwhile Jaz drew out what I thought at first was a large black book, and propped it on the table: speakers for her iPod.

'Are we having music?' I asked, with some slight anxiety. Jaz's tastes could be off-beat.

'Uh-huh,' was all she said.

While she scrolled and fiddled with the cursor, I set to unfastening Matty's reins. He hardly registered my interference, so focused was he on separating two blocks. I thought, That's changed too. He wouldn't have been able to concentrate at that level three months ago. Then, out of the speakers, a ribbon of violin started, so pure it was like a pang of grief.

'Bing Crosby,' said Jaz, 'Pennies from Heaven.'

'Oh, Jaz,' I said. Even Matty paused to listen for a few moments as Bing's low voice cut in over the orchestra.

'Thought it might cheer Grandad up.'

Both of us shifted our chairs round so we were half-facing him, and I took his hand. His eyes stayed fixed on the feeder. 'Matty's here,' I said. 'And Jaz. Come to see you.'

'Plus, I don't like it when it's too quiet,' she said.

'Your generation, you need a soundtrack wherever you go.'

'Silence does my head in after a bit. Doesn't it yours?'

'When you live on your own, you have to make friends with silence. I rather like it.' Bash bash, went Matty. 'Although, when he was away . . .'

The music played on, sweetly.

'I've been thinking,' said Jaz, 'about when I was little. Did you know, Nick was brought up by his grandparents? His mum and dad were missionaries. Like Victorians or something. And where they were working wasn't always safe, so they left him with his mother's parents, which was fine with him because he loved it there. He says that family is the most important thing there is, after God. Family's a gift. People don't appreciate what they have.'

Matty was gathering his blocks together, corralling them into a pile in the centre of the carpet.

Jaz said, 'I think I can understand now what you were trying to do, Mum. When you let Ian see Matty behind my back.'

A fearful hope surged inside my chest. 'Can you?'

'I told Nick about it, and he said I hadn't thought it through. What might have happened if I'd shut Ian out completely, how he might have retaliated. The damage. To all of us. I couldn't see that.'

'That's what I was worried about; I tried to tell you.'

'I know. You still shouldn't have done it, but—'

'And David. David was only ever trying to help.'

'He's just a git.'

'Why do you hate him so much, Jaz?'

'Why do you *like* him so much, Mum?'

She held my gaze till I looked away.

Suddenly Dad cleared his throat and we both jumped. Bing was 'Ac-Cent-Tchu-Ating the Positive', a track I knew was one of his all-time favourites.

'Gosh, can you remember Grandad singing this in his shed?' I asked. Jaz still eyed me suspiciously, but I carried on. 'It was a summer afternoon, probably a couple of years after Grandma died; you'd have been about eight. He was making some sort of rack for his beans, working with the door open because the day was hot, and you and I were on the lawn making daisy chains, except you couldn't because your nails were bitten to nothing and you couldn't split the stems. There'd be a burst of hammering, then a couple of lines, then more hammering. It made you laugh. And later on you were asking about the picture on the syrup tin he used to keep his nails in, and he told you the story of Samson killing the lion, and the bees making a nest in the carcase.'

'*And out of the strong came forth sweetness.* God, yes, I do remember that. I used to love going to Grandad's. He always did fun things. I was never in trouble at his house.' She was leaning over the arm of the chair, in a posture that reminded me of how she used to ask for a bedtime story. 'I wish I could remember more from that time. You think you'll never forget something, or that it'll never end, and the next minute it's gone. Why do we let the good stuff slip away?'

'That's why I take my photographs,' I said. 'Pin down the past.'

Jaz closed her eyes. 'Tell me about when I was little, Mum.'

'What about it?'

'Anything, really. I want to see if I can get it back again.'

So I told her, off the top of my head, some random memories: taking her when she was a toddler to Eileen's, and finding her in the kitchen eating cat biscuits from the bowl; about Mojo hanging by his teeth off Phil's thumb; her first words, how she learned to swim in the sea at Weymouth, the llama in Paignton Zoo that spat down Eileen's coat, the time she made a Hallowe'en mask and accidentally cut a hole in the bed-spread beneath. While my dad gazed out of the window, and Matty sorted and re-sorted his bricks, the past pulled up the past the way roots pull up soil.

In turn she told me about wetting her knickers once when we were on a picnic, and throwing them in a hedge. How she'd watched Phil pour Coke on next door's lawn, and how he'd sworn her to secrecy and given her five pounds to keep schtum. How she'd killed my lobivia cactus out of revenge because it had spiked her. She talked about seeing us in the audience at the school play, and how it had distracted her but she'd also been pleased we were there. She recounted a sledging session with Eileen, and how Nat had once tried to get her to bleach the ends of her hair with Toilet Duck.

Matty moved between us, sometimes offering Duplo to me, sometimes to his mum. At one point he dropped a piece and, in pursuing it, he bumped into Dad's knee. He might as well have walked into a table leg, and I ached for the acknowl-edgement that would never come: the freckled hand coming down to caress the curls, the friendly word.

'Let's not leave Grandad out,' I said.

'No.'

Jaz moved her chair again till it was very close, and spoke into his face. 'Do you remember when you let me practise bandaging on you, Grandad? And I did your arm in a sling and I made you keep it on all through teatime?'

'I didn't know about that,' I said.

'Oh yeah. I wanted to do him up like a mummy, head to toe, but there wasn't enough bandage.'

'Otherwise he'd probably have let you do it.'

'And those pigeons,' she went on, speaking loudly as though he was deaf. 'Do you remember taking me to see your friend's racing pigeons? We had to go down this long path between people's gardens and then there was a massive shed, and all this noise coming out. You said it sounded like a bunch of Grandma's friends, tutting and moaning.'

'Car,' said Matty. 'Car, Mummy.'

Jaz indicated over her shoulder at the bag on the floor. 'Oh, could you get it out for him?'

'Of course.'

I knelt down and opened the bag, and Matty shuffled in next to me. Together we made a performance of peering inside. 'Uh-oh, I think there's a mouse in here,' I said, making my hand scuttle under the canvas. 'Watch out!'

When he giggled, I whipped my hand out and tickled him so that within seconds I had him shrieking with laughter, bucking and flailing against me, butting me in the chest with his head. I put my arms round his solid little body and squeezed him to try and restore some calm, but he still wriggled like a demon. 'Watch out,' he said, making his own mouse and aiming it at my stomach. 'Watch out, Nanna!'

'Honestly, you two,' went Jaz, behind me. Part of me was screwing myself up against a telling-off, but she only said, 'Get that car of yours, Matty, then you can run Nanna's mouse over if it starts being naughty again.'

I laughed, partly from relief.

You let her rule you, I heard Phil say again. Yes, I thought, perhaps I do. Perhaps other grandmothers don't tread on eggshells the way I have to. But I'm so damn grateful to have Matty back, and so petrified she'll take him away again, that I'll do anything it takes not to rock the boat. She can impose any condition she likes. I'll drain the pond dry, cut my hours at work, have him any nights she decides, at the drop of a hat. She only has to name her terms. If that makes me feeble, then that's too bad.

I knew now there was no way I could carry on seeing David. His gentle kindness and support belonged to a very particular time that was gone. Already some of the memories were patchy and imperfect, though I could still conjure the modulations of his voice, his confident stride, the detail of his mouth and eyes. I should have taken some pictures of him, but there were too many events and revelations in those months that I didn't want to acknowledge; photographs would have fixed them more firmly into reality. Jaz was right, the bad images would hang around longer, but it would all pass away eventually. Everything would go. New hurts and new happinesses would overlay each other, till the weeks without Matty, with David, were almost nothing. That was the way it had to be.

'And you used to have this joke about the coasters I made for you,' Jaz was telling Dad, 'the little felt ones with the cross stitch round the edge. You'd pick one up and you'd go— Oh, Mum, look! *Look!*'

Panic shot through me as Jaz bent forward. What could she see on my father's face? A heart-attack? A stroke?

She drew back from him and turned to me, her face triumphant. 'He's rocking himself to the song, Mum. He can hear it. He knows it.'

'*Don't fence me in,*' crooned Bing.

'Dad?' I said, touching his fingers lightly. His eyes were still vacant, but there was no doubt about it, he was marking time to the music.

'Isn't it fantastic?' Jaz said. 'Has he ever done this before?'

'No,' I said.

We sat entranced by the tiny movement of his shoulders, as though we were witnessing some incredible feat of gymnastics.

Meanwhile Bing spoke of wide skies and blissful solitude, of a life at ease and without boundaries or grief.

The song played out its jaunty amble, and I let myself imagine, for those two minutes, my dad's spirit roaming free across any landscape he cared to call up. Inside his silence, he must still be moored by a thread of memory; not floating, lost and nowhere. Even if he wasn't with us, he was himself, somewhere.

A weight lifted in me for the first time in ages.

'I have my uses, don't I? I'm not just a thorn in your side,' said Jaz over the closing chords. She passed me a tissue from Dad's locker, and I dabbed at my eyes.

'Rewind it, oh please, rewind it.'

'See,' she said, bending once more to the iPod, 'how something good can happen even after you've given up hoping?'

It wasn't till hours afterwards that I saw the irony of what she'd said. And I don't think Jaz got it at all.

CHAPTER 33

Photograph 352, Album Three

Location: Carol's dining room

Taken by: Carol

Subject: Eileen's birthday. A triple celebration because the biopsy seems clear, she's been promoted at work, and today she's twenty-one for the nineteenth time. Jaz brings in plates and cutlery, sets them down, and Eileen catches her hand playfully. 'Why do you bite your nails?' she asks.

Jaz raises her eyebrows. 'Why don't you get your roots re-touched?'

'Touché,' laughs Eileen.

At the far end of the table, Carol's stomach turns over with jealousy.

'You're so good with her. I bet she wishes you were her mother,' she says that evening, when Jaz is in bed and both women have had a fair bit to drink.

'Don't be daft,' says Eileen. 'I'm more like a substitute granny. I just hover on the edges. I'd be a useless mother. I'd be a useless wife.'

'You would not,' protests Carol. She'd like to know why Eileen thinks this, and also why there have been so very few

359

boyfriends over the years. After all, she dated at school. This is a bright, sparky, good-humoured woman with a decent figure and all her own teeth. 'Not the marrying kind, your Eileen,' Carol's mother once remarked. Meaning what? Now, under this friendly gauze of drunkenness, might be the time to probe. But in leaning forward to pursue her point, Carol knocks her glass off the chair arm. By the time they've mopped up and re-poured, the moment's gone. Some instinct tells her not to return to it.

It was only when I came to trawl through my hard drive to make up a special album, a thank you to Jaz, that I realised how many photographs I'd actually taken of Matty. Already there were hundreds.

Of my own first twenty-three months of life there existed just two snaps. One was a studio portrait of me as a baby, which my mother only had done because a friend was getting one of her little girl and wanted the company. The other shows me as a toddler in a knitted pixie cap with ear flaps, and an A-line coat. I'm holding onto my father's hand and we're outside church watching a neighbour's wedding. Heaven knows who took the photograph, or how we came by a copy.

It's difficult not to feel hard done by when I flip between that early album and the most recent. My childhood versus Matty's. There *are* snaps from the Fifties and Sixties, but they're pretty much all holiday vistas, rarely troubled by human figures. Very occasionally the minute form of my mother appears at the bottom of a sweeping landscape or a historical monument. Later on I pop up in a couple of beach shots, once underneath an archway in Ludlow Castle, and in the entrance to the Blue John Cavern. But the ordinary, everyday activities – the sort of thing I snap Matty doing, and treasure – never merited recording.

I just don't think there was the same level of interest in children then. Eileen and I used to play in the quarry, and round the lonely deep pond in the middle of Copper's Field, and clamber over farm equipment and throw branches at pylons. What freedom, you might say, how lucky we were. I know for a fact, though, that a lot of my personal liberty stemmed from my mother's indifference. Stop ironing and play a game? Switch off the vac and go for a walk? Don't be soft. She'd no more have got down on her knees to be a growly lion than she would have performed a striptease down the nave of St Stephen's. The nearest she and I ever came to spending quality time was when I became old enough to learn baking, sewing and cleaning (and there's not much entertainment to be had out of a wad of Duraglit, I can tell you).

What was it about those decades that made mums and dads so blasé? My mother thought I was mad to rush to Jaz as soon as she cried. Couldn't understand why I was cutting trailing ribbons off her baby clothes, shifting bottles of bleach out the way, screwing the bookcase to the wall. 'You wonder how any of us managed to make it through infancy,' she used to scoff. *Your bloody good luck*, I'd think.

I let myself be frightened; stoked it, revelled in it. My reasoning was, if I remembered to be consciously grateful for Jaz from the moment she was born, then some Higher Power might recognise my appreciation and keep her safe.

I realise now you can't make bargains like that. Fate laughs in the face of such tactics.

I asked David to meet me by Pettymere Lake. I couldn't face seeing him in private, where heaven knows what might get said – or in a public place like a restaurant, with other people listening in. The wide bowl of the Moss was the only space I felt I could cope with.

We were both early, but I'd got there first and was able to watch him walk from the car park, round through the bare trees and across the bridge to the bench where I was sitting. I'd rehearsed a hundred lines and still I didn't know what to say. As he came towards me, his hands in the pockets of his big overcoat and a scarf at his neck, my mind went as blank as the sky. I was all October cloud and chill.

When he reached the bench, he didn't kiss me or say any kind of greeting. He sat down next me, his eyes on the lake.

'Shall I begin?' he said after a few moments.

Pointless to pretend I didn't know what he meant. I nodded.

In cool, straightforward terms, David spelled out what I'd been about to say: that I couldn't contemplate a relationship with him because I was scared of my daughter.

'It sounds so cowardly when you put it like that,' I said.

He made no comment.

'Let me try and explain,' I said. 'It's not just that I *love* Matty – obviously I do. It goes right beyond that. When I'm with him, it's almost as though I'm – I'm taken out of myself. I don't mean he makes me young. He makes me *no* age, and I can act how I want, I don't have to watch the implications of every damn thing I say. I see the world through his eyes and it's new and magical, and we're discovering it together. I go into the garden and Matty's pointing out, oh, spider webs, as though they're the most brilliant creation ever, and it lifts me right up. It's a kind of energy he gives off. Or happiness. I'm recharged. When he was away it was . . . well, you know what it was like. I was lost. A really important part of me was missing. So I daren't contemplate being without him again, I really daren't. I don't know what I'd do.'

'I can't possibly compete with that,' he said.

'You're Matty's grandad. Don't you feel the same way?'

'I don't think I do, no. Not to the same degree. I love my grandson, too, of course, but not so – ferociously.'

What had Phil said? *He's not your child. You're obsessed.* Why could neither of them understand?

I tried a different tack.

'OK, look at it this way, David. Are you prepared to risk all the ground we've won?'

'It wouldn't come to that.' He spread his palms in a dismissive gesture. 'I know what you're trying to do here: bargain with the future. Sacrifice one happiness against another. But it doesn't work like that. You can have both.'

'I wish I could be so confident.'

'Try it, Carol.'

Dead leaves lay clumped round our feet, rotting into blackness; bare branches scraped against each other.

'You know,' he went on, 'some people would say you've hung me out to dry.'

'That's not fair!'

'Tell me, what is fair about this business?'

On the other side of the lake an elderly couple walked a dog, a retriever or a golden labrador, which ran back and forth excitedly along the water's margin. As I watched, the woman stopped and spoke to her companion, and in response he held out his arm to her while she leaned against him and shook a stone from her shoe. It was one of those small, tender, everyday gestures that you take for granted when you're in a relationship, but which viewed from the outside can strike you through your breastbone with longing.

'I feel terrible enough as it is,' I said. 'I *do* understand what you did for me over the summer, of course I do. Do you honestly think I've forgotten the phone calls and chats and meals? The fact you drove me all the way down to see Tomasz and back again, found out all that information on legal rights, offered me money? I will *never* forget those things. How you talked Ian round. Jaz and I couldn't have managed without you. I count my blessings every day that you were there to help us through. Whatever else, please don't think I'm not intensely grateful.'

'It's not gratitude I'm after.'

'This is hurting me, too.'

'And I'm supposed to be pleased by that?'

At every turn he blocked me. The lines I'd prepared, I didn't dare deliver. I sat there with the cold slats of the bench digging into my back, feeling like the meanest woman born. My only consolation was my own, deserved, pain.

I said: 'You know, I spent two dozen years married to a man who never listened. Unless you've lived in a relationship like that, you have no idea how lonely it is. Every serious conversation I ever started, he'd derail with his jokes and daft asides, till eventually I stopped bothering; I used to get more sense out of Jaz. And that was in the days when we were getting on, never mind what came later. Then I started talking, really talking, to you, and I found I could tell you things I'd not told anyone since Eileen died.'

'But isn't that exactly—'

'Wait,' I said. 'Let me finish. It's worked the other way, too. I've got so much out of listening to you. Some of the things you've said have gone right through me, and changed me. You've made me feel more confident in myself, I've been better at making decisions. Essentially, you've become the best friend I've had in years. Although I know it's more than friendship.' I blushed. 'And I never thought, after Phil—'

Say it, went Eileen. *You owe him*. But I couldn't get the words out.

'You're making me sound awfully altruistic. Do you think I've got nothing back from this relationship, Carol?'

'I don't know.'

'Oh, for God's sake. Why do you imagine Jacky left me? Can you really not guess?' I shifted my gaze away from him, embarrassed. 'It was because I "wouldn't commit". Her words. She was right. I admired her, we got on well, but for me it went no further. She wanted more and she got fed up of waiting. So she went. Like the others. Do you see?'

'Not really.'

'I thought, when Jeanette died, that was it. That I'd been incredibly lucky to have met her and to have had that time with her, and the flipside of that was that I'd never experience anything like it again. Every woman I've dated since then has confirmed that belief. Until you.'

'I don't see why I'm so special. Compared with someone like Susannah.' I meant her long, poetic face, that sleek hair, the expensive coat.

'There you go again. I'll tell you what the difference was: she didn't have your warmth, Carol. I look at you and I see a woman who's natural and instinctive and straightforward and true, and, when you're not tying yourself up in knots over Jaz, damn good company. You don't hold back, or scheme or calculate. There's nothing *artful* about you. You have this tremendous warmth, it just pours out of you—'

'Holds me hostage,' I said.

'Yes, but it *needn't.*'

I laughed bitterly. 'You're the one who believes people are born as they are. Well, I wish I wasn't. I wish I could turn my emotions off. I wish I was cool and calculating and all the rest of it, because it would be a damn sight less distressing, that's for sure.'

At last he lifted his arm and put it round my shoulders, and the simple pressure was so comforting I wanted to cry.

Laverne's voice came through the muddle of noise in my head: *Imagine the hassle of dating again. I'd hate to start over, wouldn't you? The stress of someone moving into your house. Or you moving into theirs. Interfering with your systems, always around you. Seeing you in all states. The s-e-x.* It was true, it would have been hard to begin all that business after so long on my own. I would have been prepared to face those fears for David, though.

I made myself shift away from him, out of reach of his arm. Probably he knew then.

'David, it's taken me a long time to get where I am. Settled, I mean, and calm. I had a difficult marriage, years of trouble with Jaz, this latest upset. Finally I can see a bit of clear water ahead. What I have is enough. And although I do want to be with you – believe me, you have no idea how much – I can't risk losing what I have. I daren't. I really daren't. You don't know my daughter, even now.'

'I see.' He clasped his hands in his lap, a man defeated.

'I'm sorry.'

'Yes, I know you are. Is there anything, anything at all I can say to persuade you?'

'I don't think so.'

'Then I shan't drag this out any longer. It's unpleasant for us both.' He rose and stood, looking down on me. 'Thank you for being honest, at least. I shan't bother you with it again. Next week I'm off to the States for a few months to see my sister, so that should give us all some space to recover. I'm sorry if I've distressed you; that was never my intention. But will you do one thing for me, Carol?'

'What?'

'Will you try and make Jasmine confront what she's done? What she did to you when she took Matty away, and what it's cost you this afternoon? And what she means to you, how much it matters that she's fair and decent in her dealings with you. I don't think she sees any of it, and she needs to.'

'She's not a bad person.'
'Will you speak to her?'
'I can't promise.'
'Then you won't have any peace till you do.'
And he turned and walked away into the trees.
Waste of time crying for the moon, said my mother's voice.

CHAPTER 34

Photograph 67, Album One

Location: outside Phil's mother's terraced house, Tannerside, Bolton

Taken by: Phil

Subject: The other Mrs Morgan, Betty, stands with her arms folded and a cigarette between the index and third finger of her right hand. She reminds Carol slightly of Eileen's mother – a slattern – but where Eileen's mother is built on a large scale, Phil's is little and shrunken. She's older than Frieda, but dresses younger, to ghastly effect.

No one's really expecting this visit to be a success.

Husbandless Betty's on a lower rank to start with, and she knows it. There was never any point in trying to impress. So she doesn't. 'You've to take me as you find me,' she says, elbowing Frieda jocularly in the ribs.

Engagement celebration it may be, but they eat across two folding, clothless tables, while ITV plays in the background. The first course is potted meat barmcakes, during which Betty tells a joke about a man refusing to eat tongue because he doesn't like the idea of anything that's been in an animal's mouth and so asks instead for a nice boiled egg. Frieda absolutely does not laugh; the room is filled with the loudness of her not-laughing. Bob pretends absorption in the exploits of Black Beauty. Phil laughs uproariously, even though he's heard the gag before, because he means to show whose side he's on. He's fed up of Frieda's narrowed eyes scrutinising, finding fault; she must think she's the Queen or something.

When Carol finally gets the joke, she laughs too, and Phil loves her for it.

Dessert is tinned pears plonked in cereal bowls and eaten with soup spoons. By now Phil and Carol have got the giggles and cannot stop. Pear juice comes out of Phil's nose, and despite the pain and disgrace, he remains helpless.

By Sale of the Century, everyone's had enough and the coats are brought back in. Carol stands looking round the room, tries to imagine through Frieda's eyes the matted shagpile rug, the collection of trolls, the porcelain cat climbing the green brandy glass, the unravelling raffia plant-holder. The Whites are not well-off, by any stretch of the imagination, but they make a better fist of things than this. She feels simultaneously proud of her mother, and ashamed of her.

'Come again, it's open house,' says Mrs Morgan, flicking ash into a chrome-plated pedestal ashtray. Carol suspects sarcasm, but passes Phil the camera anyway. It's unlikely there will be any more visits between the in-laws, so they'd better commemorate this one.

I pulled the car up outside Phil's place, and sat, considering.

In all the years he'd lived there, I'd never once been inside. There was no need. It wasn't as if Jaz was a kid and needing to be shuttled between households. Phil's new life was all his own, I didn't want any part of it. *I haven't even a washing machine*, went Phil, making me think of a derelict flat I'd seen on TV the night before. What would it be like inside, the place where my husband had chosen to set up home with his spiteful, lumpen mistress? For everything she'd taken with her, would there still be evidence of her decoration, her tastes?

Did I dare go up and ring the bell?

And what if he'd been lying, and she was still there? What in God's name would I do then? For a few moments I let a fantasy run of Penny opening the door and me punching my car keys into her face. *Ha! Weren't expecting that, were you?* Perhaps if I'd carried on like that from the start, kicked and screamed and fought, brawled in the street like a fishwife, I'd have saved my marriage. If I'd wanted a husband brought to heel that way, if I thought he'd wanted such a wife.

I'd have given anything to turn the keys in the ignition now and drive straight up to Chester, and David.

But that was a chapter closed.

I needed to see my ex.

He wasn't expecting me; I didn't want to give him chance to hide anything. As soon as he let me through the door, though, I could see he hadn't been lying.

'It's a mess,' he said.

There were gaps everywhere, and dirty marks along the walls. Sometimes you could guess at what had been there before: some sort of arched dresser in that corner, a bureau or bookshelf along that side. There were dents in the door where it must have opened repeatedly against a table edge. 'How much a month do you spend on car magazines?' I asked because random stacks of them rose up everywhere, some on the floor, others on chairs or balanced on the windowsill. Despite the clutter, the middle of the room felt empty; there was no sofa, though you could see from the hollows in the carpet where one had been. No curtains, either. He followed my gaze. 'I keep meaning to get a blind,' he said. 'This weekend. Maybe. I don't spend that much time in here.'

The kitchen wasn't as bad as I expected in that, although the drainer was full, the sink was empty and clean, the lino swept.

'I'll get sorted in the end,' he said.

'I thought you said she'd taken the washing machine.'

'It's new. I wasn't going to start mauling with launderettes. Funny, in some ways, it's quite nice to have everything stripped away. Makes you re-evaluate what you need. It's almost like you could start again.' He looked hopefully in my direction.

'Or not.'

'Yeah, well.'

There were only tall stools to sit on. I tried perching on one but it felt unnatural and exposed so I got up again and stood, shuffling my feet.

'Where's she gone?'

'She's at her mum's. That's where she was headed, first off. Although she might have gone on somewhere else, I'm not sure. It's nowt to do with me any more. She can go camp on the moon as far as I'm concerned.'

'So that really is it?'

'It really is.' He licked his lips nervously. 'Listen, do you want to come through?' I wasn't sure what he meant. Then it clicked he was talking about the bedroom. 'Only I'm all set up there. This is no good, in here. I promise, no funny business.'

He was inviting me to see the room where he'd lain with Penny.

For a second I was too appalled to answer, but I didn't want him to see that. 'I came to give you the latest on Jaz,' I said.

'About Ian mending her hot-water tank? Yeah, she told me. Hopeful, eh? She was round earlier.'

'What, here?'

'She dropped in for half an hour with Matty. I played bowls with him, Matty-style. You know, crash, fling, wallop, thump.' He nodded at a small cardboard box that I hadn't noticed before because it was tucked between the bin and the wall. The flaps of the box were pushed half-open by a selection of cheap toys, bright and out of place in this shabby kitchen. 'She'd never come round when Pen was living here, but now she's popping in every week or so. I keep that lot for the entertainment of his lordship.'

'Oh,' I said. 'Great, that's great.' It shouldn't have been a surprise that Jaz was visiting her dad, that Matty was getting to know his grandad better. It was a good thing. It just felt odd.

'Come on,' he said. 'Let me take you through.'

And suddenly the compulsion to see the life he'd led without me was overwhelming.

'OK,' I said, shrugging in case he thought it was a big deal.

When I saw the bedroom I understood at once why the lounge was so neglected. This room was almost twice as big, with a (curtained) bay window, a two-seater sofa, TV, computer workstation. It was moderately tidy, too, though the television screen was dusty and the window panes could have done with a wipe.

'You have made yourself at home, haven't you?'

'It's all right.' Phil seemed pleased, shyly proud.

I made myself turn and look at the bed.

'That's new too,' he said. 'Brand new.' He walked over to the swivel chair by the monitor and sat down. 'You won't find anything of hers anywhere.'

'Makes no odds to me.'

'I'm only saying. It's all how I want it now. Everything around me, to hand. I can put something down and it stays there. Hey, I've even a mini-fridge next to the bed. In fact, do you fancy a can?'

He urged the chair forward on its rollers and leaned down to open the fridge door. 'Ice cold, yeah? It's really good.'

His naked delight amused me. 'No, thanks.'

'Oh, go on. You used to love a cider. When we were first married, it was your tipple of choice . . . Do you remember the White Swan in Alnwick? That swanky dining room that had come off an old ship? I can see you now, in your leather coat, all those grand fittings round you, sipping half a pint of Woodpecker. Yeah? You remember that, Carol?'

I did. As soon as he'd mentioned it, I could see the wood panelling and the gracious columns, the thick red carpet and the snowy tablecloths. Afterwards we'd gone for a walk up to the castle where he'd run about the grounds, re-enacting scenes from Robin Hood, till an elderly couple told him off. So then he stalked them, pulling faces, till they stropped off to the car park and we collapsed, hysterical with laughter.

'Sure you won't have a little sip?' said Phil, waggling the can at me.

'Oh, go on, if it'll shut you up. But I can't have much, I'm driving.'

He grinned, and tossed the can over to me. I settled into the sofa and tried to ease back the ring-pull without the contents exploding. Phil selected a bottle of Stella for himself.

He said, 'It is weird, though, isn't it?'

'How do you mean?'

'Well – life. How are you, in yourself, Carol? What are your plans?'

'Keep my head down, now Matty's back. If I can just untangle things between Jaz and Ian.'

'Yeah. I meant, how are *you*, though?'

'I'm all right. Don't try and be clever.'

'I'm not. I'm only asking.' He sighed. 'Looking back to when you were starting out, you know, in your twenties and such, did you have any idea your fifties were going to be like this?'

'Like what?'

'A bit of a fucking shower.'

'Speak for yourself.'

'Aw, come on. You know what I mean. Is this what you envisaged when you imagined yourself at fifty-odd?'

'What do you think?'

Again he sighed. 'It's a bugger, isn't it?'

The can flexed cold under my palm. 'I always thought your middle age was a time of calm and wisdom,' I said slowly, 'when you'd have everything important in its proper place. I never dreamed there'd be any of this – this upheaval. There are days I feel I don't know who I am, which is ridiculous at my age. Like some confused teenager. I said to someone this week I was a coward, and I waited for them to disagree and they didn't. Served me right.'

'That's bollocks,' said Phil. 'Who was it? Laverne?'

'No one you know,' I said hastily.

'Well, it is bollocks. God, when I think of some women.'

'Don't bring *her* into it.'

'The way you dealt with Jaz growing up . . .'

'You were always criticising me for that!'

'How you coped with your dad's illness, how you supported Eileen at the end. You were a rock. And putting up with me. Even I can see I must have been a tricky sod to live with.'

His expression was so rueful it was almost funny.

'Don't think for one minute that admitting it wipes it all away,' I said sternly.

'As if. Seriously, though, the last thing you are is a coward.'

'I am with Jaz.'

He seemed to consider this; at least he took another long swig of lager, and then stared up at the ceiling rose. 'You're not a coward. But I've told you before, you don't stand up to her like you should. You've got balls, but sometimes you need to strap them on a bit tighter.'

'Charming turn of phrase.'

'It's true. You forget, I've known you since forever. The daft thing is, she'd respect you more if you did take a bit of a harder line.'

He was so wrong. I thought of Jaz's face twisted with fury, her fist gripping Ian's jacket and shaking it like a dog. The memory still made me feel sick.

'I asked Dr Page if she'd got religion – trying to find my bearings. He said not as far as he was aware, but he thought she might have developed a better sense of perspective. Maybe if I understood her more . . .'

'What's to understand?' He waved his bottle. 'Understand yourself, Carol. Put yourself first, for once in your life.'

'Thank you, Marjorie Proops.'

This time it was he who laughed. 'I reckon we could both do with seeing a trick-cyclist. Family therapy. What do you say?'

'Bog off. I do owe you a sort of thank you, though.'

'How's that?'

'Well, you never once said to me, "I told you so", did you?'

'Over what?'

'Letting Ian come round and see Matty. And you had every right.'

He scratched his neck. 'You were trying your best – do you think I'd have done any better? You're the one who knows how people work. I look at our Jaz and I haven't a bloody clue.'

Phil had been edging his chair back across the room till he was by the computer. He wiggled the mouse and, after a few seconds, I heard music.

'Hey, what do you reckon to that?'

'What is it?'

'Shh. Listen.'

A jaunty guitar riff, punctuated by claps, then Marc Bolan's reedy voice: 'Ride a White Swan'.

'Good God, this takes me back,' I said. 'What year was it? Were we still at school?'

'I think so.'

'Yes, we must have been, because I remember Eileen and me going into town after last lesson to buy the single, and being embarrassed because we were in our uniforms. She'd pulled her shirt open and had her tie wrapped round her wrist, I don't know what we must have looked like. And we went to that little record shop in St Andrew's Square, do you remember it? I bet it's long gone now.'

Phil took another swig, wiped his mouth, and said, 'This mess we're in, do you think there's any good to come out?'

'With Jaz and Ian?'

'You and me.'

I put my can down on the carpet. 'Oh, Phil. I'm too tired to argue.'

''Cause it wasn't all bad, was it?'

'No, but the bad bits spoiled the rest.'

'What I'm saying is, though, you don't have to make that the last word. You don't *have* to let the past rule your entire future. We're not the same people we were, even this time last year, are we? Are we?'

I found myself feeling with my left thumb for the tiny dent that still marked my ring finger.

'You think,' he went on, 'what a team we made when we went to fetch Matty back. I'd never have managed without you. I don't think you'd have managed without me. We did it together.'

He stood up, and my heart began to beat faster. Keep away, I thought. But I stayed where I was.

'All I'm asking, Carol, is that you give it some consideration.'

'I have considered it. The answer's no.'

With extreme care he lowered himself down next to me, a man keen not to make any sudden moves. Nevertheless, his hip was against mine, and I felt the contact acutely. 'I'm just trying to be honest with you. I thought it would help if you knew where you stand. No messing, I'm telling you: I'll do any-thing at all—'

He took my hand. Still I didn't pull away.

'See, the man I was then isn't who I am now, any more than you're that girl in her teens or twenties. You're not, though, are you? And it's madness to let that hang over us when we could make a fresh start. The time's right. Jaz is home, she's back with Ian – kind of – you've got Matty. Everything's how you want it. But you're more than a "grandma" and a "mum" anyway. You have a life of your own.'

I do have a life, I wanted to say. *Don't unbalance it again.* And another part of my brain was saying, *Why did you come round here, Carol? What were you expecting?*

'Are you really saying you want to shut the door on this?' He leaned in and kissed my hair. 'And this?' He put his lips to my forehead. 'And this?' He kissed the side of my mouth. By now I'd closed my eyes to shut him out, but that only made the sensations more intense. His fingertips crept round to caress the back of my neck, circling the top vertebrae, smoothing along the collarbone. A groan stifled in my throat. When someone's that familiar with your body, they know exactly what works.

Stop, oh, stop, I said, but no words came out.

'I tell you, we're different people now,' he said again, breath-ing into my hair.

You're wrong, I thought. I am that girl in her teens, her twenties, her thirties. I'm fooling with a scarf on the motorway bridge, waiting outside the Odeon, being snogged against a tree, walking up the aisle, crying in your arms, passing you your baby daughter, cracking your photo over the newel post. I'm a blank-faced future me, watching.

He pulled away, and the unexpected action made me open my eyes. His brow was creased with hope.

'Oh, please, Carol,' he said.

At last, the power was all mine.

CHAPTER 35

Photograph: unnumbered – loose inside an old Bunny-Bons toffee tin, Sunnybank

Location: Blackpool

Taken by: Phil

Subject: Eileen leans against an iron railing with the sea at her back. Her hair is blowing about, her fun-fur coat flattened down one side by the strong breeze, and her grin is as wide as the Golden Mile. This weekend she has the Key of the Door; all her life stretches in front of her, starting with this coming Saturday night.

Newly-married Carol should be standing next to her, in her long leather coat, only she's been cut off the photo. You can just make out the crook of her elbow, and the fluttering end of a belt.

It was my last chaotic area. This afternoon I was determined to have one big push, clear the shed, and then at last that small aspect of my life would be under control. As usual I was equipped with my three sets of bin bags – Keep, Throw and Charity Shop – and this time my mood was ruthless. Space had to be forged, my house reclaimed from the past. A new era beckoned.

I dragged the first box towards me and flipped it open.

There's a displacement activity, if ever there was one, went Eileen.

You'll be telling me to take a cold shower next, I said to her.

When you live alone and don't date, your body learns to accept the situation, and deals with it accordingly. The dying days of my marriage had run my libido down for me; nothing damps your sex drive like living in simmering resentment month in, month out. Then, after the divorce came Jaz's illness, plus the stress of losing both Eileen and, after a fashion, my dad. By the time I felt anything approaching normal, my hormones had shut down. Sex seemed an activity I'd grown out of, the idea of me stripping naked in front of a man ludicrous, remote and petrifying.

Now, though—

Are you really saying you want to shut the door on this? I heard Phil say again. And my own response, *I'm not taking Penny's leftovers.*

'Not worthy of you, Carol,' he'd said. 'Pen left because she couldn't compete. We both know it's always been you. That's why I couldn't leave you, why you had to kick me out. I didn't want to go – I've missed you like hell. It's been crap.'

This kiss should have been David's had come into my head and I thought, If I spoke that out loud, it would really hurt you. 'Tell me again why Penny left,' I'd said.

Something clattering onto the floor made me jump. In moving the box I'd disturbed a pile of refuse sacks, and they'd been gradually sagging against one of the shelves, shoving the contents towards the edge in the manner of one of those coin waterfall arcade games. A tin of Back to Black lay rocking on the concrete with its cap off.

I looked down at the box I was supposed to be sorting. It was full of crumpled newspaper, which I knew meant crockery:

Dad's. There was no need to go through it because I remembered the kind of thing he kept in his kitchen cupboards towards the end – mis-matched pieces from the Sixties and Seventies, ugly and utilitarian. He'd made me take the best when Mum died, said he was frightened of breaking them. Of course I should have slung this lot as soon as he moved out, but I couldn't bear to. Getting rid meant he was never coming back.

But he wasn't coming back. He was where he was, ambling across some great twilit plain towards a dark horizon. With one hand I opened the door, and with the other I pulled the box right out of the shed onto the flags. Perhaps a charity shop could use old plates and mugs, or a homeless shelter. Jaz might know of somewhere.

The next bag was his clothes. When I cleared out Dad's wardrobe, it seemed to me he must have kept every garment he'd ever worn in his life. The care home's always sweltering, so we only took a handful of outfits, light summer wear, and bought him new where necessary. But here were his old overalls, stained with creosote, and his gardening boots, and his rough tweed jacket. He used to sit in that jacket rolling cigarettes, I could see him now. Once he caught me on the lawn with a square of blotting paper, trying to construct a tube out of bits of grass and clover. Not long after that, he quit smoking.

The box behind, when I tore it open, was solid with books: Alistair MacLean, George MacDonald Fraser, Dennis Wheatley, the old familiar covers. I wasn't getting rid of these, for all the spines had softened and the pages swelled. Dad loved his paperbacks. I felt guilty for leaving them out here in the damp for so long. *The Ka of Gifford Hillary* I lifted out, and it flopped open unresistingly. 'They make paper out of rags,' I remembered him saying. The edges of the pages were furry, like felt.

Underneath the top layers I found, not action novels, but a more eclectic mix of sizes, conditions, bindings and genres. Strange books I didn't recognise. Perhaps Phil had packed these away. *The Grapes of Wrath*, I uncovered; *Brave New World*, *Sons and Lovers*, *Middlemarch*. They had me frowning because, to tell the truth, I couldn't recall anyone reading the classics at Pincroft. But these had been read, you could tell by their state. *A Room of One's Own* was positively tatty, dog-eared, the picture of the woman on the front creased right down the middle. Delving deeper, I found Doris Lessing's *The Golden Notebook*, A. S. Byatt's *The Virgin in the Garden*, Fay Weldon's *Down Among the Women*. There was something severe and grand about these titles, despite their dated fonts and colour-ways, as if they knew I hadn't read them and held me to account for it. One had been covered with brown paper in place of a jacket; when I opened it to find out what it was – Margaret Drabble's *The Millstone* – I saw, not my father's, but my mother's name inked possessively on the flyleaf. I put it down and picked up an ex-library copy of *The Selfish Gene*, only to find she'd gone further, marking sections with pencil underlinings and crabbed, illegible notes. Frieda White versus Richard Dawkins.

I hadn't known her as a reader. When had I last seen her absorbed in a book? All I could conjure at that precise moment was my mother up a stepladder shouting for curtain clips; holding her forearm under the cold tap where she'd caught herself with the iron; hacking viciously at the lilac which hung over our front path. Or sunk against the hospice pillow, her drip swaying on its tall stand. They might almost have been memories of someone else's mother, or a character from a drama on TV. At the very bottom of the pile was a battered paperback edition of *The Second Sex*, which I put gingerly to one side, as if it were a grenade.

To my relief, the next box turned out to be not Dad's, but Jaz's: schoolbooks and ringbinders and coursework folders. I flicked one open and my heart gave a twinge at the rounded, childish handwriting, at the doodles in the margin of cartoon bombs and eyes and wasp-waisted women. 'What would Jaz say if she could see us now?' I'd asked Phil as he tried to kiss my neck.

'Stop thinking about her,' he'd said. 'You always think about her first. Think about yourself.'

I managed to dispatch two more boxes (old books and ornaments, tea towels and bedding) and three bags of clothes before Phil intruded again. This time it was a memory of very early sex, a clumsy attempt to use a condom that wouldn't roll down because it was on inside out. I honestly thought I'd die of embarrassment, but he made me laugh, and it was OK. It was always OK in those first years (and, God, we were young when we started out). He was still the only man I'd ever slept with. That counted for something, whether I liked it or not.

What would David say about that? If we were in a room, kissing, and I broke away and said, 'You should know, I've only ever been with my husband.'

I needed to keep telling myself, though. He wasn't mine: Phil was.

Take all the time you need, Phil had said. *I'm going nowhere.*

I hadn't slept with Phil, but I knew I was going to, sooner or later.

By the time I'd stopped for lunch and washed up and put away, I knew I only had another four hours before dark. The shed floor was now clear and I was about three-quarters of the way through the mezzanine section; this despite the voices in my head keeping up a hysterical and disjointed commentary throughout. I replayed Eileen's advice about how I should treat Phil's affair like a battle, and on no account let this other woman take him off me. 'You've come too far, you belong together,' she used to say. So un-Eileen-like, in many ways. Then it was Moira, talking about her ex and how she blamed herself for the break-up because she got obsessed with wanting a baby. And Faith from the gym, confiding to a general audience that her husband complained she put the children first, which is what Phil always said I did. I still couldn't see how that was wrong, so perhaps I had been a bad wife. Perhaps I did bring it on myself.

Towards the end wall of the boarded-off section I discovered a small disaster. A drum of varnish Phil had used to renovate the bedroom floor had fallen over and emptied itself. Everything in the immediate vicinity, I could see at a glance, was ruined – the fan heater, the fish tank, Mojo's cage, the spare shower head. Worse than that, the varnish had soaked into the hardboard and dripped through the join.

I came down to investigate the damage below. This was an area of the shed I hadn't bothered looking at before because it was all Phil's odds and sods, tins and jars of loose screws, nails, nuts, staples, bolts, drill bits, unidentifiable twists and fragments of metal. 'Don't *ever* move my gear around,' he'd warned me repeatedly. But it was clear that a lot of it was now covered in a film of varnish, and that the contents of the top two shelves at least would need throwing. There was no point leaving it when I had a rubbish pile going. I picked up an open Walkers Shortbread tin and tipped it experimentally. Nothing inside moved. The mess of panel pins was stuck solid, like flies in amber.

So I set to, working my way down the wall where the varnish had flowed in a sticky river, tossing into the centre of the floor anything that was beyond redemption. If Phil had wanted any of it, I reasoned, he should have come and taken it years ago. Sealant tube was welded to bracket, brush to bottle, sanding disc to match pot. In one corner a batch of oily rags had soaked up some of the varnish, and now they were stuck fast against the wall, and crispy. I had to pull hard to get them to lift, and even then they only came because the varnish cracking tore some of the threads. I was thinking, Phil'll need to get a chisel to this, when they ripped completely away, and I half-lost my balance and knocked a tin nearby right off.

It seemed to fly in slow motion, while my hand swiped ineffectually, striking against glass jars, skinning my knuckle on the sharp metal edge of the shelf. The tin crashed to the floor and the lid popped open, spilling out the contents. *Riley's Bunny-Bons* said the ancient label, over a badly scratched picture of a rabbit in a top hat and spats. Pre-war toffees, it must once have held. Now it seemed to be full of postcards and clippings.

I squatted down, turned over the first piece of paper.

It was an old photo, from the early Seventies, of Eileen and Phil together. He was dressed in a Homburg and a mackintosh, while she had on a man's pinstriped suit and a bowler hat. I recognised the occasion at once: Stackholme Grammar End of Year Review, and the Social Classes sketch from *Frost Over England*. They'd cast me as Common Man, in my dad's flat cap and muffler, and I remember it wasn't a role I was very comfortable with because it seemed to me they were mocking people like Dad, decent ordinary folk who kept their heads down and worked hard and were the backbone of the country. Every time I had to say the line 'I know my place', it made me wince. Phil and Eileen hadn't been able to see the problem. In fact, they found rehearsals so wildly hilarious I used to wonder how we'd get through the actual performance.

I should have been on the end of this photograph, but someone had cut me off.

I drew the print aside, only to find that under it was another photo of Eileen, this time on her own, in our garden.

Then Eileen in her Vauxhall Viva, waving through the windscreen.

And underneath that, there were dozens more pictures of Eileen, not one of them put there by me.

Nowhere is as lonely as the middle of the night. While Matty slumbered upstairs, I sat on my living-room carpet reviewing the hundred thousand lies inside my photo albums. All those Eileens, smug with secrets. All those Phils with their scheming sideways glances and their hearts entirely full of self.

At ten I'd called my ex-husband and told him what I'd found.

'Was it Eileen, or you?' I asked.

'I haven't looked at them for years,' he said.

'Was it Eileen, or you?'

'Nothing happened, I swear.'

'Why should I believe you?'

'It just didn't. As God's my witness. On my life. On Jaz's life.'

'Don't you *dare!*'

'I'm trying to get you to see. I never so much as kissed her, nothing. She wouldn't let me. I made a pass, she said no. That's it.'

'And the photos?'

'I had a little crush for a couple of years.'

'If she'd said yes?'

No answer.

And there I'd sat, feeling I should have been relieved, when in fact hearing the truth was more painful than I could have imagined.

'Don't blame her,' Phil had said.

I'd slammed the receiver down on him.

Twenty-six pictures he'd stored in his bloody tin. In some he'd physically sheared me off with scissors, so I was no more than an arm, or a scrap of material, or a shadow. Once, unforgivably, he'd cut away Jaz. I never knew betrayal could go so deep.

Eileen stared back at me, sometimes darkly, sometimes sunny and mischievous. There she was holding my arm, my wedding bouquet, my baby girl. You knew about this, I said to her, and you kept quiet. Why? Eileen tipped her head to one side and smirked at something lost to the camera. At least when you were dying, you could have told me then, I said.

What purpose would that have served? she said.

I'd have known where I stood!

You weren't ready.

It would have been honest of you, then.

Is honesty always the best policy, Carol?

I flung the album from me by its spine but I couldn't stop the photographs chattering. They had their own agenda.

CHAPTER 36

Photograph: unnumbered, loose in a Bunny-Bons toffee tin

Location: Grimeford Lane, Tannerside

Taken by: Phil

Subject: nothing except the empty road, stretching up towards the moors.

Phil wants this photo for a souvenir. It's the best he's going to get. Eileen refuses to be in it, doesn't want to be here, is livid with him. She can't imagine why he'd want a reminder of this day.

She thought she was coming up to help him take pictures of childhood haunts, as a surprise for his wife. 'You invited me here on false pretences,' she rages. 'If I'd had any idea you were going to start spouting this rubbish, I'd never have come near.'

Because he's claiming he's in love with her suddenly, à propos of nothing at all. He's sorry about the lie, but he's desperate.

'Don't be so stupid,' she tells him.

'You know what I'm talking about,' he says. 'You've felt it too. We're two of a kind. When we were at school—'

'When we were at school,' says Eileen dryly, 'you had

388

every opportunity. But you chose Carol. She thinks the sun shines out of you.'

'What if I made the wrong choice?' he says.

'Too late,' she says.

'It might not be,' he says.

'It is,' she says. 'Sod off.'

Eventually she convinces him to go, and he drives away, watching her grow smaller in the rear-view mirror. He has no idea what he's doing. Is he simply scratching an itch? Is it just a crush, a product of post-wedding-panic? If she'd said yes, would the affair have burned itself out? The years are his to wonder.

Eileen walks alone across the fields to the station and catches the train home.

No one must ever know what it's cost her to turn this man away. You can't help who you fall for; he may be a fool, but he's a bloody handsome one. From the Second Form up, she thinks she's been in love with him. Not that he's ever looked at her in that way. Till now.

She prays she was convincing enough, so that he feels too embarrassed to try again, because she doesn't know if she'll be able to resist him a second time.

It was half-past midnight when I heard my doorbell go. Luckily I was still up, pottering about doing a final tidy because I hate coming down in the morning to a messy room. I can't sleep if I know there's washing not put away.

My heart jumped at the sudden noise. I dropped the pile of tea towels I was holding and ran out into the hall. It crossed my mind that the shape behind the glass might be a criminal, a madman come to rape me in my bed, except from what I understood, such types didn't tend to announce their arrival and formally request entrance. The letterbox opened, a pair of fingers poked through and Josh's voice went, 'Carol? Are you there?'

I let him in at once.

'What in God's name are you up to?' I asked.

He grinned sheepishly. 'I got locked out.'

'Your mother locked you out?'

'Sort of.'

'Is she not in?'

'Oh, she's in.'

I was having some trouble with the idea that if Josh was out after dark, Laverne would be tucked up peacefully in bed. Impossible.

I brought him through and switched the main light back on. Josh was wearing a jacket I hadn't seen before, and his T-shirt was tucked in on one side only. 'You've not been in a fight, have you?'

He shook his head. 'I was round my girlfriend's.'

'I didn't know you had a girlfriend.'

'Yeah, well.'

'Not that one I saw you with at the bridge?' I remembered that sneering female shout, and shuddered inwardly.

'God, no, not her. Sheesh. Not her. Kirsty's *nice*.'

'OK. And where does Kirsty live?'

'Near the park. Bargates.'

'So what happened?'

'That's it.'

'And your mother knows you're out?'

Josh treated that question with the contempt it deserved. 'Can I borrow your front door key, Carol?'

'You went out without a key?'

'No, I have a key, but it's to the back door and Mum's put the bolt on. I left via the front. I failed to think my strategy through.' His face was very open and friendly, the way it used to be when I gave him lifts to school. He might have been asking me to help with a tricky piece of homework.

'But you'll wake her up, she'll hear you.'

'No, she won't, because she's taking sleeping tablets and they knock her out. She had one tonight, I watched her take it.'

'And then you sneaked out?'

'Yup.'

I noticed that all the while he was talking, he was struggling not to smile. I didn't know what to make of it.

'But if she wakes up and I'm not there,' he went on, 'she'll freak. The shock'll send her mental. Then she'll be on tranx as well as sleeping pills.'

That was true enough.

'Oh, honestly, Josh. Right, listen, I will let you in, *this once*, but for Laverne's sake. And I'm not thrilled about being put in this position. You're not in any sort of trouble, are you?'

'Do I look like I've been in trouble?'

'You look a bit drunk, if I'm being honest.'

'I'm not. I've not been near any booze. Smell my breath.' He opened his mouth wide and huffed over me.

'No thanks,' I said, stepping back. All I could pick up were mints and body-spray.

I left him in the lounge while I went to fetch from the kitchen the biscuit tin with Laverne's key inside it. When I came back he was grinning to himself again.

'Hey, do you like shortbread, Carol?'

'Why?'

''Cause I can get you a load from Healey's. A carrier bag full, if you want. They throw them when they get to their sell-by date, and there's nothing wrong with them.'

'I don't want paying,' I said sternly. 'Especially in dodgy biscuits. You know, you're damn lucky I was awake.'

'Mum goes to bed at ten.'

'Well, I had a few things on my mind this evening.' I extracted the key and put the tin down. 'Do you absolutely promise me you've not been doing anything illegal? Because you're putting me in a very difficult situation here.'

Josh hung his head. 'I know. You're a mate, Carol, you really are. I just lost track of time, that's all it was, I swear.'

'And this girl's parents?'

'On holiday.' Again, that smirk.

'You know, you could try asking your mum straight out whether you can go round to your girlfriend's house.'

'I could, couldn't I?'

I held out the key to him. 'Wherever did that good little boy who used to live next door go?'

'He got wazzed off at being pushed around all the time.'

'I see.'

'So he pushed back and found he liked it.'

'And while we're on the subject, that teacher who used to make bother?'

'Oh, the Hungarian? Currently the subject of a formal complaint. With any luck, he'll be suspended, his career in ruins. Couldn't happen to a nicer bloke. I'll post your key back tomorrow.'

'You'll open up and then you'll bring it straight back now,' I said.

I waited on my front step, listened for his trainers crunching along their path, silence, the clicking of metal against metal, his footsteps coming back.

'And if your mum finds out,' I said, 'I shall claim you stole my key. I'm not being held responsible. She'll have my guts for garters.'

He flicked his fringe to one side, roguish in my porch light. 'In that case, you'll just have to stand up to her, won't you? Don't let yourself be bullied, Carol. That would never do.'

Then he turned and disappeared into the dark.

The evening after Matty's second birthday, Ian and Jaz brought him round for his usual Saturday night sleepover. I had everything ready for him, the curtains were drawn and the fire lit.

Ian carried him in, swooping him round the room like a human battering ram before dropping him onto the sofa. This kind of treatment always made me wince to watch, but Matty loved it. For a split second I remembered Phil holding a squealing infant Jaz upside down, the ribbons on her bunches streaming down his trouser legs. Then the image was gone. Matty was standing against the back of the settee, holding up his arms for more.

'How's he getting on with his electronic book?' I asked. They'd bought him a device to help accelerate his reading, a ring-bound contraption with a wand that spoke the words as you pointed at them. Terrifically complicated, it looked to me.

Jaz pulled off her coat and laid it on the chair arm. 'Not shown much interest in it yet. It does say "age three or over", but he's bright, I thought he'd be able to cope with it.'

'Don't wish his time away,' I said. 'He'll be there soon enough.'

'He likes the bead frame you bought him, though. He's never been off that.'

'Wanted it in the bath last night,' said Ian, sitting down opposite her.

'Did he?' Jaz smiled.

'Oh yes. I had to distract him with Squirty Fish.'

'Well, I hope Squirty Fish confined his exploits to the tiles, and not the carpet or the wallpaper like last time. You should have seen the state, Mum.'

'It was him,' said Ian, pointing at Matty. 'He led me on.'

They were laughing together, just like a real family.

'Are you staying for a drink?' I asked hopefully.

A signal passed between them.

'No,' said Ian. 'I have to get off. I'm working tomorrow, this project where they've brought the deadline forward and we're all scrambling to get it finished. So I need to make tracks. Sooner it's started, better chance we have of nailing it.' He ruffled his son's hair, and stood up. 'Bye, Mattster. Be good.'

Jaz stayed where she was. 'See you Tuesday,' she said. Then she saw my expression. 'We came in separate cars, Mum. I'll have a coffee, if you're making one.'

Looking back, I suppose that's the point I should have twigged.

After I'd got Matty in bed, I came down to find Jaz standing by the back window with the light off. She'd opened the curtains and was staring across the garden.

'I was checking out the stars,' she said. 'It's a really clear night.'

'Frosty.'

'I'll say. It was bitter coming over.'

'Has Matty got a hat?'

'Yes, Mum, he's got a hat. And mittens, and a quilted coat and boots and a scarf. So no need to worry.'

'My mother once accidentally locked me out on a night like this, then blamed me. I was too small to reach the door knocker. A neighbour let me in, in the end.'

Jaz snorted. 'She always sounds a bit of a cow, does Grandma.'

'I think she was just one of those people who's born discontented. And maybe I was a disappointment to her.'

'In what way?'

'I don't know. We never talked about things like that. She just gave that impression.'

'Am I a disappointment to you?'

'Oh, love,' I said, 'how could you think so?'

She spoke without turning her head. 'Ian and I are getting a divorce. I'm sorry.'

The stars beyond my daughter's silhouette stayed where they were, unblinking.

'He's OK with that?' I managed to make myself say.

'We've spent a long time talking it over and he can see it's best. I'm not being awkward, Mum. I need to start again. With someone I can trust, if there is anyone out there. I'd never be able to trust Ian again, not totally, and I can't stay in a marriage like that. It would destroy me. I'd rather be on my own.'

Tears threatened, but I fought them back. This was not the time to load her with my distress.

'Matty can see his dad when he wants?'

'Oh, yeah, that's key. I figure it'll be less damaging to him if he grows up knowing we're separated, than if we try again and Ian and I split later. Two houses'll be normal for him because it'll be all he's ever known.'

'You know you'll need to cite this woman in the divorce papers, like I had to do with Penny. You'll have to see her address and everything. It'll rake a lot back up again.'

'Yeah, I know. It's got to be done, though.'

I sat myself down in the armchair.

'You always said I should have divorced when you were little, Jaz. I want you to know that I would have done if I'd seen – the whole—'

'Oh, that's the past, don't beat yourself up about it,' she said carelessly, as if she couldn't hear how those words echoed round the room, rebounding off walls and colliding against themselves till it hurt my head.

Or perhaps she did realise, because she came away from the window and stood by me. Her hand came out of the dimness and touched my shoulder.

'You're being really good about all this. I thought you'd have hysterics or something. Did you already guess?'

History was splitting off into decisions made and not made. Other versions of my life spooled out against the gloom.

She bent and peered into my face. 'Are you OK?'

'Yes.'

'Look, I'm going to pop upstairs and check on Matty,' she said. 'Then we'll talk some more.'

I don't know how long she was gone, it could have been a minute or an hour. When she came down she said, 'Someone's letting off fireworks on the cricket field.'

I glanced over at the window as a spectacular rocket burst, on cue, into a golden chrysanthemum. 'Early for Bonfire Night. Mind you, that seems to last about a fortnight these days.'

Three glittering green stars bloomed, and faded.

'It might be a wedding reception, or a party,' I said. 'Draw the curtain right back so we can see properly.'

'Why don't we go out? I could put the monitor on the patio.'

'We'll freeze.'

'Stick your coat on. I could do with breathing some cold air,' she said.

We leaned over the back fence. The larch lap panels were already glistening with ice.

'You can smell the cordite,' she said, 'or whatever it is.'

'They must have a bonfire, too. You can see the glow.'

Fireworks screeched upward, little bright nuggets tracking across the wide sky, to explode into fleeting brilliance. The night cracked and whistled around us.

'There was something else,' said Jaz, below the whine of

rockets. Her face lit red, then green, then was dark again. 'Sam's been in touch with me.'

'It was when I was looking for you,' I said quickly. 'I was trying any avenue I could think of.'

'What did she tell you?'

'About some of the things that made you leave university.'

'The abortion?'

'Yes.' My breath came out in a puff of white.

Jaz shifted against the fence, and I wondered if I should put my arm round her.

'I know what you want me to say, Mum. You want me to say it was terrible and I was really upset, and it's haunted me forever after.'

'Oh, Jaz, you know I'd *never* wish for that.'

'Didn't you think I'd "let you down"?'

'No! Good grief, no. Just sorry I wasn't there to help you. Have you any idea how it made me feel, as your mother, hearing that you were upset and frightened, and I wasn't with you? There's nothing worse, believe me. You wait till something happens to hurt Matty and you can't make it better. See how that cuts you up.'

'You need to hear how it was,' she said, and it was a kind of challenge.

Smoke hung in a pall over the far gardens, like the remnants of a battle.

'It was dire, Mum, having to go to the clinic. It's quick, the actual . . . but there's a lot of stuff beforehand, talking to people, which churns you up, and then you feel pretty shit for a few days after. I wouldn't have managed without Nick and Steph.'

'They've been good friends to you.'

'You think I don't know that? But the abortion wasn't anything compared with the rest. It was Tom who broke my heart. That's what did the damage.'

'And the boy who died?'

'Sam told you about him too. Oh, God.' She buried her face in her hands. Then she raised her head and said, 'It's like it never goes away. Will it ever go away?'

This time I did touch her arm. She stiffened immediately.

'I don't want your sympathy, I'm just telling you how it was because you need to hear. It was really, really shit. I couldn't think about anything else for weeks, Sam just kept going on and on about Andy dying, and I was sick in case Tom told her what I'd done. But I only lied to Andy because I was desperate to get her out of the way. I thought she quite liked him. I thought if Sam was hooked up, she'd leave Tom alone, and then— None of us knew Andy was ill. And a lot of it was Sam's fault; she didn't have to be so fucking vile with him. Trying to impress Tom, mocking Andy because she thought Tom would find it funny. I actually said to her, "Don't be such a bitch." He didn't deserve it. He didn't deserve any of it. It was so fucking awful, what happened.'

'Oh, Jaz,' I said. 'I can see why you got poorly, keeping all this to yourself.'

'Then, when I came home, you didn't understand.'

'How could I, love? I didn't know! Why didn't you tell me?'

'Because.'

I closed my eyes for a moment, thought again about Andy Spicer's parents standing in that courtroom. But the picture hardly touched me. The instinct to protect my own child obliterated any connection with their pain, to a degree I never could have credited. 'Have you talked about this with Nick?'

'He says it wasn't my fault, people get knock-backs every day but they don't all take their own lives, and how could I have known? That if I'd had any idea of the result, I'd never have taken that course of action.'

'Well, then.'

'But if I hadn't made up the story. I keep coming back to that.'

'Jaz,' I said, feeling for the right words, letting my breath rise and fall in time with hers, 'you have to believe me when I say it was pure horrible awful luck.'

'No, Mum.'

'*Yes*. You might just as well have spoken to Andy and had him laugh in your face or tell Sam to get lost or drink himself into oblivion for two days and then be fine. The leap to – to that particular outcome was one you could never have anticipated. Not everything links up to this person's fault or that person's action. Most events just happen. The idea you can trace them back and make yourself responsible's a fallacy. David taught me that.'

She turned on me. 'Oh, *David*. Well then, it must be true. I suppose you told him what I did at Leeds?'

'Not the private stuff, not the things you hadn't confided to me yourself. Honestly, Jaz! I didn't even tell your dad about the boy who died.'

'Because it was that shameful.'

'No, because there was no need. Who would it have benefited? It's in the past, it's terribly sad but it's done with. As Nick said.'

Rockets were blasting the sky apart in front of us; there was no pause now between explosions. At my side, Jaz was shivering.

'Let's go in,' I said.

'Wait,' she said. 'You know, it's been hard in the past to talk to you about anything upsetting. You're so bloody cheerful, Mum, so bloody brave. Even when your life's falling apart, you're smile, smile, smile. It's outfacing.'

'Seems like I can't do right for doing wrong,' I said.

'I'm only trying to explain.'

An aeroplane passed over the far rooftops, navigation lights winking red and white. 'When you were little, you used to think planes at night were Santa's sleigh,' I said.

'That's a long time ago,' she said. 'Look, the fireworks are over.'

I took her hand and led her across the lawn, back to the house.

CHAPTER 37

Photograph 35, Album One

Location: 22 Manchester Road, Tannerside, Bolton

Taken by: Mr Ainscough from the Black Horse

Subject: the village snow plough, at the junction of Halfacre Lane and Church Street. This is the winter of 1947, and the snow lies in drifts that reach some second-storey windows. When Frieda's mother went shopping this morning, she tripped over the rung on a gas lamp post, that's how deep this snow is. The children have been forced to pick coal off the slag heap on the Brow, while the men cut down hedges and trees to burn. The roads are impassable.

But here comes the plough, so perhaps the worst is over. Two cart-horses pull not only the wooden wedge but half a dozen children, who've been invited to sit inside for ballast. Frieda watches, half-jealous. She's too old for such activities now, although a snowball fight isn't out of the question, especially if it's with a certain young man living six doors down. She fizzes with energy and excitement at the thought.

One thing's for sure: never, never will she moan about

snow, the way old people do. Why they can't see the magic of it is beyond her.

It was with gladness I made up the spare bed for Jaz, unwrapped a spare toothbrush, laid out fresh towels, located Kitten. 'I'm too tired to drive back now,' she said. 'My head's all over the place.'

I said, 'I meant it when I said you could always stay here for a while, till you get yourself sorted. This is your home.'

She closed her eyes. 'I need to be moving forwards, not backwards. So do you, Mum.'

The next morning, while I was feeding Matty his breakfast, she had all my photograph albums out. I picked up straight away a sort of giddiness about her, a relief that last night's confession was out of the way.

'Oh my God, look at this,' she said, as I brought Matty in and plonked him on the sofa.

Reluctantly I craned my neck to see. I'd been avoiding photos recently.

It was a picture of the four of us: me, Phil, Jaz and Eileen, standing on Chester city walls. It must have been a hot day because all of us were in short sleeves and Phil was wearing sunglasses. 'How old were you there?' I asked her.

'Fourteen, fifteen. That was the afternoon you dropped your earring and we had to go all the way back round. We found it, though. It was on the steps by the river.'

I switched on CBeebies for Matty and he settled back, sucking his thumb. 'Who took the picture, then?'

'Some old granny in a sheepskin coat. Do you not remember? Dad said she must have been walking round with an ice pack strapped to her vest.'

The day was a void as far as I was concerned. 'Eileen looks pleased with herself.'

Jaz went to turn the page, but I stopped her. 'What?' she said.

'It's just—' Phil's real expression was hidden by the glasses. Eileen stood, honest-faced, her arm draped round Jaz's shoulder.

'What, Mum?'

'Sometimes I think she'd have made a better mother for you.'

Jaz glanced my way. 'You're not serious?'

'You got on better with her, a lot of the time.'

'Oh yeah. You know what she used to say to me? That if I'd been hers, she'd have kicked me out on the streets. Handed me a washbag and a tenner and told me to sod off.'

'She didn't say that.'

'She bloody well did. She was a laugh, Eileen, but pretty useless in the maternal department. Once I asked her advice about some girls at school—'

'When?'

'You know. When I was getting bother, when you went in and saw the Head. Not long after this photo, as it happens. Half of that mess was Eileen's fault, because she told me to fight back so I did and I got into more trouble than the bullies. It was the crappest tip ever.'

'You confided in her, rather than me?'

'Only because she overheard me and Nat talking.'

'And she didn't think to let me in on it.'

'No,' said Jaz patiently. 'It wasn't like that. What she made me do was promise to speak to you myself if I couldn't sort things on my own. Which I did. Jeez, Mum, what's eating you?'

'I've been wondering about her and your dad,' I muttered, pushing the album away.

'What do you mean? Oh!' This time Jaz laughed out loud. '*Eileen?*'

'It's possible.'

Jaz was shaking her head. 'No way. No *way*! I always assumed Eileen was gay. Wasn't she?'

'No. She had boyfriends sometimes.'

'Did you ever ask?'

'Don't be ridiculous.'

'Well, gay or straight, she certainly didn't have the hots for Dad, absolutely not. She couldn't stick him. Used to call him all sorts behind his back. If she did fancy him, Mum, she was a bloody good actress.'

'What about if he fancied her?'

'Makes no odds, if she wouldn't play ball, does it?'

The sick ache in my stomach eased fractionally, for the first time in weeks. I leaned over and hugged her.

'What was that for?'

'Being my daughter.'

She sighed, like someone who endures unimaginable provocation. 'Big fan of yours, Eileen. Always going on about what a great mother you were and how I should be thankful, not that it made much difference . . . Hey, look at Dad, here,' she said, lifting the book up for me to get a better view. She was pointing to a group shot of herself, Solange Moreau, Nat and Phil, all crowded into the hall. Solange's suitcases were by the door; it must have been her last day. Behind Nat's head, Phil held up two black dinner plates to give her Mickey Mouse ears. 'He was funny, Dad. Do you remember the Exploding Taco?'

'I do.'

'He made us laugh.'

'Sometimes.'

'It wasn't enough, though, was it?'

'No, it wasn't.'

Flick, flick went the pages. I glimpsed a photo of Mum holding my new baby like a sack of potatoes; Dad pushing Jaz's

Christmas bike through tiny islands of melting snow; Prom Night, and Jaz kitted out like a trollop.

I said, 'You know that first time you ran away, when you were still at school? Where was it you were headed?'

She didn't look up. 'I have no idea.'

'Please. Since we're clearing the air.'

'Honestly. I didn't have a clue.'

'You weren't meeting up with someone?'

'Nope. I was bored, I was getting hassle from some girls in my class, I took off. That's all it was. Teenage dramatics. I told you at the time.'

'You told me a lot of stuff,' I said.

She closed the book and set it down.

'I'm sorry. I'm sorry for all the crappy things I've done to you, Mum. All right?'

Now would have been my chance. I could speak out, tell her my side of events, tip the balance back. If she could be made to see—

I glanced at Matty, rolling his head against the sofa arm, and my courage evaporated into nothing. 'Someone's still a bit sleepy this morning,' I said. I got up and sat close to him, so that his small feet were in my lap. 'You used to like having your feet tickled, do you remember? You'd poke me with your toes every time I stopped. You were a devil for it.'

Jaz began to pile the albums back onto the shelf. 'Do you think he'll turn out optimistic, like you, or gloomy, like me and Grandma? Dark and light. It's like a pattern. Each generation reacts against the other.'

'I think my optimism's been fear, a lot of the time. Not being able to face the worst possibility.'

She pushed the last album home, then came over to the sofa and squeezed in on Matty's other side.

'Matty'll grow up to be what he'll be,' I said. 'And he'll be a little treasure.' I gave him a cuddle, and got no reaction at all. On television, a man in a pink sweater waved over the battlements of a pink castle. As I watched, he became Eileen, speaking Eileen's words: *You and Phil belong together.* Then Phil: *Not even a kiss. Don't blame her.* What had Jaz said? *If she did fancy him, Mum, she was a bloody good actress.*

'So what was it David was on about?' asked Jaz suddenly, jerking me back to reality.

'David?'

'What you said last night, about events not being causal. What was he referring to? Was it me?'

'Oh,' I said. 'No.'

'What, then?'

'It doesn't matter now.'

The TV showed two small girls spreading glue on purple sugar paper. One had her neck in a kind of metal brace, but she seemed to be coping all right. The children took dried leaves from a pile at the side and stuck them down randomly. Then we had a short film showing frost on hedges, trees, grass and cobwebs, while Prokofiev's Troika played in the background. When the cameras came back to the girls, they were dribbling glue on the leaves while a lady bent between them with a saucer of glitter. The next shot was a close-up of their fists against the saucer. 'We're like Jack Frost,' said the one wearing the brace. I put my hand against Matty's leg to stop him kicking.

'When's he back from the States?' said Jaz, her eyes on the screen.

'I don't know.'

The lady helped the girls hold their pictures up and shake them onto paper. Swathes of glitter fell away, leaving random lines and blobs of sparkle across the brown leaves. "It's a winter picture," said the second girl, as the camera closed in.

A sharp rap on the window made us both jump. When I looked up, Laverne was peering through the glass.

'I've come to ask if you're around over Christmas,' she said, as I was leading her through to the lounge. Josh shuffled in behind her.

'We're thinking of booking a mini-cruise,' she went on, perching herself on the chair arm. 'One of these last-minute deals. Only I don't like to leave the house without someone to keep an eye on it. So, would it be possible for you to pick up my post from behind the door, check my pipes haven't frozen, that kind of thing? It would stop me worrying.'

'Of course,' I said.

Jaz had turned in her seat and was staring at Josh. I knew what she was thinking. His outline had changed. These days he filled the doorway, and no longer with puppy fat.

Laverne was still talking. 'I know we usually go to my sister's at Abersoch in the summer, but I think it's time for a change. Josh has never been abroad, have you, love? And all his friends go on about France, and America and – You have to keep up, these days.'

'How's the job going?' I asked him.

He shifted his weight from one foot to the other. 'All right.'

'You're loving it, aren't you?' said Laverne. 'And he's loving his drama group in the evenings. And he's got himself a little girlfriend. Little Kirsty. She's very nice. I know, I know, I shan't go on – he gets embarrassed – but you're enjoying this school year a lot better, aren't you? One boy he didn't like so much has left, and another one who was – You've palled up with him, haven't you? Mind you, he's not getting quite such good reports as he was, so I don't know whether that's altogether a good thing. Detention last week, his first ever. I was mortified. He wasn't, though. Took someone's rugby kit out of their bag and filled it with lost property, so when they got off the coach, all they had—'

'Mum,' said Josh, warningly.

I looked from one to the other. Against him, she was tiny and frail. Lines were forming round her eyes. He looked as if he could swallow her up in a single bite.

'Not my little boy any longer, is he?'

'That's the way it goes,' I said.

Matty sneezed, and for the first time Laverne seemed to notice him properly.

'Ooh, look at this young man here. Hello, Matty. Are you watching television? Who's that? Is it La La?'

'Wrong programme,' said Jaz.

'And did he enjoy his birthday party?'

'He did, yeah. He loved the Talking Thomas: thanks.'

'It's nice to have someone small to buy for. They're not babies long. You need to make the most of every minute.'

Laverne and I exchanged the glances of women who've been through it, and know.

She stood up. 'Well.'

'Have you heard any more about how Alice is getting on?' I asked as we got to the front door. Josh made good his escape, slipping through ahead of us.

'Oh, yes. The baby's home.'

'He's better?'

'Better than he was, but he's still needing all sorts of specialist care. Tanks of oxygen, tubes. They're seeing how he goes.'

'And long term?'

'I don't think they can tell yet. Connor, his name is. Bonny little boy, really blond hair. Has Dorothy shown you the photos?'

'No.' I pictured again her young, scared face. 'Oh, poor Alice.'

'I keep thinking, you know, if it was me, I'd never manage.'

'If you had to, though. If it was your child. Maybe when the absolute worst happens, you do just get on with it.'

We stood in silence, two mums trying to imagine how we'd cope if fate had charged to us a desperately poorly baby.

'I suppose—' Laverne hovered on the step, frowning as she tried to frame some idea of a way forward, some positive comment where almost nothing positive can be said, 'I suppose all she can do is love, and hope.'

Which is really all any of us can do, I thought, when it comes to it.

I shut the door against the world, and went to sit with my family.

CHAPTER 38

Photograph: unnumbered, part of a postcard-sized wedding album, wrapped in a tea towel inside a Fox's biscuit tin

Location: St Stephen's C of E Church

Taken by: Imperial Photographic Studios, Chapel St, Adlington, Lancashire

Subject: Frieda and Bob's wedding day. The couple stand in the centre of the picture, flanked by family from both sides. What an abundance of middle-aged women there are, too, all in their hats and gloves and long flared coats. 'Smile,' Frieda's mother hisses from time to time, when she thinks no one's listening, but once again she could do with taking a leaf out of her own book.

If I'd been able to talk to you, thinks Frieda furiously, I wouldn't be in this situation. I wouldn't have accepted an offer of marriage I didn't want.

Has it been poor nutrition, or stress, or simply being underweight that's caused Frieda's periods temporarily to stop? In these post-war days there are girls so slender they move in and out of fertility, the way the sun passes through clouds. Since no doctor's been involved, they'll never know. At any rate, when her monthly visitor does show up again, it's much too late to cancel the church.

'You'd better not mention this to anyone,' says her mother when Frieda hands her the laundry basket with its bloody news. 'Just be glad. You've been lucky.'

'But I don't want to get married,' says Frieda hopelessly.

'What's wrong with Bob all of a sudden?' says her mother. 'You liked him before.'

'Nothing. I just don't want to get married. Ever. To anyone.'

'Don't talk soft,' her mother snaps, shaking the dirty clothes into the tub. And with that, the subject's closed and Frieda finds herself prematurely vaulted into womanhood. She must put away her girlish dreams of – what? It doesn't matter now. A life circumscribed by Windolene and Brasso awaits.

For now, she's a vision in white, clutching hard at the arm of a young man who has no idea the world is anything but grand. On her other side stand Aunties Edie and Flo, her mother and her grandmother, like a set of disapproving Russian dolls.

'Where's Matty?' I asked as Jaz climbed into the Micra.

'With Nat. Brewing up a cold and pretty grouchy about it; I didn't think any of us would enjoy ourselves if he came along. Plus it's forecast snow. He's better staying in.'

'Is he OK to leave?'

'It's a cold, Mum. I've got my phone.' She unbuttoned her thick coat and pulled the seat belt across her body, slotted it home. 'Have you got your camera?'

I'd had an idea to make an illustrated family history, with Jaz, for Matty. He'd appreciate it when he was older, I'd said to Jaz. And if she helped, it'd be her chance to get the story down right.

So a trip to Tannerside was needed, for background. We hadn't been up there for nearly five years.

'Will there be pages about Ian, too?' she'd asked.

'That's up to you. Only, it's for Matty, remember. What do you think he'd want?'

She'd looked away, out of the window. Yes, I thought, one day he'll be grown up and standing there like a recording angel, listing all your deficiencies. Missing photos won't be the half of it.

The place I grew up in had gone from being an unpicturesque village, built off the back of cotton and coal, to one of the remoter suburbs of New Enterprise Bolton. Building developments had sprung up everywhere; the fields I'd played in had vanished under housing estates and bypasses and supermarkets. Streams we fished and poked about in had been culverted, trees we used to swing from chopped down, their roots blasted out. You couldn't blame Dad for becoming disorientated. When they erase key landmarks from your childhood, it becomes harder to trust your own memory.

Tannerside's original vicarage was now an old people's home, with a bungalow where the main lawn used to be. Jaz and I stood at the bottom of the drive, underneath leafless horse chestnut trees, reading the sign.

'Is this where you want putting when you reach your dotage?'

'You're to stick me on a cruise ship, you know that.'

'Why do you want a photo of this place, then?'

'It reminds me of your grandma,' I said. 'They used to hold Mothers' Union meetings here, and let us kids loose in the garden. It was terrifically grand. For Tannerside.'

Between the upper and lower lawns there'd been wide stone steps, but we always chose to run down the grass bank instead. Every visit began with a game of hide and seek. Round the back of the house, near the kitchen, I remembered a compost heap where Joseph Critchley found a nest of grass snakes and threw gravel at them till the vicar's wife made him stop. There were fruit canes at the back, too; one time Margaret Wardle ate so many raspberries she vomited red on the doorstep, and panicked because she thought it was part of her insides. We always got a high tea before we went home, with miniature sandwiches and fairy cakes, so it was almost like going to someone's birthday party. Uneaten food was parcelled up for us to take home. Eileen was never part of these afternoons because her family didn't go to church. For some reason my mother, normally a keen recruiter, would never approach hers. So to make up, I'd share any stale sponge left over and give Eileen a blow-by-blow account of what we'd all been up to in the vicarage grounds. I did try to include her that way. Perhaps, in retrospect, it might have been better if I'd kept the details of our revelry to myself.

St Stephen's Primary was now a private residence called 'The Old Schoolhouse', had a black and gold name plaque on the gatepost. 'Boys still got the slipper in those days,' I said to Jaz, bringing the gable end into focus through my viewfinder. 'Girls just lost their playtime for being naughty. Though your dad once famously got both.'

'What for?'

'He carried one of the reception class up to the top of the oil tank and left him there.'

'Why would he do that?'

'Oh, he never needed a reason. It was me who went to get a teacher, but I've never told him that. Don't you say, either.'

'Like it matters now.'

Greenhalgh's was still there, still with a queue coming out the door. Hot pasties glistened in the window.

'You're not taking a picture of a bakery, Mum?' said Jaz.

'We used to go there every Friday dinnertime to get the bread for the weekend. Never cake, though; your grandma made all our cakes herself. Drop scones, she was always very good at. I've still got her griddle. One day it'll be yours.'

'Gee, thanks.'

We strolled on down to the wool shop, but it was a chiropodist's.

'How much do you remember of your grandma?' I asked.

Jaz shrugged. 'Nothing, really. She walked with a stick.'

'When she got poorly, yes. Nothing else?'

'Don't think so. She wasn't very nice to you, was she?'

'She did what she was capable of.'

'You've got a bit of an issue there, haven't you?'

'I wouldn't say so.'

At the start of the next terrace was Eileen's old house, unchanged except for a satellite dish above the upstairs window. I'd meant to stop, take a snap, but as we drew near I changed my mind and kept my camera by my side. Bevelled glass doors, the smell of hairspray, plastic flowers and charity shop shoes with dirty insoles bring her mother back to me. 'By the time I turn twenty-one, I want to be out of this village,' Eileen had told me. But it was me who'd left first, for Phil's job.

As we passed the low front wall I had a sudden memory of Jaz returning from a sleepover at Nat's and saying, 'I'm glad I live here and not there.' I think she may even have hugged me, although I might be imagining that.

St Stephen's Church looked the same as ever from the outside, but when we went in I discovered the interior had been dramatically refurbished. There were now indoor toilets, and a proper enclosed meeting area, and what looked like a crèche. The austere feeling I remembered from childhood had gone, banished by deep orange carpet in the entrance hall and proper heating. My mother would have hated it.

'I knew you'd come here,' said Jaz, putting her bag down by the baize display board.

'I wanted a shot of the village quilt,' I said. 'If it's still on display. Come and help me find it.'

Two years it had taken the Mothers' Union to complete the quilt and they'd hung it in the Lady Chapel, with a spotlight of its own. It depicted historical landmarks of Tannerside, bordered by scenes from the Christian Year. In the top left-hand corner, the Nativity hovered above a set of pit winding gear; bottom left were harvest sheaves, veg, fish, and the original council offices with their bowed walls and cobbled front. St Stephen's itself had been given centre spot, along with Cappelthorne Hall where they started holding the church fete after the old vicarage was sold off.

'The middle right side is Grandma's,' I said, pointing. My mother had used a mixture of embroidery and appliqué to render the Passiontide: a basin and towel, a bag of coins, a whip, a sword, a crown of thorns, some nails, a sponge, a blindfold and a sign saying *King of the Jews*.

'How neat is that?' said Jaz.

'Oh, she was a whizz with a needle, before her hands got bad. She taught me to sew when I was still in the Infants.'

'You never taught me.'

'I tried. Anyway, you can manage the basics, can't you? You can mend a seam, sew on a button.'

Jaz smirked. 'Nat's got this thing with buttons.'

'How do you mean?'

'I'm not sure I should say in a church.'

So we went outside into the freezing graveyard, and while

I hunted for ancient family headstones, she told me how Nat liked to secretly cull a button from every man she slept with. 'She keeps them in a box,' said Jaz.

'Good grief. How many are we talking about?' I was picturing something the size of a shoebox, filled to the brim.

Jaz sketched cigarette packet dimensions with her fingers. She was grinning.

'Well,' I said, 'I don't think that's very nice.'

'I know, it's cheap. I wouldn't do it. Not that I'd have a lot of buttons in the first place.'

'If it was me, it'd be the one button only. I'd need a single compartment of a pill box, that's all.'

She goggled at me. 'God, honestly?'

'Yes.'

'Only my dad?'

'Yes. Stop looking at me like that.'

'No one else, before or after? Jeez. That's amazing.'

'Not really.'

She followed me as I picked my way through stone memorials.

'I suppose there's a lot of stuff like that I don't know about you,' she said.

'I'm your mum. There's nothing else for you to know.'

I stood for a moment in front of my Great-aunty Florence's grave and thought about the drive to the crematorium after my mother's funeral, then all those po-faced elderly ladies standing round the chapel foyer. *You'll not remember me, Carol, but I lived next door to Flo Viner* . . . Phil stiff and awkward in his suit; Dad with his head bowed over the pew, one hand laid across the other. Moira had looked after Jaz that day. I'd been so glad to get back to her.

'Do you think I should start going to church?' said Jaz.

I tried not to look taken aback. 'If you want to.'

416

'Why did you stop going?'

'I was too busy.'

'That's rubbish.'

'All right: I lost heart, then. Things got in the way.'

'But Nick says—' She saw my expression. 'Obviously it's your choice.'

'It is.'

'Can we talk about it sometime?'

'Yes, but not today,' I said, clicking the lens cap back into place. 'Today we have other fish to fry.'

The rendering on Pincroft's top half had been re-painted pale yellow and the front lawn paved in that compressed concrete they have nowadays. I thought of my mother's continual war with grass and dandelions and lilac and privet, how she'd don a pair of pink rubber gloves and re-do the bedding from scratch every season, and wondered whether she'd have been pleased at the innovation. It's possible she might have approved.

'Haven't you got photos of the house already?' asked Jaz.

'Not of the front, looking from the road.'

'Is it the same people Grandad sold it to? They were going to move the bathroom upstairs.'

In my head I was clearing piles of old newspaper from under the stairs while Dad, his shirt hanging loose from his trousers, paced anxiously up and down the hallway. The next instant I was sitting on the back step in my Ladybird nightie cutting the robin motifs off a box of starch.

'It's a strange process, getting old,' I said.

'Do you want to have a look inside? Shall I go knock on the door?'

'No!'

'Go on. I'll do it, you can wait here. What's there to lose?'

'I don't want to see what they've changed, Jaz.'

The grey carpet with black, white and red drizzles would have gone for sure, and the kitchen cupboards with their rickety sliding doors, and the old Fifties bathroom suite. Probably everything I knew would have been stripped and junked.

'It's not my house any more.'

'Fair enough,' she said. 'Can we get something to eat soon? I'm frozen and I'm starving.'

She let me take her arm and we retraced our steps towards the High Street. There was a café-cum-gift shop I'd noted, where, as well as having a snack, I could check out product lines and displays to report back to Moira. After lunch I intended taking Jaz along the canal, see if the woods were still there, and the stone dovecote, and we could loop back via the main road to where the car was parked, taking in Cappelthorne Brow where Dad once took me blackberrying when the works were on strike.

'You look nice today,' she said, as we drew near the church again. 'Your hair's so much better than it was when you used to try and do it yourself.'

'Job's complimenter.'

'The jacket's neat, too. I've not seen you in that colour before.'

'It's funny,' I said, pausing before we crossed the road, 'you might think you'd get to an age where you'd have sorted your style for good. You'd just know what suited you, and that would be it. But actually, the older you are, the more need there seems to be for reinvention and makeover. I can't decide whether that's a positive thing or not.'

'I'm getting old,' said Jaz. 'I'll be thirty in a couple of years.'

I made a mock-swipe at her, and she laughed.

Together we stood outside the gift-shop window, eyeing the pearlescent vases and floral pigs. Behind the front shelf our reflections hovered.

'You know,' she said, 'Nick's a friend, not a rival. He really rates you.'

'That's lucky, then.'

'It's been fun today, hasn't it? We could do it again, with Matty when he's a bit older.'

And I thought, This is my reward, this is my life as it is now. It's enough. I'm happy. I am.

CHAPTER 39

Photo 185, Album Two

Location: the lounge, Sunnybank

Taken by: Carol

Subject: It's Christmas 1983 and Frieda's stationed in an armchair, clasping a cerise paper hat to her bosom. How did she get here? she's thinking. Who are these people gathered around her? Perhaps this is how dementia begins. Not with a lack of recognition, exactly – that woman there's her daughter, that man there's her no-good son-in-law – but with a lack of explanation for your life. What has this scene got to do with who she is, and the things she wanted? She could surely have done more with these past four decades than shift dust from surface to surface, wring out the days over a Belfast sink.

If she closes her eyes, she feels it: only the thinnest of filaments tethers her to this room and this family.

Now Carol's talking, she's offering round a box of Eat Me dates, but it's as if she's stretching her hand out from a mile away. Bob's taken refuge in a nap. Even the jolly piano music to All Creatures Great and Small *fails to provide its usual faint comfort. The only object that stirs Frieda*

*here is the little girl playing on the hearthrug. She can't say
why.*

It was dark by the time we got back to Jaz's.

'I hate these winter evenings,' she said as the car pulled up.
'After I've put Matty to bed.'

'I'm only ever a phone call away, you know.'

'Yeah. I've got to learn to cope, though, haven't I?'

I couldn't answer her. Bloody rotten shame, I was thinking,
when she'd had it all, their lovely first home just how she
wanted it, and no mortgage or rent to pay so they weren't
struggling like so many young couples; happy and loved and
safe and optimistic. Sometimes these sudden and massive
waves of anger against Ian still knocked me off-balance: the
injustice, the waste. What must my daughter feel every time
she unlocked the front door of this flat to be presented with
grubby walls, worn carpet, other people's post?

When we got inside, Nat was feeding Matty chocolate buttons in front of the TV. The arms of the sofa were covered in
scrunched-up tissues. 'How's he been?' asked Jaz, bending to
kiss his filthy face.

'Snotty,' said Nat.

'Apart from that?'

'Yeah, fine. We went into town, looked at the Christmas
lights. But it was brass monkeys so we didn't hang around
long.'

'Shall I go run his bath?' I said.

Jaz nodded. 'That would be a help. I'll be there in a minute.'

I made my way to their poky bathroom and started the
water running, then I went next door to Matty's room to collect his slippers and pyjamas. Those I laid out on the bathroom
floor ready, and then I thought I'd have a quick tidy round
while I was there. I was on my knees cleaning the base of the

sink pedestal with a sheet of baby wipes when Jaz appeared, carrying a pile of towels.

'I keep thinking about Grandma,' she said.

'What about her?'

'That she can't have been happily married if she was always such a misery-guts.'

I struggled to my feet and dropped the wet wipe in the toilet bowl.

'So I reckon,' she continued, 'it *is* a pattern. I'm unlucky in love; you were; Grandma was. It's genetic. Either that or I'm cursed.'

'Don't be silly,' I said. 'Grandma and Grandad got along fine. It may not have been a movie-style romance, but they stuck it out for thirty-six years. Anyway, Grandad's lovely, he'd never have done anything to hurt Grandma, never. And Ian – Ian's situation isn't the same as your dad's. For all sorts of reasons.'

Jaz sighed, opened the airing-cupboard door and began to stack the towels on the top shelf.

I said, 'I understand the urge to look for a broader explanation, but sometimes there is none.'

'I'll go get Matty,' she said.

She kept his bath toys in a colander near the taps, so I picked out a few I knew he liked – a polythene kitchen jug and funnel, a wind-up turtle, a flannel frog – and dropped them in the water. Matty burst in, trouserless, and peered over the edge while I swirled the water round. 'Froggy all wet,' he said. He bobbed against the bath rim in anticipation.

'Let's get your top off,' I told him.

He stood, jiggling impatiently, while I knelt again to undo the press-studs at his neck. His mouth was smeared with chocolate and his nose was running. When I reached for a wipe, he saw it coming and jerked his head away.

'No, come on, be a good boy, let Nanna clean you up.'

'Determined, isn't he?' said Jaz, poking her head round the door and watching us wrestle.

'Oh yes. I can't think who he reminds me of.'

While Jaz moved back and forth between rooms putting away dried washing, I whipped off his nappy, hooked my hands under his armpits and lowered him gently into the bath. 'Not too hot?' I asked him. For answer Matty grabbed the jug and splashed it base-first into the water.

'Watch out,' he said. 'Watch out!'

I pretended to duck, and shake my hair, which pleased him. He splashed some more, rubbed his eyes, then his attention lighted on the soggy frog. He pulled it out so it lay across his leg.

'Is Froggy having a rest from swimming?' I asked.

Matty said something I didn't understand, and raised his knee so the frog slid off with a plop. 'Oh dear,' he said. Then he scooped the frog back out and repeated the exercise. I got hold of the turtle and began to wind its key.

Suddenly he raised his head and said, 'Where Swir-Fish, Nanna?'

I looked about me. 'I'm not sure, love.'

'Swir-Fish.'

'Let's see if he's in the colander.' I reached over and rummaged about.

'Swir-*Fish*, Nanna.'

'I know, sweetheart, I'm doing my best.'

'Swir-Fish!'

I stood up and cast my eyes around the room; there wasn't much room for even a small toy to hide itself. Without much hope I peeped inside the airing cupboard, but there was nothing in there except towels and toiletries.

'Nanna!'

'OK, OK, I'll just nip and have a look in your room,' I told him.

Matty's bedroom was probably no smaller than his old one had been, but it felt cramped because Jaz had put a lot of her belongings in there. Some of it was boxed and some wasn't: some of it spilled out over the floor. A pile of clothes lay across a pair of speakers, and behind those she'd stacked half a dozen framed prints and a weekly planner blackboard. There was a suitcase labelled *imp docs*, another labelled *cupboard 2*, and a beaten copper umbrella stand she'd filched from Sunnybank and seemed to be using to store DVDs. She'd pushed piles of foreign language books between the end of Matty's bed and the wall. His dismantled cot she'd shoved down the side of the wardrobe. And overlaying all this was what looked like an upended bin-full of toys and toddler equipment. I didn't know where to start.

Speedily I began to work my way across to the bed, shifting this bag of Duplo, that basket of trains, this dislocated drawer of socks, that bundle of parenting magazines. The item I was trying to locate was only three inches long, but on the plus side, it was bright orange.

Something I trod on mooed, and a tower of boxed games fell over. I gained the low bed where Dawg lay flat on his back, legs splayed as though pinned for dissection. Then I pulled down the sheets and scuffled a few teddies aside. Nothing. I lifted the pillow, and there was the blessed fish. 'Got him!' I called.

Jaz met me at the bathroom door. 'You shouldn't leave Matty on his own in the bath,' she said.

'I went to get this,' I said, waving the toy at her. 'He was asking for it.'

'Then you should have called for me.'

'I was only gone thirty seconds.'

'More than that. It's OK, I've been here, I saw you go so I

left the washing and came to watch him. But don't do it again, Mum.'

'I was twenty steps away.'

'Makes no odds. You shouldn't leave him in water even for a moment.' She must have seen the upset on my face because her tone softened. 'Like I said, I was here, he's all right. Just, in future—'

Limply I held out the plastic fish. 'I'm really sorry.'

'OK, well. I'll see to him now. There's no harm done. But you really mustn't leave him unattended like that, ever – yeah?'

I nodded.

'After all,' she said playfully, 'I don't want to have to cut you off again, do I?' She pulled a mock-tragic face, and disappeared into the bathroom.

For a moment I couldn't take in what she meant. Then the impact of her words hit me, and I had to steady myself against the wall. I could hear Matty twittering, and Jaz responding, the slosh of water, the gurgle and clunk of the plug coming out. I pictured her lifting him up, setting him on the bathmat, wrapping the towel around his pink body. Her tone was bright and cheery, untroubled. And all the time the heat of rage was spreading over me like a fever, leaving my throat tight, my breath shallow. After a minute, she came out carrying him, his pyjama bottoms draped over her arm. 'These have got porridge stains down them,' she said as she passed me. I stayed where I was.

His bedroom light went on again, then dimmed as the curtains rattled against the rail. His musical bear-lamp started up, and when the tune finished, I could make out the story she was reading, *Runaway Bunny*. Found myself mouthing the words, while inside my head raged and whirled. Silence after, as she closed the book, took him over to the bed, then Matty asking some sort of question, too low for me to hear, Jaz murmuring something soothing. She'd be kissing him now, patting Dawg, pulling the cover up tight. I waited.

I caught her as she was closing the door.

'Oh!' she said. 'You made me jump.'

'How dare you,' I said.

'What?'

'How *dare* you joke about it.'

'How dare I joke about what, Mum? What's up? You look—'

'Joke about cutting me off from Matty. Stopping me from seeing him. *It's nothing to joke about.*'

Jaz's eyes had gone wide with surprise. I let her steer me away from Matty's bedroom door and round the corner, into the lounge.

'Sit down,' she said.

'No.'

She hovered uncertainly by the sofa. 'Look, I'm sorry. It was a stupid thing to say. Obviously I didn't mean it, I wouldn't take Matty away again.'

'How do I know that, Jaz?' I shouted. 'How am I supposed to know? I never guessed you were going to do it before! Why should now be different from then?'

She began to say something, but I swept on.

'You have no idea, *no idea* what it did to me when you and Matty went on the run. I didn't know where you were, whether you were safe, whether I'd see either of you again. You could have been lying dead somewhere – anything. You'd told me I'd never see my grandson again – yes, you did, it was your parting shot, don't deny it. And you meant it.'

'I didn't.'

'You did when you said it.'

I'd backed her up against the edge of the sofa; she had nowhere to go.

'I didn't, Mum. I was just really angry. I get angry, it's the way I am.'

'We *all* get bloody angry, Jaz! *I* get angry! What am I supposed to do? Swallow it down, smile? Carry on pretending it doesn't matter; forgiving-and-forgetting? Oh, I forgot, that's another of my failings, isn't it, stoicism? Well, I've *had* it. I'm sick of you taking advantage of my honest concern. You turned your own son into a weapon, your own son, it's unforgivable. What you did to me was horrible. You took my love and used it to hurt me, when you know I'd do *anything* for you and Matty, lay down my life if need be, and that's not being dramatic, it's a simple statement of fact.

'You had no *right* to threaten me that way! Not answering my calls, no word, nothing. If you'd planned for weeks, you couldn't have hurt me more profoundly. You need to be told. It was beyond cruel.'

Behind Jaz, on the cushion, I could see one of Matty's socks, sky blue with a penguin motif on the ankle. For a second I imagined him next door, his lashes fluttering against his cheek, his thumb in his mouth, and my momentum faltered. What in God's name was I doing, risking everything after I'd been so careful all these months to keep control?

But this wasn't just a matter of indulging my temper. I thought of a letter in a problem page I'd read a few days ago, where a woman had written in to ask about tackling agoraphobia. 'It's like a bully,' the agony aunt had told her. 'Step back to give it room, and it'll only advance further.' The comparison had stuck in my mind. If I spent the rest of my life avoiding confrontation with my daughter out of fear, I'd always be in this same place: a click of her fingers away from losing Matty. David was right. I had to make a stand.

'Since you were born,' I said, 'you've been my first priority. Everything I've done has had you as the central consideration.

You must know that. If I've made mistakes, it's not because I haven't cared, it's because I'm human, and we all make mistakes.'

I saw again Jaz raging about my living room, kicking my albums, barking accusations at me while Matty cowered behind the long curtain. Gathering now were all the lines I'd rehearsed over and over, the defences I never got to deliver, till they'd become a litany which sent me nearly mad. 'Good God, love, how could you possibly accuse me of not sticking up for you or protecting you? You've been my *life*. I've done my damnedest to give you the best of everything – maybe I tried too hard and spoiled you, that's what your dad always said. But to claim I taught you to make bad choices, just because I was trying to protect you! Would you really have been happy if your dad and I had split up, like Nat's parents did? No, you wouldn't, and you'd have blamed that on me as well. Oh yes, you would. I'm sorry, desperately sorry about what happened with Ian, but to argue it's somehow my fault is as ridiculous as it's insulting. And the idea that I'd *ever* deliberately want to hurt you – it would be like hurting myself, Jaz, only worse.

'I would *never* betray you, I would never stand aside and watch someone cause you pain. How could you even contemplate those things? All I've ever wanted, from the moment I first held you when you were a tiny baby, was your happiness. That's been my focus and my direction. I can't imagine how you could ever think otherwise. To say the things you've said to me, to treat me the way you have – it's got to stop. Enough. I don't want a medal, I just want you to be fair and decent, *the way you were brought up*.'

Jaz hadn't moved at all while I was speaking. Her face was rigid now, her pupils shrunk to tiny unreadable points. I needed my words to have gone below the surface, snagged somewhere in her conscience. Out of nowhere I remembered

Dad reaching through brambles to get me blackberries, pulling his hand back and there being a line of welling red beads across his knuckles.

A swoop of dizziness passed over me and I knew I had to get out. Without waiting for her to respond, I grabbed my coat and turned towards the hall.

The last detail I saw, out of the corner of my eye, was the kitchen door opening a fraction, and Nat's shocked face peering out. I'd completely forgotten she was there.

CHAPTER 40

Photograph 315, Album Three

Location: Jaz's bedroom

Taken by: Nat

Subject: a head and shoulders shot of Jaz, draped in a red velvet dressing gown, her hair crimped and swagged up on each side with enamel combs. Today she is the Lady of Shalott, because they have been doing it at school and Jaz thinks it is the most tragically beautiful story she has ever heard. The death scene's obviously interesting, and the hazy circumstances of the curse, but it's the twist in the end that's bothering her most, the fact that Lancelot kills her and he doesn't even realise it. How could you inflict that amount of damage on someone and not be aware of what you'd done? How might he be made to find out, and pay? She's been turning the question over in her mind ever since.

Nat's plain bored with the whole Camelotty business. She thinks Jaz is only going on about castles and webs and greaves and mighty bugles because of Mr Bryant. All the girls (except for Nat) are in love with Mr Bryant.

'How old do you think he is?' asks Jaz dreamily.

'Dunno. Twenty-three?' Nat has no idea how long teacher

training lasts, but Mr B looks like a student to her. He wears
tour T-shirts under his jackets, and a leather strap round his
wrist. 'You just want to shag him,' says Nat, seizing her
chance with the crimpers.

'Already have done,' says Jaz.

It's an idiotic boast. She's still only fourteen, hasn't even
French-kissed yet.

'You can get into trouble for making up stories like that,'
warns Nat. Tirra Lirra by the river. It's all bollocks, all of it.

For years I've had a recurring dream where I come across a
whole set of extra rooms to Sunnybank I hadn't realised were
there. Sometimes it's a bedroom suite, sometimes a dining room
featuring a great banqueting table; once I discovered, against all
logic, a sea view. Even though I love my house, it's always a
mild disappointment to wake up within its real confines.
Disorientating, too. For a day or two after, I'll flick through
home improvement magazines till the sensation passes.

You get to my age, you think you know yourself pretty well.
But in that half-hour at Jaz's, I'd found a side to my personality I'd never suspected. I strode out of her flat and climbed into
my car without hesitation. As I drove back through the sleety
darkness I began making plans: how, if the worst came to the
very worst, I could contact Grandparents Apart, engage a
mediator, get myself a lawyer, take my access case to court. Re-
mortgage Sunnybank if I had to. *You mustn't ever think you're*
powerless. You should never assume there's no hope, I heard David
say again. Then: *I'll be right behind you.* 'I can do it on my own,
you taught me that,' I said out loud into the night, and the
windscreen wipers marked the seconds between what I'd done,
and the consequences.

When I got home I had a glass of brandy, spent three hours
on the internet researching useful organisations, then took

myself to bed. Against all the odds, I fell into a deep sleep that took me through till morning.

I woke with a crushing sense that I'd done something awful. But when I recalled the details, I didn't panic. I made myself breakfast, using some of my mother's Royal Worcester that normally lived in the back of the cupboard and never saw the light of day. I took the time to set the table properly. I opened a jar of posh jam I'd been saving, and I read the opening chapter of a Mavis Cheek novel while I ate my toast. Then I set off for work. What I didn't do was go rushing to the phone to plead my daughter's forgiveness, or trawl round the house stroking Matty's things, or pore over his albums, weeping.

How long I'd be able to keep it up I had no idea. Was I confusing courage with numbness? Had I been brave, or unbelievably, irredeemably stupid? Would I be spending Christmas alone? I had no way of knowing till Jaz made her move, whatever that might be.

Days passed, five of them, and I heard nothing. She could have been in her flat, or she could be at the other end of the country. She could be carrying on as normal, unconcerned beyond a lingering sense of annoyance, or beside herself, downing pills with the curtains closed and daytime TV on for company. She could even now be applying for Matty's passport, with a view to emigrating thousands of miles away. That would teach me.

She won't cut you off, you're too useful, said David's voice, reasonably. And another voice, possibly my own: *Come on, you're her mother, she loves you.* 'Then why hasn't she been in touch?' I asked the woman frowning back at me from the mirror. None of the voices in my head had a convincing answer to that.

In my bleakest moments, I found myself wondering how long it would take for Matty to forget me entirely. Time operates differently for two-year-olds. Within the space of a few months, I guessed, those hundreds of hours we'd spent together would evaporate to nothing. By the time he started school, he'd have virtually no recollection of his grandma. Fifty-four, I'd be, then. Sixty-one when he went up to secondary school, sixty-six by the time he sat his GCSEs. How old when he married? I tried to picture it but the image was too remote. Matty was just a misty shape and the only Jaz I could conjure was younger than she was now, a sulking, flash-eyed teen. I couldn't get near either of them.

Repeatedly I forced my thoughts away from the worst possibilities, but even so, the temptation to at least phone Nat or Ian and check up on her was continuous and almost overpowering.

I started re-organising the loft, took more clothes to the charity shop, and binned all my mother's old recipe books and magazines. For all her hours spent carefully copying out ingredients, what use were they now? *Everyday Eggless Cooking*, for God's sake. Her other books – the novels, the de Beauvoir, the annotated Dawkins – I stowed in my bedside cabinet because one day I did intend to read those, if only for themselves.

On the Wednesday evening, when I should have been having Matty to stay, I retrieved the photograph of Penny and, without looking at her, folded it in two and dropped her on the fire. A brief yellow flare and she was gone. She really didn't matter any more. So little did, when it came down to it.

I was in freefall, I could have been any woman except the one I had been.

On the sixth day I was in Healey's picking at my ham sandwich when Josh came over and plonked a plate of sponge cake in front of me.

'I didn't order that,' I said.

'No,' he said, 'but you looked like you needed something. And we're not allowed to serve alcohol.'

He winked at me, and I was just thinking what a lovely boy he was after all when suddenly his head jerked up and I saw him mouth 'Fuck off' in the direction of the window. I turned to see three youths flicking Vs and grinning. When I looked again at Josh, he was grinning too. He snatched my laminated menu and held it with his middle finger up the back, towards them. The boys jostled each other, slapped the glass, jeered, and carried on past the window.

'You won't last long if you start making obscene gestures at the public,' I observed.

'I won't do it to real customers.'

'You'd better not.'

'Madam.' He draped a serviette over his forearm and bowed deeply. 'Sometimes a waiter's got to do what a waiter's got to do. Enjoy your cake.'

I did my best to eat it, but the buttercream was an inch thick and tasted oily. Only last week, when Jaz was still at primary school, she'd stood in my kitchen sifting cocoa powder and icing sugar into a mixing bowl to decorate her first ever batch of fairy cakes. You know these years are going to come to an end, but you don't believe it. One day Matty would be a stroppy, gangling youth, and Jaz would be stranded out of time, bewildered and unsure.

I was trying again to visualise an adult Matty, when the café door tinkled open and Nat walked in.

Nat didn't come in Healey's, it wasn't her sort of place. Was she here for me? Did she bring bad news? I didn't know if I dared meet her gaze or not, but I had no chance to pretend indifference because she came straight over to my table and sat down.

'That woman in the shop told me you were here,' she announced.

I swallowed nervously. 'Everything all right?'

'With Jaz?'

Of course with Jaz. Good God, what else would I mean? 'And Matty.'

'Oh, they're fine. Matty's still got a cold so he's off nursery. But he's all right.'

'They're – around?'

'She hasn't gone off anywhere. She's in the flat. I thought you'd want to know.'

'Yes, yes I do. Thank you.'

''S all right.' A brief twitch of the lips that was Nat smiling.

'What state's she in? Is she angry?'

'She was, yeah. Now she's just, sort of crushed.'

That single syllable was like a stab to the ribs. 'Depressed?'

'I dunno. She wants to say sorry,' Nat continued, 'but she can't, you know, make the move.'

'So she's sent you?'

'God, no. She doesn't know I'm talking to you. You mustn't tell her. She'd be – shit. No, don't say anything.'

I watched her fidgeting, nudging the salt and pepper pots around with her French-polished nails. Two narrow strips of bleached-white hair hung down around her cheekbones. She said, 'I'm a little bit frightened of Jaz, to tell you the truth, Mrs Morgan.'

I don't want your confidences, I thought, I haven't the energy for them. In and out of Sunnybank for years, this girl had been; she was part of Jaz's childhood. There should have been a connection between us, but I looked at her and felt nothing.

'What should I do?' I asked.

Nat shrugged. *How should I know?* her expression said.

'Is she very upset?'

'She was crying last night. She needs you.'

I felt like the worst mother in the world. 'You're a good friend to her,' was all I could think to say, and that nearly choked me.

'Yeah, well.'

Nat was studying me with narrowed eyes. Clearly there was something else she needed to add.

'Do you remember,' she said at last, 'when I used to come round your house?'

'Well, yes.'

'I bet you don't, really.'

'Of course I do,' I said.

'Not all of it. Like, in the summer, going to school, yeah, if it was hot, you'd put suncream on Jaz and then you'd put some on me too.'

'That was no—'

'My mum never bothered. And sometimes you cleaned my shoes when you cleaned hers. And once I didn't have the stuff I needed for Food Technology, and you sorted me out, pots of butter and that.'

Dimly I recalled standing in the kitchen amongst the breakfast remains, hunting out Tupperware boxes while the girls hovered behind me.

'And if it was a non-uniform day and I'd forgotten, you'd let me wear Jaz's clothes. And you lent me a hat for the Year Seven play, and you made me a packed lunch for a trip when my mum hadn't done me one. I think you paid for a trip, too, didn't you? Because I had to have the cash that morning or I wouldn't have been allowed on the coach and Jaz didn't have anything in her money box. Did you ever get that back? I don't think I ever paid you back.'

'It was no trouble,' I said. They were light, unthinking kindnesses I'd barely registered.

'You don't even remember, do you?'

'Some of it. I'm glad if I helped.'

Her face was irritated, disappointed. 'I used to love your house. I tried to say about it to Jaz, sometimes, but she just laughed at me. She didn't get it.'

Nat paused there. If it had been anyone else, I might have put a supportive arm around them.

I struggled for a moment, decency against instinct, and then I withdrew my hand from under the table and laid my fingers across hers. Her brow pinched into its usual tight lines. Then she pulled away, scraped back her chair and got to her feet.

'Basically, my mum's never been able to give a shit. Far as I can see, Jaz is bloody lucky.'

I stared down at the uneaten cake, embarrassed.

'It's very nice of you,' I began, but when I raised my head she was already halfway to the door.

So on the seventh day I went to my daughter because she was unable to come to me.

I stood in the porch, surrounded by thick cobwebs and dead leaves, stamping my feet with nerves. When Jaz came to the door I took a deep breath and said, 'Does Matty want a walk to the back field, see the horses?'

There was old gritty make-up round her eyes and a tiny smudge of ink under her chin, but I was relieved to see she was properly dressed, that her clothes and hair were clean. She was OK.

She said, 'Shouldn't you be working?'

'Moira's in this afternoon. I'm back again this evening for late-night opening.'

'Oh,' she said.

'I thought I could take him off your hands for an hour.'

'I've got this translation to finish,' she said, her voice gruff and tired-sounding. 'So that would be good, yeah.'

I waited on the doorstep while she got him ready. At last he trotted out, his face small between thick folds of scarf and woolly hat. His mittened hand reached straight up for mine and I took it and clasped it.

'I've got my phone,' I said, patting my pocket.

Jaz nodded and stepped back into the hall, but she didn't close the door. She leaned on the jamb, watching us as we picked our way down the stone steps, and I knew without turning round that she stayed like that till we reached the end of the road.

The traffic was busy and I kept Matty well away from the kerb. We used the pelican crossing, Matty pushing the button, and shouting when the green man lit up. We looked both ways till we got to the other side.

An alleyway between two houses took us onto the broken tarmac of the public footpath, and there were iced-over puddles to step on, and a holly hedge covered in berries, and someone had dumped a wheel trim in the grass that needed investigating. We saw a flock of small birds land on a telegraph wire and take off again, and we heard a police siren far away, and just before we got to the field we discovered a wall with an air vent that was belting out a column of steam. I lifted Matty while he swiped and blew at it, but the effort made him cough so we left it and moved on.

Soon we came to the end of the estate and the path became cindery gravel, then opened into fields. 'This is where the horses live,' I told him. 'If they're around today.' There'd been horses here as long as I could remember; I used to take Jaz to see them when she was six or seven. She'd clamber up on the gate to reach, and stroke them confidently down their noses and flanks. The grey one she liked better than the black because he was smaller and friendlier. She'd given them names, and made up stories about them.

Here came two horses now, both tall and glossy-brown, sleeker than their predecessors but making those same chomping, clodding, huffing noises, their breath coming in cloudy snorts. 'Look,' I said to Matty. 'They want to say hello.'

From my bag I extracted an apple and showed Matty how to offer it, palm flat. 'So they don't accidentally bite your fingers,' I told him. I held the apple over the gate and the lead horse dipped his head, nostrils flaring. The next moment, the apple was snatched off my hand and crunched to slobbery pulp behind black rubber lips. The horse behind shuffled its hooves and tried to push nearer.

'Shall we give his friend one?' I asked. Matty jigged up and down excitedly.

I loved the rippling sheen of their coats as they shifted on the hard, rutted ground, and the expressive way they swivelled their ears. I presented the second apple.

'Horsey's hungry,' said Matty.

'He is, isn't he? Goodness. What a big wet mouth. I think Nanna might need to wipe her hand with a tissue, don't you?'

'Bleauh,' said Matty.

When Jaz was little, I used to pretend the horses were answering back. I'd a high voice for the grey one and a low voice for the black. It always made her laugh.

Matty pulled dead beech leaves off a twig, and I extemporised about the stable the horses slept in at night, and the people who came to feed them, and the wild animals who sometimes visited the field. I don't know whether he was listening or not. Snack time over, the horses drifted away to the side of the field and I was able to hoist him onto the top bar of the gate for a better view. I put my arm round his shoulders to steady him. 'I won't let you fall,' I said.

Footsteps crunching behind us made me look round: it was Jaz, walking towards us in her long black winter coat with her hands in her pockets. Her head was lowered, but I could see she'd scrubbed the make-up off her face and her eyes were pink and bare. She looked clean and young and penitent. I knew then it was going to be all right.

She came up against the gate, on Matty's other side. For a while all three of us stood there, watching the sky change from bright to dull to bright again. There was, when I looked across at her, something in her profile, in the earnest set of her jaw, that put me in mind of an old wartime propaganda poster. *Women of Britain Fight On!*

Matty began to tell her in his garbled way about the horses and I stayed where I was, my hand against his back. I'm sorry, Mum, she would say, I will never take your grandson away from you again. I understand how you must have felt. I know you were only trying to help.

And I might explain how horrible it was to have to say goodbye to David, to have such a decent man think of me as a coward and an ingrate, and how I didn't blame her for it but that she needed to know what it had cost me to turn him away.

Not quite yet, though.

With infinite gentleness, she slid her arms round her son, drew him off the gate, set him back down on the ground, steadied him, and took his hand. I came up and took his other one.

Then, still without speaking, we began to make our way home, swinging Matty between us every few paces. Anyone watching would have thought we were the most normal family in the world.

CHAPTER 41

Photograph 839, Album Six

Location: Carol's spare bedroom

Taken by: Carol

Subject: Matty asleep in his cot with Dawg and the gourd-rattle

I'm not naïve, whatever Jaz thinks. I know my albums are more than just memory prompts. I'm well aware I've been manipulating history to make it more upbeat. In that estimation, she was right, and I make no apologies for it.

But even edited narratives don't remain stable for long. Event overlays event, it's impossible to view any incident in isolation. Some hurt or failure here, a triumph there, the cutting of ties, a resolution or a reunion, every experience creates another version of the past. Sometimes I remembered Jaz's boast, how one day she would make an album which told the Real Truth. Good luck with that, I thought.

I took albums two and three and went through them, systematically removing all the photos that included my ex-husband. I scanned each one, cropped him out, and replaced it on the page with a Phil-free version. Although the idea of a bonfire or tearing-up session was tempting, I found myself keeping the originals for the same reason I'd never excised him before: my marriage was too big a part of my history. But neither was I prepared any longer to give him an official place in my book of memories. You can't undo the past, but you can choose how you move on from it.

On the last page of album five I added, defiantly, a portrait of David, taken from one of the wedding shots. Twice I'd written to him since he'd left, once to say thank you again for all his support, and then to tell him some of the things I'd said to Jaz. He hadn't replied to either letter. Which was an answer in itself, of course. *You've made your bed*, went my mother.

Meanwhile.

Matty learned how to run, kick a ball, climb the stairs one at a time if I was behind him. He could speak in almost-sentences, and if you gave him a felt-tip and paper, he'd do you a circular scribble, holding the pen in his fist like a dagger. I bought a cardboard wallet to keep his pictures in, and Jaz laughed because I'd spent so many hours clearing the house and here I was, filling it up again.

Jaz and Ian met at a solicitor's office and agreed terms of contact and maintenance. Jaz filled in the first set of forms and submitted them. Ian returned the form that acknowledged receipt. Jaz completed an affidavit confirming his signature, and sent it back to court.

Dad caught another chest infection and needed antibiotics.

Moira changed the opening hours of the shop so we started at ten. Our rent went up. The main window had to be replaced after it got smashed by drunks.

Gwen at the gym handed in her notice to train as a firefighter.

Josh was in the local paper for saving a woman customer from choking. *Service with a Thump* said the headline, which

Laverne felt trivialised the incident. The woman wanted him entering for a Local Heroes competition, but Josh refused.

Connor went back into hospital, and came out again.

Dr Page and his wife had a baby girl called Amelia Catherine.

Dove at Beavers announced she was getting engaged.

I had an awful, awful dream about Andy Spicer.

Jaz had her hair cut short, like a boy's.

I went to strim the ugly dead reeds from round the pond, and there were already new green shoots coming up underneath. I cried for a little bit, but then I was fine.

Spring had been a long time coming. The crocus bulbs Matty and I planted in December had come up, flowered, and died away to a purple slime. I'd cleared out the winter bedding and installed lobelia plugs and primulas, snapdragons and petunias. All the shrubs I'd hacked back hard a few months before were flushing into leaf again. We watched a blackbird build a nest in Laverne's hedge, and we took in half a handful of frog spawn so we could see it developing. 'I wish we'd had a pond when I was little,' said Jaz, watching a tadpole suck on a fragment of beef. She's never been good at identifying irony, for all she's clever.

Mostly she was up – more buoyant than she'd been for a year – but there were days she was as snappy and downbeat as ever. I had those too. When I knew she was going round to Phil's, for instance. I bore it, but I no longer bothered pretending it didn't get to me. This was the new understanding I'd reached with my daughter.

One warm May morning we were walking across the centre of Nantwich to deliver Matty to his dad.

'You know Penny's back on the scene, do you?' said Jaz over her shoulder, as we cut through the lawn of St Mary's Church, me pushing the empty buggy behind them.

I think I might have stumbled; in any case, Jaz turned round and halted. Matty tugged at her hand but she ignored him.

'Oh, Mum.'

'It's all right.'

'I shouldn't have said anything.'

'No, really, it's all right. I should have guessed he'd go that way.'

She squatted to adjust Matty's coat. 'I've told him he's a fool. Pen's moving her stuff back in, the place is a tip. You know, the daft thing is, they don't even like each other.'

'So, why?'

'Scared of being on his own, isn't he? It's pathetic. I'm not scared of living alone. You're not. The trouble with Dad is, he's never grown up.'

Pigeons stalked near us, curious and hopeful. I said, 'Do you mind if we don't talk about him?'

'Nope,' said Jaz, and stood up.

The market was on, so we took a stroll through that.

'Need any more sheets?' I asked, pointing to the linen stall. 'Or tea towels, dish cloths? Have you a pair of oven gloves? I'll treat you.'

She laughed. 'I'm fine. In fact, I'd say I've got the flat pretty much as I want it. Well, aside from the décor, but I'm not shelling out for new wallpaper when I'm only renting. That would be mad.'

'When you've your own place again, we can make it like a palace.'

'I'm not rushing, Mum.'

As we walked past a stall selling carpets and runners, Matty spotted a sheepskin oval and broke free from his mother's grasp to bury his face extravagantly against the wool. We had to haul him away, with apologies. 'Thank God he doesn't have a cold,' I said. 'Then we'd have had to buy a snotty rug.'

Next door was a stand of baby clothes and equipment.

'Did I tell you, I sent a parcel of Matty's old sleepsuits to Nick and Steph,' said Jaz, pausing to finger the little vests. 'They'd hardly been worn, it seemed a shame to have them sitting in the drawer.'

'You don't think you might be needing them again sometime?'

Immediately she dropped the giraffe bib she'd been examining. 'Let's not even go there, Mum. Hey, I know what I meant to ask. How's Alice doing?'

'She brought the baby round, little Connor. He's gorgeous. Except he's got this tracheostomy, this tube taped to his throat.'

'Oh, God.'

'He smiles, though. He's got a beautiful smile. Libby tickles him and he just beams.'

'What does she think of her brother?'

'Libby? She's very good. I was nervous about holding him, but Libby went, "He won't break, you know". It's something she must have heard her mum say.'

'And Alice?'

'Tired to death, strung out. But getting on with it. Mind, I don't know if she has any other choice. He's scheduled for an operation when he's a bit bigger, and that should improve his breathing.'

'Must be awful,' said Jaz, drawing Matty nearer and stroking his hair.

'It's a tough road ahead, that's for sure.'

I thought of Alice sitting in my armchair, her face grown older than her years, older than mine somehow, yet how the dark shadows under her eyes melted away when she smiled down at her baby and he smiled back. A very different sort of family, with very different problems and tensions and struggles and fears, but as full of love and the possibility of ordinary joy as the next. 'Well, he's gorgeous,' I'd said to her, not because I felt I ought to say it, but because he was. 'He is, isn't he?' she said, shining with pride. 'And so is Libs.' And with her free arm she'd reached out and hugged her daughter, and I'd felt the brittle tension of all their gathered hopes, like a bright glass ball surrounding them.

'What time is it?' asked Jaz. 'Only I said I'd be in the park by eleven.'

'We've still got twenty minutes,' I said. 'Do you want to stick Matty in his pushchair?'

'No. He naps better in the afternoons if he's had an active morning. See, I'm that considerate of my ex.'

The precinct was busy, but we weren't in a hurry.

She said, 'You know, Ian's thinking of having counselling. He reckons his personality was subsumed by his dad, and that's why he has no confidence. He's decided the input of a professional might help.'

'Oh, we're all failed parents now, aren't we?' I flashed. 'For God's sake! Everyone's a victim. Alternatively, Ian could try taking full responsibility for his actions as an adult.'

Jaz eyed me, then let Matty pull her away to the centre of the square where a man was selling balloons. I was left on my own to stew. It took some deep breathing, and a run-through of my eight-to-twelve times tables before I was calm enough to catch them up.

'All right, are we?' asked Jaz.

I ignored the tone. 'What are Ian's plans for the weekend? Has he said?'

She nodded. 'He always gives me a run-down of where he's going. I do the same for him, as much as I can. Making the point. So it's back to the house this afternoon, and then tomorrow he's taking Matty to one of these farm shops where they let you stroke the lambs and feed the chickens.'

'He'll be in his element. I hope Ian takes some photos.'

'Yeah.' Her hand went up to fiddle with her hair, but her new style was so short there was nothing to play with. Perhaps she was hoping to break a lifetime's habit. 'What'll you be up to this weekend?'

'The usual. Visiting Grandad, getting the food shop in. I want to price up fence panels because that section behind the shed's on its last legs, and I said I'd pop round and see Moira's new house, have lunch there.'

'A packed programme?'

'I shan't sit around and pine for Matty, if that's what you're worried about. I appreciate he needs time with his dad.'

She flashed me a grateful look. 'It's hard, sharing him out.'

You're telling me, I thought.

We were making our way down Mill Street when she said, 'Tell me to mind my own business, but did you ever hear again from David?'

'Mind your own business,' I said pleasantly.

I'd been ahead of her because she was trailing Matty, but she caught up and came in close to my side. 'I deserved that, didn't I?'

'Well. Yes. It doesn't matter any more. Truly.'

Jaz looked down at her feet.

'It'll be awkward for you, seeing him again.'

'If I ever bump into him, yes, it'll be awkward. But I know he'd go out of his way to make things as easy as possible, because he's like that.'

I half-expected a response to that, a rebuttal, but again she said nothing. Good, I thought. We've got somewhere.

The main road was busy and we had to wait a long time for a gap in the traffic. Neither of us spoke till we'd got Matty safely across, then Jaz halted on the verge and cleared her throat. Again her hand moved to her head, seeking tresses that were no longer there.

'Mum?'

'Yes?'

'I need to warn you about something.'

'What?' That instant shot of dread.

'David's back. I didn't tell you before. He's here.'

'You mean, in the UK?'

'Over there, with Ian.'

A few yards in front of us lay the shelf of the riverbank, then a stretch of green, a bench, a path, a line of trees bright with new leaf. It was under these trees that two figures stood. One was tall and lean, his hands in his pockets and his shoulders hunched forward. The other stood straighter, was shorter and more solidly built.

My legs started to tremble. 'Oh,' I said.

I'm not prepared, I wanted to say. *You ought to have let me know in advance. Ian should have rung and tipped me off. I look a mess!* If I could have had half an hour, even, to get myself together.

'He knows you're coming.'

'Does he.'

'Are you OK?'

'I don't know.'

When I'd rehearsed the moment of reunion, I thought the only real emotion I'd feel would be embarrassment. I assumed I'd have to force myself to approach him and then I'd be standing like an idiot, struck dumb under the weight of shaming memories. I'd not counted on this rush of painful pleasure, so intense it made me light-headed. There he was, in plain and shocking sight, and all I wanted to do was go to him.

'Ian was saying he's only been back a couple of days—'

I swallowed hard, touched my daughter's arm. 'Can you take the pram?'

'Mum?'

'It's all right,' I said.

'What are you going to do?'

One, two, three, four swans I counted on the grass ahead. *All mouth and trousers, your swan*, Dad used to say.

I'll tell you what I'm going to do, I thought. I'm going to take a stupid long-shot chance. I'm going to walk over there and tell him properly, to his face, that I was wrong to make him go, that I regret my decision and I wish like mad I had the power to undo it. I don't care who's listening in, Ian or you – let everyone hear. And if David sneers or shouts at me, or worse, if he's kind and shakes his head and says gently that it's too late, then I'll have done my best. I'm no worse off.

I thought of my mother, a life spent skewered on her own mar-tyrdom, it occurring to no one around her to ask what was wrong, not that she'd have spoken up anyway. I thought of Dad, shack-led for decades to a woman to whom he was patently unsuited, and without any form of romantic consolation. I thought of the years I'd wasted with Phil. What Jaz said was true: I wasn't afraid to be alone. It was the risks associated with commitment that scared me witless. But at this moment I wasn't motivated by fear. It was purely and simply a need to set something right.

'Jaz,' I said. 'Listen, I have to speak to him. I have to try and take this opportunity to make good. I don't know whether I can – I'm fairly sure it's too late, actually – but I want him to know I appreciate the chance he gave me, and how much I regret its loss. If you don't agree with that, then I'm sorry, but I still have to do it, and you really should be supporting me because I've always tried so hard to support you, and I'd never deliberately stand in the way of your happiness, especially if you wanted to start again with a new man, which is damned hard to do when your confidence has been knocked into the ground the way mine has, and yours, both of us, really—'

I ran out of breath.

'Jesus,' she said, frowning. Matty pulled on her wrist impatiently. 'I was going to tell you to go. If you must.'

And with those brief syllables, I was suddenly left to fend for myself.

When I looked over, David's face was turned in my direction, waiting. I tried to read his stance: was it disappointed, defensive, calculatedly indifferent? The space between us was wide and unobstructed, the clear sky gave no cover.

I began to pick my way across the lumpy grass, all too aware of how clumsy I must look, lurching on weak ankles, clinging onto the shoulder strap of my bag as though it were a parachute ripcord. The skirt I'd chosen, a dull corduroy thing, was riding up over my knees, my coat flapping open. My lipstick needed re-applying. Ill-equipped fiftysomething, floundering.

The field seemed to elongate as I struggled on; two swans whipped their heads up and hissed me spitefully on my way. What would happen when I reached him? He might use any one of a dozen put-downs, all deserved. He might say, 'You'll have heard about—' and then some woman's name, some American piece whose hair was not in desperate need of re-colouring, and who was smart enough to hold onto a good man when she saw one. Perhaps he'd pull out a photograph of them together for me to admire, while my insides dissolved in acid remorse. If I was going to get my speech out, I'd need to say it quickly. Or would that be worse, blurting out my feelings with no idea of their appropriateness? I lowered my gaze and concentrated on where I was putting my feet, so at least I didn't go sprawling in front of him.

When I dared look up next I was near enough to see David's face. What struck me first was his tanned skin, and the fact that his hairline seemed further back than I remembered. His expression was stern and my confidence faltered. There was no hope. He had not replied to my letters because there was nothing more to say. This whole exercise was a pointless humiliation.

It might be better never to speak again.

Suddenly he broke into a grin and said something to Ian, who smiled too. Was it a real smile, or a mocking one? Were they just amused by the state I'd got myself into? Somehow I made myself keep going towards them, until at last I could make out the expression in his eyes. Then I knew.

'You know it's a myth about a swan being able to break your arm,' I panted. My chest was heaving and sweat prickled between my breasts.

David took one step forward, and opened his arms for me.

'God, I'm such an *idiot*,' I said.

'Shh, shh,' he went, holding me tight against him.

'It's taken me till now,' I said. 'All this time. Did you get my letters?'

'I did,' he said.

And?

In the background I could hear Ian beginning to exclaim in that exaggerated voice grown-ups use with small children, Jaz calling instructions about nap times and clothing and pick-up. Underneath ran a piping descant from Matty, thrilled once more to be with his dad, too young to understand that for every reunion there must also be a parting. There was this child, surrounded by adults, all trying their best to build a world around him that made sense, even when their own didn't.

I touched the side of David's face, still terrified he hadn't understood.

'Can we go somewhere and talk? I've all sorts I need to tell you.'

'I'd say you and I could go anywhere you like, when you're ready,' he said.

EPILOGUE

Photograph 899, Album Seven

Location: the park, Nantwich

Taken by: Carol

Subject: It is a glorious spring Saturday, the culmination of a week of unseasonably warm weather. People are calling it a reward for last year's wash-out summer. But meteorology doesn't go in for checks and balances, thinks Carol, as she attempts to trap her family inside the camera's viewfinder. For the previous half-hour she's been sitting on a bench holding hands with David, a pose she's found simultaneously foolish and thrilling, given it's in the presence of her daughter. Hovering at the edge of her consciousness comes an ancient memory: the mortifying moment her dad opened the front door and discovered her mid-snog with Phil. But she waves the image away because those days are long gone, irrelevant.

'Why didn't you reply to my letters?' she asked, as soon as they were out of earshot.

'I wanted to be sure you meant it. I thought you might be just surfing a wave of guilt, and you'd change your mind back again as soon as you were challenged. I don't think I could have stood that.'

'But the silence. That was cruel.'

No consoling reply. All he'd done was take her hand possessively.

There's something steely and triumphant about him; she's noticed the sideways glances passing between him and her daughter. God knows how they are going to work this. Another picture comes: Dad showing Jaz the lion on the syrup tin, tracing the minuscule lettering with his soily finger. And out of the strong came forth sweetness.

Jaz and Ian are talking, or not talking, over by the river's edge; Matty is mooching about halfway between bank and bench.

'Every time you let yourself love, it's like being held hostage,' Carol observed earlier. 'Laying yourself open. We must be mad to do it, and keep on and on.'

'And yet we do,' he said.

David observes her now. Matty is plodding over to his grandma, holding some suspicious brown nugget between his finger and thumb. He has the air of a naturalist, discoverer of rare and significant species, who's anxious to log his findings with a colleague.

'Look, Nanna,' he says, holding it out to her. 'Snail's gone.'

'No,' says Carol. 'He's hiding in his shell because he's frightened. That's what they do. He'll come out soon, though, you wait.'

Matty drops the snail on the grass and crouches, frowning, waiting for the future to unfurl.

Carol raises the camera again. She has forgotten everything outside the viewfinder. Just before she presses the shutter, her face is illuminated.